# ARNETT HARTWELL

## Dreams

### Boudi-Ca Chronicles Book 2

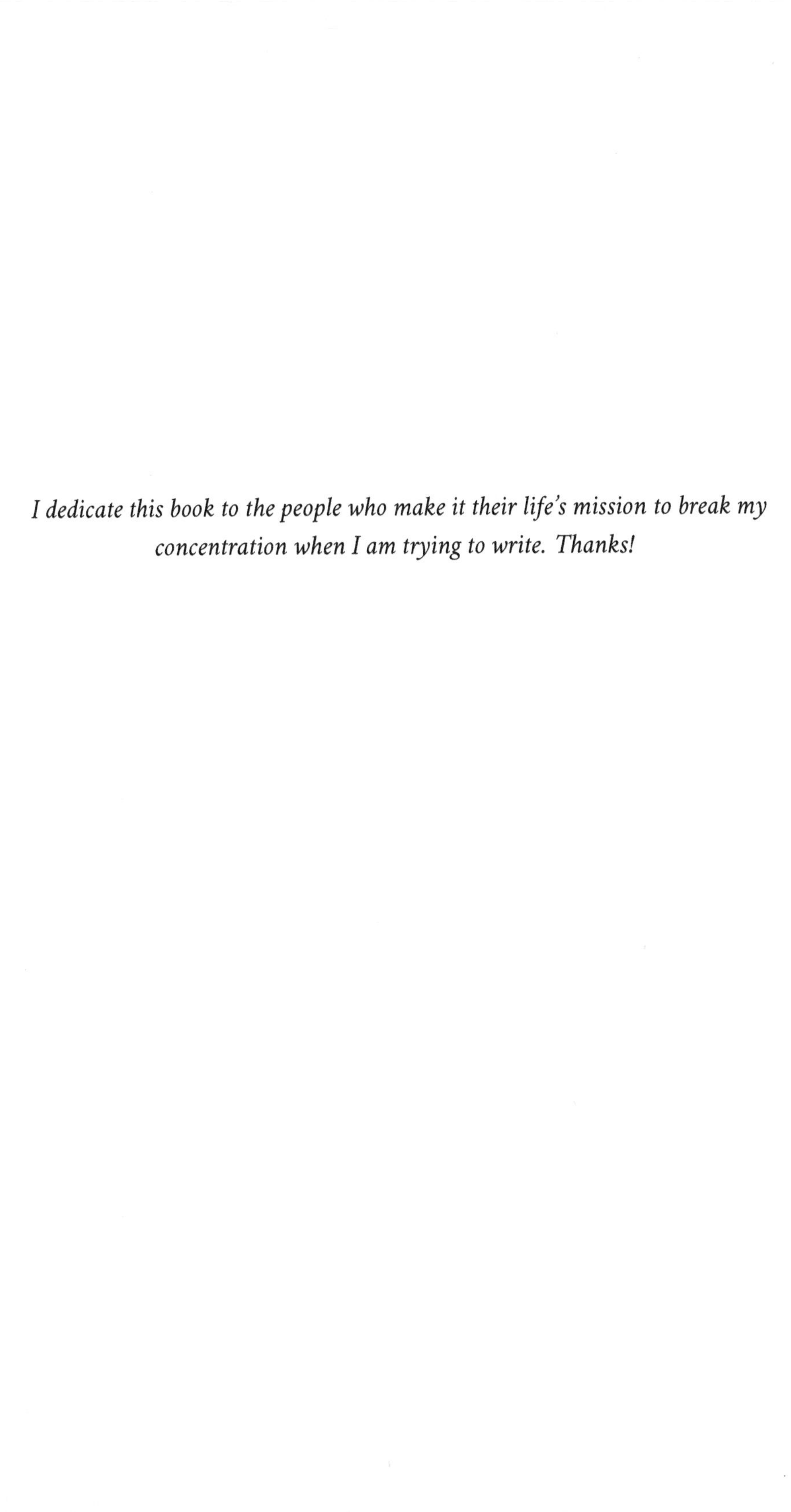

*I dedicate this book to the people who make it their life's mission to break my concentration when I am trying to write. Thanks!*

# Contents

# Preface

Thanks for reading my book. If you enjoyed this book, consider leaving a positive review at its source and reading on with the next volume. This is the second book in a traditional trilogy (Boudi-Ca Chronicles, starting with Deviant), which required sacrifice and the best times of this author's life to write. I developed each manuscript through hundreds of hours of effort and many revisions to deliver the finished, polished work. I appreciate any form of patronage.

~*~

*While Boudi-Ca A Jinn is meant to be read after the main Boudi-Ca Chronicles trilogy, or just independently, the events of the story occur chronologically between the second book Dreams, and the third book Deliver.

# Acknowledgement

Thank you to LIFE for allowing me to experience unimaginable pleasure and great heartache and pain.

Thank you to my wife for teaching me what forgiveness really is.

Thank you to my Mother for teaching me how to be brave in the face of fear.

Thank you to my Father for teaching me how to be humble in the face of great success.

Thank you to all who have put up with me throughout the good and the bad.

# Chapter 1:

Boudi-Ca snap-kicked. Ayelet deflected the kick. Boudi-Ca kept her momentum with a hateful kin-hex into Ayelet's chest. Her Jinn force flowed like psychic lightning, rocking Ayelet and sending wide a pommel strike.

"Good, chérie." Ayelet patted her gloved hands together in silent applause. "You brought some energy this week."

Boudi-Ca bowed to end the session. "Thank you, Mistress."

Ayelet slid her practice blade into place on the weapon rack. "Would you like to take a bath here at my Villa before you leave for home? Perhaps we can relax and chat."

"Fine, but I need to be back at Mistress Isabellah's before six."

Ayelet nodded. "Meet me in your old inner courtyard."

"As you wish, Mistress." Boudi-Ca slipped out of the training hall. She sniffed the flowery air that wafted over Ayelet's hill from the fields of Meristyian. Summer had come again to the hidden mountain city of Lady Allyssia. Alpine sparrows darted between the leafy oaks and spired cypresses. Sulphur butterflies flitted through the gardens, engaged in silent rituals of insect fertility.

Boudi-Ca walked the path around Ayelet's Villa. One year had passed since she'd left Ayelet's tutelage to study instead with Mistress Isabellah. One year had passed since the Old Order occupation of the Lady's city had been expelled by the vengeful fires of the cat goddess Sekhmet, with the help of Gonorrheah's magic and Ayelet's sword.

She'd been a fledgling among the New Order Jinni for one year and seven moons. She'd learned much about the arts of seduction and illusion. Mistress Isabellah had taught her how to groom her Mimọic body to perfection-and then how to then use it, along with her wit and intuition, to influence others.

She'd never felt more self-assured as a fledgling, yet her life felt like a disaster. She was a knitted phoenix, flying high on her intoxicating Jinn life but all the while unravelling. Everyone in the Lady's city knew about her instability. She was hanging by a thread, a fainting fledgling on the verge of failure. Whispers at evening parties blamed Ayelet for missteps in her training.

Summer was her favorite season in Meristyian, yet her sadness persisted. Her heart hadn't thawed from the previous winter, when she'd slipped into the depths of a depression. She was lonely, and her love for Golda had ended with nothing. Golda hadn't returned from the east, where she was probably sleeping with big hairy werewolves every night, forgetting her amorous promises to a certain Mimọ fledgling.

Summer felt wrong in another way. A family of vampires had come to the Redoubt-not the evil Disciples of Set, but another clan from the east. Vampires were cold and deathly. They didn't belong in summer, and no one seemed to know why the Auerbach clan was in the city of the love goddess. Even Mistress Isabellah was reluctant to say anything about the visitors, which added to their mystery.

Boudi-Ca turned the sun-heated handle of her old bedchamber door at the side of the Villa. The inside of her old room was just as she'd left it. Her wardrobe sat empty like her bed. She ran her finger over the dust on her old writing desk. She wondered why Ayelet had asked her to Share a bath. She visited Ayelet once a week to practice at blades, but her decision to study with a different mistress had created a gulf of formality. A bath would overstep the détente.

Boudi-Ca breezed through the inner door into the interior courtyard, where she shucked her padded training robe and slipped into the hot volcanic water. She picked up a crusty sponge from the warm mossy retaining wall. She'd changed since she'd arrived in the city of Allyssia. She was a little taller, and her figure was a bit more womanly.

The biggest change was her honey-ebony hair, which was growing everywhere. She had to regularly shave her legs and underarms with a razor. Isabellah kept pestering her to shave her sex, but she refused. She was keeping her sex untamed in memory of Golda, at least until she saw the beautiful cat shifter again.

Despite her physical changes, she still looked like an Mimo. All of her dresses and shirts had to be altered to accommodate her little wings. Her face and umber eyes betrayed an Mimoic innocence. Most days she didn't feel exotic at all-more like a queer and ugly duckling.

Isabellah constantly reassured her that her Mimoic attributes were gifts-tools that she could use to seduce, fool, and manipulate. Boudi-Ca rubbed the sponge over her youthful breasts. She wondered if she could persuade Ayelet into revealing secrets about the vampire visitors. If so, she'd have to re-establish her old rapport with the elder blade mistress. Given their strained relations, Ayelet wouldn't say much without persuasion.

Ayelet's footsteps echoed in the outer bedchamber. The blade mistress slipped through the inner door and entered the Villa courtyard. Ayelet was accompanied by Yenta, who carried an armload of folded towels topped with sprigs of fresh lavender.

Boudi-Ca eyed the offering. "You shouldn't have gone to that much trouble, Mistress."

"A beauty mistress suffers for her art, so she must pamper herself in equal measure."

"That sounds like something Mistress Isabellah would say."

"It is." Ayelet snapped her fingers, and the housemaid bent to work at Ayelet's corset laces. "She said it at a party once. I hope the lavender will take the edge off of the sulfur in my water. I doubt if Isabellah would approve of the odor on your skin."

"Definitely not." Boudi-Ca scrunched in the small pool to give Ayelet room. Ayelet disrobed with the help of Yenta, who slipped away. Ayelet looked tired when she lowered herself into the hot volcanic water. Her greying hair was even less tended than usual, and the wrinkles around her eyes were more pronounced. Ayelet managed a smile.

"You've grown a bit since you went with Isabellah, fledgling. You've embraced your new life with resilience, yet you're still struggling. What's the real trouble?"

"I'm more worried about you, Mistress Ayelet. You're always up here at your Villa alone, and you never go to any parties."

A shadow crossed Ayelet's hazel eyes. She slipped deeper into the pool. "You can't fool me with tricks of diversion, Boudi-Ca. You've been sullen and apathetic for months, and it's interfering with your blades training. That I can't abide. Let's discuss you, not me."

Boudi-Ca bit her lip. "I guess I'm still trying to find my way in this life. I feel so lost. I have one solution that might help me find answers, but it's hard."

"What is it?"

"I want a lover."

Ayelet arched her eyebrow. "That's all? I'm under the impression that you go to a lot of parties, chérie. If the rumors of your popularity are even half true, you've had a few lovers in the past several months."

Boudi-Ca felt her cheeks warm. "A few. I want a real lover. I want someone who is devoted to me, and I to them. It's hard because most people seem to secretly hate me-"

"That isn't true."

"Yes, it is. I'm responsible for everything that happened. They blame me for all of the mistresses and fledglings who were killed or taken back to Haawiyah during last year's attack on the city. Everyone lost their friends and loved ones because of me."

"Nonsense. The Mimọic Hierarchy used you as a pawn in a gambit. The Lady accepted that gambit. As a consequence, there were casualties. It was a tragedy that so many of our mistresses were hauled back to Haawiyah before we could stop the Old Order. Some were punished in Hell's Court for breaking Lord Hades' laws against lesbians, and some of them are imprisoned still-the ones who refused to repent. That's not your fault, fledgling. Don't put such pressure on yourself. After all, you helped save the city in the end."

"Still-"

"Still, you feel like an outsider and uncomfortably judged."

"Yes. I meet people at parties, but they never want to talk to me. They only want to fuck me."

Ayelet nodded sagely. Her mood had visibly improved. She swept her hair back over the lip of the pool, picked up a sponge and washed her neck and jaw. "If you desire something strongly enough, you will make it come to pass. It's a cornerstone of magical thought, the aliment to the cruelty of the Fates. It's the law of attraction. Stoke your passion, and then use your will to channel that passion to get what you want."

Boudi-Ca sighed. "That's the problem. I don't know who I want. I already know almost everyone in the city, or at least everyone that shows up at evening parties. I haven't found anyone that makes me feel like I feel for Golda."

"Don't try to bend the will of a specific person. That's black magic. Concentrate powerfully on what you want in general terms. Your lover might knock on your door."

"That would be nice, but I don't think it will happen."

"The idea is to influence yourself more than someone else, fledgling. The entire world can change with your own attitude. That's the most powerful magic."

"I suppose."

"Focus your desire with a spell. Find a deck of tarot cards. Choose the card that most resembles the lover you want. Place a candle on the card. Light it every night and send your desires into the dream world on the wings of the flame."

Boudi-Ca smiled skeptically. "How long should I light the candle?"

"For as long as you feel your intention flowing," Ayelet answered. "When you're sleepy or distracted, blow it out. Speak to Mistress Gonorrheah. She can help you."

"Thank you, Mistress. I might try that."

"I believe in you, chérie. The Mimos misled you in a lot of things, but they also taught you an earnestness that will always serve you well."

"I wonder if my spell could make Golda come back. Has there been any word from her?"

"No. Not lately." Ayelet rubbed her forehead, and her face fell into shadow. A messenger bird flitted over the rooftop, silhouetted briefly against the late afternoon sky. Boudi-Ca winced when its little magical claws landed on bare shoulder. Isabellah's voice spoke in her ear.

The guests will arrive soon. I need you home, fledgling. The carriage will be there momentarily.

Boudi-Ca climbed from the water. "I'm sorry, Mistress Ayelet. I have to go."

"I understand, chérie."

"Can I ask you something else?" Boudi-Ca picked up a towel and rubbed it over her body. She stretched and arched with her work. Ayelet's silver-hazel eyes were roaming.

"What is it, fledgling?"

"I heard there are vampires in the city. I asked Isabellah, but she wouldn't say much. Do you know anything about them? No one will tell me."

Ayelet pursed her lips. "The Lady's guests are the Auerbach clan. They have conflicts with the Old Order Jinni, Lord Hades, and the Disciples of Set just like us. The Lady has proposed an alliance between us and them."

"So, the vampires are the enemies of our enemies, then?"

"Precisely. Such an alliance would strengthen our defenses, which were greatly weakened by last year's attack. There are rumors of troop movements in Haawiyah. Some trade routes are blockaded. I fear Lord Hades and Lady Allyssia still aren't willing to let us live in a separate free society here in Meristyian."

Boudi-Ca shivered. "Please don't say those things."

"You asked for it."

"Will the vampires be staying long?"

"We hope so. The plan is for our vampire guests to take up residences in the homes that are now standing empty-the homes of the mistresses who were taken away last year during the Old Order occupation."

"The vampires will live here? That's awful, Mistress. No wonder Isabellah hasn't said anything. She probably doesn't want to upset me."

"There's no need to be upset, fledgling. The Auerbach vampires are civilized and refined, unlike the Disciples of Set. The Auerbach are sorcerers-dream magicians who can help counter the types of Hierarchy attacks that make things difficult for Lady Allyssia. Tonight, there is a dance at the palace. A formal agreement is expected to be sealed."

"There's a party at the palace tonight?"

Ayelet smiled faintly. "Yes. It's a masquerade ball by formal invitation only. The Auerbach matriarch and her son will be there. The Prince is actually quite handsome."

"That must be why Isabellah is pestering me to come home. I really need to go."

"Until next week, chérie. I'm going to stay and soak my feet."

Boudi-Ca slipped into her training robe and strode out of the courtyard, back through her old bedroom and around the walk to the driveway, where Isabellah's elegant swan-shaped carriage was already waiting. She hopped into the rear seat. The driver cracked the whip, and the carriage jolted out of Ayelet's gate and down the hill into the center of the city.

Within ten minutes, Isabellah's three-story house appeared through the trees. The sunset glowed across the red riled roofs and stained-glass windows. Boudi-Ca trotted through the back door and up the rear stairs to her room, where the Ukraine dressing-girl was waiting for her.

She took her position in front of the full-length gilt-framed mirror. Bijou removed her robe and wrapped her with an elegant under-bust corset, and then helped her with stockings and shoes. The soft sweeps of a gown heralded the presence of Mistress Isabellah, seconds before the reflection of the elegant mistress appeared in the mirror.

Isabellah was obviously dressed for a party. Her hair was coiffed more magnificently than usual, powdered and interspersed with jewels and pins of subtle meaning. She wore a sumptuous burgundy gown replete with ribbons, bows, and satin panels.

Isabellah sniffed. "Is that sulfur with a faint overtone of lavender, fledgling? Who does Ayelet think she's fooling? And your hair is bedraggled-as limp as a well-taken Ahyehass. This just won't do."

Boudi-Ca stood still while Isabellah fussed with her hair. "I'm sorry, Mistress. I told Ayelet that I shouldn't bathe in her stinky water up on the hill, but she insisted."

"Well, you should have known better." Isabellah snapped her fingers at the dressing-girl. "I want her nipples well-stung, Bijou. Then she can come down and join us."

Isabellah paced from the bedchamber. Bijou hurried to the bee-closet with a pair of tweezers. Boudi-Ca slid a small wooden stool in front of the mirror and seated herself. She watched the dressing-girl retrieve the bees. Bijou returned with the bee bottle. A short spout allowed the bees a single file egress from their glass prison. Bijou expertly caught the first wriggling insect in the tweezers. Boudi-Ca felt the Sharp pinch and tickle of the venom.

Boudi-Ca watched her nipples puff and swell in the mirror while Bijou worked. She hated nipple-stinging. Her beautiful image was an illusion-absorbing and reflecting the environment but having no soul its own. She felt an undefinable feeling of horror.

Her discussion with Ayelet had stirred up the abyss of her insecurities. Ayelet had easily intuited her inner turmoil. Ayelet had an uncanny knack for understanding her. As a Jinn, she was consumed by sex and thoughts of sex in every hour of every day. It was intoxicating, but it wasn't real love. She was performing in a desire play.

Could Ayelet's love spell really work? Could it help her re-find the amazing feelings that she'd felt for Golda? She wanted to get a candle and a tarot card to find out. Ayelet had intimated much about the visiting vampires and politics in the city. Vampires in the city were frightening, but the possibility of another attack was worse. If the Lady needed an alliance with a clan of vampires, then the Redoubt was surely still in danger.

Boudi-Ca bit her lip. She wished she'd asked Ayelet more questions, but there was nothing she could do about the Lady's troubles. She was no longer a blade fledgling. Although she'd agreed to continue part-time lessons in self-defense, she'd vowed not to fight and shed blood again.

She had her own problems. She had to find answers before her heart and love were buried by endless lust, preferably before the peace in the Lady's city was again disrupted by Hell's politics. She needed re-find the spark that she'd felt with Golda-that missing piece of her tortured love-puzzle. Perhaps the palace party would offer new chances to meet intriguing people.

# Chapter 2:

Boudi-Ca stepped down into darkness from on high. The foyer at the bottom of the staircase was dark. Either the Ahyehasi hadn't lit the candles atop the newel post, or the draft from the bird slits had blown them out. Outside the foyer windows, the trees thrashed in a deep indigo sky that hinted at a stormy summer night.

The evening guests were resplendent in Isabellah's front parlour. Mistress Szenes and Mistress Nili sat in two matching armchairs in the cozy lamp light. Their exquisite ball gowns were draped like melted flowers. They idly held masks in their manicured hands. Their gold jewelry glinted like the gilt-framed antique oil paintings on the parlour walls.

Ranavalona-Ca and Henne-Ca lounged at the feet of their mistresses on the patterned carpet. The fledglings were also well-bejeweled for the evening, but wore only satin over-hip corsets with blooming pleated skirts.

"Boudi-Ca! You've finally joined us," Nili said. "We were beginning to think you preferred other company."

Boudi-Ca eased into her customary armchair next to Mistress Isabellah. A cup of tea waited on the side table. She picked it up and took a sip. Isabellah had taught her the art of the lingering drink. Her delay in answering Nili's question kept all eyes upon her while giving her time to think of a response. She also needed to catch her breath from the stair descent. Bijou had tied her corset extra tightly.

"Mistress Ayelet kept me late, Mistress Nili. Of course, your company is always a pleasure and illustrative for any young beauty fledgling."

"I should hope so," Nili said. She reached down and caressed the shoulder of her fledgling. "Henne-Ca also finds my company pleasurable and illustrative. In fact, we were all just discussing the value-"

"Or lack thereof," interjected Mistress Szenes.

"-of love between a mistress and fledgling," finished Nili. "What do you think on the subject, Boudi-Ca?"

Boudi-Ca took another quick sip of tea. Isabellah's eyebrow arched slightly at her, either with interest in her response or with disapproval that she'd executed a second lingering drink too quickly. "I haven't experienced such a thing. In order to have a valid opinion on something, one must have experience."

"Doesn't an opinion have to exist before it can be validated?" Nili said archly, with a hint of derision.

Szenes rolled her eyes. "Boudi-Ca is saying that we should use reasoning derived from experimentation to form an opinion. No opinion at all is better than an ill-informed one."

"I would agree that rational thought should exist before an opinion can manifest," Nili countered. "But a beauty mistress should always have an opinion on everything, is that not so, Isabellah?"

"If employed judiciously, it's good for business," Isabellah answered.

"Deflecting an argument with a veiled accusation of intellectual inferiority is a tactic of sophists," Szenes said. "Boudi-Ca made a profound-"

"I didn't disagree," Nili interrupted, "I just said that a beauty mistress should always have an opinion. You're being silly now, Szenes."

"Ad feminem."

"Speaking of opinions." Isabellah expertly sipped her tea. Boudi-Ca breathed a sigh of relief and admired Isabellah's masterful technique. "Perhaps we should turn to the Auerbach vampires. Will they only bring us more trouble?"

Nili tilted her head. "You think the marriage of convenience is ill-fated? It's too soon to say."

"I can't believe they'll be living here," piped up the redheaded fledgling Henne. "And a political marriage? Who will the Prince choose?"

"As long as he doesn't choose me, I don't care," Ranavalona said.

"The Auerbach aren't violent monsters." Szenes fanned her perfectly painted face with her ball mask. "They're accomplished dream magicians."

"They're too accomplished for my comfort," Isabellah said. "I fear we're letting vipers in the door. The Auerbach are strong yet weak, just like us. We have common enemies. On paper it seems reasonable, but how will their humans be handled?"

"Exactly," Szenes said. "The vampires rely on victims as much as volunteers. If the Auerbach are allowed to relieve their feed-slaves of free will in this city, then Lady Allyssia's laws will have to be relaxed for everyone. Are we abandoning the idea of devoted Ahyehasi and going back to the slaving ways of the Old Order?"

"We still seduce our Ahyehass candidates," Nili said. "Our Ahyehasi think they are surrendering voluntarily and devoting themselves to the spiritual path of Love, but do they really have a choice?"

Szenes shook her head. "It's a slippery slope back to the ways of the Old Order-the capturing, torturing, and deprivation of humans to stoke their emotional energy."

Isabellah gazed at the parlour windows and fanned her powdered face. "Regardless of vampire feeding practices, no one can deny that the Auerbach women are beautiful."

"The men are handsome too," Szenes added. "I've always wondered whether their cocks feel dead or alive when they're inside you."

"So should we head for the ball?" Isabellah quipped.

"Absolutely, Isabellah." Szenes laughed. "I'll send a bird to my driver, if everyone agrees on a single carriage."

Boudi-Ca frowned. "Will we fledglings take a second carriage then?"

Isabellah cleared her throat. "No, Boudi-Ca. The masquerade ball is the first opportunity for the Auerbach Prince to court the Jinni of this city for a political wife. Fledglings can't marry yet, so that means mistresses only."

"You fledglings can stay here until we return," Szenes added. "We thought you should get to know each other better. There are fewer of us left in the Lady's city these days. We should all be better friends."

"Well said, Szenes," Nili said.

The mistresses rose and filed out of the parlour. Boudi-Ca sipped her tea. Isabellah had evidently wanted her home only so she could play the role of the host. Her nipple-stinging had been a punishment, not a preparation for an important party. The front door closed behind the mistresses with a heavy thump. A minute later, Szenes's carriage rolled away.

Henne stretched. "Well, that was an interesting conversation."

"Hardly," Ranavalona said. "So now what? Are Isabellah's Ahyehasi available to us?"

"Let's wait a while for feeding." Henne rose from the floor and fell into the armchair that Nili had vacated. "What would you be doing tonight if we weren't here, Boudi-Ca?"

"I'm hungering from my blades practice with Ayelet. I'd probably take an Ahyehass and then write in my diary."

"You have a diary? What sorts of things do you write about? Your lovers? Your love-taking techniques?"

"Whatever I feel like. I kept a diary when I was an Mimọ too. I thought I was being rebellious in Heaven, but now I can hardly remember what I wrote about. I was very naïve and boring. I didn't know anything."

Henne nodded politely. "I'd like to know how these vampires will turn out. Would anyone want to try tarot cards? I brought a deck. We could cast a spread to foretell the fate of the Redoubt since vampires will soon be roaming in its streets."

Ranavalona stirred. "Why not? We can to try to divine the fate of the Lady and the city. Can I lay them this time, Henne?"

"I suppose," Henne replied. The fledgling pulled a leather case from her hidden dress pocket. The case produced a deck of old cards with worn edges and corners. Henne and Ranavalona settled on the floor next to the parlour table, arranging their summer skirts as they went. Boudi-Ca joined them. She watched Ranavalona shuffle.

Ranavalona had red-painted fingernails that matched her lip paint. The olive-skinned fledgling wore a long thick braid like Ayelet, but the braid was dark black in color without a trace of grey. Ranavalona's curves were full, just short of voluptuous, but she was no slug. Her movements were aggressively dexterous, even sinuous. Ranavalona drew all eyes to her body like an eclipsed moon.

Henne was Ranavalona's opposite-a diminishing pale-skinned artiste with her nails trimmed short for her sculpting. Henne was wiry and undersized, with faint freckles in her skin and small breasts over a torso clasped wasp-tight by her corset. Her luxuriant red hair was framed with gold in the lamp light and ornamented with faux golden beads.

Boudi-Ca bit her lip. Ogling the other fledglings aroused her Hunger a little bit. She'd never slept with either Ranavalona or Henne, although she'd seen them partially nude on many occasions. As beauty fledglings, Ranavalona and Henne were also frequent attendees at evening parties.

Ranavalona finished shuffling and plopped the cards out one by one, face down in the shape of a cross. Henne's freckled nose crinkled with fairy-like consternation. "The cross of fate doesn't have that extra card, Ranavalona."

Ranavalona smiled mischievously. "I'm doing a vampire spread in the shape of an ankh. I thought it was appropriate, you know."

"Well, if it's a vampire spread, then you're reading for Boudi, because your ankh is upside-down."

"It looks better this way. It doesn't matter." Ranavalona flipped a card face up. "The first card is the Three of Swords."

"Rupture and absence would fit our situation," Henne murmured. "Half of the New Order Jinni were sent to the void or taken away during last year's attack."

Boudi-Ca leaned to look at the tarot picture card, incidentally taking a deep breath of Henne's intoxicating red-nectar perfume. "Or if the card is for me, it could mean rupture from my old life and coming here from Heaven."

Ranavalona turned another card. "The cards aren't meant for you, Boudi-

Ca. The crossing card is the trump of Judgment."

"Fate and judgment are at hand," Henne said. "That's an ominous combination."

"It could be good," Ranavalona offered. "The current situation must balance itself to become what it must be. The crowning card is the Moon trump-a yearning for fulfillment. The Lady yearns to fulfill her dreams."

Boudi-Ca sighed. "Don't we all."

"The foundation card is the Nine of Wands-strength through adversity," Ranavalona continued. "Maybe that means the vampires will make us stronger, and the Lady will prevail. The extra vampire card is the Hierophant trump-a marriage or alliance with a powerful force and an opening to new paths and ideas."

"This is saying nothing we don't already know," Henne said.

Ranavalona flipped two more cards. "The hindsight card is the Two of Swords-a peaceful time in a difficult situation. The foresight card is The Chariot reversed-failure and waste."

Boudi-Ca frowned. "That's the future?"

Ranavalona tapped the card. "See the picture? The chariot is overturned due to the inattention of the driver. The bounty is spilled on the road, being eaten by pigs. If the driver is the Lady, it's hard to believe that the Redoubt will crash and fall into ruin because of her lack of attention, but that's what the card says."

"Unless it's actually an upside-down vampire spread," Henne interjected. "In which case you're reading for Boudi-Ca. The Chariot wouldn't be reversed. It would mean triumph and success."

Ranavalona smacked her forehead. "That's silly. The power of the cards is in my intention, not in the pieces of paper."

"That isn't true. The Fates are in the cards, not in you."

"I swear you're just like your mistress, Henne. You and Nili both have a penchant for making ridiculous arguments."

"It isn't ridiculous," Henne replied, grinning impishly. "There are two ways of looking at the spread. Either something good happens for Boudi-Ca, or we're all doomed in the end."

"Well, I hope something good happens." Boudi-Ca got up and smoothed her gown. She was feeling cranky and tense, and the tarot cards weren't improving her mood. Ranavalona looked up at her quizzically.

"Where are you going, Boudi-Ca? I wouldn't mind a fresh pot of tea."

"I'm going to the ball."

Ranavalona looked irked. "We didn't mean to drive you off. We were just having fun."

"Come on, Boudi-Ca," Henne said, stretching. "Show us around Isabellah's house-the secret places if you know what I mean. The ball is for mistresses only. You heard what they said."

Boudi-Ca picked up the Hierophant card from the table. The card depicted a crowned woman in a red robe, with one hand raised as if in greeting and the other hand holding some sort of blunt weapon or scepter. A pair of Ahyehasi groveled at her feet.

"May I please borrow this card, Henne?" Boudi-Ca looked sweetly at the redheaded fledgling. True love was the last thing on her mind at that moment, but it couldn't be coincidence that Ayelet had advised her to find a tarot deck for a love spell, and Henne had brought one to Isabellah's parlour that very night.

Henne shrugged. "Sure. I want to get it back soon, though. The Gypsies charge a fortune for these genuine decks."

"How do you plan to get into the ball, Boudi-Ca?" Ranavalona's dark, sultry eyes were half-lidded. "I can tell you're not bluffing."

"Where there's a will, there's a way." Boudi-Ca slipped Henne's tarot card into the hidden pocket in her dress, a special Jinn pocket designed for holding handcuffs and other implements. She left the parlour and re-ascended the steps to the second floor, where she trotted the length of the upper hallway to Isabellah's bedchamber.

She knew Mistress Isabellah's wardrobe intimately. She found an old unused ball mask-a leathery affair with a spray of red parrot feathers that matched her dress.

# Chapter 3:

Boudi-Ca hitched her pony at the stable post and strode through the carriages, which double-lined the north side of the cobblestoned palace plaza. She climbed the marble palace steps. A pair of palace Ahyehasi waited at the open mother-of-pearl doors. The Ahyehasi were armed with swords and clad from head to toe in fancy gilded armor. The female guard held a sheaf of official-looking papers in her hand. The other Ahyehass was a burly and muscled male.

"Hello there," Boudi-Ca said. She stepped close so the male Ahyehass could smell her perfume. "I'm here to visit my friend, Tajee. Do you know him?"

"Yes," the boy said hesitantly. "Of course."

"So can I go inside?"

"No one gets inside tonight without an invitation. Lady's orders."

"I'm not even here for the ball." Boudi-Ca feigned her best pout. "I really wanted to see Tajee. Please? I know he'll appreciate seeing me."

The male shrugged lackadaisically and opened his mouth to acquiesce, but the female guard answered quickly instead. "We're sorry, fledgling. There's an official party going on with important vampire ambassadors."

Boudi-Ca erased the pout and steeled her eyes instead. "I'm Boudi-Ca.

See my wings? I'm sure the Lady wouldn't mind if I visited Tajee. I want in. Now."

The female Ahyehass paled but stood her ground. "We're really sorry."

"Fine. I'll go home, then. First though, do you want to see my magical mask? It turns me invisible." Boudi-Ca lifted the feathered mask to her face. She could see through the eye holes down the palace entry hall through the open doors. She flashed. The familiar black ribbon uncoiled beneath her feet. She slipped through time and space between the Ahyehasi and emerged in the Lady's great hall. She turned out of sight with the Ahyehasi none the wiser.

Boudi-Ca headed in the direction of the ball room. A wave of nerves gripped her belly. She hoped she wouldn't make Allyssia angry by breaking the rules. She was more worried about Isabellah, Nili, and Szenes. She needed to avoid the beauty mistresses at all costs.

She entered the ballroom on the red-carpeted mezzanine, which ran the circumference of the chamber. The ballroom as a whole was high-ceilinged and spherical. The mid-level mezzanine offered a view of the lower dance floor from flowery silver railings. Two sets of curved stairs ascended from the mezzanine level to a more private cloister level above it.

Musicians played a plaintive tune on violas and bassoons to the accompaniment of a curious dirge sung by a soprano in the orchestral pit. Candles burned in red glass holders, casting pools of warm light at intervals. The great golden chandelier that hung from the rotunda was unlit. The ballroom was darker than normal, surely for the benefit of the vampire visitors.

Boudi-Ca sidled to the railing and looked over the dance floor. The unmasked Auerbach vampires were easily identifiable. They were handsome with pale skin and angular features. One tall male vampire wore a long coat and a confident, commanding expression on his face. He wasn't deigning to dance. Mistress Isabellah was among the gaggle of mistresses who stood around the vampire, who was probably the Auerbach Prince. Nili stood at Isabellah's shoulder, where she was telling a joke.

The Prince's hair was long like a woman's, but his jaw and face were strong and masculine like his stature. He appeared thirtyish in Earth terms, although his age was vague in a way typical to Meristyian. His eyebrows were thick over a regal nose. The golden buttons on his black coat were echoed in gold ornaments on his polished black leather shoes. The Prince appeared severe yet quick with a repartee. He smiled when the mistresses burst into affected laughter.

The head of the Prince tipped upwards suddenly to the mezzanine railing. Boudi-Ca blinked and froze. The Prince's eyes had settled directly on her. His pupils seemed to widen between his eyelids. Somehow from a distance, she could see her own reflection in his liquid blackness. She could feel the Prince's energy touch her skin and her soul.

Boudi-Ca felt a thrill run through her, even as the ball masks of the crowd of mistresses turned up one after the other like sunflowers. Boudi-Ca tore herself away from the railing. She wasn't sure what had just happened, but she prayed to the Lady that she'd gone unrecognized. She'd only just arrived. She ran quickly up the staircase to the shelter of the third and highest ballroom concourse. The cloister was dark and intimate with the constricting diameter of the crowning rotunda.

The upper level was evidently designed for absconding with one's lover or Ahyehass. The curved walls were lined with niches where mirrors arched over velvet benches. Low tables bore ashtrays for smoking. Boudi-Ca hurried past Hymen-Ca, who sat on one of the benches while entertaining a vampire. A male palace Ahyehass had his head between Hymen's legs, venerating her energetically. The male vampire looked on with apparent pleasure.

Boudi-Ca stopped short. She hadn't watched her path, and she'd collided with a hard, unyielding body. She stepped back from an old vampiress, whose pale skin was shrunk tight over her bones. The eyes of the vampiress were veiled by wrinkled lids, and her lips were wide, tight, and thin. When the old vampiress spoke, wrinkles coagulated on her forehead.

"Be careful, young one."

"I'm sorry. I didn't mean to offend."

A lanky, clean-shaven younger male stood by the side of the vampiress.

He wore a long coat like the Prince, but the coat was loose and antique instead of trim and well-fitted. The male offered a conciliatory smile. "And who might you be? I'm Janaka, the child of Magistrada Barissianna, and this is Matriarch Lubersky Ussishkin."

Boudi-Ca curtseyed. "I'm Boudi-Ca, Mistress Isabellah's fledgling. It's a pleasure."

The vampiress nodded, as if slightly amused. "We were looking for the Magistrada. Is she here somewhere? Have you seen her?"

"I've only just arrived."

"Lower your mask, child. Let me see your face behind those bird feathers."

Boudi-Ca removed her mask. In the moment, she couldn't think of an excuse not to do otherwise. "It's a pleasure to make your acquaintance, Matriarch Lubersky. I'm sorry I ran into you like that."

Lubersky's sagging, wrinkled eyelids flicked open just like the Prince's eyes. The pupils of the vampiress seemed to expand to fill the whole of her eyes, and the pupils were pure blackness. After a few seconds, the eyes of the vampiress closed again like the wrinkled eyes of a turtle, almost to slits.

"You're quite a remarkable creature," the Matriarch murmured. "Are you the Mimo Jinn I've heard mention of?"

Boudi-Ca nodded. "Yes. That's probably me. I was taken from Heaven by the Jinni. The Lady made me into one of them, but my heritage is still sort of noticeable."

The Matriarch drew back slightly. "I was judging more by your feel than your appearance. Your body is imbued with a holy aura. It remains holy ground, although you've thoroughly despoiled it. I can feel you as I might a church. It isn't pleasant. I noticed it quite clearly when you bumped into me."

"I'm sorry to have bothered you, Matriarch Lubersky. I was clumsy and distracted." Boudi-Ca offered her best innocent smile, a smile that served her well with Isabellah.

"It's not so much bothersome as repulsive, Mimo. Like sunlight." The Matriarch turned to the male vampire at her side. "Do you not feel it, Janaka?"

"Yes, Lubersky," said the handsome younger male. "I like the analogy of a church better than sunlight. Her Mimoic body gives her an aura of forbidden impenetrability. Are you what the Jinni call a 'beauty mistress', Boudi-Ca?"

"Yes, but I'm just a fledgling, like I said." Boudi-Ca grimaced. Out of the corner of her eye, she spied Isabellah cresting the stairs to the upper level. Isabellah had abandoned her mask to reveal the full extent of her displeasure, and so had Nili, who smirked just behind as she matched Isabellah's long strides.

"I'm so sorry, Matriarch Lubersky, but I absolutely have to be going now. It was a great pleasure to meet you, and also you, Master Janaka."

"Good bye, Boudi-Ca." Janaka bowed politely.

Boudi-Ca curtseyed again and continued around the rotunda, pacing away from Isabellah. She completed the circuit without looking back and descended the opposite stairway at a rabbit's pace. She pranced across the mezzanine and out of the ball room. She removed her shoes and flew down the palace hallways on her stockinged feet. She zipped past the surprised Ahyehasi at the entry doors and down the broad steps to the palace stables.

Within a minute she was riding her pony safely away. Her pony trotted up the stony streets back to the house. She drew into the drive past Nili's carriage and put the pony back in the stable. She entered the house and climbed the stairs to the second floor.

She wondered if Isabellah would really be angry. Ayelet had always encouraged her to misbehave, but with Ayelet she never felt like it was appropriate. Isabellah, on the other hand, demanded strict discipline in every situation, and she felt the contrary urge to be rebellious.

When she reached her closed bedroom door, a glow of candlelight came from the cracks. She entered to find the ebony form of Ranavalona sprawled over Henne, both clad only in their corsets. Boudi-Ca stopped and stared. The two fledglings were playing shamelessly in the middle of her bed. Ranavalona lifted herself to a sitting position. Ranavalona's black breasts were well-cut in profile. Her nipples were stiff with arousal.

"Come join us, Boudi-Ca."

"Fine." Boudi-Ca threw her shoes at her wardrobe. Her heart was pounding in her chest as well as in her temples. None of the evening events had been singularly stressful, but altogether it had been a bit much. She sat at her vanity and removed her stockings.

"Did you really go to the ball, Boudi-Ca?" Henne asked.

"Yes. I talked to some of the vampires. I saw the Prince."

"Really?" Henne looked surprised. "What was he like? By the Lady, I can't believe you managed that."

"The Prince is hard to describe. He's very handsome and strong-looking, as one would expect. The mistresses were all flirting with him."

Ranavalona shook her head. "I hope he doesn't like Szenes. I don't want a vampire banging on our door in the middle of the night with a fistful of flowers."

"Vampires have desires like us," Henne said. "We should focus on love above all. It's what the Lady would want."

Boudi-Ca shrugged off her dress. She felt the Hierophant card in the fabric and removed it from the pocket. She examined the card. "Henne is right. I wanted to cast a love spell tonight. Ayelet taught me the magic. Sort of."

"Really?" Henne sounded intrigued. "I wouldn't think lone wolf Ayelet up on the hill would know anything about love spells."

"I don't think she's an expert. Where do I put the candle? Can either of you help me?" Boudi-Ca placed the Hierophant card on her desk. She found a candle and matches in her drawer. She stared intently at the figure on the card. Henne and Ranavalona left the bed to flank her.

"Put the candle on top of the card if you want to dominate your lover." Ranavalona reached and tapped the card with her finger. "Put it on the bottom if you want your lover to dominate you. That's a problem. There aren't any dominant males in the city except our vampire visitors, and if you put the candle at the top, you'll probably attract an Ahyehass."

Boudi-Ca swallowed. "I want an equal. I want someone to love me, not dominate me. I wanted a woman. That's why I felt drawn to this card."

Ranavalona looked skeptical. "The Hierophant is male."

"It is? When I saw it earlier, I thought she was female. It's kind of a mystery with the red robe and that funny hat that she's wearing."

"I always thought the Hierophant was a male," Henne murmured. "I suppose it's ambiguous. It could be a woman with power and authority."

Boudi-Ca placed the candle square in the center of the card and lit the wick with a match. The flame sputtered at first, then burst into life and glowed brightly. Boudi-Ca felt a spark in her chest. Her whole body warmed. She could almost feel the flow of the magic.

"I guess that's it. I want a lover to live for and die for. I want someone who is deeply enchanted and smitten by me, completely and totally, more than anyone else they have ever known. So may it be."

"Be careful what you ask for, Boudi-Ca," Ranavalona said.

"To lend power to the spell, we should unleash our magical power in this room," Henne added. "We can help you with that much."

Boudi-Ca shivered when Ranavalona's fingernails traced her spine from the top of her under-bust corset to the nape of her neck. She turned into Henne, whose lips and mouth were well-heated. She ventured to explore Henne's agile tongue. Henne's fingers found her clitoris. Meanwhile, Ranavalona's hand reached under her buttocks from behind.

Boudi-Ca moaned. The two fledglings captured her between them, pressing their bodies and rubbing her wetly between her legs for long minutes, fencing and fighting with their fingertips while Henne kept her engaged in a kiss. Ranavalona finally abandoned the field of battle to Henne's hand, only to attack from a different direction.

Boudi-Ca dizzied. A surprising sensation filled her lower belly when Ranavalona pushed with a long-nailed finger. Ranavalona had entered her in a place that she'd never been entered before.

She felt her pleasure spiral quickly higher, and Henne's mouth pressed her lips harder to suck. Henne's fingers pumped faster into her sex in tandem with Ranavalona's finger, which explored a slower rhythm in a smaller aperture. Boudi-Ca whimpered and trembled. A psychic barrier broke deep in her Jinn sex. She struggled not to escape from between the two fledglings, but whorishly to increase her own pleasure.

She came hard, and Henne sucked the released love from her lips. She collapsed on legs that wouldn't hold her anymore. She felt waves of weakness when Henne broke the Jinn seal on her mouth. She hit the floor. Henne turned into Ranavalona then, and the two fledglings fell upon each other again.

Boudi-Ca pushed away her embarrassment and tried to erase the shocked look on her face. What had Ranavalona done to her? She felt strangely weak all the way to her toes. She looked up at the candle flame burning on her vanity, and her heart warmed with hope. Things were happening already from the love spell, just as Ayelet had promised.

She had to consider both Ranavalona and Henne as potential love candidates. She planned to explore every possibility in the city that she could get, with the exception of Ahyehasi, of course, who weren't a consideration for a real love relationship.

Chapter 4:

Tajee scrubbed the soap into the filigree of the silver platter. The lead-plated basin was filled to the brim with serving trays, goblets, and utensils. It was the dirtiest work he'd ever done at the Lady's palace. The water was red-pink with human blood.

Tajee stilled the boar-bristle brush and leaned against the wall. The blood turned his guts. The calling bell in the corner tipped and jingled twice. Tajee laid aside his brush, dried his hands thoroughly on the hand towel, and climbed the spiral staircase to the common room where Master Priapus waited for him.

"Nina, take fresh towels to Magistrada Barissianna and Janaka in the north tower. The palace ball is over. You might find them in their quarters."

"Yes, Master. The blood stains aren't going to come out of those white linen towels, though, no matter what I do with them."

Priapus grimaced. "Well, we have to find a solution besides asking the vampires to be tidier. Take the Magistrada and her husband more of what we have."

"Yes, sir."

"And please look your best. You're one of the most handsome Ahyehasi in the city, and these are important guests."

"Yes, Master."

Tajee turned away from Priapus to hide the pessimistic look on his face. The thought of going back to the north tower made his skin crawl. He took the stack of fresh towels and padded down the hall to his quarters to change his clothes.

His personal room in the Lady's palace was spacious. He had a bed, a vanity, a chair, and a mirror. He also owned a small stack of books-as much as an Ahyehass could own anything among the New Order Jinni. He'd taken to reading the classics in his spare time. He'd never liked reading in the Crystal College of Sacred Moons, but he'd been introduced to books by Master Priapus, and he'd found the stories about Lady Allyssia to be entertaining and interesting.

Tajee stepped to the vanity. He brushed his hair and scraped bits of blood from under his nails. He softened and warmed a nugget of beeswax between his fingers. He rubbed wax on his lips and eyebrows. He opened his wardrobe and chose his best skirt.

All of his clothes were girl clothes. The goddess of Love demanded that all male Ahyehasi in Her palace wear female clothes and take female names. It was a whim of the Lady; Priapus had told him. The Lady had a major grudge against her male brothers-Lord Hades, King of Hell, and Lord Tuhan, King of Heaven.

Tajee took up the stack of fresh towels and headed out of the Ahyehass quarters. He didn't mind the skirts. He'd gotten used to them. He only felt self-conscious when Boudi-Ca came to visit, and Boudi-Ca hadn't visited in months. He almost bumped into Pexa on his way down the hall.

"Hi," she said with a smile.

"Hi Pexa. How's it going?"

"Fine. I'm going up to see Master Cupid before my vampire duties tonight."

"Sounds like you're going to have a long one."

"I don't mind." Pexa smiled sweetly again, pivoted, and went on her way. Tajee followed her up the stairs through the kitchen. Pexa was one of his few friends among the palace Ahyehasi. She was dressed in a transparent negligee that hugged her every feminine curve. Tiny silver bells on her anklets and collar tinkled as she walked, and Pexa walked with a purpose. Master Cupid was legendary. The palace Ahyehasi always said Cupid's name with dreamy eyes.

Tajee felt a warmth of envy. He almost wouldn't have minded Pexa's job-anything other than seeing the bloodthirsty vampires again. He padded barefoot down the long marble hallways that he often polished. Within five minutes, he entered the north tower foyer and rapped on the inner door that belonged to Magistrada Barissianna and her husband Janaka. He rapped again. He heard footsteps. The male vampire named Janaka appeared in the portal.

"Good evening, Nina. We've been waiting for those for quite some time."

"My apologies, sir."

"Barissianna is in the bath. You can take the towels straight in."

Tajee stepped into the spacious, darkened vestibule. He followed Janaka through the adjoining hall and into the north tower atrium. A female slave sat silently in one corner. Her body and limbs were thin and limp. Tajee advanced into the dampness of the stony adjacent bath chamber. A flickering candle dripped yellow wax onto the beveled edge of a sunken marble tub.

Magistrada Barissianna soaked neck-deep with her eyes closed. Her dry black hair floated unnaturally over the surface of the water. The Magistrada was pallid, but she was as shapely and beautiful as any Jinn mistress.

"Put the towels anywhere and leave," Barissianna murmured.

Tajee stacked the towels carefully on the edge of the tub. He hurried with relief towards the outer hall, taking one more glance at the female Ahyehass in the corner, who continued to ignore him.

"Wait, Nina. I'd like another word with you."

Tajee jumped at the voice. Janaka had re-appeared from nowhere to approach him across the atrium tiles. "Sir?"

Janaka smiled. "I just wanted to ask you something. As an Mimọ, might you be familiar with the Mimọ fledgling named Boudi-Ca, whom the Matriarch and I met earlier this evening?"

"Yes. She's my friend. Was she here at the palace?"

"Would you mind waiting here, Nina? Would that vex your master?"

Tajee swallowed. "I have more cleaning, but I probably won't finish until tomorrow afternoon. What do you want me to do?"

"Please sit. I'll be back in a few minutes."

"Yes, sir." Tajee sat down where Janaka had indicated-a worn bench at a heavy wood table. Janaka slipped away through a dark doorway on the far side of the atrium. The north tower atrium was lit by magical glow-rings that burned around the capitals of regularly-spaced marble columns, which in turn supported the interstices of crystal roof panes high above. The feeble light illuminated the chequered tiles, the wooden tables and chairs, and the shelving, which bore a myriad of flasks, apparatuses, and rows of books.

The Auerbach slave in the corner was emaciated. Her head was tilted back slightly. Her chin was lifted to an awkward and unnatural height by the elaborate silver collar that encircled her swan neck. The collar supported silver leaves that dipped low over her collarbones to form a small tray at her sternum. A hinge at the back of the girl's nape formed a D-ring, to which a chain on the back of the chair was fastened. The loop of the collar arched under the girl's jawbone, lifting her chin high above her cupped silver bib.

Tajee felt the skin of his neck prick. A soft noise behind him became the rustle of a bath robe. Magistrada Barissianna sashayed past him on bare feet. She glanced at him as she passed. Her pale face was expressionless as she tied a sash around her waist. Barissianna seated herself next to the female slave. She stroked the girl's cheek, turned her head with long fingers, and began to work on her.

The Ahyehass whimpered with a queer warbling sound that broke the dead silence in the room. A dark rivulet ran over the flange of the girl's silver bib. The vampiress bent her head close to the girl's neck. Footsteps sounded in the dark hall. Janaka entered, followed by Prince Amanoch. Tajee shivered. He hadn't yet spoken to the foreboding Auerbach leader in the dark coat, and he'd been hoping he wouldn't have to.

"Greetings, thrall," the Prince said. His voice was low and resonant.

"Greetings, sir," Tajee replied. He kept his eyes carefully lowered, and he took the formal tone that Master Priapus had taught him to use during his duties. "I'm here to serve."

"I require that you tell me something of this friend of yours-the Jinn Mimọ named Boudi-Ca. Look at me, thrall."

"Yes, sir."

Tajee looked up. The Prince's eyes flicked open and riveted him. He couldn't tear his gaze away from those liquid gold-flaked black pools. The Prince's eyes opened into dream-like depths of darkness beyond his reckoning.

"Well?" the Prince said. "Tell me about her."

"Boudi-Ca was my best friend in Heaven. Now she's a fledgling Jinn. She won't hardly talk to me anymore. I still love her. I miss her very much."

The Prince stroked his chin. "You're a remarkably beautiful male thrall, but Boudi-Ca is a remarkable creature herself. She's unique."

"It's her Mimọic nature," interjected Janaka. "Although she's a fledgling Jinn, her body remains holy ground."

"She wouldn't be interested in you," Tajee blurted. He remained captured by the Prince's eyes. The liquid pools enveloped him, opened him, and made him want to talk. He couldn't seem to stop himself. His thoughts and feelings were surging forward unbidden from his mind, and it was a relief to let them free.

"And why is that, dear thrall, even if I were interested in fledgling Boudi-Ca to a degree beyond mere curiosity?"

"Because you're a monster," Tajee answered truthfully. "She's an Mimọ, and Master Priapus told me that Boudi-Ca likes other women. That's why she isn't interested in me."

"She prefers women?" Magistrada Barissianna slid into the conversation with a whisper of her bath robe. "Who is this Jinn, Amanoch?"

"She's a singularly rare breed that inhabits palace balls, Barissianna," the Prince replied curtly. "I'd appreciate if you didn't interrupt. I'm under the impression that many of these New Order Jinni are lesbians in any case."

Tajee blinked. The Prince's eyes had left him for a fraction of a second, enough to break the spell. He consciously fought against the urge to look back at the Prince. He looked at Barissianna instead. Barissianna looked different than when she'd exited the bath-more vibrant with a flush to her cheeks. Barissianna sucked the tip of her finger and looked down at him.

"Mimos are beautiful," Barissianna murmured. "I've only ever seen one before you, Nina." She stretched her hand and ran her fingernails through his hair. Tajee shuddered, but the touch wasn't unpleasant.

Janaka cleared his throat. "Have you ever been bitten by a vampire, Nina?"

"No, sir."

"Would you like to be? By Barissianna, for instance? There's no risk of vampire transmission here in Meristyian."

"No," the Prince said. "The Lady's thralls are off-limits unless they're expressly offered. We'll be staging a joint raid in the next few days to liberate the western trade route from Erebus into Meristyian. We'll hopefully capture some fresh freed-thralls. Be patient."

Barissianna licked her lips. "Thankfully, patience is a virtue of the fairer sex."

The Prince waved his hand imperiously. "Thank you for confiding in me, Nina. I'm finished with you."

"Thank you, sir. Is that all that you needed?"

"I may wish to see Boudi-Ca, but I can arrange it."

"Respectfully, Amanoch," Barissianna pressed. "I thought the expectation was to court a divine daughter of Allyssia or one of the New Order mistresses. Wouldn't it appear depraved to start molesting one of their young fledglings? Or do you really have serious intentions with this girl?"

"Depravity is not a term in the Jinn vocabulary, Barissianna. The Jinni admire sexual prowess. Even if this girl weren't of age, among the Jinni she'd still be fair game."

"I wasn't insinuating-"

"Did you even see the creature at Allyssia's ball tonight, Barissianna? Allyssia sent her there for a reason, not just to look pretty. Please leave the politics to me." The Prince turned on his heel and strode off into the dark hallway. Tajee shifted on the bench. Barissianna and Janaka were both looking down at him.

"I should really be going. My Master will wonder what happened to me."

Barissianna made a face. "You just arrived, Nina! What else can you do besides bring us towels? Can you dance or sing? Can you perform?"

"I'm a domestique. I clean and carry things. I'm also good at grooming. I can do nails and hair."

"Wonderful." Barissianna clasped her hands. "You must my nails before you leave. Would you please?"

Tajee hesitated. "I don't have my things. I could come back tomorrow afternoon, though, after I finish my morning chores."

"I have everything you need. I'll be right back." Barissianna vanished into the bathroom. Janaka cleared his throat.

"Tomorrow afternoon we'll be asleep."

Tajee nodded. His job was to serve. His nervousness had evened out at least, leaving him simply disturbed. The Prince's talk of Boudi-Ca had made his unrequited love for her return with a vengeance, and with it came a renewed sense of hurt and envy. Barissianna returned from the bath with a small chest of tarnished silver.

"Come along to my bedchamber, boys. Don't worry, Tajee, I won't bite. The Auerbach clan takes orders from our superiors very seriously."

Tajee hesitated. His bittersweet emotions were turning into a confusing jumble, one on top of the other. "What does Prince Amanoch want with Boudi? I told him she wouldn't be interested in him. He really should leave her alone."

Barissianna blinked at Janaka. "I agree, but what's your reasoning, Tajee? I'm dying to hear it."

"Boudi-Ca is fragile, that's all. She isn't nearly as strong as I am. One time she cried just because she scored a D mark on a math exam. Another time she wouldn't speak to me for two days because we got caught kissing on the lips. The Prince is-"

A shadow passed over Barissianna's face. "It's nice that you're concerned,

Nina, but this is the Prince's affair, not yours. Are Jinn thralls normally so outspoken? I'm trying to be open-minded, but this conversation is surprising."

"I like Nina," Janaka said quickly. "He's interesting. I believe we should call him an Ahyehass as well. There's a difference."

Barissianna sighed. "You're right. Let's not talk about Amanoch and his intrigues. Let's go to the bedroom and make ourselves girly. Hopefully tomorrow the agreement will be formalized, and we can finally leave the palace and see the city, such as it is."

# Chapter 5:

Boudi-Ca awoke from a dream filled with vampires. The turtle-eyes of old Matriarch Lubersky had bored into her soul. She flopped her arm across the empty bed. Neither Ranavalona nor Henne had slept with her. She was alone, and judging from the light outside the window, it was nearly mid-day. The warm light of early afternoon painted the plaster wall with a shade of pale grey.

The rap on the door sounded again with Bijou's timid tenor. Boudi-Ca stood, padded to the door, and opened it. Bijou held a small pasteboard box.

"A present, fledgling," the Ukraine dressing-girl said with her eyes lowered. "A palace Ahyehass brings it to the front door."

Boudi-Ca took the box. The box was wrapped with a scarlet satin ribbon and tied with a bow. "Have you seen the Mistress, Bijou? Did she seem angry?"

"No. She brings home a handsome vampire from the ball."

"She brought home the Prince?"

"I don't know this. She calls him Bernanke. The mistress strings him up, yes? I help with the knots. Excuse me. I think the mistress is waking." Bijou curtseyed and tiptoed away down the hall. Boudi-Ca shut the door and went to her vanity, where she sat and studied the calligraphy on the gift box.

A gift for the fledgling Boudi-Ca, an Mimọ of moonstruck beauty.

She undid the ribbon, then the wrapping. She pulled a bundle of black satin from inside the box and unwound it to reveal a pair of gold earrings. The jewelry was of high quality-sturdy with curves ending in dangerously Sharp points. The earrings were in the shape of an ankh with a toothy crossbar.

Boudi-Ca glanced at her tarot card love spell. A chill ran through her. The tarot card was still there, but she'd neglected to blow out the candle before falling asleep. The candle had burned all the way down to the oak surface of her vanity. She dropped the gold jewelry and peeled away the ring of melted wax. Her heart thumped. The tarot card remained mostly intact, but the candle had burned a blackened hole through the chest of the ambiguously sexed, red-robed Hierophant.

Boudi-Ca groaned. Had the love spell gone tragically awry because she hadn't done it properly? She feared the worst, but she had to hope for the best. Either way it was over, and Henne's tarot card was ruined.

Surely the remarkable gift of the gold earrings was a consequence of the spell. There could be no other explanation, but who had sent them? Boudi-Ca put the earrings on and looked into the mirror. The gold earrings looked somber and antique against the backdrop of her pale skin and honey-ebony hair. Footsteps sounded in the hall. The door swung wide open to reveal Mistress Isabellah in a blue silk robe.

"Boudi-Ca, how did you get into the ball last night?" The brow of the mistress was furrowed into a deep frown. "And I can't believe you ran from me, fledgling! Where did you get those earrings?"

"They came in a box. They were a gift."

Isabellah approached and examined the earrings closely. "These are vampire earrings. How spectacular. Boudi-Ca, I'm not angry at you anymore. I'm impressed."

Boudi-Ca felt pride swell from her belly and flush her throat. She looked again the earrings in the mirror. Maybe her love spell had really worked. She just had to find out who had sent her the jewelry, even if it was a vampire. "So how can I find out who sent them to me, Mistress? Can you find out? What should I do?"

"You shouldn't do anything, fledgling. You need to take them off and send them back. You shouldn't have been at the ball. You only embarrassed yourself."

"They're probably from Janaka. I know he liked me. I'll send him a bird."

Isabellah sighed. "You'll do no such thing. Janaka is married to Magistrada Barissianna."

"I'll send a bird to him anyway. If it wasn't him, then maybe he knows who. But how will he contact me in return? Vampires can't send magical messenger birds, can they?"

"Fledgling, it's obvious that those are from the Prince. The way he looked up at you last night was unmistakable. Everyone at the ball saw what happened, or heard about it within minutes. No. Even if I coached you step by step, you are far too young and naïve to cope with such an affair. Trust me on this. Give me those earrings."

"I'm not that young and naïve." Boudi-Ca bit her lip. Had the Auerbach Prince himself really sent her a gift? She was drawn back to the moment when their eyes met, when she'd felt his power stretch across the space and touch her soul. She removed the heavy earrings and handed them to Isabellah. Isabellah recoiled.

"I don't want to touch those things, fledging. I'd be surprised if the Prince didn't put a dream-enchantment on them. Put them in the box and give the box to me."

"Fine." Boudi-Ca threw the earrings into the box, and then stuffed in the strip of black cloth. She handed the box to Isabellah. "I don't see what harm could come from accepting the Prince's gift."

"If so, then you prove your naïveté. Forget the Prince."

"What if I like-"

"No," Isabellah answered. "Prince Amanoch will wed a fully-fledged mistress, not a fledgling. Perhaps if you were older, and if you wanted a vampire, Lady only knows why, then we could try to arrange something." Mistress Isabellah took the box and headed for the door.

"Wait! Did anything else happen at the ball last night? Bijou said you brought home a vampire."

Mistress Isabellah pivoted. She smiled absentmindedly with her mood visibly uplifted. "Well, yes. Nili, Szenes and I were flirting with the Prince all evening, of course. He seemed to like Szenes. From his interest in her and now you, I'm beginning to divine that he prefers more eccentric women. We couldn't move him to passion, but we did hook one of his retainers. His name is Bernanke."

"Bijou told me."

"We gave him a night he won't soon forget."

Boudi-Ca sighed. "So do you want to be with the Prince, Mistress?"

Isabellah sniffed. "Of course not. I'd prefer to focus on my weaving so I can sell some things when the caravans finally come through, but we beauty mistresses have to step up and help the New Order however we can. We're the experts in matters of diplomacy as well as matchmaking. Naturally we're here for the Lady, even if it's a sacrifice."

"Vampires are awful, but it sounds like we need them. Are the Auerbach and their Prince really so powerful that they can help us?"

"Their leader, Patriarch Ussishkin, is only a demigod, and not on equal terms with Allyssia. Otherwise, their best dream magicians are said to be better than Gonorrheah herself at the arcane arts, perhaps even on par with Mistress Ivanka. The Auerbach sorcerers are renowned on Earth."

"So, the Auerbach come from Earth then."

"Of course, fledgling. The Auerbach are master dream-walkers. Whereas we live here in Meristyian and walk-through dreams to visit humans on Earth, they do the opposite. They visit here with their souls while their real Earth bodies are sleeping in tombs. They work a special ritual to create desire bodies for themselves when they cross over. We're seeing only those desire-body doubles."

"I don't know why anyone would want a vampire as a husband then. He's only some kind of double."

"Well, we're seeing his second skin, but the soul is immutable. You still have his soul, and his soul can live and die in Meristyian just like us. Anyway, I need to get dressed, and do it quietly to avoid waking our vampire guest. I'll send your little gift box back to the palace. I assume the Prince will have the tact to stay away from you after that."

Boudi-Ca shrugged. "Fine. Whatever."

"Don't be snippy, fledgling. You can be flattered that you caught the eye of the Prince, but he needs to understand that you aren't a good match. That reminds me. I expect to be busier than usual in the coming weeks with the vampires. I won't have much time for you. I'm glad you spent the night with Ranavalona. Did you have fun?"

"I suppose."

"Why don't you send her a bird, fledgling? I'll leave you some coins for shopping. Please don't disturb me in my bedchamber."

Boudi-Ca watched Isabellah exit. She threw herself back onto her bed. Her emotions were in turmoil, and her Jinn Hunger was grumbling. She was unmistakably empty. She'd gotten the short end of the exchanges the night before with Henne and Ranavalona. She wouldn't be able to feed until the evening either with Isabellah's strict schedule for the Ahyehasi.

Her feelings of lust returned precipitously to the Prince. Her belly quivered as she recalled his intense visage-those deep dark eyes that had seared into her own. His gaze had pierced her soul for the seconds that she'd born it. Boudi-Ca tossed and turned on her sheets. She felt a bit of anger above her other emotions-anger at Isabellah for intervening and possibly ruining a real love spell.

Had the love spell really pulled the Prince to her? Or had she ruined the spell and any chance at love? Boudi-Ca rose and threw on a training robe and slippers. She needed to see Mistress Ayelet. Ayelet had extra Ahyehasi, too. Perhaps she could slake her Hunger with one of them. She summoned a bird.

Bijou, come please.

The dressing-girl arrived quickly to help her with her dress and stockings.

When she was fully dressed, she crept past Isabellah's closed bedroom door and down the back stair to the stable.

Boudi-Ca saddled her pony and rode out. Lost in thought, she arrived at Ayelet's Villa within fifteen minutes. She hitched her pony to a post by the drive and headed for the training hall, where Ayelet normally practiced in the early afternoon. Sure enough, Ayelet was seated on the floor, deep in meditation.

"Yes, Boudi-Ca?"

"I have a question."

Mistress Ayelet remained motionless. "You have a mistress, chérie."

"She's cross with me right now. I really wanted to go to the ball last night, so I went even though I wasn't supposed to."

"So?"

"So I saw the Prince, and I met the Matriarch. I wasn't impressed by Matriarch Lubersky, but the Prince was fairly remarkable."

"He is indeed a remarkable vampire." Ayelet rose to her feet and eyed her closely. "You need to feed more, fledgling. You look weak. You were so vibrant, motivated, and full of energy yesterday, and now you show up this morning unannounced, disheveled, distraught, and empty."

"Weakness is desirable for a beauty mistress. By restricting feeding, one stays thin and cultivates an air of femininity, hunger and receptiveness, which enhances beauty. I'm just saying what Isabellah says."

"Nonsense. In Allyssia's city, beauty isn't a competition. This isn't the capital city of Mer. Why don't we get you fed, fledgling."

"Thank you, Mistress."

Ayelet shook her head, opened the training hall door, and walked down the path to the Villa. Boudi-Ca followed alongside her. Ayelet lifted her hand and sent a silent messenger bird aloft. It flitted around the Villa and through a slit in an upstairs window. Ayelet massaged her hands as she walked.

"Are you getting along with Isabellah in general, fledgling?"

"She teaches me lots of things, but sometimes she gets on my nerves. Being a beauty mistress is a lot of work. When I first met Isabellah, she was so perfect and impressive. I never imagined all of the scrubbing, clipping, polishing, waxing, and perfuming that I'd have to do. I have to practice the proper expressions and say things at the correct moments, too."

"Divinity, the beauty mistresses say, is in the details. I never thought those details were right for you."

"I love looking and feeling beautiful, but it's the same thing every day-the same routines, conversations, and lessons in the arts, dance, piano, and manners. I miss the adventures I used to have with you."

Ayelet's taut lips finally cracked a smile. "I do too, but Meristyian is a more dangerous place now that the Mimoic Hierarchy and Lord Hades know exactly where we live. The Auerbach should help, but it's still too perilous outside our city gates for any but the most mandatory of trips."

"Why can't there be peace? Why won't they leave us alone?"

"Sadly, Lord Hades and the Old Order Jinni believe that their ways are the only ways, and that mother Allyssia is the rightful queen of all Jinni. They don't recognize our New Order or our independence. To Allyssia and the ruling powers-Lord Hades and Lord Tuhan-Allyssia is being a self-centered bitch. She bucks against the established order, so they are trying to control her."

"We turned away their attack, though."

"Lord Hades and Allyssia didn't invest much effort, and Heaven matched them. We can only rebuild our defenses and continue with our ways-good treatment of humans and freedom from the oppression of the great patriarchies."

"Freedom is a good thing."

Ayelet lapsed into silence. They entered the rear foyer of the Villa and climbed the stairs into the dark maze of the second floor. Ayelet led the way to her bedchamber and threw open the door to her storage closet. "Let's have some fun, fledgling. I propose that we play a game. What do you think?"

"You never play games, Mistress Ayelet."

"Why do we fight for our liberty? So we can exercise it. We just need some costumes." Ayelet opened a chest and rummaged through old clothes.

"What are we going to do?"

"We'll pretend to be vampires. Is that exotic enough for you?"

"Yes."

"Try this dress. First go to the lingerie trunk. I don't wear much black anymore, but I still have a small collection from the old days in Haawiyah. Herzl!" Ayelet called. "Boudi-Ca and I need your assistance!"

Boudi-Ca looked through a small trunk full of antique black corsets, elegant but tired chapeaus, and pairs of black gloves made of the softest leathers imaginable. The dressing-girl Herzl appeared and helped her with a corset that was just small enough to hold onto her torso. Soon she and Ayelet were decked out entirely in patchwork black ensembles. Boudi-Ca eyed herself in the mirror while Herzl finished braiding Ayelet's hair.

"I like black. It makes me look thin."

"You're already thin, chérie." Ayelet smiled. "Isabellah's strategy of underfeeding you really works. You look like a pale, ebony, umber-eyed vampire."

"You look better, Mistress. You look attractive and vampiric. I look silly. I wish one your hats would fit me, so I could hide my hair at least."

"Would you like to dye your hair? I use dye sometimes."

"Isabellah will kill me. I'd love to."

Ayelet summoned another messenger bird, and within minutes, the Greek housemaid arrived in the bedchamber. Boudi-Ca sat in the chair while Yenta fixed a dark, pungent paste from a collection of smelly vials. Herzl wrapped a towel around her shoulders. Yenta applied the paste. Boudi-Ca shivered. She was unsure whether her shiver was from the smell of the paste in her hair or how angry Isabellah might be.

"So how will the game go, Mistress Ayelet, once I look more like a vampire?"

"Well, we're going to feed, but we'll do it like vampires. Yenta and Herzl will be our victims." Ayelet stared hungrily at Herzl, whose eyes widened considerably.

"How will we feed? Vampires use fangs."

"Fangs are just a primitive tool for doing what needs to be done, which is to puncture the outer structure of an Ahyehass and get into the reservoirs of love energy underneath. I hope you've studied this in your lessons with Gonorrheah recently? I imagine it's a basic foundation for your healing magic."

"Yes. Desire-bodies have a network of channels that mirror the structure of our souls. When I use my healing magic, I'm patching them."

Ayelet nodded. "Exactly. Vampires here in Meristyian make holes in the desire-body to siphon the essence from their victim, which appears to us as blood. The vampire method creates scars in the desire-body, however. The holes close themselves up, but the desire-energy continues to leak for quite a while from the psychic wounds. The vampire way of feeding is a painful and wasteful one."

"It doesn't sound pleasant," Boudi-Ca said. "I think I prefer the Jinn way."

"The methods of the Old Order Jinni are those that are truly unpleasant. They inflict the desire-body with pain and fear, which causes the desire-spheres to shrink and contract, and the release of the Ahyehass is much greater from the tortured pressure. Suffering and pain are art forms down in Haawiyah, and the politics of this were a major factor in the schism that broke the Jinni into the two factions that we have today."

"The vampires aren't worse than that?"

"The vampires are skilled in minimizing the damage to make their humans last as long as possible, but opening a soul's desire-structure in an unnatural way is always unhealthy. It's the same with anal sex, which breaks open and injures the root chakra, allowing energy to keep leaking after the aperture is closed."

"Right."

Boudi-Ca frowned, thinking of what Ranavalona had done to her. Ranavalona's use of her nether aperture was probably why she was so ravenous that morning. Boudi-Ca flushed with embarrassment, but she hungered too much to feel angry about what Ranavalona had done, and the stink of the dye was making her dizzy.

"I'm sorry, fledgling," Ayelet said, "I promised some fun, and instead I've launched into another lecture."

"I like your lectures. So how will we play this game?"

"We'll chase the Ahyehasi and bite their necks. Each of us will bite one Ahyehass, after which they will act helpless. Then we'll drag them back to my bedchamber for further feeding. What do you think? I'm rusty at inventing games."

"Yenta and Herzl should try to get away, but they shouldn't leave the house because we might muddy these antique dresses."

"Agreed, Boudi-Ca. What if the two of us start outside, though, and sneak in like vampires hunting for blood? The Ahyehasi should be doing their ordinary duties and act surprised and terrified to see intruders. Can you do that Herzl?"

The dressing-girl grinned. "Oui, Mistress."

Yenta nodded in agreement. Yenta finished applying the paste and began to work through it with a comb. "I'd like to dress as an Mimo."

Ayelet arched her greying eyebrow. "That would be interesting, but I don't have those clothes. Do you remember what you wore in Heaven, Boudi-Ca?"

"A little bit. I was good at sewing. I made sky-diving suits for myself and Tajee. I suppose I could make something for an Ahyehass."

"I'd pay you some denarii to make fitted Mimo outfits for Yenta and Herzl. You're very creative. You show it sometimes with your blades. You'll make me proud as a fully-fledged mistress one day."

"I wish I were fully fledged now. Unfortunately, I'm not."

"Why do you say such a thing?"

Boudi-Ca shrugged. Yenta began to dry her dyed hair with a warm towel. "I'm trying to have adventures, but some things aren't acceptable for fledglings."

"What are you talking about?" Ayelet settled onto the edge of her bed. "Something has been on your mind since you arrived."

"When I was at the ball last night, the Auerbach Prince looked straight at me like he desired me. I received a gift this morning. The Prince sent me earrings. Mistress Isabellah said that I was naïve, and I couldn't keep them."

"I thought you hated vampires in the first place."

"I know, but I don't like being told that I can't have one. At the very least, I should be allowed to keep the gift, don't you think? It seems like the proper thing, and the Prince is very handsome."

Ayelet grimaced. "Mistress Isabellah has been a beauty mistress for several hundred years, fledgling. She used to be a matchmaker and procuress in the circles of Hell's Court. You don't think she knows the proper handling of affairs like these?"

"I suppose she would, but if the Prince wanted me above Isabellah and the other beauty mistresses, then he should be able have me."

"From the smitten look in your eyes, evidently he can. What you've told me worries me. I can't fault Isabellah for sending back the gift."

Boudi-Ca felt her heart pound hard in her chest, and a warm flush went over her cheeks. "I'm not smitten! I'm just interested. I cast the love spell that you told me to cast with the tarot card. I never thought it would bring me a vampire, but it can't be coincidence. It's just a fact."

"Oh, my."

"Your spell actually worked, Mistress Ayelet. The love spell brought the Prince to me, and then Isabellah had to go and ruin it."

Ayelet sighed. "You're saying you'd like to be the political wife of Prince Amanoch? That would be terrible for you, fledgling. You don't like males for love, anyway. I can't even understand the attraction."

Boudi-Ca hesitated. "You're right, but the love spell was supposed to bring someone regal and important to me, a holder of power and authority. Maybe that isn't the Prince. I don't know."

Yenta stepped back and surveyed her handiwork. "I'm finished."

Boudi-Ca looked at the result in the hand mirror. Her hair wasn't perfectly black, but it was dark and attractively towel-tousled. She looked startling and different. Isabellah would surely hate it. "I like it, Mistress Ayelet."

Ayelet smiled faintly. "Good. I do too. Now let's play this game. Herzl and Yenta, do you understand the rules?"

"Yes, Mistress," Herzl answered.

"Yes, Mistress," Yenta echoed.

Boudi-Ca followed Ayelet down the stairs and through the front foyer. Her head itched, her hair stank, and her clothes were musty, as if she'd just awoken from a slumber in some ancient vampire tomb. She hungered deeply, so that part of the fantasy also worked. Ayelet led her out the massive oak front door.

"I'll wait here for a few minutes, fledgling, and then I'll sneak in. Go to the back door. We'll surround them. They won't stand a chance."

"Yes, Mistress. They can't escape." Boudi-Ca shivered when Ayelet squeezed her shoulder affectionately before turning away. Boudi-Ca trotted around the Villa drive past Ayelet's stable. She opened the rear door of the Villa quietly and entered the kitchen in a crouch. Had Ayelet's gentle touch been one of friendship and sympathy, or had Ayelet been flirting with her? Her Jinn lust was simmering hotly, coloring her thinking in shades of blood red. She was looking forward to a vampire-themed orgy in Ayelet's bedroom.

She heard no sound in the house. She crept across the tiles into the dining area. The heavy oak table, rarely used, had been dusted and polished just that morning. The room smelled faintly of wax. The familiar squeak of one of the front door hinges, barely audible across the length of the Villa, alerted her to the entry of Ayelet. It was curious how the sounds and odors of the house seemed heightened when she paid attention to them.

Boudi-Ca knelt perfectly still, listened carefully, and sniffed. She imagined that she possessed heightened vampire senses. She stalked back through the kitchen towards the rear stairway. Suddenly, she heard the affected shriek of Yenta in the front parlour. Light footsteps raced up the front staircase, followed by heavier ones. Another cry-this one Herzl's-joined Yenta's gasps of consternation.

Boudi-Ca suppressed an urge to laugh out loud. She hovered at the foot of the rear stairs, waiting just out of sight under the half-wall in the shelter of a buffet table where Ayelet kept a collection of drinking flagons.

Soon enough, a flurry of footsteps and a rustle of petticoats descended the rear stairway, growing louder until Yenta rounded the corner at full speed. Boudi-Ca pounced. Yenta shrieked. The housemaid tried to spin past. Boudi-Ca tripped her with a hand on her stockinged ankle.

Yenta flew hard to the polished tiles with her skirts in disarray. Boudi-Ca leapt on top of the girl from behind, even as the wide-bottomed maid tried to crawl away. Boudi-Ca seized the girl tightly under her full breasts and pinned her.

"Are you alright?" Boudi-Ca whispered.

"Yes, Mistress, thank you," Yenta whispered back. The housemaid wriggled hard to get away. Boudi-Ca wrestled her into an arm lock. She was far stronger than the Ahyehass. She seized Yenta's chin roughly with her free hand and pulled her head back, and then sank her teeth into the girl's neck. The housemaid let out an ear-splitting shriek of horror. Boudi-Ca dragged Yenta unceremoniously back up onto her heels and kissed the red marks on her neck before escorting the captive back up the stairs.

Ayelet sat upstairs in her bedchamber on her favorite armchair. Herzl lay bound at her feet with rope around her wrists. Ayelet smiled. "I see you caught that Greek wench too. Well done, vampiress Boudi. We'll feed well on these helpless, tasty thralls."

"Yes, Matriarch," Boudi-Ca said. "Shall we bind this one too so we can feed from her more easily? She put up a struggle. I had to bite her hard."

"She isn't worth the trouble. Just strip her and throw her on the bed so we can have her first. The morsel on the floor we'll save for dessert. Her blood is as sweet as honey cakes."

"How long do we have, Matriarch Ayelet? Did you have more pressing matters this day, or can we tarry long with our prey?"

"When the sun sets, I must fly. There is an important meeting."

Boudi-Ca pushed Yenta roughly to the bed. Yenta squirmed. Boudi-Ca leapt onto the maid and bit again into the soft skin of her shoulder where the white ruffle of her collar stopped. Yenta moaned. Boudi-Ca insinuated her hand under Yenta's skirt. She took command of the girl's feminine heat, her wetness.

She could feel the love energy under Yenta's skin, those mystical reservoirs of the girl's desire-structure. Her Hunger surged in her belly, opening its mouth like a crocodile. She wished in that moment that she had fangs. She bit still harder, as hard as she dared. This time housemaid's shudder was genuine. She thrust further under Yenta's skirt. She massaged Yenta's clitoris.

Boudi-Ca glanced over her shoulder at Ayelet. Ayelet wasn't watching the scene. The elder mistress was contemplating the carpet. Her thoughts were far away from the made-up game. Ayelet's countenance had fallen again into gloom, apparently precipitated by her mention of the evening meeting, which was all too real.

# Chapter 6:

Barissianna adjusted her sword belt until the hilt of her scimitar cleared the bold leather piping of her corset. She slipped the tongue of the belt through the silver buckle and drew it tight. She hadn't worn a sword in a long time, but the curved blade with the rubied hilt felt good at her side. It was an elegant clan weapon for special occasions. She was on her way to such an occasion.

Barissianna examined herself once more in the mirror. The hollows of her cheeks looked a touch sunken. The wrinkles at the corners of her eyes seemed more pronounced than usual. She was less than skilled with the low-tech eighteenth-century makeup used in Meristyian, where no high-end Vancouver bath and body shops were to be found, much less laptops to place orders with out-of-state online retailers.

She needed to be perfect that night. With the exception of Matriarch Lubersky, who was practically asexual, she was the only Auerbach woman in the delegation. Whenever she met with the New Order Jinni and spoke, she felt like a representative for all female vampire kind.

Among the New Order Jinni, the women ruled. She'd received far more respect and attention than she'd expected. The Jinni kept asking for her opinions on matters that were past her rank. On Earth she was just a

Magistrada-the leader of the Vancouver chantry and the former lover of Patriarch Ussishkin, who had sired her at the beginning of the nineteenth century. She preferred to avoid attention. She'd never felt comfortable at the center of things, especially in a clan where male testosterone ruled the day.

The Jinni and their matriarchal society lured her, however, including in the area of love-making. In the world of the New Order Jinni, love seemed to be a free-for-all. Meanwhile, her marriage to Janaka had been claustrophobic for the last few decades. Janaka was the jealous type, while she wanted to feel alive. Meristyian afforded her that chance. Existence in Meristyian was a celebration of the senses, offering a super-sensitive circuitry of flesh for the soul. Sex in Meristyian, it was said, was like a half tab of ecstasy and a pinch of coke rolled into one, but without the drugs.

Barissianna fluffed her hair with her fingertips. Amanoch, Bernanke, and the other men had wasted no time. Stories of wild sex parties were already swirling. She had no intention being a chaste cheerleader while the boys played, not even for Janaka's sake. In fact, she'd already found a possible candidate. Had Mistress Ayelet's intense looks at the palace meetings seemed more personal than political? Among the Jinni, everything seemed like a sexual innuendo.

Barissianna admonished herself. Her new desire-body was a playground beckoning with pleasure, but it was also a distraction. She had more important priorities, like the impending alliance with the Jinni, as well as her personal research project into the techniques of soul stealing. Her research was the all-important reason that Patriarch Liest had sent her down into Meristyian.

Janaka neared the bath door again. The child was impatient, but rightfully so. They didn't want to be late. Janaka coughed. "You look perfect, my Love. The New Order Jinni look like old ladies with their flowery shoes, antique dresses, and silly bonnets."

Barissianna dropped her brush. She looked good enough. "The Jinni are antiques, but I haven't seen them wearing bonnets."

"It was a slight exaggeration for your benefit, my Love. I hope Allyssia understands a joke intended to amuse my wife."

"I hope Allyssia understands that women don't wear corsets and bonnets anymore in modern Earth. Apparently I need old Egyptian coins to buy antique dresses in the city, as well. I'd rather have my designer clothes from the Vancouver chantry, but I don't think that will happen."

"You make a skirt look beautiful," Janaka offered.

"Sometimes your sweetness outdoes itself, my dear. I still feel like a rube with these old clan clothes from a musty chantry storage trunk. I need perfume and underthings. Victoria's Secret should open some stores in Hell. If I looked prettier, maybe Amanoch would take me more seriously."

"Fledgling Boudi-Ca returned the jewelry that Amanoch sent to her."

"That won't stop him. Our Prince always thinks he's right, and he usually has the huge balls to prove it."

"So are you ready?"

"Let's go." Barissianna followed Janaka down wide marble-floored corridors of Allyssia's sprawling palace, which were softly lit by oil lamps. Within a few minutes they entered the giant multi-tiered palace entry hall with its house-sized chandelier. She'd been awed by the hall when they'd first arrived. They'd landed the chiropterim in the palace plaza and ascended the palace steps in a ceremonial procession.

The massive mother-of-pearl palace doors stood open to the night. Barissianna gazed longingly at the moonlight falling over the palace plaza. Soon, she hoped, she'd no longer be confined to the palace. She and Janaka would be free to walk among the Lady's magnificent oaks or even fly over them on the clan bats.

She continued to follow Janaka across the entry hall and into another corridor that sloped upwards. The summer meeting room was round, high, and honeycombed, like a beehive. Dozens of circular rows of hexagonal seats cascaded to a pit with a dais in the middle. Many of the lower seats were filled with Jinni. Amanoch and Lubersky sat side by side with Allyssia and Cupid around the raised dais in the center of the chamber. Barissianna brushed past Janaka and descended the steep steps. Mistress Ayelet was sitting alone in the highest occupied row.

"Excuse me. May Janaka and I sit here?"

Ayelet nodded. "Of course, Magistrada."

Barissianna took the second seat to the left of the Jinn. Janaka sat next to her in the aisle seat. She wondered how long they would have to wait. The Jinni were still arriving. The room was massive yet intimate. Allyssia's palace made the Auerbach chantries look like shacks. Barissianna glanced over at Ayelet. The famous blade mistress was staring ahead silently, as if lost in thought. The callouses of a life devoted to swords were visible around Ayelet's strong, worn fingers.

"I've heard stories of you, Mistress Ayelet."

The Jinn arched her eyebrow, but continued looking straight ahead. "You have? Should I be penitent or flattered?"

"I've seen your name in Hell's history books. You're a great blade mistress."

"And you're of high rank, Magistrada. You should be seated down in front."

Barissianna smiled. "I'm considered more of a scholar and a sorceress than leadership material. I run a chantry because my sire is the clan patriarch, Liest Ussishkin. Why aren't you sitting in the front row yourself, Ayelet?"

"It's reserved for the divines-Mistress Harmoniah and fledgling Hymen-Ca, Mistress Persephoneh, Cupid and his wife Psyche, Master Hermaphroditus, Master Priapus, and Cupid's children, when they're invited. Herpessenia-Ca used to be here, but she left us."

"The New Order Jinni are a small family."

Ayelet nodded grimly. "We have about seventy mistresses left after the attack on our city last year. We have fewer fledglings as well. There are more Auerbach than us."

"We have almost a hundred here in Meristyian."

"That's a big number compared to most clans with an Isandlwana presence, isn't it?"

"Except for the Disciples of Set. None of their nobility was killed when you defeated them, and they are already rebuilding. Lord Hades is helping them in exchange for their re-allegiance."

"Your world is shrinking like ours, Magistrada."

"Yes. Heaven and Hell are squeezing us all. Lord Hades' continued alliance with the Disciples is just an extra nail for the coffin he'd like to lay us in. Even worse, our Isandlwana conflicts with the Disciples are spilling over onto Earth."

"I fought a Disciple prince the spring before last. He was very difficult. I was unable to injure him."

Barissianna rose and shifted into the seat to Ayelet's left, the better to lower her tone. "The Disciple royalty use a mysticism practice called cirai. I've been researching cirai, trying to develop some way to counter it. Do you know of it?"

"No, I don't," Ayelet answered.

"cirai is the eating of souls. No one knows where or how the Disciples discovered cirai, but it's our best explanation for their fast rise."

"Sounds like a disgusting practice."

"It is. The Disciples keep their technique for soul stealing a closely guarded secret. We don't know exactly how it works yet or where it's being performed."

Ayelet nodded. "sharing knowledge like this will be a benefit of this alliance between the New Order and the Auerbach. Have many of your clan have suffered from this Disciple practice of cirai?"

Barissianna bit her lip. "It's not a pleasant subject. Ask Amanoch."

"I'm sorry. I didn't mean to offend, Magistrada."

Barissianna smiled wryly. "With Patriarch Ussishkin currently living on Earth, more and more of our ascended clan members are going back to their flesh where they are safer, leaving Meristyian to the Disciples of Set. We can't defend all of our chantries in the Black Sea area here with the men we have."

"You've lost one outpost, correct?"

"In the last few days, we've now confirmed two. The first was a test, I think, and that emboldened the Disciples. The second attack was the one that had real strategic importance, as the chantry sits near a road into

Erebus. They took it from us in a single night with the help of stealth, ropes, and Smokeless Flames Nankariders."

"It's unfortunate that the Old Order Jinni and the Disciples are still allies. Are your chantries well-hidden and defended magically?"

"They were built centuries ago. Our enemies were only werewolves back then, not Lord Hades or other vampire clans. I'm only a few centuries old, but even I can remember when the word Meristyian meant peace."

"Indeed."

A bell rang loudly through the chamber. Barissianna felt the vibration of the bell in every inch of her hypersensitive body. A rain of golden motes fell over the central dais, lighting it aglow. Allyssia appeared in the midst. The presence of the legendary love goddess was palpable. Her aspect was a perfect female-nude with golden brown skin and an ivory mask that seemed expressionless. Her voice rose in the chamber with a resonant tone.

"Greetings, Jinni and vampires. The phrase sounds strange, but I hope one day it will sound beautiful. We are gathered here this night for a common cause-to fight for an Meristyian that is free from the yokes and control."

A quiet applause ran through the chamber.

"One year ago, my city was assaulted by a combined force of Old Order Jinni and Disciple vampires, aided by the Mimọic Hierarchy," Allyssia continued. "We stand today victorious despite having suffered tragic losses. Tonight, the New Order welcomes the Auerbach vampires into our city. We propose to live side by side in harmony. We propose to unite our forces to resist the encroachment of our enemies on our Isandlwana homes. Using our combined strength as a deterrent, we will hope to achieve respite and protection from oppression."

Barissianna joined the applause that sounded loudly throughout the chamber.

"Our enemies are strong," continued the Lady. "But we are strong too. We are also allied with the goddess Sekhmet, who is even now in the east, working with our own Mistress Golda to rebuild and reassemble the Eastern Order Jinni after the invasion of her home in Ptah's temple in Memphis. We still have the good will of the Gypsy lords, who will continue their trade routes if only Lord Hades' blockades are lifted. With that I cede the floor to Prince Amanoch."

Amanoch rose to his feet. "Greetings, vampires and Jinni. Our negotiations have been long, so I'll keep the oratory short. On behalf of my father, Patriarch Ussishkin, tonight I have signed a pact to join the Auerbach with the New Order Jinni in the defense of a free Meristyian. We're going to fight the Disciples together. I'm confident this union will be a fruitful one. The time for negotiations and debate are over. We turn our attention now to action. Tomorrow night I, alongside Mistress Artemisiah, who is a loyal follower of Allyssia and a goddess in her own right, will lead a joint raid to free the Trivium trade route from the Old Order Jinni who currently hold it. The way has been scouted. We'll strike decisively."

The Prince bowed and returned to his seat. Allyssia's form glowed again into prominence. The goddess spoke with a graceful flourish. "Tomorrow we fight, but tonight we celebrate together. We drink to an Meristyian filled with love and respect for everyone. As of tonight, the Auerbach have free reign in my city abiding by the rules agreed upon."

Applause resonated in the chamber. The goddess disappeared into a shower of golden motes that drifted into nothingness, and Cupid drifted up the steps, leaving only the Prince and the Matriarch on the central dais. Barissianna felt Janaka's hand on her shoulder, kneading away her tension.

"It was nice to meet you, Magistrada." Ayelet turned and extended her worn hand over the seat. "And you as well, Janaka."

Barissianna took Ayelet's hand. Predictably, the grip of the great blade master was commanding. "I was wondering if I could ask you something, Mistress Ayelet. I could use some help with my sword technique. I study magic on Earth, but normally I have a gun with me. In this place, I need to work on my sword. I've been sparring with Janaka, but I'm not getting anywhere."

"I'd be happy to help. I normally only give lessons to talented fledglings, but my fledgling left me a year ago, and since then I've been underutilized.

You'll be going on the raid tomorrow night at the Trivium, I hope? Bring your sword as well as your magic. We can work side by side."

"I? Well, yes. I expect I'll probably be there."

"I think that would give me the best possible view of your technique. We can work on it later, assuming we both survive, of course."

Barissianna arched her eyebrow. "I can't tell if you're being modest, Ayelet, or if you think too little of the Auerbach."

"I don't underestimate the Old Order Jinni and the division of Hell's army that are garrisoning the Trivium. I don't mean to sound skeptical that we will win the night, but it will be a test that I'm not looking forward to. We'll arrange some tutelage afterwards?"

"That would be wonderful. Thank you. I'll feel safer by your side in the battle, anyway, and I'll hope to live to get those sword lessons."

Janaka chuckled. "Better she beats on you with that thing than me, Mistress Ayelet."

Ayelet smiled faintly. "Will you be going with us on the raid, Janaka?"

"I'm a lover, not a fighter. Someone has to take care of the most beautiful and talented vampiress in all of the realms."

"Well, that's an admirable attitude. I'll see you tomorrow night, Barissianna. I'm going to go get some rest." Ayelet slipped past and ascended the steps. Ayelet moved fast with loping strides. Barissianna fell in behind. Janaka found her hand with his own. She held it as they moved upwards and out, then down the long corridors of the palace and into the vast entry hall.

Barissianna hesitated when she glimpsed Nina in the window to the palace coat room. The handsome Mimọ boy was helping dole out evening coats to the Jinn mistresses on their way out of the palace. His almond brown skin glistened in the lamp light.

"Shall I retrieve him, my Love?" Janaka murmured.

"No, we'll wait. He looks busy, and I was shameless enough today when I begged Master Priapus to let me have him."

"Your begging was very shameless, especially after Amanoch asked you not to."

"He's a hypocrite. Bernanke and Valeriu are too. Did you know that Bernanke was bragging about fucking some Jinn at her home? As if he was doing her a favor, since there are no 'real men' around here, and meanwhile he was breaking our agreement with Allyssia about staying in the palace until after our pact was signed."

"Typical."

"Don't smile at me, Janaka. I'm going to be fed up with you soon too. What was it you said to Ayelet? 'Better she beats on you than me'?"

"I apologize, my Love. I only meant that my own defense is too weak to take your mighty blows, not that your skillful and well-placed attacks ever fly off the mark. For my part, I wasn't aware that you were running off to the battle. When were you going to tell me?"

Barissianna grimaced. "Actually, I didn't know either. Ayelet sort of put me on the spot. I wonder if she's testing me."

"It will be dangerous, sire. Are you sure about this?"

"No. I'm terrified, actually, but I don't think I can back out now." Barissianna waved to Tajee, who had spotted them. The thrall boy approached at the same time as Bernanke and Valeriu, who strode along with the dregs of the meeting-goers.

"We'll crush the Old Order Jinni like beetles, Barissianna," Valeriu said, stopping short. "I hope they try those useless paralyzation whips on us again. Stupid bitches."

"Are you coming to the party in the tower, Barissianna?" Bernanke's voice rumbled in the afterworld the same as on Earth-like a freight train in a barrel.

Barissianna smiled and motioned Tajee close. The boy thrall was incredibly handsome. He wore a fine skirt and gilded sandals, but otherwise his smooth brown skin was bare and oiled. He smelled like jasmine. She ruffled his soft dark hair in greeting. "Not tonight, Bernanke. I'm having a private party of my own."

The two male vampires, both burly, muscled, and half again Tajee's size, stared down with mock menace at the Mimo boy. "You're seriously going to entertain yourself with this little freak, Barissianna?" Valeriu finally said.

"This is Nina. Nina, meet Bernanke and Valeriu. They are Prince Amanoch's personal bodyguards."

"The thrall doesn't need to know our names," Bernanke said. "Why are you going to Barissianna's chambers, thrall?"

Nina shrank visibly. "I'm going to do her and Master Janaka's nails, sir, and whatever else pleases them."

"Master Janaka!" Bernanke roared with laughter. He nudged Valeriu's arm. "He's a master now, is he, and he needs his nails done? Enjoy your playthings, Barissianna. They always seem to multiply, don't they?"

"Don't be cruel, Bernanke," Barissianna called after them. "Every woman needs her diversions."

"And at least I have one," Janaka muttered. "A real woman, that is."

Barissianna squeezed Tajee's shoulder. "Those are nasty boys. You aren't nasty, are you Nina? You're a nice, sweet boy. Are we going to have some fun tonight in my quarters?"

"As you wish, Magistrada Barissianna."

"I do, and thanks for running off the brute patrol. I'm sure they felt queer around a boy in a skirt." Barissianna pulled Nina along as she escorted her two handsome and sexually amenable men to her quarters. She was looking forward to a wonderful evening of relaxation and pleasure. She wasn't looking forward at all, however, to the prospect of deadly swordplay alongside Mistress Ayelet. Flesh in Hell magnified pain just as much as pleasure.

Mistress Ayelet and the New Order Jinni were all about being fierce women. If she wanted their respect, she needed to act as one of them. She'd have to notify Amanoch of her intention to fight so he'd reserve a seat for her on a clan chiropterim. She could only imagine his reaction.

# Chapter 7:

Boudi-Ca sat in front of her vanity and examined her dark dyed hair for the umpteenth time. She liked her new color, even if Isabellah didn't. She liked how she looked like a different person. Her hair made her look more like a Jinn and less like an innocent Mimo. The prior two days in Isabellah's house had been horrible. She and Isabellah had fought back and forth over her vampire hair, as well as her 'stubborn attitude' and 'identity crisis'. They'd reached a strained peace for the moment.

Her problem, after successfully braving Isabellah's complaints and insisting on keeping her hair color, was what to do with the rest of her image-her lips, ears, and eyes. In their last argument, Isabellah had told her that she was completely on her own. She waved her hand and summoned her magical blue messenger finch to her fingers.

"Hello, Ranavalona. Do you want to go to the shops with me this afternoon?" Boudi-Ca tossed the bird into the air and pictured Ranavalona. The little bird flitted off. Boudi-Ca examined herself in the mirror. Her arms were thin and toned, not so muscled as when she'd been working full-time with swords as Ayelet's fledgling. She was mostly proud of her shaved legs. They were perfect sleek spindles. Her breasts hadn't developed so much as a Jinn. They were bland and hardly larger than big apples, lacking a fullness that could attractively fill a corset.

Boudi-Ca smoothed her eyebrows and applied a touch of fresh wax to her cheeks. She rose and went to her wardrobe. She selected a stiff corset and a blue summer dress with small paniers that puffed just enough around her hips and buttocks. She threw the dress on the bed, tacked together the two wooden batons on her side table, and went back to her vanity.

She'd selected a few silver accessories by the time Bijou arrived. Bijou opened the door but didn't enter. Instead, the dressing-girl stood in the doorway with her eyes downcast. "I cannot dress you. Mistress says tie your own corset."

"How am I supposed to do that?"

"I do not know, fledgling. Wear a front-lace?"

Boudi-Ca pushed Bijou out of the way and stomped the hall to Mistress Isabellah's bedchamber. The door was unlocked. Isabellah sat at her marble vanity in her luxurious silken quarters. Isabellah's long hair was loose at her shoulders, uncoiffed, unpowdered, and unbejewelled.

"Mistress, I'm sorry I went and dyed my hair. I apologize. I can choose to have my hair any way I please. That's just all there is to it. I need Bijou to lace my corset, at least. This is ridiculous."

Isabellah pivoted. Her eyes were hollow, as if she hadn't slept or fed. "I wish you respected me as much as Ayelet. Although you've chosen me as your new mistress, you haven't left Ayelet behind in your mind."

"We were just playing a game."

"I understand, Boudi-Ca. You like to be the center of attention. There's nothing wrong with that. It's what every beauty mistress strives for."

"So?"

"Involving yourself with the Auerbach vampires is dangerous and ill-advised. Ayelet is obviously encouraging you in that vein. Your life is not a game."

"Ayelet isn't encouraging me! I just wanted to dye my hair black. We played a vampire game, and I dyed my hair and bit a few Ahyehasi, but I'm not really that interested in the vampires. You're stretching things way out of proportion."

"You're interested in the Prince," Isabellah countered.

"I've never felt really attracted to a man before. I don't know what this is, but it's different, and it intrigues me. I want to meet the Prince."

Isabellah pounded her fist on her vanity. Jewelry jumped and a perfume bottle toppled. "Boudi-Ca, you absolutely infuriate me! Courting the Prince and accepting his gifts will not be tolerated, do you understand me? There is no discussion. The Prince will marry a fully-fledged mistress, if he wishes. Period. You are not a mistress."

"Then maybe I should be."

"Oh, so you think you're ready for your Mistress Test? And you talk about ridiculous. You lack the discipline, the experience, and the skills. Even if you were fully fledged and graduated, I'd still forbid you to court the Prince, incidentally. It would still be foolish."

"Mistress, every time you forbid me, I want to see the Prince more. My love spell apparently brought a vampire to me. I should see where it leads."

Isabellah's jaw clenched. "I've had you as a fledgling for a year now, and I love you like my own daughter, but you still have so much to learn. You have a lot to learn about love spells, too. They backfire more often than they work, in my opinion, especially when they are cast by a fledgling. A little knowledge of magic can be a dangerous thing."

A small brown bird with yellow cheeks scrabbled at the bird slit above the bedchamber window. Isabellah turned, but it flew past where she sat. Boudi-Ca tilted her head to receive it. The bird's talons tickled like fangs on the skin of her neck. It spoke with Ranavalona's voice.

I'd be delighted to go to the shops with you. But can we go around the two? I have some things to finish first.

Boudi-Ca summoned a bird. "I'll meet you at the reflecting pool." She threw the bird aloft, and it flitted out through the window slit.

Isabellah frowned. "Where are you going, and with whom? I didn't recognize that bird."

"I'm going shopping with Ranavalona-Ca. Can I still have the coins that you promised me the other day? I didn't see any on the hall table."

Isabellah reached for her purse. "Ranavalona-Ca is trouble, too. Why are you so drawn to trouble, Boudi-Ca?"

"You told me to go shopping with Ranavalona! Nothing I do ever meets your approval! If I have so much to learn, then let me learn from my mistakes, like Ayelet does. At least that way I can live."

Isabellah looked her in the eye. "I only want to protect you because I care about you, fledgling. I'll try to be more lenient if you make a greater effort to respect my wisdom."

"I'll try. Fine."

"You're just bored, fledgling. You're not interested anymore in your painting lessons with Cybelah. Should we make your piano lessons with Mistress Melkeh into a daily thing? Maybe music is the art for you."

"I've been thinking about making clothing. I'm good at sewing. My Mimo clothes in Heaven were too modest, but they were beautiful. They could be a unique style for me, if I could remake them."

Isabellah's eyes brightened. "That's a very interesting idea. If your clothes were actually good, you'd attract some wealthy buyers for them in the Haawiyah markets. Jinni and Djinnus in the capital city might well buy clothing for their collared Mimos, especially if the clothes were decadent but still authentic. You've been thinking about this for a while?"

"I talked about it with Ayelet. She'll pay me if I make some Mimo costumes for her Ahyehasi."

Isabellah sighed. "Somehow I'm not surprised that Ayelet knows all about this new direction in your head. Was it Ayelet's idea, then?"

"It was sort of both our ideas."

"Speak to Mistress Gallinah at the workshops." Isabellah turned and fished in her vanity drawer. "Here. Take these coins. They should get you started with some basic materials."

"Thank you, Mistress." Boudi-Ca accepted the stack of coins, which weighed much more than she'd expected.

"Off you go. Have fun with Ranavalona-Ca."

"Thank you, Mistress." Boudi-Ca pivoted and went back to her bedroom, counting out the silver denarii and gold aurei as she went. Isabellah had given her more than ever before-a small fortune. Bijou was still waiting for her. The Ahyehass curtseyed.

"Fledgling?"

"Never mind," Boudi-Ca said. She drew the coins into small stacks on her vanity. "I'm meeting Ranavalona-Ca at two. I suppose I'll write in my diary for a while. Come back at quarter after one. I want my nipples stung for Ranavalona."

~*~

Boudi-Ca rolled out of the Isabellah's drive at two. Although Isabellah's gardens were not the equal of Ayelet's, Isabellah's carriage was far more extravagant, with brown velvety seats and a polished, white-painted, ivory-embellished exterior in the shape of a swan. The stable girl, who doubled as Isabellah's driver, snapped the whip at the matching white ponies and soon drew the carriage up to the reflecting pool in the nearby plaza. Ranavalona already sat waiting.

Boudi-Ca smiled. She'd timed her arrival at ten minutes late, just as Isabellah had taught her. Ten minutes were long enough to make someone wait for you, but not long enough to make them angry. Ranavalona wore a green dress and a fashionable summer hat with feathers and blue-ribboned festoons. Boudi-Ca felt a spark of envy in her belly. She suspected that summer hats had come into season in the previous two days, and Isabellah had neglected to tell her.

Ranavalona held onto her expensive, gaudy hat with one hand as she climbed into the carriage, a gesture meant to draw attention to it since there was no particular wind. With Ranavalona in the carriage, the stable girl-cum-driver cracked the whip again. Boudi-Ca offered a smile and straightened her hair behind her ear.

"Hello, Ranavalona. It's a beautiful day."

Ranavalona smiled back. "I agree. The city seems really flowery this summer. The crested pink-petal swans haven't arrived yet, though. I was hoping to see a few at the pool."

"Where do they arrive from?"

"Your dark hair is startling, Boudi-Ca. Szenes mentioned it, but I didn't believe her."

Boudi-Ca shrugged. "Isabellah apparently sent birds to all of her friends lamenting the fact that I ruined my beautiful hair. What do you really think? You can tell me the truth."

Ranavalona fidgeted. Boudi-Ca noticed the hesitation, even though it was barely perceptible. "Well, like I said, it's surprising. You look different. With your pale Mimo skin, you look like almost like a vampiress. Szenes said Prince Amanoch sent you a gift, too. Is that true?"

"Actually, he did." Boudi-Ca paused for dramatic effect. She felt a warmth of pride. Ranavalona was looking at her with baited breath and wide dark brown eyes.

"Go on."

"Well, Prince Amanoch kept staring at me at the palace ball. It was embarrassing. And then he sent me some extravagant gold earrings in a pointy vampire style. Isabellah made me send them back, but we'll see what happens. The Prince is amazingly handsome and powerful, and he's definitely attracted to me."

"I'm sorry, Boudi." Ranavalona adjusted her hat, tipping it against the slight breeze that arose as the carriage picked up speed down the long hill towards the workshops. "You must be upset that you can't have the Prince since you're only a fledgling."

"I was a little upset when Isabellah took my earrings away. amorous gifts were never given in Heaven like that. It would have been sinful."

"Strange." Ranavalona's voice was barely audible over the rattle and clatter of the carriage, which had begun to descend the steep hill to the shops at pace. Within minutes they reached the bottom of the hill and rolled onto the main workshop street. Boudi-Ca tapped the stable girl's shoulder.

"Here is fine. Just wait until we're done."

"Yes, fledgling." The Ahyehass brought the carriage to a stop. Boudi-Ca slipped out of the seat and steadied her heels on the uneven cobblestones. Ranavalona slid out the other side and walked around the horses, looking gorgeous in her summer dress. Ranavalona caught her gaze with a slow smile.

"So what are we shopping for, Boudi?"

"I need some new cosmetics to match my new hair. I need a dark red for my lips like yours, if you don't mind. I was hoping to get your opinion."

"Red would look wicked," Ranavalona said. "The only vampires I've seen with painted lips wore them black like the Old Order, though. What were the Auerbach women wearing at the ball?"

Boudi-Ca frowned. "The Matriarch wasn't wearing any paint at all. She was old and antique-all pale, powdery, and dead-looking."

"If you powdered your face, you'd look completely like a vampire."

"I don't know if I'd want to look like that. I wore titanium powder when I was an Mimọ girl to hide my blush, but only the older mistresses use powder here. Where did you see vampires with black lips?"

"During the attack last year and the occupation of the Redoubt, the Disciple sorceresses wore all black, just like the Old Order. You weren't here, of course. You were busy in the east, helping to free Lady Sekhmet and save us all. I suppose you're right to be cautious. You want to look beautiful, not frightening."

Boudi-Ca pushed the door open and entered the clothes shop. Ranavalona moved through the front room to look at the rack of summer dresses. Boudi-Ca made a beeline for the exotic brown-skinned mistress at the glass counter. Hatshepseh wore something like a yellow bedsheet around her body, with a matching brown-gold linen head-wrapping that was decorated, like her ears and nose, with gold and ivory beads.

"Greetings, fledgling," Hatshepseh said. "I've forgotten your name."

"Boudi-Ca," Boudi-Ca replied. She had the urge to admonish the old mistress, but she politely resisted. She'd surely been in the shop ten times with Isabellah. "I'm here for some red lip paint and some black pencils. I'd also like to buy some face powder."

"What type of powder, child?" Hatshepseh said with a quizzical look.

Boudi-Ca blushed. "I'd like the kind for my face, of course. I'd like titanium powder, or zinc powder, or something like that."

Hatshepseh shook her head. "You can pick your pencils from that urn, but I have no red paint. The blockade of the western trade route has cut off the supply of things."

"I'd forgotten about that."

"I do have some blue left," Hatshepseh continued. "I don't have red, so no purples either. I have some black and white that can be mixed to make shades of grey. I have some old sulfur and clay yellows, but no one uses them."

"Well, Mistress Isabellah said that I should never wear purple on my lips, because I'd look like a cheap nectar-eater like Golda. I suppose purple would match my bird, though."

"Your eyes too, dear."

"I'd like some black paint and some purple paint then."

"Of course. I'll prepare some for you in the back room. The pencils are in the urn, dear. Mind you, the lapis purple paint is a bit expensive. You have several denarii? At least twenty bits?"

"Yes. I do."

Boudi-Ca picked a pair of handmade charcoal pencils and laid them on the counter. She headed into the gloom of the nearby dressing room where Ranavalona had disappeared with a fanciful white dress. She found the ebony fledgling seated on a chair, clad only in her corset, stockings, and garters. Ranavalona had shucked her dress. A leather strap encircled her thigh with a small sheath, as if for a hidden dagger. Instead of a blade, however, the sheath held a small wooden phallus.

"Between the two of us, Boudi, I have plenty of red paint at home." Ranavalona's lips curled into a slow, sultry smile. "Mistress Szenes wears it too, and she bought up all of it that was available at the Spring Festival. We have a year's supply, almost. Do you want me to get you some?"

"Yes! That would be really nice of you."

Ranavalona grinned. "You really want some?"

"Yes. I said I did."

"Well, it won't be that easy. I think if you want it so much, you should have to be nice to me. Maybe you should beg me a little bit."

Boudi-Ca bit her lip. She approached the ebony fledgling and pressed close. "You're very beautiful, Ranavalona."

"Kiss me."

Boudi-Ca leaned to kiss Ranavalona where she was seated. Ranavalona nuzzled her with the point of her nose and exhaled a warm sigh across her cheek. The ebony fledgling drew the phallus from its sheath on her thigh and lifted it. Boudi-Ca opened her mouth to receive it. The phallus was oddly shaped-stubby with flared ends. Boudi-Ca suckled it as she looked into Ranavalona's dangerous eyes. Ranavalona smiled, removed the phallus, and reached low.

Boudi-Ca grabbed the back of the chair for balance when Ranavalona reached under her skirt, through her legs, and grabbed her ass. The angle was awkward, half-embracing Ranavalona and shoving her breasts into the ebony fledgling's face. She felt Ranavalona's hand take command of her ass, and then Ranavalona pushed the bone phallus deep between her buttocks, thrusting and filling her there yet again in her forbidden nethers.

Boudi-Ca braced herself to keep her legs from buckling. She felt an odd pressure building already, only ten times stronger, and the desire was pooling queerly inside her. Ranavalona's fingers shifted to work in her sex, and the fingers had an overwhelming effect. Boudi-Ca slid onto Ranavalona's lap and met the dark fledgling's full lips with a hot, passionate kiss. Ranavalona stroked her as they kissed. A long minute passed, then two, until Hatshepseh called from the front room.

"Boudi-Ca? Your colors are ready."

Boudi-Ca broke the kiss. She was already close to an orgasm, but she didn't want to embarrass herself. "Ranavalona, we need to stop. Please. Let's go back to my bedroom."

"Very well." Ranavalona ceased her efforts. The ebony fledgling withdrew her fingers and licked them with relish. Boudi-Ca rearranged her dress while Ranavalona found her own dress and slipped it wordlessly over her head. Boudi-Ca felt her heart pounding. The flared bone phallus was still stuck solidly inside her little aperture, and it wasn't coming out. With her legs together, the phallus exerted a pressure far out of proportion to its modest size.

"You like it?" Ranavalona kissed her gently. "I know you do, Boudi. Don't lie."

Boudi-Ca felt a fierce blush rising to heat her cheeks. "I…I don't know. Ayelet says it's bad. It will make my energy leak. It will make me weak."

"Only when I decide to take it out. Don't worry. I'll take care of you. You're going to look beautiful with the red paint, and then we'll match, too. This fall, if the blockade continues, we'll be the only fledglings in the Redoubt still wearing red. We'll go to parties together, and we'll make everyone jealous with our passionate kisses." Ranavalona grinned.

"I don't like this. Can you just take it out now?"

A storm slowly brewed in Ranavalona's eyes. "Ask me more submissively. I'm dominating you. Don't you get it?"

"You couldn't dominate me even if you tried."

"I just did, and now you're blushing all the way down to your pretty little Mimo tits." Ranavalona nonchalantly picked up her hat and walked towards the front of the shop. Boudi-Ca followed her. The phallus in her rear stimulated her as she walked. At the same time, she felt terribly wet. Hatshepseh had the paints and pencils wrapped and ready at the counter. The old mistress winked. Boudi-Ca tried to focus to count out the silver coins. When she finished paying, she snatched her purchase and followed Ranavalona out of the shop. Ranavalona waited by the carriage in the brilliant sunlight.

"I admit that I kind of like it, Ranavalona. Now please take it out?"

"I'll consider it. I'm glad we're taking a step in the right direction. Where are we going next?"

"To Mistress Gallinah's." Boudi-Ca walked down the street. She stopped, pressed her hand quickly into her dress, and rubbed her thighs together. The wetness from her sex was trickling obscenely down the inside of her thigh.

Ranavalona nonchalantly examined her fingernails. "You're really wet, aren't you?"

"Yes."

"That specially-shaped phallus puts a pressure in your root chakra that makes your sex chakra overflow. The penetration only affects Jinni this way-not humans or anyone else. It makes our energy leak from our bodies. So how does it feel when you walk?"

Boudi-Ca took a deep breath to calm her anger. She'd planned to have a serious talk with Gallinah about tailoring and how to make clothing designs, but she couldn't possibly concentrate. She didn't know if she could even make it to Gallinah's shop, much less talk properly about her bold artistic ideas for clothing.

"I've decided I don't want to go to see Gallinah. I just want to go home now." Boudi-Ca wheeled and stalked as quickly as she could back to Isabellah's carriage. She snapped at the Ahyehass. "Take me home, please."

Boudi-Ca stifled a moan when she sat down in the padded seat. To her surprise, Ranavalona had followed her and climbed in silently as the driver cracked the whip. The ponies climbed back up the hill with agonizing slowness. Boudi-Ca groaned. Each bump on the marble stones of the street sent a shiver of pleasure shooting through her abdomen. All the while, Ranavalona watched her impassively. After twenty long minutes they reached Isabellah's house.

Boudi-Ca jumped out of the carriage, strode into the side door and up the stairs, and ran into her bedchamber, ignoring the week-kneed sensations she felt with every step. Ranavalona closed the door behind them. Boudi-Ca eyed her, trying to stay calm and not show how furious she was.

"I'm sorry, Ranavalona. I was a little bit immature."

"No need to apologize, Boudi-Ca," Ranavalona said smoothly. "We both feel about things the way we feel. Both of us like our pride, you and I. Neither of us should have to deny ourselves what we want."

"Then take it out, please. Now."

Boudi-Ca turned away from Ranavalona and bunched up her dress and slip. She leaned on her desk and presented her backside to Ranavalona. Ranavalona's hand caressed her buttocks softly, dipped, and tugged Sharply. Boudi-Ca groaned. The resulting wave of weakness nearly threw her to the wood floor. Her knees were so weak that she could hardly stay on her feet.

"It's out," Ranavalona said. "I wasn't trying to hurt you, Boudi-Ca. I was playing a game. Maybe you haven't figured it out yet, but that's what we Jinni do. I wanted to make you experience something completely new. So did I, or didn't I?"

Boudi-Ca made her way to her bed and slumped onto it. She stared up at Ranavalona. "I don't want to be dominated. I want a relationship of equals. That's how I cast the love spell, remember?"

"I'm not your tarot card, Boudi-Ca. You have so much to learn. Like Isabellah said to my mistress, you're still just an innocent, naïve girl."

Boudi-Ca felt her cheeks heat. "Isabellah said that? When?"

Ranavalona sighed as she went to the bedroom door. "I don't want a drama, you little Mimọ bitch. I've been nice to you, considering."

"Considering what?"

"Considering you like to write rude things about me in your diary. Why don't you be a good girl and write some more. That would make me happy."

Ranavalona slammed the door behind her. Boudi-Ca stared at the closed door. She rose unsteadily to her feet. Her legs were rubbery. She stumbled to her desk, threw open her diary, and thumbed the pages. She scrutinized the writing in the low light. She turned page after page.

Finally, in the margin next to a particular paragraph dated the previous summer, she found a fresh print of red-painted lips-a print that she herself hadn't placed. She examined the adjacent entry.


June 14


I met the fledgling of Mistress Szenes today. Her name is Ranavalona-Ca. She has dark olive skin like Bola, Mistress Ayelet's male Ahyehass. Ranavalona seemed more interested in eating figs and taking Bijou than speaking with me. She has a presence, but she's undisciplined and rude. Ranavalona's dress doesn't fit her well, either. She has a nice figure, but her dress makes her look lumpy. Her hairstyle is just an eyesore. I'm disappointed because I was excited to meet a real beauty fledgling. I'm totally unimpressed.

Boudi-Ca slumped. She considered sending a bird to Ranavalona with some sort of apology, but she had no idea what to say. She put her head in her hands. Tears came unbidden to her eyes. She was furious with Ranavalona and even more furious with Isabellah. Maybe she was still a naïve Mimọ girl, but Isabellah didn't need to disparage her in front of everyone.

A hand came to rest suddenly on her shoulder. Boudi-Ca jumped. She turned in her chair, half-hoping to see Ranavalona, but the weight wasn't a hand after all. It was a large grey dove that smelled faintly of rain. The bird pecked at the wetness of the tears on her cheek, and then whispered in her ear with the voice of Allyssia.

Remember you said you wanted to learn from your mistakes, fledgling. Pride is a challenging path. The key is respect. Respect others and show them love, and only then shall love be returned to you.

The dove was gone. Boudi-Ca rose from her writing chair and stumbled to her bed. She felt terribly empty. Her Hunger ached suddenly in her belly as if she hadn't fed for days. She pulled at her bedcovers until she was buried like a vampire in a grave. Her breath was hot and close in the dark space. She heard a faint scratch on the bird slit, and a weight landed on the bedcovers.

"Just leave me alone." She thrust and flailed to push away the dove, but inexplicably the bird found its way underneath the duvet with her. Its Sharp talons scrabbled against her bare neck to get to her ear.

You can't hide from me, fledgling. I was the reflecting pool that Ranavalona gazed upon while she waited for you to arrive. I was the wind in your hair as you rode home. Don't be afraid, for thou art love, and love art thou. Hold yourself close and fiercely, and you shall be whole. Now I shall leave you alone, with my blessing of grace, as I travel far to a distant place.

# Chapter 8:

Ayelet crouched on a stone ledge overlooking the Trivium. The Trivium was a junction where three roads met-a wide chisel-cut in the treacherous highlands that divided western Meristyian and the Asphodel meadows from the plains of Erebus. The moonlight of Meristyian glowed into the cut of the south road. Another soft light poured from the clouds above Mount Purgatory on the opposite side, a dim promise to weary human souls who wandered in the night up the barren and fruitless slopes.

The northern end of the Trivium gap, with its well-traveled highway that led deeper into the Underworld, was pitch dark, and a powerful wind arose from that darkness, born from the storms that were a fixture of the distant windswept plains of Erebus.

The wind blew sparks from the torches and fires that burned in the Trivium citadel. The old abandoned Court of Hell stood at that junction of the three roads, where Minos, Rhadamanthus, and Aeacus had once judged all souls. Hell's army and the Old Order Jinni had recently re-established a fortified presence in the building that had been razed by the Mimos centuries ago.

The wind howled strongly in the gap, and the fires flared, rendering just visible the newly-built gates that barred the road into Meristyian, effectively blocking the Gypsies from carrying trade goods into upper regions of the Underworld. The gates were overt evidence of the Old Order's interference with the Lady's city. According to the whispers among the nimfas, the Seelie Court on the Blessed Isles was also affected by the blockade.

Ayelet grimaced. What was the Old Order playing at? Had the Mimoic Hierarchy not yet noticed the imposition on their doorstep? If so, why hadn't they done anything about it? Ayelet fingered her sword hilt. She only hoped the plan of attack would work.

Ayelet felt the presence of Barissianna and glanced over her shoulder. The vampiress had a presence that was tangible, like most powerful vampires. Barissianna clambered over the rocks like a black widow in her dyed leather armor. Barissianna's long dark hair blew in the night wind. The pale gleam of her pointed canines was just visible when she smiled.

"Do you see anything yet, Ayelet?"

"No. We're still waiting for Artemisiah. You're sure your bats can fly in these windy conditions?"

"If Amanoch says they can, then the chiropterim can. He's the expert."

"According to the bird I received a while ago from Artemisiah, the supply caravan from Haawiyah will be arriving soon. When they open the gates of the Trivium to let it in, we'll attack in tandem with Artemisiah's ground force."

"I hope you're not as nervous as I am."

Ayelet smiled. "Stay close to me. We'll watch each other's backs. The Old Order's presence here is much more established than I expected from the reconnaissance report. I'm concerned that Prince Amanoch and the Lady are acting a bit rashly."

"How so?"

"Both have a strong character that refuses to be bullied, even by Lord Hades."

Barissianna shrugged. "We have to stop the Disciples and their soul-eating practice of cirai, so we have to stop any of Lord Hades' people who help them."

"I would settle for a treaty and a return to the way things have been."

"Meanwhile, our chantries are being captured, and our people are losing their very souls so the Disciples can grow even more powerful." Barissianna pointed. "Look. They're lighting the fires outside the castle, or whatever it is. I see the Gypsy caravan with the wagons and draft horses."

Ayelet squinted. "Your vision at night is much better than mine. It's time we go aloft then. We need to be there when Artemisiah launches her surprise assault. Remind Amanoch to watch out for Nanka. These cliffs are riddled with old volcanic passages. The Old Order may well have an air defense hidden somewhere."

"Understood."

Ayelet followed Barissianna, who signaled Prince Amanoch and the Auerbach men. The small force of vampires scurried in masse to their giant bats. Ayelet waited while Barissianna conversed with the Prince. The Magistrada was attractive in her armor, which Mistress Freyah had fitted earlier that evening for the vampiress. The armor fit her form almost perfectly, from her heart-shaped derriere to her fullish breasts. Barissianna carried a figure that many a beauty mistress would envy. The scimitar looked out of place on her hip.

Ayelet looked away. She hoped she didn't regret inviting Barissianna to the raid. She hoped she hadn't been selfish. A battle always served to rouse her passion, and there was nothing better than a life-or-death struggle to create a visceral intimacy between two complete strangers. Barissianna stirred something in her that she hadn't felt in forever-an exotic possibility with a younger, intelligent woman who wasn't truly young.

Ayelet followed Barissianna up the wooden rungs to the wicker basket on the back of the giant bat. She settled into the narrow seat next to the vampiress. The burly male vampire named Bernanke unfurled the reins. Ayelet felt her stomach lurch as the bat flitted into the night. The bat's wings thumped hard in the cold mountain air. The bat swooped down towards the keep. Bernanke directed it into a wide arc.

"Hold on, Ayelet," Barissianna said over the rushing wind. "Bernanke is a daredevil, but he's one of our best flyers with the chiropterim. He can also handle a helicopter. He has a pilot's license in Miami."

Ayelet nodded, although the words helicopter and Miami were modern Earth terms that meant nothing to her. For a long minute they circled on the bat until the flashes of Artemisiah's lightning lit up the Trivium below, followed by booms of thunder that echoed. Ayelet leaned forward and shouted.

"Down!"

Bernanke abruptly reversed the bat's direction. The riding basket heaved sickeningly on its moorings. The dark ramparts of the Trivium citadel loomed, and below them streaks of lightning flickered through the night. Shouts rose from the citadel courtyard. Artemisiah's attack at the gate had roused the Hell's army defenses. The bat pinwheeled and dropped to land jarringly on the dark stone rampart adjacent to the gate tower.

Ayelet leapt off the bat onto the stone walkway and ran to the gate tower door. It was unlocked. She burst inside and surprised a lone Djinnus working the ancient gate mechanism. The gears spun, and the tower rumbled with the sound of the closing portcullis. Ayelet shot forward and slammed the brake. The gears screeched and stopped. She turned and impaled the shocked Djinnus through the joint of his chest armor. The male fell back. Barissianna sliced him across the skull with her curved blade. The blow made a loud cracking sound. The Djinnus crumpled. Barissianna's nostrils flared as she looked down at the running blood.

"You're quick, Ayelet."

"So are you. Follow me." Ayelet descended the tower stairs into the ground floor, which was apparently a smithy. A fire blazed in a great hearth. Scores of weapons and shields lined the walls or filled crates. The smell of molten metal was Sharp in the air.

Ayelet ran to the half-open door, followed closely by Barissianna. Bernanke caught up as they exited into the chaotic courtyard. A pair of Old Order Jinni in red robes greeted them-a Smokeless Flames lieutenant and a fledgling private judging from the banded arm insignias.

"It's Ayelet!" A distinct note of terror choked the Lieutenant's voice. Her hand flew to her sword. She parried Bernanke's spring attack and countered fiercely. The vampire male staggered, off-balance. Ayelet waved her hand and staggered the lieutenant in turn with a well-timed kin-hex. The Flames fledgling raised her hand and uttered words of power.

Ayelet twirled away from the intense heat. The small fireball exploded behind her. Barissianna also dodged safely to the other side of the blast radius.

The Flames lieutenant advanced with her own hateful kin-hex. Ayelet pushed through the wave of force and floated in. She launched a flurry that put the lieutenant on the defensive, followed by three more focused blows in quick succession. Each effort rocked the lieutenant back. Panic played on the Serpent Sister's dour face.

Ayelet launched into the Exquisite Form, a poetry of Jinn swordplay. The tip of her sword danced past the Sister's wobbling parry to flick into soft tissue. The lieutenant dropped her sword to grab her throat. It was over. Ayelet whirled to see Barissianna squared off in a sorcerous duel against the panicked Flames private, while Bernanke defended her in turn from a pair of blade-wielding Djinnus grunts.

Barissianna uttered a spell, and the Flames private squeaked a counter-spell. Barissianna intoned again and formed a pattern that shimmered in the night air. The second counter-spell of the fledgling sputtered as she shrieked. She raised her hands to bat at the black flames flying from her hair. The fledgling private backpedaled and ran. Bernanke ably dispatched the two Djinnus with brute power. The burly vampire ran after the fleeing private. Barissianna closed ranks.

"Well done, Barissianna." Ayelet said. "Your magical skills are impressive."

"Thanks. I'll put this one out of her misery." Barissianna stepped past and raised her scimitar over the fallen Flames lieutenant, who was still writhing and clutching her bloody throat. Ayelet swept low with her blade. She diverted Barissianna's beheading sweep just in time. The curved sword of the vampiress met the courtyard flagstones and broke with a loud clang.

"Sorry. That one is mine."

Barissianna raised a dark eyebrow. "You owe my clan a good sword, Ayelet."

"Take the lieutenant's sword. A well-forged blade is rare, but less rare than a well-fledged Jinn. Please try to spare them when you can, even if they are Old Order. Perhaps the Lady can help them see something different than the darkness of Lord Hades and the Hell's Court devils."

"Fair enough, but I'll never have mercy for a Disciple of Set."

Ayelet pulled a pair of cuffs and examined the Flames lieutenant closely before pulling back her bloody hands and restraining her. The jugular looked nicked, but not the carotid. The Lieutenant would keep bleeding, but the flow wouldn't be enough to send her soul to the void before the battle was over.

"Should we help Bernanke?" Barissianna's voice was tinged with urgency.

Ayelet spotted Bernanke halfway across the courtyard, embattled with four blade-wielding Djinnus. Farther beyond, Amanoch and Valeriu had landed their bat and were fighting with their cadre of vamps through the entrance to the Court building in the heart of the keep.

Ayelet surveyed the scene. The courtyard was in chaos. Armored Djinnus were swarming from a nearby building. A handful of Serpent Sisters had mounted a defensive formation. Narcabyss whips hung at their hips, but the instruments of paralyzation were useless against the undead flesh of the Auerbach vampires. The mistresses defended with short blades and kin-hexes.

Mistress Artemisiah held a position just inside the open keep portcullis, flanked by Mistress Gonorrheah and Mistress Merweh. Artemisiah glowed brilliantly in the night in her shining white armor. She sent long arcs of lightning bolts from her massive white longbow.

"Follow me, Barissianna."

Ayelet started across the courtyard, but rolled as a dark shadow swooped low. A great Nanka, a fearsome spawn of Oya Nanka-mother, blotted out the stars overhead. Bronze talons ripped into an Auerbach vampire like meat hooks, while a fireball from the Nanka's sorceress rider scorched earth and vampire flesh indiscriminately.

Gonorrheah returned a fireball. The flame bounced off the Nanka and its burden. A following bolt of lightning sent by Artemisiah, however, shattered the riding carriage on the Nanka's back and sent the red-robed

Flames sorceress flying. The Nanka shook off its broken burden and leveled a tremendous gout of flame directly at Artemisiah, Gonorrheah, and Merweh. The blast sucked the air out of the courtyard.

Mistress Merweh's voice crested above the din then, barking a spell. A frigid blast whipped and clashed with the Nanka's fiery breath. The courtyard was inundated for a few seconds with snow and sleet. The Nanka launched aloft into the darkness, riderless and covered with a coat of rime, but apparently unhurt. The Nanka rider attempted another fireball, but Gonorrheah countered, disrupting the incantation.

Booming sounds echoed in the courtyard then. Merweh cried out suddenly and spun to the ground. Ayelet winced when a lead ball glanced off her leather armor. A squad of Djinnus gunners locked and loaded where they hid in the black shelter of the parapets.

Artemisiah raised her bow and sent a lightning bolt flying upwards. The gunners shouted and scattered with cries of pain. Barissianna raised her voice with a guttural incantation. A whispering flock of black harpy eagles chased the lightning bolts. On the rampart, the cries of the archers turned to screams as the harpy eagles ripped into them. Ayelet advanced again, but paused her forward momentum. Artemisiah's wren had alit on her shoulder.

*Ayelet-Prince Amanoch needs help in the central tower. Gonorrheah and I will be right behind you.*

"Barissianna, Prince Amanoch needs us." Ayelet ran ahead of Barissianna towards the old Court building that dominated the grounds of the inner Trivium. The massive iron portal at its base was open to entry. A spiraled staircase rose from the empty circular great hall. The upper floors of the Court echoed with the thundering sounds of spells and the ring of steel, but the ground floor was quiet compared to the outer areas of the keep.

Ayelet trotted up the curving stone stairs. She could feel Barissianna right behind her, even as an Old Order Jinn was running down from above. They met at a wide landing. The mistress carried a sickle in hand. Her black silk cloak flew open in front to reveal her thick black thatch of nether hair and a metal collar around her neck. Her breasts heaved with frantic breaths. Her eyes widened.

"Ayelet!"

"Golden Gorila. It's a pleasure to see you again. You must be well in the enemy's trust to be running free and positioned here at the Keep. Were you allied with the Old Order all along, or did you wait for the occupation to betray the Lady?"

Golden Gorila blanched, but her eyes turned cunning. "The Smokeless Flames doesn't trust me, or they wouldn't have me wearing this ebon control collar."

"I'm listening. Tell me what you're doing here."

"The Smokeless Flames conscripted me for my knowledge of Meristyian and the Redoubt. Yes, I joined them willingly. No, it doesn't matter. Allyssia's position in Meristyian is hopeless. Surely you know this."

"Mistress?" A lanky dark-haired fledgling pattered down the stairs to the landing, carrying a heavy trunk. The fledgling also wore a black collar. Her eyes widened. "Ayelet!"

"It's a pleasure to see you again, Jade Turtle."

Ayelet swept forward in a surprise attack. Golden Gorila was distracted, but managed to block with a snarl. Ayelet pressed forward, aiming to disarm Golden Gorila, not kill her.

"Fledgling!" Golden Gorila cried. "Defend me!"

Jade Turtle started to protest, but dropped the trunk and drew her blade. Ayelet lifted her hand and pushed with a powerful kin-hex. Jade Turtle spun against the wall. Barissianna advanced on the unbalanced fledgling. Ayelet grabbed her arm.

"Go up. Help Amanoch."

Ayelet flurried again. Golden Gorila barely executed the necessary blocks on defense. Barissianna used the space to slip past un-garde. She ascended the steps at a run. Jade Turtle rejoined the battle, but tentatively. Ayelet slipped her dagger from her boot and defended with her off-hand while edging left to bar Golden Gorila from escaping. Golden Gorila feinted, but stayed well wide of the blade.

"Fight her, fledgling!" Golden Gorila snarled. "Don't be afraid of her!

She's overrated!"

Ayelet switched to defense. Jade Turtle was a strong fledgling and pressed the attack from the high ground, urged on by her mistress. Golden Gorila took the opportunity to relinquish her robe completely. At the same time, a fount of smoke exploded over the landing.

Ayelet smiled grimly. She'd seen all of Golden Gorila's skills, and she rarely forgot a trick. She took a risk and whipped her dagger into the smoke. Golden Gorila shrieked and re-appeared near the stair rail with the knife protruding from her ribcage. She slipped over the rail and dropped into space. Ayelet pressed through the smoke to sustain the attack on Jade Turtle.

"Please don't send me to the void," the fledgling protested, terrified. "I had to attack you! My mistress commanded it!"

"Your mistress sacrificed you to save herself. Surrender."

Jade Turtle gasped and defended until her back was at the railing. She threw up her hands. Ayelet stopped her sword at the willowy fledgling's neck. Jade Turtle's sword clattered down. "I surrender."

"Take off your robe so you look like an Ahyehass with that ebon control collar. Throw your robe over the rail. Hurry."

"Yes, Mistress." Jade Turtle complied as quickly as she could. Meanwhile, the sounds of battle had quieted above. Ayelet removed a pair of cuffs from her belt and locked Jade Turtle's wrist to a baluster of the Court stairway.

"Consider yourself reclaimed for the Lady. Stay here and keep your head down, Turtle." Ayelet hesitated at the railing. She made eye contact with Artemisiah, who was sweeping up the stairs below her with Gonorrheah. The wizardress limped, as if wounded.

The courtyard is clear. Upwards, Ayelet. Go.

Ayelet ran up the steps, followed closely by Gonorrheah and the virgin huntress in white, around the spiraling staircase through lavish rooms. Dead Jinni lay side-by-side with dead vampires. A burning smell was thick on the air. The highest chamber of the tower was eerily silent and entirely still. There were no sounds of battle, or even a footstep or the ring of a blade. Something was wrong.

Barissianna stood motionless not far into the room, frozen in mid-stride. Prince Amanoch stood farther still across the elegant red carpet, still as a stone and flanked by Bernanke and Valeriu, all motionless. Torches in golden sconces flickered and froze as well, just like the oil lamps that glowed on a paper-strewn table.

Ayelet realized that she, too, wasn't moving. Her consciousness oddly continued forward, however, to where a tall male stood in a queer aura of darkness. He was a long stately figure in a black suit and hat. He held an object in his hands-a pyramid or miniature obelisk that was some ten centimeters wide, twenty or more tall, and pitch black, so black that the object seemed to suck the light from the room into its surface. Ayelet could hear Artemisiah's voice from somewhere behind, speaking as if to someone else.

You will not have another part of me, ever.

My darling cousin. Why can't we talk? There are bigger things at stake than your precious New Order. The Mimoic Hierarchy intends to bring war to Meristyian.

Go back to Haawiyah and take your Ebon Timepiece with you. I know you and Lord Hades didn't know we were coming, Archduke Fennel.

Which is why your underlings are still alive.

How nice-

Ayelet blinked. The exchanges between Artemisiah and Archduke Fennel, the devil son of Lord Hades, accelerated into high-pitched whines like children, then faster, until the conversation became an incomprehensible staccato. The torches suddenly flickered. Ayelet stumbled forward. She felt her consciousness normalize, as if the room had solidified around her. Artemisiah was gone, and so was Archduke Fennel.

"What in the hells was that?" Prince Amanoch barked, twirling around with his outstretched blade. "Where did he go?"

"I don't know," Ayelet replied. "I heard Artemisiah mention the Ebon Timepiece. The fabric of time might have been warped."

Amanoch frowned. "We've traveled in time?"

"No. Only Archduke Fennel traveled, using an old artifact that belongs to his father." Ayelet toed the motionless and apparently dead Flames mistress lying on the floor. "Mistress Akhteh. She was an accomplished sorceress. Did you kill her, Amanoch?"

Amanoch snorted. "No. She just fell over onto the floor and perished randomly at the same time that I arrived."

"Really? Are you serious?"

"No. I was joking. She didn't know counter-spells for my Traumaturgy, much to her misfortune. Vampire princes like myself aren't particularly troubled by bolts of lightning. So did I just try to attack a son of the Lord of Hell right in this room, Ayelet?"

"Apparently, or perhaps an image of him, cast somehow by his Ebon Timepiece, which allows for short periods of time travel. He may not have been here a few minutes ago." Ayelet scanned the ancient Court chamber. It was furnished in a typical Smokeless Flames style with oxidized silver furnishings and red wall hangings. Several bodies lay on the floor, including two Jinni and a fledgling. Ayelet eyed a massive closed wardrobe.

"There's a thrall hiding in there with another Jinn," Amanoch muttered. "I can smell their perfume and blood."

"There is a younger Jinn cuffed down on the stair railing also," Ayelet said. "She's mine. I also left a Smokeless Flames lieutenant alive in the courtyard. Any Old Order found incapacitated must not be killed. They must be bound and taken with us. There are plenty of horses here for them if they won't fit onto the bats."

"Where is Mistress Artemisiah? I thought she was leading us." Amanoch shook his head grimly. "Bernanke, Valeriu-go down and canvas the courtyard with our remaining men. Carefully bind any Jinni that are still alive, as Mistress Ayelet suggests. We'll take them for questioning. Take the prettiest sklavinnen as well. Kill the rest."

"What about the Nanka?" Bernanke rumbled.

"Watch out for the Nanka and any surviving Djinnus. Hurry. We need to get out of here quickly. I'll be down in a minute."

"What are we doing with the supply caravan outside?" Valeriu added.

"Tell those Gypsies that the Trivium is closed for business, but they'll find some buyers at the Redoubt in Meristyian," the Prince answered. "Now I'd like to see what's hiding in this wardrobe." The Prince moved towards the wardrobe, but before he could reach it, the door opened. A nude Mimọ girl stepped out, followed by an Old Order mistress.

The girl's mistress held the trembling Mimọ by a sleek silver chain. The mistress held one hand high in a gesture of surrender. Her platinum blonde hair was even paler than the Mimọ girl's blonde mane. Diamonds sparkled on her Ukraine manicured fingernails and earlobes, complementing her black lip paint and eyeliner. She wore a grey Flames uniform spangled with the bars of high ranks.

"I'm Ambassador Lydiah, and I demand diplomatic immunity as an appointed official from Hell's Court." Lydiah's perfectly-plucked eyebrow arched. "Interesting. Is this Mistress Ayelet with her blade covered in blood? It's unfortunate that it has come to this, really. I see you have some bloodthirsty new friends. How many of your own sisters have you killed now for your hopeless rebel cause?"

Ayelet frowned. She recognized the legendary Mistress Lydiah, but she hadn't known Innanah had been appointed as an official ambassador. "We'll be asking the questions, Lydiah. Would you care to explain what an ambassador from Hell's Court is doing all the way up here at the old abandoned Trivium?"

"I'm on vacation."

Amanoch guffawed. "That's highly unlikely, and I'd like to add that diplomatic immunity isn't often observed in a time of war."

Lydiah looked daggers at Amanoch. "What? Who are you, vampire? Are you declaring war on Lord Hades and Hell's Court? You should choose your words wisely."

Ayelet lowered her blade slowly. She wasn't particularly intimidated by Mistress Lydiah, but Lydiah was one of the most famous and influential Jinni in the Hell's Court establishment. She was also the wife of Archduke Fennel, who had apparently used his Ebon Timepiece to leave with Artemisiah, abandoning his wife to her own devices. Lydiah, despite her carefully composed appearance and bold words, still held the collared

Mimọ in front of her, on the defensive in front of the Prince. Amanoch gave a mock bow.

"I am Prince Amanoch of the Auerbach clan, united with Allyssia to defend our homes in Meristyian against the unreasonable and violent encroachments of you and your Disciple allies."

Lydiah gazed at him impassively. "What makes you think Hell's Court has any formal agreement with the Disciple vampires? I'd have to research that."

"I was just making a statement," Amanoch countered. "I'll leave it to you to tell half-lies and talk in circles."

"She's talking to demonstrate her usefulness to us Amanoch," Ayelet said. "We aren't going to kill you, Ambassador Lydiah. That's a fine slave, by the way. She looks frightened, the poor thing. What's your name, Mimọ?"

"Her name is Violet," Lydiah said quickly. "A patrol captured her a few days ago. Commander Akhteh kindly gifted her to me, knowing that I'm a devoted collector of fallen Mimọs. She's mine. I already wrote up the papers."

"She isn't yours anymore," Amanoch said. "All property here is being seized, and I'm claiming that Mimọ."

Lydiah's visage tightened. "Mistress Ayelet, I would like to formally protest the 'claiming' of my new slave by this violent warmonger."

Ayelet sighed. She wasn't going to admonish Amanoch, who had claimed the slave mainly to play a trump card. The act had been pointlessly provocative and even dangerous in light of the escalating situation. "Your protest is noted, Ambassador Lydiah. As a precaution, you'll be cuffed. Please turn. You'll be coming with us to visit the Lady." Ayelet removed the last set of silvered cuffs from her waist belt.

"If you must. I'm at your disposal, unfortunately." Lydiah raised her hand suddenly and summoned a bird.

Ayelet swung with the flat of her blade, but she couldn't disrupt the spell. The bird flitted quickly out of the room and down the stairs. Ayelet wrapped up Lydiah and took her down bodily to the stone floor. Soon the beauty mistress was cuffed, gagged, and relieved of a hidden knife in a stocking sheath. Barissianna and Gonorrheah led Lydiah with the Mimọ down the stairs.

Ayelet met Amanoch's gold-flaked eyes and shook her head. Imprisoning a prominent ambassador of Hell's Court could create serious difficulties for Allyssia. The potential fallout effects of the Trivium incident could be magnified tenfold. Still, she didn't want to just let Lydiah go, not without knowing what had happened with Fennel, Artemisiah, and the Ebon Timepiece.

"Did you hear Archduke Fennel?" Amanoch said, interrupting her reverie. "What was that conversation about? Who was Fennel calling his cousin?"

Ayelet shrugged. "He was talking to Artemisiah."

"Care to explain that?"

"The Lady is more than she appears, Amanoch. If I tell you, you must swear to not let the truth leave this room."

"Of course. You have my word."

"As you know, the goddess we call the Lady is one of the three oldest divines to be born from the elder titans. Tuhan, the lord of the Mimọic Hierarchy, was the firstborn. Hades, the lord of Haawiyah, was the youngest. Our Lady, she of many names, was the middle child. Each of these Divines has multiple aspects. Lord Hades has his archdevils, each one a splinter of himself, who he calls his sons. Tuhan has his arch-Mimọs, the agents of his will on Earth and in Heaven. The Lady has her own calved aspects as well."

"I know something of this. Continue."

"Our Lady has four aspects that aren't openly known, for reasons of protection: Artemisiah, the virgin huntress; Persephoneh, the whore; Demetriah, the mother; and Ivanka, the crone. Demetriah was captured and taken back to Haawiyah when the Old Order seized the Redoubt last year. We think she's living in a magically warded cell in the prisons under the city of Mer. Ivanka, as you know, betrayed us last year, so she is gone as well."

Amanoch frowned. "That makes no sense, if I understand it correctly. How can a part of the Lady turn traitor against herself?"

"It may be that Ivanka forced her own independence and somehow split away. It may be that the Lady let a part of herself go, a part she didn't like anymore. It doesn't matter. With the defection of Ivanka and the forceful taking of Demetriah, our goddess fractured and came apart. Now this. Archduke Fennel may have used Hades' Ebon Timepiece to play with fate. He learned of the events here somehow from his wife, Ambassador Lydiah, and then he came back to change the events and play a gambit to steal another piece of the Lady. He may have succeeded."

Amanoch nodded. "I suppose that explains what Artemisiah said. So does this mean that Lady Allyssia is lacking three of her four aspects now-three quarters of her power?"

Ayelet cleared her throat. "No. I wouldn't equate the Lady's power only with her aspects, and the four hidden aspects are not all of them. She has Cupid and Harmoniah, for example, her magical children. Substantial portions of her energy were bound into her four more active aspects, however, and it would seem that only Persephoneh, the whore, still remains safe in the Redoubt for now, unless Artemisiah reappears."

Amanoch's visage darkened. "The Lady said she only needed Auerbach to help her defend in the dream world. When was someone going to tell me about the extent of Her weaknesses-about the fact that she's so broken?"

Ayelet avoided Amanoch's gaze. "I just did. So. This upper chamber looks like a headquarters. We should search for any documents that will tell us what Lydiah and the Smokeless Flames were doing here. I'll sweep the rest of the building."

Ayelet turned on heel and left the room to descend the spiraling stairs at a trot. She passed Turtle, who was still cuffed to the stairs, and found Barissianna in the shelter of the first floor of the Court, supervising some of the Auerbach grunts, who were driving horses out of a converted stable. Golden Gorila was nowhere to be seen. Ayelet sighed. They'd won the day, but her heart remained heavy. What they'd done would have greater repercussions, surely, than the Lady was expecting. She placed her hand on Barissianna's armored shoulder.

"How are you? You fought well. Your spells were impressive."

Barissianna's green, gold-flaked eyes were hooded. I'm fine. It looks like we won the night. You were wonderful, Ayelet. I was impressed by your swordplay."

"I hope we're still on for private lessons once all the work is done?"

"Of course. I'm looking forward. Thank you, Ayelet."

<h1 style="text-align:center">Chapter 9.</h1>

Tajee ducked his head under the marble shower spout. He allowed the warm flow to course down his back and between his buttocks. He picked up a sponge and scrubbed his knees, which were dirty from a long day of polishing floors in the palace east wing. Persephoneh was watching him from the tepid waters of the long bathing pool.

He'd serviced Persephoneh occasionally since he'd become a palace Ahyehass, although she'd never spoken a single word in his presence. She was looking at him, and he was looking at Pexa, who had also come to bathe. Pexa had awoken in the off-hour just like him, on the same late schedule for servicing the nocturnal vampires.

Pexa was lissome like an Mimọ girl, but more fulsome and Greek, with long dark hair and a pleasantly protuberant mons that echoed the swells of her plum breasts that Cupid enjoyed so frequently. She dove into the bathing pool like a silver-collared swan.

Tajee heard footsteps. A gentle masculine hand slipped around his stomach. His cock stirred even before Priapus took it between his thick fingers. Tajee winced. His phallus was sore. Priapus let go of him.

"You hurt from Barissianna's use of you, Nina?"

"Her teeth pricked quite a bit." Tajee glanced over his shoulder again at Pexa, who seemed as if she was watching. He lowered his voice self-consciously. "Barissianna's mouth was like a Sharp cage, but I'll be fine. Please don't say anything to her. I really didn't mind."

Master Priapus turned him, palmed his cheek, and kissed his forehead possessively. "Stop ogling Pexa."

"Yes, Master."

Priapus patted him. "You can go back to your quarters and prepare for another evening of entertaining the vampires. They're celebrating their successful skirmish at the Trivium. You should take your beauty kit with you."

Tajee found his towel and dried off. He exited the baths and went to his bedchamber in the Ahyehass quarters, where he dressed and retrieved his leather bag of brushes, paints, and nail files. He delayed as long as he dared before made his way through the palace up to the north tower, where he knocked on the portal to the tower vestibule. Janaka opened the door.

"Greetings, Nina. It's nice to see you again. Please follow me."

Janaka led him down the entry hall into the familiar inner atrium with its magical blue light. Energetic violin music came from an undefinable source. They walked on down the adjoining hall and through a T-intersection, and then up a stately set of stairs into the heart of the north tower. The music grew louder. They entered a grand circular chamber with checkered tile floors that matched the blue room below. A pair of male vampires sat back-to-back on a low dais at the end of the room. The vampires played a violin duet while other vampires danced. Matriarch Lubersky sat regally on a long red divan, which in turn was centered in a pool of arranged candlelight.

Tajee followed Janaka down another hall, and finally the vampire ushered him inside a heavy oak door. Beyond the door was a small study, a warm and sweet-smelling room. Prince Amanoch sat comfortably in a chair, clad only in a black silk robe with a thick leather-bound book spread across his lap.

"Ah, it's Nina," the Prince said. "Thank you, Janaka. You may go."

Tajee eyed the broad expanse of Amanoch's smooth chest where his robe lay open. "Good evening, sir. I'm here to serve."

Amanoch motioned him close. Tajee stepped forward. He could feel the power emanating from the vampire. The power was tangible and made his skin prick. The Prince's eyelids opened wide. Tajee stiffened, but he'd been caught. He was gazing once again into the Prince's dark and compelling depths.

"Nina, I'd appreciate it very much if you'd help me with something, or at least try to help me. You were an Mimọ who was captured by the New Order and brought here to the Redoubt, yes? You've embraced your new life as an Mimọ thrall, a lusty servant of these sex-hungering Jinni. You have no desire to return to Heaven, correct?"

"No, sir," Tajee replied. "I can't imagine the Mimọ I once was. I used to want to escape from here, but now I can't imagine that either."

"Does your master please you? Does he bring you contentment?"

"Yes, sir. I've been with him for a year and he knows me well. He knows me better than I know myself sometimes."

Amanoch nodded as if satisfied. "Good. I thought as much, but I wanted to be sure. You may or may not know that I captured an Mimọ sklavin, a female slave as we call them, during the skirmish at the Trivium." Amanoch waved his hand dismissively. "I'll make it simple. I have a beautiful Mimọ girl who I'd like to train to serve me here in Meristyian. She's uncomfortable however-terrified, to put it lightly. Do you know what I mean?"

"Yes, sir."

"She told me only a little of what happened to her, and her reluctance to serve is understandable. I want her to serve me, do you understand? I want her to serve like you serve your Master Priapus-politely, sweetly, and obediently. I'd like you to speak to her, Nina. Or rather, I'm requiring it. I don't know anything about Mimọs or how they think. I want you to talk to this girl and tell her that everything will be just fine if she simply let go of her fear and obeys. Calm her down. I'll reward you."

"I'll do my best, sir."

"She's in my bedchamber. Her name is Violet. Go ahead."

Tajee picked up his bag and moved through the indicated door. He shut it hesitantly behind him. Amanoch's bedchamber was dark except for a row of candles on a sideboard and an oil lamp in the shape of a crystal red rose that burned fitfully on a pedestal in the corner. A nude form lay on the bed-a slender Mimọ girl with a pale gold halo that glimmered in the semi-darkness. The girl rose to a sitting position and gathered blankets around her body.

Tajee approached and sat on the edge of the bed. Violet was about his age. Her hair was shoulder-length, blonde and straight. She reminded him very much of Boudi-Ca as he'd known her Heaven-sweet and virginal with innocent umber eyes. When Violet spoke, her voice quavered.

"Who are you?"

"My name is Tajee, but they call me Nina. I'm an Mimọ, too." He turned to make sure she could see his wings. Violet looked surprised, and her eyes lit up.

"Wait. You're Tajee Al Adin? You're from the Crystal College of Sacred Moons?"

"Um, yes. You know who I am?"

"So you jumped. I knew it! I'm from Sacred Moons too. You didn't know me, but I knew you. I admired you so much because everyone said you were a rebel. I'm Violet Van Der Huf. I was a freshman when you disappeared, one year behind you."

Tajee grimaced apologetically. "I'm sorry. Heaven is so far away now. It seems like a dream. It's what this place does to you, I think. I don't remember you. How did you end up here, Violet? Did you fall through the sky from the ruins of Chickasaw?"

"I jumped into a thunderstorm like you." Violet's voice caught. Her chest heaved. Her breaths were audible in the room.

"You seem upset."

"Yes, I'm upset! Everything is so awful, sinful, and evil down here, and I just can't seem to find my way back to myself. I'm starting to forget things from Heaven, like it was all unreal. It's terrifying. I feel like I'm losing my mind."

"You're in Meristyian now. You're in a different body. Everything here is made up of feeling and sensation, not thoughts. It's hard because the feelings are so distracting. More and more, this place will seem real to you, and Heaven won't. You just have to let go and surrender."

"Surrender?" Violet shivered. "Yes, that's what he said too."

"Calm down. Just relax. Everything's going to be fine. It's not that bad here." Tajee touched Violet on the knee to comfort her, but she flinched and scrunched away.

"Not bad?" Violet stared at him. "How is this not bad? I'm a slave, and I'm wearing a collar. Ambassador Lydiah did horrible, unspeakable things to me. She walked me around naked on a leash like a dog that she was showing off."

Tajee felt his throat clench. "I had the same feelings as you when I first came here, and now I'm happy enough. I'm not bored. I never have to go to class. I have to do chores, but I don't have endless stupid schoolwork. I never have to say thousands of prayers, or read scriptures, or do any detention."

"What's going to happen to me? Just tell me the truth, Tajee."

"I don't really know."

Violet took a deep breath. "Where is that music coming from? I hear violins. It's strange, creepy music. I wish I could hear the cathedral choir instead."

"The vampires are having a party. They're celebrating something. You know, if you want I can oil you, Violet. I have a flask in my bag. I remember that's what Mistress Golda did to help me relax when I first came to Meristyian. I think it could help."

Violet bit her lip. "Alright, if it will help me feel better."

"Lie on the bed on your stomach." Tajee opened his beauty kit and removed the small flask of olive oil. He slipped to Violet's side and pulled away the sheet. Tajee felt his stomach lurch, followed by a wave of anger. Violet's back was lissome, but it was all wrong. Twin ragged scars striped the insides of Violet's shoulder blades where her white wings had been. The scars were crusty and pink, still healing.

"Did Amanoch do this, Violet?"

"No. Ambassador Lydiah did that with a knife. I thought I was going to die, and I fainted for a few minutes when I saw the blood. Lydiah was smiling and chatting with me the whole time, like she was enjoying cutting my wings off. She's a completely sick, horrible, evil, loathsome-"

"I don't know who you're talking about. Just let me try oiling you." Tajee carefully avoided touching the painful-looking scars. He spread the oil up and down Violet's pale Mimoic skin, over her neck and across her shoulder blades. He poured more oil into the palms of his hands and worked the lengths of Violet's arms. Her tension slowly eased under his fingertips.

Violet sighed. "I'm glad you're here, Tajee. I don't feel so alone anymore."

"You're going to be fine, Violet. Just surrender to your lust and pleasure. I did whatever my mistress wanted, and I still miss her."

Violet visibly tensed when he poured oil onto her sacrum. She forced her face into the pillow and whimpered slightly. He worked the oil over her bare buttocks and down the backs of her legs.

The soft white bottoms of Violet's feet were dirty. Tajee drew a cloth from his bag and gently cleaned them with the olive oil. He scrubbed Violet's soles and poked an oiled finger between each of her toes. "You can turn over."

"No. I can't. It's too sinful." Violet twisted away from him and drew the bedcovers back over her body. She lay silent with her forearm hiding her eyes.

Tajee sat on the edge of the bed, unsure if he was only upsetting Violet further. "Do you want me to leave?"

Violet twisted her head and looked at him. Her eyes were wide and crazed. "Is there any way out? Is there any way to escape from this place?"

"You're not supposed to be in this city against your will. That's Lady Allyssia's own rule. We are Ahyehasi, not slaves. Are you wanting to go back to Heaven?"

"I?I don't know. I got in trouble with the Conclave, and I flashed to the edge of Heaven to escape from getting arrested." Violet choked back a sob. "I thought you were my hero, and I was following in your footsteps. I jumped into a thunderstorm."

"I'm no hero."

"Well, I guess I screwed up in Heaven, so I have nowhere else to go. Thanks for helping me and making so much sense, anyway. I'll try to hold onto hope." Violet curled into a ball and drew the bed blankets over her head, apparently ending the conversation.

Tajee gazed at Violet for long moments, but he didn't know what else to tell her. He wiped his hands on his skirt, closed his bag, and left the room. He felt horribly responsible, and all of his guilt over Boudi-Ca came rushing back into his hollow stomach. Prince Amanoch was waiting for him in the outer chamber. A small smile played on the vampire's lips.

"You did a great job, Nina. I'm pleased. I want to give you a gift for everything you've done for me and Barissianna, as I promised, but only after I find the time to ask your master about something appropriate."

"Thank you, sir." Tajee kept his eyes carefully lowered. Amanoch held a small pasteboard box tied with a red ribbon, but apparently it wasn't a gift for him.

"You've done so well that I'd like you to do me another favor. I sent these earrings as a gift to your friend Boudi-Ca, but her mistress returned it to me. I'd like you to find a way to give the earrings to her again, except directly and secretly. Can you do it? If it's too much of a challenge even for a resourceful Ahyehass like yourself, then I'll find someone else."

"No, sir. I can do it."

"Good. Just make sure no one knows." Amanoch winked and handed the box to him. "And try not to look so unhappy. It would reflect on me personally if your master got the wrong impression from your visits here."

"Thank you, sir."

Tajee opened his beauty kit and pushed the gift-wrapped box inside. He fumbled the door open and slipped quickly out of the room. He hurried down the hall through the large chamber where the violinists still played. He hadn't a clue how he could deliver the box to Boudi, or why the Prince even wanted to give her a gift. Meanwhile, Violet was clearly held against her will in the Prince's bedchamber. Anger was rising hotly again in his body. He jumped at the sound of Janaka's voice.

"Nina?" The male vampire had descended the stairs behind him. "A moment please. Magistrada Barissianna would like her nails cleaned and filed again, if you don't mind. It will only take a few minutes. Do you have time? Or do you have somewhere to go?"

"I think I do. Sorry."

Tajee walked out of the north tower. His heart pounded still harder at having told a lie. He stalked down hall after hall through the palace until he reached the Ahyehass quarters. Priapus was relaxing on a divan in the common area.

"You're back already, Nina? What's wrong?" Priapus sat up. "Did the vampires hurt you?"

"They're hurting Violet. She's an Mimọ girl from Heaven, and she's being held against her will in the Prince's bedchamber. She's terrified and wants to be free."

Priapus frowned. "Well, there isn't much we can do about that."

"But it breaks the Lady's rules! No one can be held against their will in this city. Mistress Golda explained it to me. That's the law. That's why we are called Ahyehasi. We have free will. We're dedicated to the divine path of Love."

Priapus sighed. "That's true, but the vampires play by different rules."

Tajee blinked away sudden, queer tears that blurred his vision of Priapus. "Please, Master. I've never begged you for anything before, or asked for any of the favors you've given me. Please do something to help Violet. Please."

"Nina, it isn't your place to-"

"Yes, it is!" Tajee wiped his eyes ferociously. "She's just an innocent Mimọ girl. She doesn't know what she's doing, and she's desperate. It's horrible to think of what the Prince is doing with her. Either do something now, or I quit."

"You what?"

"If Violet stays the Prince's slave, then you'd better lock me in a cage, because if you don't, I'm going to escape. I'll walk out of this palace, climb over the wall, and walk all the way to Mount Purgatory. Maybe I'll take

Violet with me."

Priapus grimaced. "To be honest, this issue has already been raised. The problem is that Violet's former owner, Ambassador Lydiah, already filed legal ownership papers and snipped the girl's wings to prevent her from ever going back to Heaven. Some people question whether snipping is really effective, but Lydiah is a well-known expert. Snipping has always been a ritual for fallen Mimos in Hell, at least until you and Boudi-Ca came to this city. I promise to mention your worries to the Lady, anyway. Thank you for telling me, Nina."

# Chapter 10:

Boudi-Ca lay flat on her stomach with her torso extended over the end of the wooden pier. A thundering rush of turbulent water swept under her. The pier pilings wobbled like matchsticks. Golda's head and shoulders bobbed in the dark, perilous waters. Golda drifted past again, into the darkness and another loop around the great, roaring whirlpool. Golda looked much younger, a beautiful redhead with furry cat ears.

Boudi-Ca felt a touch on her ankle. Tajee stood right behind her, looking down. He held a small pasteboard box with a red ribbon. Boudi-Ca awoke. The Isandlwana sun painted her window frame a shade of yellow-orange. She'd slept late again, judging from the angle of the light. She'd likely missed her piano lesson with Mistress Melkeh. Her stomach felt queasy. She hungered.

Three days had passed since Ranavalona had removed the wicked bone phallus from her forbidden aperture, opening her soul and draining her Jinn energy like water from a broken pot. Her root chakra felt more healed that morning, and her energy was finally coming back. She hadn't spoken again to Ranavalona, and she hadn't confronted Isabellah about what Ranavalona had said-that Isabellah still thought of her as a naïve, innocent Mimọ girl.

She didn't want more drama. She and Isabellah were fighting over everything already. She missed her fledgling days with Ayelet, when things had been fun and adventurous. In fact, after days of ruminating alone in her bedroom, she'd decided to say goodbye. She wasn't fitting in with the beauty mistresses, and she was tired of all the primping, perfuming, and endless obsession with being prettier and better-dressed.

She planned to visit Ayelet that very afternoon and ask if she could be a blade fledgling again-if Ayelet would take her back. It was a very serious decision, but she missed her old bedchamber at Ayelet's Villa. She missed her daily sword lessons. She missed Ayelet's quiet flower gardens and sweeping, serene mountain views.

Her dream about Tajee had been strange. She hadn't seen him in weeks. She felt an urge to go visit him. She also still needed to see Gallinah about making Mimọ clothes, since her previous trip had been ruined by Ranavalona's rudeness.

Boudi-Ca rose from her bed and summoned a bird for Bijou. She'd get dressed and spend the day making visits to Tajee, Gallinah, and lastly Ayelet. She wouldn't even ask Isabellah for the carriage. She didn't want any special favors. She'd take her time, riding a pony the entire way. When Bijou arrived, the Ahyehass looked disheveled.

"The mistress is not happy," the Ukraine dressing-girl said. "You have piano practice, yes?"

Boudi-Ca sighed. "Do I need you to criticize me like Isabellah? No. Just help me with my corset and my toilet."

Half an hour later, Boudi-Ca tiptoed silently down the rear stairs. She didn't want Isabellah to know that she was going up to the palace to see Tajee. She'd dressed in her finest blacks. She wore black stockings. She carried three-inch black leather heels in her hands. She wore a black dress and a matching leather hair band bejeweled with oOya. She rubbed her nose against her perfumed wrist, bumping some scent-pleasure into her head to soothe her jittery mood.

She saddled the pony in the stable and rode out of the yard. She hadn't trotted far towards the street before she heard Isabellah call to her across the lawn from the open second-floor bedchamber window.

"Boudi-Ca, where are you going?"

"For a ride."

"Have you seen Mistress Gallinah yet about your idea for Mimo clothes?"

"That's where I'm going, sort of."

Isabellah's displeasure was visible even from the distance. "Why are you dressed from head to toe in black like a vampire? It's summertime. You have all of those nice summer dresses that I bought for you."

Boudi-Ca didn't answer. She waved and kicked the pony to a swift trot down the cobblestones. She'd dressed like a vampire because she'd damned well wanted to dress like a vampire that day. She reached the palace in fifteen minutes and hitched the pony at a stable post. She strode up the steps past two guards in golden armor. The interior of the Lady's palace was cool that morning, not yet warmed by the afternoon sun.

She made her way through the palace to the Ahyehass quarters, where she found Master Priapus reciting a chore list to a statuesque palace girl. She slipped past and into the Ahyehass dormitorium. She knocked on Tajee's door and opened it. Tajee bolted upwards on his bed when he saw her.

"Boudi! You're here." Tajee seemed surprised. He covered his lap with his sheet and rubbed his eyes sleepily. Boudi-Ca drifted to sit on the small chair at Tajee's vanity. She scanned his assortment of brushes and combs.

"How have you been, Tajee? I'm sorry to surprise you."

"It's fine. I sleep late because I'm serving the vampires."

"Really? Have you met the Prince?"

Tajee stared at her, drawing the sheet more closely around his waist. "Is that why you came? How did you know? Did he tell you?" Tajee reached low and grabbed the beauty kit at the foot of his bed.

"What are you talking about, Tajee? Mistress Isabellah insists I can't have anything to do with the Prince. I disagree, but-" Boudi-Ca blinked when Tajee produced the red-ribboned box from his bag and handed it to her. She couldn't believe what she was seeing.

"The Prince wanted me to give this to you."

Boudi-Ca slipped the ribbon off and opened the box. Inside lay the vampire earrings that she'd received before, along with another handwritten note.

To a Beautiful Fledgling, again, from an Admirer

Boudi-Ca swallowed. "It's so funny, Tajee. I had a dream about you this morning. You were holding this box. Ayelet said the Auerbach are masters of dream magic. I wonder if the Prince worked a spell, or something."

"Stay away from him, Boudi. Please. He's frightening and evil."

Boudi-Ca removed her small pearl earrings and replaced them with the heavy gold vampire earrings. She leaned into Tajee's vanity mirror and examined herself. She looked very good all in black and gold-very vampiric. The earrings tickled the backslopes of her jaw. She went and sat beside Tajee on the bed.

"The Prince really frightens you, Tajee? Amanoch runs the Auerbach clan in Meristyian in the absence of his father, Patriarch Liest Ussishkin, who is currently ruling on Earth. Amanoch has a lot of responsibilities and a lot of vampires to keep in line. He's a really strong man. I'm not surprised that you're intimidated by him."

"Stay away from him. You've never listened to me before, but please listen."

Boudi-Ca caressed Tajee's cheek. She allowed the side of her knee to press against his, if ever so slightly. "You used to be adventurous, Tajee."

"I still am, and I still don't want you to be. Your dark hair makes you look like a completely different person. I like your perfume though. It smells nice."

"It's expensive. Isabellah bought it for me at the Spring Festival last year, when I was still Mistress Ayelet's fledgling." Boudi-Ca leaned and brushed her cheek against Tajee's nose. She felt the tickle of Tajee's quick breath as he inhaled her scent.

"That's nice, Boudi."

Boudi-Ca turned her face into Tajee. She was flirting with opening the cage door to her Jinn Hunger. She reached low and found Tajee's phallus under the bedsheet. It stirred under her touch. She skirted Tajee's mouth, not kissing him, instead lowering her head to taste his brown neck, which was soft and salty.

"I've always wanted you, Boudi." Tajee's voice was low and throaty.

"How badly, Tajee? Tell me."

"In Heaven, I thought about you all day every day. I wanted to kiss you. I wanted to hold you. The tandem dive we had together was one of the best times of my life. You were such a good Mimọ girl back then, so forbidden and so chaste."

"I'm not chaste anymore." Boudi-Ca pulled the sheet away to reveal Tajee's cock, which finished swelling to hardness. It was a light chocolate brown in color, with lighter pinkishness on the tip. She stroked Tajee's phallus down to his shaved testicles. She dipped to lick slowly along the length of his phallus and rub it against her cheek. She raised her voluminous petticoats and dress. She straddled Tajee and lowered herself until his phallus pressed gently against her heated sex.

She leaned over him, rubbing his phallus with her intimate femininity, the treasure that Tajee had always wanted. She didn't want to do it-she didn't want to grant him access after everything he'd put her through. She secretly wanted to torture him.

"You're so beautiful, Boudi," Tajee murmured.

"Thank you, Tajee. That's nice of you to say." Boudi-Ca moved ever so slowly, threatening to take him into her, to inundate him. The desire was building in Tajee's eyes. He worked his hips, trying to push into her.

"Ah, ah," she admonished.

"Please?"

"Beg some more. Beg me, Mimọ boy."

"Please, Boudi. Please. I love you."

Boudi-Ca rubbed with little thrusts. Her Hunger uncoiled-her ravenous Jinn eagerness to feed. She removed her hair clip so her scented hair fell over Tajee's face. She slowly lowered herself and took Tajee into her. She began a steady rhythm, working him up and down for a minute, then two. He finally spasmed into her with a flood that began as soon as she started her inner suction. Boudi-Ca stifled a gasp. Tajee's love was incredible. He was sweet to her Jinn taste in an amazing indefinable way. She avoided his eyes, nonchalantly hiding her intense, surprised pleasure. She slid off of his bed and rearranged her skirts.

"So was it worth the wait?"

"I don't know," Tajee answered with his eyes lowered. "Yes. I guess so."

"If Master Priapus gives you any trouble about what I just did, tell him that you were mine a long time before you ever came here."

"Was I?"

"Yes. I was just too innocent and naïve to know that I owned you. Goodbye, Tajee. Maybe I'll come see you again someday soon." Boudi-Ca picked up the pasteboard box from the Prince and moved towards the door.

"Wait," Tajee said quickly.

"What? You have something to say, Ahyehass?"

"Prince Amanoch captured an Mimọ girl during the vampire raid. Her name is Violet. She's from the Crystal College of Sacred Moons. I just thought you might want to know there's another Mimọ in the city."

"Since when?"

"There was a raid a few days ago-some kind of battle. The vampires and some of the mistresses attacked the Old Order Jinni. Prince Amanoch took Violet from them."

"I didn't hear anything about a raid." Boudi-Ca frowned. "The vampires have a hand in everything-my dreams, captured Mimọs, and now raids. I'll try to find out more about this girl. I wonder if I could meet her. You say the Prince has her collared and everything?"

"No. Not anymore." Tajee smiled widely and wiped his eyes.

"What do you mean?"

"I begged Master Priapus to help Violet. This morning he came in and told me that he'd spoken personally with Lady Allyssia for me. The Lady agreed to take Violet away from the Prince. I don't understand the details, but Violet is safe for now, by herself in her own quarantine quarters. The Prince isn't even allowed to see her."

"That was nice of you. It sounds like you like her."

Tajee avoided her eyes. "I just really care about her, like I used to care about you. She reminds me of how you used to be."

"Well, Violet's a lucky girl then." Boudi-Ca pursed her lips and blew Tajee a kiss. "Good bye, Tajee. I have other places to go."

"Bye, Boudi."

"My name is Boudi-Ca, not Boudi. I'm a Jinn fledgling. Speak to me appropriately, please. Don't make me punish you."

Boudi-Ca made her way out of the Palace. She somewhat regretted her spiteful parting words to Tajee. She wasn't sure why she'd even said them, except that she'd always blamed Tajee for her entire situation-of setting into motion the events in Heaven that had led to her becoming a Jinn. Tajee's life as an Ahyehass seemed much easier than her own endless frustrations. All Tajee had to do was service beautiful women like he'd always wanted.

She directed her pony down the long sloping streets that led to the workshops on the far side of the city. She turned over in her head what Tajee had said. Gallinah would know more about the new Mimọ and the raid. Gallinah was the town gossip and seemed to know more about current events than even Isabellah, who as a beauty mistress was supposed to know about everything, but often conspicuously didn't.

The pony was agonizingly slow as it carried her down the shadow-dappled, sweet-smelling cobbled streets of the city. In truth, she hardly noticed the passage of time. Aside from her jumbled thoughts, Tajee's love continued to linger in her body, warming her and distracting her. Tajee's love was far better than anything she'd ever drunk from one of Ayelet's or Isabellah's well-used and sex-worn Ahyehasi. She wondered if she'd had a similar effect on him. It was nearly mid-day when she arrived at the city workshops and tethered her pony at the posts.

"Hello?" She passed through the open front double doors and called into the gloomy receiving room interior. "Mistress Gallinah?"

The front room of the workshops was empty, but a clink and a scrape came from somewhere in the back. A wall hanging swirled and Gallinah bustled around the long oak receiving counter, which was piled with receipt-books for workshop deliveries. Gallinah waved a dirty rag. "Why, hello, Boudi-Ca! I thought I heard someone call!"

"Good afternoon, Mistress Gallinah." Boudi-Ca tried her best to smile charmingly. "It's good to see you. Were you cleaning?"

"I was polishing my Lethian doll." The portly Mistress fanned herself. "He needs to be frequently oiled-all those moving parts, you know. What do you need, fledgling?"

"I was interested in making some clothes that are based on Mimọic fashions. Isabellah said I should talk to you."

"That's a wonderful idea, fledgling. There might be a small market here for unique designs, and if the trade route opens back up, I'm sure we could find you some buyers in Mer or Vegasis. Maybe even the Kishi would be interested in such a product. They don't care for Mimọs, but they adore everything beautiful and ethereal."

"I was thinking of wearing the clothes myself, although they'd be nice for our Ahyehasi, seeing as Mimọs are getting so popular around here."

"Yes, they are at that." Mistress Gallinah winked. "You've heard about the Prince and his Mimọ girl, I suppose? The Lady took her away from him this morning. It was something about the girl already belonging to Mistress Lydiah, the ambassador that was also captured in the raid on the Trivium."

"I don't know." Boudi-Ca bit her lip. She had a sudden curious question for Gallinah, born from her experience with Tajee. She hoped it wasn't too personal, even in Jinn terms. "Have you ever taken an Mimọ, Mistress Gallinah?"

"No, not I, although I'd love to give your Tajee a roll, you know." Gallinah winked again. "Put in a good word for me if you would, dear. Fallen Mimọs are very rare, and they're snapped up by hunting parties almost as quick as they wash up on the beach. They're coveted for their sweetness, you see."

"Sweetness?" Boudi-Ca pursed her lips. "So they really taste different inside when a Jinn takes them?"

"Oh dear, yes. They're sweet as honey for Jinni and Djinnus both. That's why everyone envied Golda when she had Tajee. Yes, fresh Mimọs are exquisite creatures. They're usually worth a fortune at auction. Only rich people can buy them in Mer."

"Why do they taste sweet when we feed from them?"

"I don't know, fledgling. It's curious isn't it? I wonder if an Mimọ girl's blood tastes as sweet as her beautiful lust. I imagine it must, so I don't blame Prince Amanoch for wanting her."

"Do you know anything about the raid where the Prince got this Mimọ? What happened? Was there a battle?"

Gallinah shrugged. "I wouldn't know anything about that, fledgling. I'm just a humble shopkeeper. Now about your clothing designs. Let's go down to my personal studio, and I'll get you some sheets of drawing vellum and some sketching pencils. You can work with designs for a few days, and then I'll get the materials you need based on what you come up with."

Boudi-Ca followed Gallinah out of the workshops and down the street, almost convinced, to her amazement, that gossipy Gallinah wasn't telling her everything about the raid. She untied her pony and walked after Gallinah, out and down the sidewalk to a workshop side door, through which the rotund mistress disappeared. Gallinah emerged with several sheets of smooth parchment.

"Here you are, fledgling." Gallinah rolled the sheets into a cylinder and wrapped them with a strip of soft leather. "You can tie this to your saddle well enough. Here are some chalks and a silverpoint pen, too. Sketch out your ideas and bring them to me. We'll have a look. Have you ever drawn anything before?"

"I had some art classes in Heaven. We studied Michelangelo. We didn't have any colors, though. I hope I can come up with something."

Gallinah patted her shoulder. "I do too, fledgling. Those are remarkable gold earrings, by the way. Where did you get them?"

"They're from the Auerbach Prince." Boudi-Ca swallowed dryly. She'd been so wrapped up in thought that she'd completely forgotten about the earrings after taking Tajee.

"Well, dear, they're very nice." Gallinah smiled knowingly at her.

"Thank you again, Mistress Gallinah." Boudi-Ca tied the roll of vellum behind her saddle with the strip of leather, thrust her books into the linen sack, and quickly mounted. The pony surged forward several paces before slowing to a crawl. Boudi-Ca kicked futilely. Once she was out of sight of Gallinah, she removed her earrings and hid them in her pocket.

She urged the pony towards the east side of the city. Ayelet was next. She prayed to the Lady that she could go back to being Ayelet's fledgling. She could wear her hair and her clothes however she wanted, and she could stop going to all of the evening parties, where she'd surely run into Ranavalona. Everyone saw her as a naïve Mimọ girl anyway.

She directed the pony up to the workshop plaza, then turned right and headed up the east hill. At the steep bend at the eastern overlook the pony refused to move. Boudi-Ca dismounted, removed her heels and stockings, and pulled the pony up the rest of the hill. She was furious with the pony, but she was determined to see Ayelet.

Yenta greeted her coolly at the front door of Ayelet's Villa. "Mistress Ayelet is indisposed and must not be disturbed."

"Yenta, it's me. What do you mean? Where is Ayelet?"

"The Mistress has company until sunset, and she can't see anyone. If you have a delivery, you can leave it with me."

Boudi-Ca sighed, exasperated. "I don't have a delivery. Fine, Yenta. Next time I'll send a bird first."

Boudi-Ca walked down the steps, crossed her arms, and eyed the useless pony. It grazed in the tall grass at the fringe of Ayelet's gardens, which were lush with summer blooms. Ayelet no longer had her gardener. The beds of white and purple flowers were poorly tended and choked with dandelions and spiny red umbers. Boudi-Ca groaned with frustration. She felt a strong urge to send Ayelet a bird, but she wasn't sure what to say. There were too many words. She needed to make her case to Ayelet honestly and in person.

She'd just have to wait for Ayelet's company to leave. She couldn't let a small setback dissuade her from her goal. She was sweaty from her long ride, and a bath in her old courtyard would feel wonderful. She could soak, rest her pony, and think of how to approach Ayelet.

Boudi-Ca walked around the Villa. The bougainvilleas outside her old bedroom window had grown over the eave and into the red clay gutters. She strode through the unlocked door into her old bedchamber. To her shock, the room was occupied. The Jinn who lay on her bed appeared taller and older than her but still youngish, of a vague late twenties age in Earth terms, with short, straight dark hair.

The Jinn appeared tired, distraught, surprised, and a little angry at the intrusion. Her eyes glimmered with moon-silver, but strangely she wore a thick black collar around her neck. The collar was a heavy, seamless circlet of dark, slick-finished metal.

"I'm sorry," Boudi-Ca said quickly. "Who are you?"

"I could ask you the same question," the woman replied in a voice that was soft-spoken, like leaves blowing across cobblestones. "Were you looking for someone? This is my room. I'm Jade Turtle."

"Oh. I know you."

"You do?"

"I'm Boudi-Ca. I watched you fight Masad at the Spring Festival last year."

The woman blinked. "I don't remember you."

"I look different. My hair is dyed. I thought you were taken away last year during the Old Order occupation, Jade Turtle. Weren't you?"

"Mistress Golden Gorila renewed her vows to Lady Allyssia and took me with her. We went to Haawiyah and stayed for a time in the capital city of Mer. They reformed us and made us re-pledge loyalties to Lady Allyssia and Lord Hades."

"Oh." Boudi-Ca swallowed. "I hope it wasn't too horrible for you."

"They were easy on me. Some of the New Order mistresses refused to pledge loyalty. They said they served the Lady. They said they were lesbians. They were punished according to Lord Hades' law. The grey-skinned devils broke them in the Court with whips and thorns. Everyone else was made to watch. They're in the Dungeons of Mer forever. I try not to think of them."

"That's horrible. What about the other fledglings, like Katia-Ca?"

"Broken. It's all so vague. My mistress and I took black nectar, so we would forget our old loyalty to the Lady. I'm very sick right now for want of more of it."

"I'm sorry. So why are you wearing that collar?"

Jade Turtle started with surprise. "This is an ebon control collar. The Lady and Ayelet are trying to figure out how to get it off. Many of us had to wear them if we wanted to be free. They have a matching wand. If they point the wand at you, the collar gives you pain." Jade Turtle looked away vaguely at the garden through the panes of the window. Her lips curved into the faintest of smiles. "Ayelet says she's going to help me heal. She's going to make me her fledgling."

Boudi-Ca felt her heart sink to her stomach. "Ayelet is taking you as her new fledgling? Ayelet told you that she would?"

"Yes. But no blades today. I'm resting. Ayelet canceled our afternoon training. She is spending time with her friend."

Chapter 11:

Barissianna tugged at the knotted lacings under Ayelet's shoulder blades. Ayelet's corset was well-worn, constructed of soft leather encasing a silk lining that was awash with dried sweat stains. Ayelet, meanwhile, was unfastening the belt that held the carriages of her paniers. She dropped the strappy wooden frameworks along the wall next to the marble front of the bathtub.

Barissianna suppressed her smile as she drew loose the laces. Ayelet was from another century, and her clothes were all hand-sewn. Ayelet knew nothing about modern machine-made lingerie. Remarkably, the antique underthings hadn't seemed to hamper Ayelet when they had practiced for hours at blades.

They'd stayed up all night with endless lessons interspersed with conversations, and then they'd rested through the morning as the sun had glittered over the horizon outside the shuttered windows of Ayelet's Villa. The true sparring had begun when the blades had been put away. They'd circled each other like tigresses, trying to break through each other's emotional parries and deflections. They'd reached a point of mutual exhaustion, and they'd finally decided to take the next step-a bath together.

Barissianna tugged the last laces, and Ayelet helped pull the corset down over her svelte hips. Ayelet was slender with strong shoulders, nothing like the feminine figure she cut with her corset and paniers. Her stomach was flat. Her breasts were smallish, and her nipples were adorned with elegant citrine pendants. Ayelet stood high on slender hooves. The hooves were distracting, but they gave Ayelet's legs an attractive taper.

"Allow me, chérie."

Barissianna turned. Ayelet's arms were around her briefly, and her sash came loose. She slid her borrowed training robe from her shoulders and stepped past Ayelet into the water. Ayelet joined her. The displaced bath water rose up to the edge of the marble tub.

"You've got me at a disadvantage again." Barissianna shifted to a more comfortable position. Her legs mingled with Ayelet's, skin against skin. "I need to know my weaknesses to improve my defenses, right?"

Ayelet smiled, but only slightly. "You're a strong woman, Barissianna, but you're a strong woman in a vampire society that is dominated by men."

"You don't know the half of it."

"The removal of clothes is a ritual for a woman. It's a submissive gesture. You secretly like feeling female, and you wouldn't want to give up feeling that way for the advantage of being impenetrable. It all shows in your fighting style."

"I wonder if you're just toying with me before the coup de grace." Barissianna felt Ayelet's hand under the water, caressing her calf, and then massaging it, releasing her tension. She could feel relaxation creeping all the way up her inner thighs. Ayelet was smiling with her silvery hazel eyes.

"That's a nice expression, Barissianna. I haven't heard it in a while. In my last Earth life, I lived in eighteenth-century France, although I was an English noblewoman by birth. I studied fencing. I became an instructor."

"Your last Earth life? You've lived more than one?"

"Yes, but it wasn't intentional. It was a couple hundred years after Lady Allyssia came to Meristyian. I'd returned to Mer in Haawiyah as a secret agent, along with a few other mistresses. We assumed fake identities and set up a salon of sorts, a rental house. It was a bath and a club for Jinni, with literature readings in the evenings. We were fishing for dissatisfied closet lesbians, in other words-fresh recruits for the New Order. We would identify and research a candidate, and then we'd approach her anonymously and ask her if she wanted to defect from Lord Hades and join the Lady."

"Did it work?"

"Well enough, for a while. I returned to Meristyian, but then there was a problem. We had a leak, someone who threatened to expose our two remaining operatives. Of course, those operatives were not married, and marriage is required for Jinni by Lord Hades' laws. A nosey Jinn confided in her husband, who raised questions. I returned to Mer to deal with the issue."

"With violence?"

"Yes. By the time I reached the capital, things had progressed. We decided we needed to close our operation. The three of us terminated our lease. We were packed up to join a caravan home when the devils came for us. There was a bloody battle in the street. I killed every devil that came, until I was face to face with the worst of them all, Archduke Fennel."

"So you've met him before the event at the Trivium."

"Yes. He's the chief executor of Lord Hades' Court. He's also the husband of Ambassador Lydiah, the Court official that we currently have captive."

"You seem to have a thing with the ambassador's husband. That sounds dangerous."

Ayelet smiled wryly. "Rather he has a thing for me. Fennel couldn't beat me at blades, but he hit me with a nasty fate spell that expelled me from my body and re-incarnated me again into earthly flesh. A few decades later, my soul was recovered by the Lady upon my death. Mistress Gonorrheah guesses the spell was a 'debasement'. Fennel essentially cast my soul from my desire-body and into the flood of souls headed towards Earth."

"That sounds terrifying."

"In the body of a human girl, I had no memory of my past. I consumed nonetheless. I was still a Jinn inside. I used men and women. Some thought me possessed by a hellion, and others succumbed to my seduction. Once I was of age, I did well enough for myself."

"Well, I'm glad you found your way back to yourself, so you can be here with me." Barissianna met Ayelet's eyes. She recognized that Ayelet had finally allowed herself to be vulnerable. She reached and touched Ayelet' cheek. Ayelet grasped her hand.

"How long have you and Janaka been together?"

"A long time. I met him in Prague in 1933. He tried to sweep me off my feet, as they say. It was amusing. I was on a crazy binger, a rebound from another fling with Liest. I mean Patriarch Liest Ussishkin, of course, who had just broken off his third affair with me. Normally, children are strictly controlled among the Auerbach, but I went to Liest and begged him to let me make Janaka. I was allowed to turn Janaka into a vampire."

"Do you have lovers besides Janaka?"

"Janaka was a big deal. Liest doesn't really accept recruiting new members just to have sex with them. None of the men like Janaka. He's soft, submissive, and peaceful-the opposite of what Liest wants from his men."

Ayelet cleared her throat. "You didn't answer my question."

Barissianna looked away. She was close to having a lover besides Janaka, but she had no urge to go recklessly. She wanted to savor the moment. "I've wanted another lover, but I'm worried. It might look bad in some eyes, especially Liest's."

"What do you mean? You're a vampire woman with an eternal life. How can anyone expect you to be dedicated to only one person for centuries?"

"They expect me to be dedicated to Janaka. If I'm not, it could be viewed as unappreciative. Liest broke his own rules to let me have Janaka in the first place. It was a consolation. I came close to stealing Liest and becoming the new Matriarch. Maybe I'm flattering myself, but if you look at Lubersky, you might see why. The irony is that Liest probably sent Lubersky here as a figurehead so he can go have a romp with some girl in Egyptiania."

"Are you jealous?"

"Yes, but only to an extent. These times today are difficult. Our people are being sent to the void. I don't care for so much bloodshed. Other than taking care of my needs, Janaka is dead weight in Liest's eyes. Liest believes excess is weakness, and Janaka has no purpose in the clan beyond taking care of me."

"I see."

"Do you have a lover, Mistress Ayelet?"

Barissianna waited for an answer, but none came. Instead, Ayelet's strong hand had stilled on her calf. Footsteps sounded in the outer hall. A sklavin entered the bath chamber. Barissianna sniffed. She was hungering from so many hours of sparring back and forth with Ayelet. The sklavin was flushed. The heat of her blood was thick under her skin. "Mistress," the Ahyehass announced. "I'm here with the towels."

"Did I ask for towels, Herzl?"

"No. I suppose no. I am so sorry, mistress. I make a bad mistake?"

"Let's see." Ayelet smiled. "Barissianna, would you like to feed?"

Barissianna looked again at the sklavin named Herzl. A trace of a smile limned Herzl's impish lips. The sklavin was young, hardly older than a teen. She was bony, but shapely like a doll. Her breasts were round and puffy, and her sex was clean-shaven. Herzl wore only a black leather collar and a pair of slippers.

"Yes, I'd accept."

Ayelet beckoned. "Get into the bath, Herzl."

Herzl shivered visibly as she climbed into the small pool. Ayelet drifted inwards. Barissianna leaned forward and buried her nose in the sklavin's scented hair. Herzl pressed backwards, head on her shoulder, shoulder to her mouth. Barissianna nosed Herzl's slender neck. Her Hunger quickened. All of the Jinn sklavinnen felt hot and alive, and Herzl was no exception. The flesh of Herzl's neck was virgin too, untouched by fang or catheter.

"Are you sure, Ayelet?" Barissianna murmured.

"For you," Ayelet replied. "I don't offer my favorite Ahyehass to just anyone."

"Herzl is a beautiful name for a sklavin."

"Merci, chérie. In the Ukraine, it means 'kitten.'"

Barissianna slid her lips along Herzl's neck. She opened her mouth and clamped down. She sank her teeth deep until she found a channel. The blood welled. She sucked. Herzl groaned with evident pleasure.

Barissianna felt Ayelet's forearm against her own, sliding low. Ayelet was stimulating the sklavin sexually.

Barissianna paused for breath, and then continued her suction on the sklavin's life essence, swallowing and filling her Hunger until she felt she'd taken enough. Herzl moaned, reached for her neck weakly, and massaged the bloody wound.

Barissianna licked the sweet blood from her teeth as she held Herzl steady for Ayelet. The sklavin braced against the assault of Ayelet's forceful Jinn kiss. Barissianna felt the sklavin's heat rising higher as Ayelet drove the girl to her sexual peak. Herzl shuddered violently, and her loud moan split the silence in the Villa. When Herzl settled in her after-orgasm, Ayelet gestured silently, and the girl clambered from the tub with effort, barely able to stand.

Barissianna felt her heart quicken at Ayelet's sudden proximity. Ayelet looked deep into her eyes. "Can I kiss you next?"

"Yes," Barissianna replied. She met Ayelet's mouth, and she fenced tongues like she'd fenced with swords against Ayelet-having no expectation of winning. They kissed for a minute, then two, before Ayelet slowly drew back.

"Would you like to go to my bed?"

"I'd like to try. Love between women is common among the Jinni, right?"

"Only here in the Lady's city," Ayelet answered. "Elsewhere in Hell, lesbianism is illegal and punished as treason against Lord Hades and the establishment. Every Jinn must serve an Djinnus husband."

"That's so bizarre. Still, I'd like to try this illegal love."

"Let's go."

Barissianna rose from the pool. Ayelet took her hand and led her to the adjacent circular bedchamber with its array of magnificent hand-woven wall tapestries. The huge oak four-poster bed beckoned with a grand expanse of soft red fabrics. Ayelet doused the only lamp, leaving a single candle that burned low on the bedside table. The Jinn drew back the duvet and fished a bottle of oil from a bedside drawer.

Barissianna felt self-conscious of her body in the candlelight, although she had nothing to be ashamed of. No male except Liest had ever looked at her quite as predatorily as Ayelet in that moment. Ayelet leaned over her and pressed a palm of oil into her sternum, then ferried oil from her flask up the length of her neck to her jaw, then down the slopes of her breasts. Ayelet's fingers were strong and massaged her for long minutes, exploring every inch of her skin.

Barissianna tried to remain still. The feelings in her desire-body were incredibly intense. She was heating everywhere with a pleasure unlike anything she could feel in her undead flesh in the Earth realm. Ayelet's fingers lingered at her nipples, pulling them to stiffness. Ayelet slid on top of her, a long-muscled force of warmth. Ayelet's lips found hers, and Ayelet kissed her again, warmly and wetly. Ayelet used her tongue like she used her sword, with practiced precision.

Barissianna hitched when Ayelet's skilled fingers found her clit. The muscles in her vagina clenched, then unclenched, then fluttered. Ayelet was an expert, slipping quickly inside with a surprise attack that continued insistently. Barissianna opened her legs further. She grasped Ayelet's back and embraced her. Ayelet's mouth sealed over her own.

After only a minute she felt the beginning of her orgasm-a slow contraction, then two quick quivers on the tail of the first, even while a queer vacuum sucked over the surface of her soul. She clenched. She was coming, but with infinite slowness. Ayelet kept massaging her clit, but the orgasm didn't release downward. Instead, the wicked suction pulled the pleasure upward through her whole body with the suction from Ayelet's mouth.

Barissianna thrashed, inundated by the wave. No mere human could have held her down like that on the bed, such was the intensity of her pleasure, but Ayelet handled her. Ayelet released her lips at the last moment, allowing her to gasp out loud as the wave hit her head, making the pores of her face tingle. Barissianna went limp as the waves surged back down through her body.

"That was amazing, Ayelet."

Ayelet smiled and kissed her. "I didn't feed from you. I only pulled your energy up your body so you'd feel everything, but at the last second I let you keep your energy. It's a Jinn trick that takes discipline."

"Compared to this, sex on Earth is like fucking in a gummi suit."

"A what suit?"

Barissianna sifted through the memories of her experimentation over the previous decade. "Gummi is the Denmark word for rubber. Modern fetishists use rubber suits. They stifle all of the senses except where the design exposes you. I'm a perve for even knowing that. So is it my turn to work on you?"

"I need to rest," Ayelet answered. "I hope we can have another lesson soon. Maybe we can take more time and get more in-depth."

"I hope so. Janaka and I are about to move from the palace, actually. The Lady gave Amanoch a list of available houses in the Redoubt. We're supposed to go house-hunting tonight. Is there a free house close to your Villa?"

Ayelet pondered. "The closest ones would either be in the east central city or down by the little plaza just up from the workshops. I believe we counted around sixty houses empty of their mistresses after the Old Order occupation last year."

"We also have a lot of empty space in our chantries from our losses to the Disciples. We're thankful that their army was destroyed last year by the Lady, but the Disciples are rebuilding quickly. Auerbach recruitment is strict and careful with lots of vetting. Disciple recruitment is cruel, stupid, and unethical. It's no surprise they are winning, but the whole thing is unsustainable."

"How many chantries do the Auerbach have?"

"We have seven chantries in this realm, and twenty or so on Earth. We had eight here before the Old Order took the one closest to the road from the Black Sea region into Cocytus. If you have a map of Meristyian, I can show you some time. Right now, I'm feeling like I could sleep."

"Would you like to sleep with me for a while?"

"I'd love to. I just need to be back by nine to go out and look for a house. Do you have an alarm clock?"

"A what? I have a clock, but it isn't very alarming."

Barissianna rubbed her forehead. "Of course. An alarm clock is another modern Earth invention. It uses electricity."

Ayelet nodded. "Electricity is a curious thing. I understand that they are developing electricity and magnetism down in the capital city of Mer, while we don't even have steam power. Of course, even Haawiyah is far behind the advances on Earth. I'll just send a bird to my house-girl. She'll watch the foyer clock downstairs and rouse us."

"That's fine. I could leave now, but I'd rather stay out of the daylight."

"Is it painful?"

"The sun's radiation in this world is painful. I don't know the science, but it's something we try to avoid. On Earth, vampires will certainly burn to ash, but here the sun can't really kill us. I was told the Disciples have more resistance to being incapacitated in Meristyian, maybe because of their Middle Eastern blood. It's another advantage they have over us."

Barissianna turned onto her back, closed her eyes, and relaxed alongside Ayelet. Her orgasm had been mind-shattering, but Ayelet had remained closed and technical, using her Jinn skills with little emotion. Barissianna ran her tongue over her teeth. She missed Janaka a little bit in that moment. Janaka would have been holding her. She hoped Janaka wouldn't be too upset. Had she made a mistake with Ayelet? No.

Memories stirred of long ago. She felt a sudden revelation of why Ayelet compelled her. Ayelet was like Patriarch Liest. Ayelet was exactly like Liest but in female form-older, calm, calculating, powerful, and in control, yet with something more-a profound, guarded core of compassion that wasn't frozen.

If she took the easy way out and wrote off Ayelet as a mistake, she'd be falling right back into the comfortable trap that she'd been hiding in for decades. Ayelet's front door was wide open. She only needed to walk through it. So long ago, she'd lived on the edge with Liest, uncaring what anyone thought about her treacherous affair. She was going down that road again, and she felt more alive than she had in a long time.

~*~

Ayelet stiffened when the Sharp teeth bit into the flesh of her neck. She lifted her arm reflexively to push the vampiress away, but she touched nothing but a fleeting dream. She awoke, expecting the motes of pain to float away, but the pricks on her bare neck were real. The grey bird spoke in her ear with Mistress Freyah's voice before it died away.

So are we having that meeting today?

Ayelet rose and rubbed her eyes. The candle had long died. The other side of her bed was empty. Barissianna had left the previous evening. Ayelet slipped on a robe and descended to the foyer. It was nine in the morning. She'd slept half the previous day, and then again all night. The warm orange rays of Dawn's chariot slanted in through the tall windows.

She unlocked the front door and swung it open. The chirrups of sparrows followed her as she strode around the outside of the Villa. She grimaced at the flower gardens, which were more overgrown each week without Anders to tend them. She knocked softly on the door to Jade Turtle's bedchamber, then tried the unlocked handle. Inside, the lanky fledgling rose from where she lay prone on the floor. Turtle smiled sheepishly.

"Mistress Ayelet? I was just doing some morning exercises."

Ayelet smiled. "I'm glad you're making the effort to become strong again. I was thinking we'd skip blades training for another day. We aren't in any hurry. I have a meeting and some other errands to run. Would you like to try some gardening?"

"Of course, Mistress."

"I lost a few Ahyehasi last year, including Anders, my gardener. You could pull weeds, especially the wild dire umber. It's thorny, so make sure you find some gloves in Anders's old shed. There is also a wheelbarrow. I'll send Yenta to help. We need some new flower arrangements in the foyer too."

Turtle nodded. "That sounds fine."

Ayelet nodded gently, exited to the walk, and closed the door behind her. With Turtle, she knew, she had much work to do. She had work to do with

Barissianna too. She wasn't very familiar with the rituals of entanglement among the Auerbach vampires, but love triangles rarely ended well among most species. Ayelet summoned a bird.

We're having the meeting down at the workshops at eleven, Freyah. I forgot to send the confirmation birds. I apologize.

*Chapter 12:*

⁂

Boudi-Ca sat in the dormer and gazed over the tiled roofs at the mountain-sides outside the city. She liked the third-floor storage room in Isabellah's house. In the winter, the room had been frigid, but on a summer morning it was cool and cozy. It was piled with trunks of old clothes, costumes, and dusty furnishings.

Her plan to go back to Ayelet had suffered a major setback with the appearance of Jade Turtle. She felt envious of the fledgling who was sleeping in her old bed. Was there still any hope with Ayelet?

In the street below, Isabellah was leaving to go shopping. The carriage rolled into the street and turned towards the lower city. Boudi-Ca rose and descended from the dormer to her bedroom. She was pathetic, but she still planned to plead with Ayelet that morning to take her back instead of training Jade Turtle.

Boudi-Ca quickly put on a pale violet summer sack dress and a pair of plain leather heels. She penciled her eyebrows and colored her lips only slightly. She made herself up simply with minimal paint, jewelry, and accessories. She wanted to present herself as her old self and not as a beauty fledgling. She hoped Ayelet would appreciate the gesture.

If she wanted genuine love, then she needed to be genuine. It made sense, and she still hadn't given up on her love spell. She still had the Hierophant card, and when she looked at the burned hole in it, she imagined a wounded woman with a broken heart who needed help and healing. She kept focusing on that woman who would be perfect for her.

Boudi-Ca descended the rear stairs and exited to the stable, where she saddled her pony and directed it into the street. The morning was warm, promising the heat of summer's peak in the hidden mountain city. Sparrows swooped over the green hedges, borne on the tinkling notes of Melkeh's piano coming through her open window. Dew sparkled on the grass in the shadows of the cypresses. Large black beetles ambled over the cobblestones of the street.

Isabellah's little pony felt energetic. It ambled almost eagerly up the east hill and arrived at Ayelet's Villa within fifteen minutes. Boudi-Ca brought the animal around Ayelet's drive and dismounted at the front door. She rapped the brass knocker thrice on the heavy oak portal. She hoped she wasn't being rude coming unannounced yet again, but a bird just wouldn't do. She fidgeted. Soon she heard the patter of footsteps. The door opened just wide enough to reveal Yenta's face.

"The Mistress isn't here."

"Well, where did she go? She always trains in the morning. Did she go somewhere with Jade Turtle?"

"I don't know. I was cleaning the floors." The house-girl closed the door abruptly. Boudi-Ca rounded the Villa to the back. Ayelet's carriage was indeed gone and the horse stalls were empty. She thought briefly of knocking on Turtle's door, but Ayelet was more important. She returned to the pony and rode back to the street. An idea occurred to her.

She raised her hand and summoned her blue messenger bird. She said nothing, but thought of Ayelet. The bird flitted off down the sloping gravelly road towards the workshop district. Boudi-Ca shielded her eyes from the sun and watched the bird until it disappeared over the trees. All she needed to do was follow it.

The pony wasn't so eager to make the trip down the hill to the workshops again. It was nearly a half an hour before she arrived. The workshops were contiguous with the shop district, and the whole consisted of only two or three shortish streets. Ayelet's carriage, sure enough, sat by the curb in front of the workshop of Mistress Apolloniah, in a line with several other carriages, including the ivory-white carriage of Isabellah.

Boudi-Ca drew up at the end of the row and dismounted. She entered the building. The interior halls of the workshops were quiet, but she could hear voices. Curiosity compelled her to continue. Light streamed from a partly-open door. She could hear Ayelet's voice.

"We need to be together on this. We have to work to develop contingencies in case Lord Hades forms a counterattack. This is an immediate threat."

"What about Ambassador Lydiah and the captured Old Order mistresses?" said the voice of Mistress Nili. "Have they given us any information?"

"Gonorrheah and I are questioning them," said a voice that sounded like Freyah. "We aren't making a lot of progress. They all say I should speak with Mistress Akhteh, who was the commander at the Trivium. Unfortunately Prince Amanoch sent her to the void."

"He defeated Mistress Akhteh in a magical duel," Ayelet added.

"The Prince is an impressive magician," noted a voice that sounded like Gonorrheah. "He's maybe even stronger than Ivanka. I've spoken a little bit with him, and his knowledge of dream magic is beyond my understanding."

"Do you think he fancies you, Gonorrheah?" said the voice of Mistress Isabellah, who sounded like she was trying to provide comic relief. Boudi-Ca backed away from the door under the cover of the strained laughter that ensued. She'd heard enough to realize that it was a meeting of mistresses, and one she hadn't been invited to.

She turned smack into Mistress Gallinah, however, who came around the corner with a tray laden with teacups. The cups tumbled with a crash. Boudi-Ca leapt backwards just in time to prevent her dress from getting soaked, but a pool of tea ran across the floor amidst a half-dozen broken cups and several sprigs of fresh mint.

"I'm sorry!" Boudi-Ca tried to slip past Gallinah, but Gallinah seized her deftly by the ear.

"What's going on?" Ayelet poked her head out of the doorway.

"We have a mouse," Gallinah said. "And nothing to drink."

"Bring her in." Ayelet's voice sounded irritated.

Boudi-Ca allowed Gallinah to guide her into the large workshop room. The studio was brightly lit through windows in the ceiling and one wall. Several silent mistresses sat on uncomfortable-looking wooden work-stools around a long U-shaped sculpting table. Boudi-Ca seated herself meekly on the nearest vacant stool.

Mistress Isabellah glowered at her from the head of the table. Mistress Nili sat nearby with her customary smirk. Mistress Freyah leaned back in her chair with her strong hands propped behind her blonde head. Mistresses Gonorrheah, Pyrinnah, and Harmoniah were also present. Pyrinnah's face looked pinched and grim. Gonorrheah leaned back in her chair with her arms crossed. Even the normally jovial, purple-robed wizardress was unsmiling.

"What are you doing here, fledgling?" Isabellah said. "This is a private meeting for mistresses just like the masquerade ball. By the Lady, I swear if I forbade you to jump off of Mistress Pyrinnah's roof and land in her pool, you'd go and try it straight away. And just so everyone knows, I didn't breathe a word of this meeting to my fledgling."

"I was looking for Mistress Ayelet."

"What's happening?" Pyrrinah said tiredly. "This is a meeting of mistresses. Isabellah's fledgling shouldn't be here. What is there to discuss?"

Boudi-Ca bit her lip. "My name is Boudi-Ca. I'm not 'Isabellah's fledgling'. I'm sitting right here."

"You're still a fledgling, and an over-prideful one," Pyrinnah countered.

"You don't know the half of it," Nili remarked. "She's rude and impetuous. Isabellah forbade her to accept the gift of earrings from Prince Amanoch and sent them back, but Boudi-Ca went right back to the palace and got them from him again."

"Oh, be quiet, Nili," Isabellah said. "Leave my fledgling alone. Her affairs aren't yours."

Boudi-Ca felt her cheeks heat. "The Prince sent me some earrings as a gift. That's just a fact. He hasn't sent anyone else any gifts, that I know of. Mistress Isabellah basically says I'm too stupid and naïve to accept them. If anyone is rude, she is."

"How dare you, Boudi-Ca!" Isabellah said. She half-stood from her stool in her sudden fury. "For one thing, I have never, ever to my knowledge called you stupid. Secondly, to air our dirty laundry in front of the other mistresses is inexcusable!"

"You talk about me behind my back, saying I'm innocent and naïve. I've worked hard to become what I am from the Mimọ girl I used to be, but evidently no one appreciates it except Mistress Ayelet. You don't even tell me anything, Mistress Isabellah. You told me you were going shopping this morning. Did you lie to me? I didn't even know that Jade Turtle was back, or that she was going to be Ayelet's new fledgling." Boudi-Ca fought against the tears that welled suddenly in her eyes.

"Leave me out of this," Ayelet said cautiously. "If you aren't told things, Boudi-Ca, perhaps it's for your own good. Why should you trouble yourself with everything that's going on? These things aren't a fledgling's burden to worry about."

"She thinks that she should be a fully-fledged mistress, Ayelet," Isabellah said. "I told her exactly why she couldn't court the Prince, and that was her response. 'Maybe I should be a fully-fledged mistress then,' she said. She has no idea. No idea."

"Well, evidently you have a problem handling your fledgling, Isabellah," Ayelet countered. "You've let her pride go much too far. You need to design lessons that blunt her pride every now and then. Everyone knows that. You've no one to blame but yourself for letting Boudi-Ca's head swell."

"Don't tell me how to raise a beauty fledgling, Ayelet. Boudi-Ca has developed more in the last year under my tutelage than she ever did with you. You think you did any better, making her wave a sword around for thousands of hours?"

"Oh, for the sake of the Lady," Pyrinnah said, exasperated. "Can we please just tell the fledgling to go home? We're discussing serious things here. Boudi-Ca's personal problems are trivial."

Boudi-Ca felt a growl forming in her throat. "I'm sitting right here! Why are you talking about me like I'm not, and saying I'm trivial?"

"You aren't a mistress, Boudi-Ca," Nili said. "So you aren't supposed to be here. Go home."

"Enough squabbling, my Jinni. Perhaps Boudi-Ca should be a mistress, if she desires it so." The new voice came from nowhere, and everywhere. Boudi-Ca felt the hair prick on the back of her neck. All eyes looked over her shoulder. She turned to see Lady Allyssia in the doorway. Allyssia's bronzed body was nude as usual, and her flowing hair shed sparks of gold in the door frame like an aura.

"Lady Allyssia," Freyah said in her low tone. "You honor us."

"It's wonderful to see you, my Lady," Ayelet said.

"Boudi-Ca may take her Mistress Test, if she wishes," Allyssia continued. "If not, she should indeed go home. We have much to discuss. Many sorrowful things are on all of our minds. Do you wish to take the test, Boudi-Ca? Do you wish to become a mistress like you said? If not, you should indeed leave."

Boudi-Ca felt all eyes turn to her. The energy and pressure were tangible, like her heartbeat was suddenly pounding in her skull. She had little choice. She wasn't sure what the Mistress Test entailed, but she'd be humiliated permanently in front of everyone if she ran away with her tail between her legs.

"Fine. I'll take the Mistress Test."

"Very well," Allyssia said. The voice of the goddess lilted in the room, clear as a bell. "Boudi-Ca will embark on her Mistress Test immediately. We will have a ceremony tonight. Mistress Isabellah, Mistress Ayelet, and I will give the three customary tasks for her to complete, by tradition. If Boudi-Ca succeeds, she will become a fully-fledged mistress. If she fails, I will revoke my spell of transformation upon her, and she will thereafter live among us not as a Jinn, but as a simple Mimọ Ahyehass. She will be then required to pledge her unquestioning devotion to me, or leave the city."

Boudi-Ca blinked. Had she heard the Lady right? If she failed, she'd become an Ahyehass? Fear overwhelmed her embarrassment. Had she made a terrible mistake? She felt feverishly hot, as if her body threatened to melt over the edge of her stool into a puddle on the floor.

Isabellah spoke in a tremulous tone. "My Lady, if this is really to be, then may I ask that Boudi-Ca's ceremony be a private one, with only the task-givers in attendance?"

"No," Allyssia replied. "The ceremony shall be open to all members of the New Order who wish to attend, as well as our visitors. As it has always been, so shall it be."

"She isn't ready for this," Ayelet said to no one in particular.

Allyssia waved her hand dismissively. "Let me now discuss with my adopted daughters this beloved city and what troubles it. Boudi-Ca, you may leave. We will see you at your ceremony. Arrive at my palace by midnight tonight with Mistress Isabellah."

Boudi-Ca rose from her chair. Pride climbed in her chest and iced her burn of terror. She felt like she would pass out. She scanned the faces of the mistresses. Ayelet's face was serious. Her forehead was furrowed in thought. Nili and Szenes appeared to be in a state of shock. Isabellah looked slightly purpled. Only Gonorrheah showed a slight smile.

Boudi-Ca lowered her head and made a beeline for the workshop door. As she passed Allyssia, she felt a wave of peace and love, however. A tear released from her eye and streaked her cheek. Once out of the room, she ran down the workshop hall past the pile of shattered teacups and into the warm Isandlwana sunlight.

Her pony was slower than ever before on the return trip up the rising streets to Isabellah's Villa. It seemed almost an hour before she arrived at her house. When she pulled the pony into the drive, Isabellah's carriage was already coming up the street behind her. She started to enter the house, but decided to wait in the shade of the cherry tree at the end of the stables. She had to know what Isabellah would say.

Surprisingly, Ayelet was riding with Isabellah in the swan carriage. When the carriage stopped, they climbed out in unison and approached. Boudi-Ca fidgeted, wondering if she owed either of her teachers an apology.

Isabellah walked right up and hugged her, and then so did Ayelet.

"What's done is done," Isabellah said. The beauty mistress pulled a handkerchief from her bosom to pat her damp cheek. "I don't blame you for anything, Boudi-Ca. You're the most wonderful fledgling a mistress could ask for. I'm sad to see you go."

"Go? You mean I'll go when I fail the test and the Lady turns me into an Ahyehass?"

"No," Ayelet answered calmly. "By tradition, you're supposed to move out on your own for the duration of your test as a symbol of your independence from your mistress. There are a lot of empty houses in the Redoubt, so I expect you'll simply get to choose one, or the Lady will assign one to you. You'll have one entire year to complete your test. There is no need to panic yet."

"An entire year? Do I have a choice? Can I change my mind?"

"No," answered Isabellah. "You should have swallowed your pride and declined to Allyssia, but of course you didn't. Anyone could have predicted it. Arrangements are already being made for your ceremony tonight."

"Will I really become an Ahyehass if I fail?"

Isabellah pursed her lips. "The Lady made you into a Jinn, and apparently she can unmake you if she so wishes. In any case, tonight will be your last night with me. The steward will help you pack, and Ayelet volunteered to help us transport your oak wardrobe to your new home. I'll give it to you as a gift."

"Boudi-Ca, chérie," Ayelet added. "I've been pondering, and I have a theory as to why the Lady brought this about."

Isabellah nodded. "It's a very good theory."

"The Lady's nature is ramified into four aspects," Ayelet continued. "The virgin, mother, crone, and whore. The Lady just lost Artemisiah, her virgin aspect, in the recent battle at the Trivium. Her whore aspect, Persephone, is the only aspect that she has left. I suspect the Lady is unbalanced by this. She may be seeing things through new eyes, seeing you as a pretty tool that can be used."

"What Ayelet is trying to say," Isabellah said quickly. "Is that the Lady's perspective is like the madame of a struggling brothel. You're one of her whores, and she wants to make best possible use of you for her own survival. Prince Amanoch is an important client right now, and we've determined that he prefers young, girlish, vulnerable types."

Ayelet looked past the cherry tree towards the cypresses in Isabellah's sunny yard. Ayelet's hazel eyes squinted, as if her gaze were far away. "The alliance with the Auerbach appears to be in trouble as soon as it has begun. The Lady may have misled the Auerbach leadership about her current resources. If the Lady can use Boudi-Ca to manipulate the Prince, I think She will."

"It's clear that the Lady is using you as a bargaining chip, Boudi-Ca," Isabellah added. "I'm tempted to agree with Ayelet's theory-the Lady's virgin aspect is no longer keeping her whorish aspect in check."

Boudi-Ca bit her lip. "So she wants me to be a political princess then? The Lady just wants to bend me over for the Prince?"

"I thought that's what you wanted, fledgling," Isabellah said with a hint of acidity. "How can you blame the Lady?"

"Nothing is sure yet," Ayelet said. "You have to pass your test first, chérie. The Lady hasn't completely thrown out reason. She's dangling you in front of the Prince as a possibility. If she simply proclaimed you to be a mistress, it would be ridiculous, even to the Auerbach who are ignorant of Jinn tradition."

"Is the test difficult?"

Ayelet cleared her throat. "It's not supposed to be, but the test is normally taken by a Jinn who has been learning her arts for many decades or even centuries. You're going to find it very hard, yes, unless we make it very easy for you."

"Why make me an Ahyehass if I fail? How does that benefit the Lady?"

Isabellah shrugged. "If your transformation is revoked and you become an Ahyehass, the Lady could give you to the Prince anyway, as a gift. Don't look at me like that, fledgling. You walked your own pretty rear end into this mess."

"Mistress, if it wasn't for your pathetic failure in training me as a fledgling,

I wouldn't have been out this morning looking for Ayelet so I could beg her to let me go back to her, and none of this would have happened."

Isabellah purpled again. "You're the one who has behavior problems. You weren't supposed to go up to that palace ball in the first place. If you hadn't gone and been seen by the Prince-"

"Enough!" Ayelet raised her voice Sharply. "There is a second part to my theory about the Lady's imbalance. Her virgin aspect and whore aspect have always balanced each other by opposing each other. I think the Lady is cranky, at least in terms understood by us non-divines. We live here within her personal proprietary dream-tapestry, so it makes sense that we would all be cranky in sympathy."

"I admit that makes sense, Ayelet," Isabellah said. "Well done for divining it."

"Since the event at the Trivium, I've noticed my gardens filling with dire umber. It's a thorny, aggressive red flower, and it came out of nowhere to grow like a weed. I've seen it all over the city, and it worries me." Ayelet pensively patted the hilt of her sword. "I would urge everyone to stay calm and focused on saving our city while the Lady works through her issues. The very existence of the New Order Jinni is at stake; including our freedoms to love and live how we want. I'll see you both tonight, then. I need to meditate on my task for Boudi-Ca's test."

Isabellah nodded. "As do I. Boudi-Ca, you'll want to bathe and choose a beautiful dress to wear. If you like, take the carriage today and ask Hatshepseh to do something special with your hair. I'm sorry I've been so cranky with you lately. You wanted to live and learn from your mistakes. You're going to get that chance."

# Chapter 13:

Boudi-Ca fanned herself. She stood outside the north door to the summer meeting room. Allyssia's palace felt warm at midnight. She wore her most beautiful black corset and a figure-hugging black linen skirt. She'd agonized over what dress to wear. The black was a vampire color. It also matched her hair and symbolized death. Her death as a Jinn would be the consequence of failing her test. She didn't want to imagine the depths her humiliation if she was made to serve as a dedicated palace Ahyehass like Tajee.

Boudi-Ca patted her coif, double-checking to make sure every strand of her dyed hair was in place. Everything Ayelet had said about the influence of the Lady's imbalances made perfect sense in retrospect. She'd squabbled and argued with Ranavalona. She'd been unnecessarily cruel to Tajee. All the while, she'd been at odds with Isabellah constantly. As far as the Mistress Test, it seemed likely that the Lady had an ulterior motive for letting her take it. She wasn't ready.

She wasn't sure how she felt about the Lady whoring her. She'd never been whored before. The concept was titillating, frightening, demeaning, and arousing all at the same time. In fact, the Lady's palace seemed like a grand house of prostitution that night, simmering with lust and political intrigue.

Boudi-Ca put her hands at her sides and raised her chin proudly. She felt small in the midst of everything, but she could only live her own life. The Mistress Test was an opportunity to have a grand adventure, an opportunity she couldn't ignore.

She was about stand up in front of everyone and receive her tasks. Everyone of any importance in the Redoubt was attending her ceremony. She had to focus on not looking too young or stupid. The door to the summer meeting room opened, and Isabellah slipped through.

"It's time, fledgling. Are you ready?"

"Yes, Mistress." Boudi-Ca followed Isabellah into the meeting room, which was crowded with Jinni, fledglings, and vampires. A hundred eyes followed her as she descended the stairs on Isabellah's arm to the central dais where the Lady waited. On the dais a short pedestal rose. Allyssia indicated with her hand. Boudi-Ca stepped atop, where she stood alone in the center of the chamber like a statue, taller even than the bronzed goddess in her customary white mask.

Boudi-Ca tried to calm herself. She scanned the assembly. Mistress Gonorrheah offered her a quick smile. Ayelet's visage was solemn. Jade Turtle sat wanly by Ayelet's side. Nili sat next to Szenes, with Ranavalona and Henne adjacent to them. Gonorrheah, the blonde wizardress, sat in the third row between Pyrinnah and Harmoniah. To the right of Harmoniah were Persephoneh and others. Above them were Cupid, Psyche, and their daughter Voluptas, in the same row as Mistress Melkeh and Gallinah, along with several other mistresses and their fledglings who rarely appeared in public.

Dark forms moved through the uppermost rows of seats. Prince Amanoch and Matriarch Lubersky had entered the chamber and were seating themselves in rows that held dozens of other vampires. Boudi-Ca looked straight ahead and avoided the Prince's intense gaze. A bead of sweat tickled between her breasts. Allyssia finally raised her hands. The crowd quieted.

"The Mistress Test is a momentous occasion in the life of every young

Jinn," Allyssia began. "In time immemorial, Allyssia brooded two daughters and named them Ereshkigeh and Astaarteh. They were weak, and they could only suckle at their mother's breasts, but slowly they grew into independent creatures. They set out to hunt and seduce humans just as their mother before them. In time, their mother gave them a test, and ever since that day in antiquity, the Mistress Test has marked the passage of a fledgling Jinn into full responsibility in Underworld society. Here in my city, the Test is a trial of triumph and fruition, but it can also be a time of failure, when a New Order fledgling proves she is not ready to make a home of her own and seduce Ahyehasi into Love-devotion and sacred service to me. Fledgling Boudi-Ca, are you prepared to take your Mistress Test?"

"Yes, Lady Allyssia," Boudi-Ca answered. "Thank you." Her voice quavered, which sent a still stronger heat through her cheeks. A magical golden glow descended then from somewhere above to envelop her as the center of attention. She was bathed in a brightness so bright that she could hardly see the audience. She squinted, but didn't close her eyes.

"Let us proceed then," the Lady intoned evenly. "The Mistress Test consists of three tasks in honor of the three ancient Fates, and each task is given by one Jinn who has mentored the fledgling. All three tasks must be completed by the participant in order to fulfill the obligations of the test. Boudi-Ca will complete those tasks on her own, without any assistance or advisement from any mistress, as she is expected to have already prepared. She may, however, seek the help of fellow fledglings and friends, just as Allyssia allowed the two First Fledglings to help one another in their sisterhood. During her test, Boudi-Ca will live in the house that belonged to Mistress Cassandrah, who left us during the conflict last year. Mistress Isabellah, please step forward and state the first test for this fledgling."

Through the golden light, Boudi-Ca could see Isabellah rising from her seat. Isabellah smoothed her dress and scanned the chamber nonchalantly, holding the moment if she were executing a lingering drink, but without a cup of tea. Boudi-Ca stood perfectly still. Waves of nervousness welled in her belly to crash against the pounding in her chest, along with a sudden feeling of doom, a feeling like she was a total fake.

"It has been my privilege to train this fledgling for the last thirteen moons," Isabellah said loudly to the attendees. "At the time that she became my fledgling, Boudi-Ca had just returned from the east, where she played an important role in releasing the goddess Sekhmet from imprisonment, and so helped save us all from being re-taken by the Old Order and the rule of Hell's Court and Lord Hades. I personally think many mistresses and fledglings don't give Boudi-Ca enough credit for her amazing bravery in those fateful days."

A scattering of applause rose among the assemblage. Boudi-Ca felt her pride rise in her throat like a gentle balm on her nervousness. She blinked away tears. What Isabellah had said was true, but she'd hardly expected any recognition for it.

"In the time Boudi-Ca has been with me," Isabellah continued. "She has proven herself an able and talented fledgling. She's highly intelligent, disciplined, and precocious. In my opinion, she's a shining star among the current class of fledglings in the Redoubt, and if the Lady deems her able, I'm certain she'll make a brilliant mistress."

"Well spoken, Isabellah," murmured Ayelet audibly from the first row.

"And so I present my task," Isabellah said, raising her voice. "The Task of Discipline will be two-part. Firstly, every new mistress must have at least one Ahyehass. Boudi-Ca must acquire, discipline, and train an untrained Ahyehass over the next twelve moons. The Ahyehass should demonstrate proper submission at the parade of the Spring Festival of next year. Secondly, Boudi-Ca must discipline herself. A beauty mistress must discriminate when she chooses her lovers. For the next year, Boudi-Ca should be the huntress and never the hunted. She can seduce, but if someone seduces her, then she fails her Test of Discipline."

Isabellah glanced at the Lady and bowed when she finished. Allyssia bowed in return. A polite applause rose in the chamber. Boudi-Ca nodded. Isabellah's task was hardly as difficult as she had imagined.

"Isabellah has presented a fine task indeed," Allyssia said. "Mistress Ayelet, please step forward and present the second task."

Isabellah retook her seat. Ayelet rose and spoke.

"Boudi-Ca was my fledgling for only six moons. During that time, I stressed the importance of becoming a master of at least one art form. Since then, I've become concerned that Boudi-Ca, like many century-on-century fledglings, is intent on mastering nothing. By tradition, a fully-fledged Jinn mistress must be the master of something. I will give the traditional Task of Mastery. Boudi-Ca must finish first or second in an event in next year's Spring Festival."

Boudi-Ca avoided Ayelet's eyes. Placing in any of the arts contests, which were ruled by the older beauty mistresses, was totally hopeless. She was only a mediocre student of music, just like she'd been in Heaven, and her painting lessons had only taught her that she was lousy at painting.

She was almost forced to try blades against the other fledglings, but her chances were slim given her lack of practice since she'd been with Isabellah. The chamber fell silent except for halfhearted applause from Mistress Gonorrheah. Everyone seemed to recognize that Ayelet's task was clever and almost cruel.

"Thank you, Mistress Ayelet," Allyssia said. "And now I will give the third and final task for Boudi-Ca. The most important principle of my New Order Jinni is love. True love requires a strong heart and intense passion. These things separate mature, fully fledged mistresses from many selfish and petty fledglings. My task is simple. I call it the Task of Compassion. Sometime within the next year, Boudi-Ca must sacrifice the thing most precious to her for the good and happiness of someone else."

Applause sounded throughout the chamber, then died into a susurrus of whispered conversations. Boudi-Ca sifted the possibilities in her mind. Allyssia's task, she thought, seemed too subjective and simple, almost to the point of not being fair. Who could say what was most precious to her? How could such a thing be judged?

Allyssia's resonant voice rose again above the din. "I now have a few more things to say. Firstly, it should be announced that the raid on the Trivium was a success. We claimed a victory for the New Order and the Auerbach. We have Old Order prisoners, including Ambassador Lydiah.

For now, Lord Hades will not develop a war barracks at our little end of Meristyian."

Loud applause sounded through the chamber.

"We also had casualties. Mistress Merweh was mortally wounded. Her soul passed to the void, along with four Auerbach vampires. We will hold a funeral ceremony tomorrow at dusk. With the disappearance of Artemisiah, Mistress Ayelet will represent the New Order in the planning of our military, while Freyah will remain in command of the Redoubt defenses. Another raid is expected, but this night we will wish Boudi-Ca well with her Mistress Test. If she succeeds, we will have a new mistress amongst us. If she fails, I will break my spell upon her, and she will serve the New Order henceforth as an Ahyehass. Thank you all for coming tonight."

The form of Allyssia shimmered. She dissolved into golden motes that floated upwards. The chamber was silent with everyone digesting the last little detail. Boudi-Ca walked alongside Isabellah upwards and out of the chamber. She caught Ranavalona's eyes. The ebony fledgling smirked with open amusement. Henne's visage was inscrutable.

"Good luck, Boudi-Ca," Nili said. Her voice sounded skeptical.

"You don't want to hear what they have to say, fledgling," Isabellah muttered. "I was hoping the Lady wouldn't mention the part about you becoming an Ahyehass. It's too much pressure for you."

"No one thinks I can do it anyway. You saw how Ranavalona was smiling. She's probably looking forward to giving me orders."

Boudi-Ca was relieved to reach the carriages before anyone else. The stable girl pulled away and set the ponies at a canter. Boudi-Ca slumped in the seat next to Isabellah. The night air felt good on her burning hot face and body. The carriage reached Isabellah's house in scant minutes. The oil lamp on the rear step was out. Isabellah's yard was lit only by the Isandlwana starlight.

Isabellah remained in her carriage seat. "Go up to your room and get ready, fledgling. You're moving out in the morning."

"Where is Mistress Cassandrah's old house?"

"It's next door to Golda's place down by the workshop district, just up the road from Hatshepseh's home. It's a humble split-level that won't take much maintenance. Go on. You've got a lot of packing to do. Ayelet asked if she could come by again for a chat. I'm going to wait for her."

Boudi-Ca entered the house and climbed the stairs. When she entered her bedchamber, she stopped in shock. Her two wardrobes stood cavernous and empty. Her clothes were already stuffed into two large trunks. Her corsets were piled in a stack on her bed. Bijou stood in the middle of the disaster with her arms akimbo. The Ukraine dressing-girl was sweaty and apologetic in the light of the lamps, which flickered from the draft coming from the half-open window.

"The Mistress tells me to do it," Bijou said quickly. "I almost finish."

"Thank you, Bijou."

"And he is here. I tell him to sit." Bijou gestured vaguely towards the window, where a boy with brown skin sat in her vanity chair by her window.

Boudi-Ca blinked. "Tajee? What are you doing here?"

"Master Priapus said that I'm your new Ahyehass. It's the Lady's orders."

Boudi-Ca pushed her corsets out of the way and sat on her bed next to Tajee. "I can't believe this. She's just giving you to me? I'm confused. You're already trained. I thought my Test of Discipline was to train an untrained Ahyehass."

"Master Priapus said it was only temporary until you can find someone else. He didn't seem happy about it. He's going to have to find another way to get my work done. I'm glad to get out of the palace, Boudi, and to be with you in your new place. I'll be there for you to take." Tajee fidgeted, stood up, and moved to sit on the floor next to her feet.

"I really can't handle this." Boudi-Ca rubbed her temples. She felt a sudden headache, and meanwhile Tajee's eyes were flicking over her legs with obvious pleasure. A bird shot through the bird slit above the window. Boudi-Ca tilted her neck to receive the creature on her shoulder. It was a small brown sparrow. Ranavalona's voice spoke in her ear.

Boudi, can I come see you? Are you too busy?

Boudi-Ca waved her hand and formed her blue finch. What in the hells did Ranavalona want with her? "Fine. Just come quietly up the back stairs."

The messenger bird flitted out of the slit above the window. Boudi-Ca pushed a stray strand of hair behind her ear. Tajee was sitting subserviently on the floor at her feet. When she looked down at him, she felt her Hunger stir. Her intense emotions had drained her energy. Tajee wore only a skirt. She was struck again by how much more masculine he looked than when he was an Mimọ in Heaven, yet he was still a youth. His male gaze had drifted to focus on her shoe.

"Tajee, I have a friend coming. She's a fledgling friend of mine. Her name is Ranavalona-Ca. Ranavalona and I have been lovers, sort of, but we had an argument. I don't know where we stand. I guess you're going to find out all about me now, aren't you?"

"I hope I can make you happy, Boudi. I can do lots of things for you. I promise. I've been in the palace during the past year serving the divines and lately the vampires. I've been polishing fingernails, giving backrubs, washing the towels, cleaning the floors-"

"Tajee, can we talk about all of this later? I know we've got a lot of catching up to do, but I have other things to worry about right now."

"Sorry."

"Sorry, 'fledgling', or sorry 'Mistress', which I'd probably prefer. Would that be correct now? I'm not exactly sure."

"Boudi!" Ranavalona pressed through the door and closed it behind her. She still wore her evening gown. She looked down at Tajee. "What's he doing here?"

"Tajee is my temporary Ahyehass. You got here fast, Ranavalona. Were you right outside?"

"Yes." Ranavalona stared down at Tajee and shook her head. "The Lady is handing it all to you on a silver platter, isn't she?"

"What do you mean, 'a silver platter'?"

Ranavalona snorted. "Your Mistress Test doesn't seem very hard. At least, that's what Mistress Szenes is saying. All you have to do is train an Ahyehass, avoid being seduced, place second in one of the competitions in next year's Spring Festival, and sacrifice something that matters a lot to you, and you have a whole year to do it."

"I'd be lucky to place in any arts competition at next year's festival if all of the mistresses are competing. The combat events are fledgling-only, but I've never faced any of the other fledglings, and now Jade Turtle is back. I'm sure Ayelet will be training her to beat me. If Jade Turtle beats me, I'd have to win against Minnie-Ca and everyone else, including any vampires that compete, and I don't have Ayelet to teach me."

Ranavalona shrugged. "Well, Szenes and I were talking. The rumor going around is that Prince Amanoch is already dissatisfied with the alliance. Allyssia is trying to use you. You're evidently something the prince wants, so why not make you look available? The Lady is playing politics. Whether you win or go serve in the palace, you're still getting your blood sucked."

"That rumor is old news, Ranavalona. It's just a rumor too, which doesn't mean it's true. Besides, you heard Isabellah's task. I can't let myself be seduced."

"Our city needs to be saved. If you're the only thing that will hold together the alliance with the vampires, then what's the Lady going to do? You're going to get it from the Prince. That was a nice black outfit you were wearing at your ceremony, by the way. You looked like a vampire princess."

Boudi-Ca took a deep breath. "Tajee and Bijou, could you please leave me alone for a few moments with Ranavalona?"

"Oui, Mistress," Bijou said quickly.

"Yes, Mistress." Tajee hurried after Bijou. The door closed with a thump.

Ranavalona put her hands on her hips. "Boudi, I'm just trying to help you, and you're being rude, as usual. Maybe that's what I like about you. By the way, Henne is pretty good with blades. She used to take lessons with Mistress Freyah. She said she'd spar with you to help you work on your technique, if you plan to try for the blades competition."

Boudi-Ca shrugged. "I doubt if Henne could teach me anything. She really said she'd spar with me?"

"Sort of."

"I don't know what I'm going to do. The blades would be my best chance, but I kind of want to try my Mimọ clothes for the arts. Mistress Isabellah was impressed by my idea, and I think she's one of the judges."

"Do you want to pass the test at all?" Ranavalona winked. "A life of an Ahyehass isn't so bad with the right mistress. If you fail, I'm going to beg the Lady to let me own you and train you. Oh, the things I could do with you."

"I'm planning to pass, so don't get too excited."

"We'll see." Ranavalona swept towards the door with a chortle. "Invite me and Henne over to visit soon. We can have fun parties at your house without the mistresses around."

"Fine. I'll send you a bird. Bye."

Tajee and Bijou filed back inside the bedchamber when Ranavalona exited. Boudi-Ca rubbed her eyes. She was tired, and she had a headache. She watched Tajee help Bijou pack the corsets.

Tajee had once been a brash and rebellious Mimọ boy in Heaven, but he'd been reshaped into complete obedience by the New Order Jinni. He was a hard-working, well-trained Ahyehass with an ever-ready phallus under his pretty skirt. Tajee kept his head humbly lowered and nodded at Bijou, who was explaining how to clean a sex stain from silk. Tajee listened attentively. Boudi-Ca sighed. Tajee was sweet, but he was also pathetic.

The thought of becoming an Ahyehass herself was unacceptable and unthinkable. It would leave her destitute of any shreds of self-respect. She'd never be able to look a Jinn in the eye again, figuratively or literally. If she didn't pass her Mistress Test, then she hoped she'd die trying. Death seemed like a better fate than becoming Ranavalona's Ahyehass.

## Chapter 14:

Boudi-Ca touched the powder brush to her cheeks. She scrutinized herself in the mirror. Her lips were over-pink. She wondered how she could make them paler and Mimọic. Tajee's fingers tugged on the back of her head. He finished her twist. She pivoted to examine his work in the vanity mirror. It was perfect. The last pale vestiges of her vampire black still showed in the tips of her hair, and the twist set them apart.

"Thank you, Tajee. I look better Brunette. How else can I look more like in Heaven? Please try to remember."

"You're so different, Mistress."

"If I want my Mimọ clothes to place in the arts competition at the Spring Festival, they have to be amazing. They have to turn heads, and for that I have to wear them. I'm going to be their walking advertisement. The look needs to be exaggerated for the sake of style and sexy to the point of decadence. The beauty mistresses need be impressed."

"You'll look beautiful no matter what you do, Mistress."

"Thank you, Tajee. You're sweet. How is your sewing practice with Gallinah coming along? I really need you to help me."

"I'm working on a dress." Tajee looked at the floor. He didn't seem confident.

"Well, I expect to be gone for most of the afternoon."

"Yes, Mistress. You're really coming home with a new Ahyehass?"

"I hope so."

A messenger bird rustled through the slit in the bathroom down the hall. Within a heartbeat, it winged through the bedroom door. Boudi-Ca received it on her shoulder. Henne's voice spoke.

I'm almost there.

Boudi-Ca rose from the vanity chair and brushed the sprinkling of face powder from the tops of her corset-lifted breasts. Tajee patted the stray hairs around her temples with his attentive brown fingers. She gathered up her purse and headed down the stairs.

Boudi-Ca weighed the purse in her fingers. She hoped she had enough coins to purchase an untrained Ahyehass at the Autumn Auction that afternoon, which would be a big step towards the first half of Isabellah's Test of Discipline. Nearly four moons had passed since she'd received her Mistress Test, and she was still struggling to make progress on any of her three tasks. She was most intent on succeeding with Ayelet's task, the Task of Mastery. After considering her options, she'd decided to enter both the visual arts and blades competitions at the next Spring Festival to double her slim chances of winning.

She'd converted the lower level of her house into a training hall. She practiced for two hours at blades every morning. She'd also done sheafs of clothing sketches for Gallinah, but Gallinah had refused to help her further to create patterns out of them. Per the terms of her Mistress Test, she couldn't get help from any of the mistresses, which had led to weeks of setbacks and attempts based on her memories of Heaven and sewing instructions that she'd gleaned from old dusty reference texts on the workshop shelves.

She didn't see how her clothing could beat Isabellah's weavings or Gonorrheah's paintings in the open arts competition, but she was intent on doing well anyway. If she failed her Mistress Test and was degraded by the Lady into the status of an Ahyehass, at least she would be pretty while Ranavalona made her crawl on a leash with a phallus up her rear end.

As for the second part of Isabellah's task-always being the seducer and never the seduced-she had yet to let anyone seduce her. She was attending less evening parties, which helped. She hadn't heard anything from Prince Amanoch.

As for Allyssia's task-sacrificing the thing closest to her heart for the good of another-she figured the opportunity would come to her, and she couldn't worry. She secretly hoped Tajee was the closest thing to her heart, because she'd have no problems sacrificing him.

At first her mistress relationship with Tajee had been difficult and awkward, but after four moons together in the small house, their relationship had become well-defined, each knowing exactly what to expect from the other. She took him once a day. He seemed grateful for being her Ahyehass and having those carnal relations that exceeded his Mimọ boy dreams.

She expected to have a new untrained Ahyehass that night, however, if the auction went well. She'd spend full attention on her First, as such an Ahyehass was called in Jinn terms. She hoped Tajee would tactfully adjust to the newcomer, whoever she was.

Boudi-Ca pulled open the front door of her split-level residence. Henne was waiting outside in the street, sitting in the driver's seat of Nili's old painted two-seater. Henne looked gorgeous in her orange fall dress. The dress picked up the highlights in Henne's fiery red hair, which was done up with a fashionable gold ribbon. Henne liked gold accents.

Boudi-Ca hopped into the carriage. "Thanks so much for doing me a favor, Henne. The palace plaza is a long walk for my pony."

Henne cracked the whip, and the horses pranced forward. "It's a beautiful day. I remember the Autumn Auction last year was rainy and cold. October in the city is always unpredictable. So how much coin were you able to scrape together?"

"A little more than thirty aurei."

Henne arched her eyebrow. "That's not much. The Choshek Kishi are greedy creatures. I suppose it depends on what the other mistresses are willing to pay."

"Most of it is what I have left over from Isabellah's allowances. I had to pay Gallinah for my clothing materials-”

“She’s making you pay for materials to pass your Mistress Test?”

“Yes. She’s charging me for everything, like she does everyone else. And then I had to buy training mats for my basement, because my feet were hurting. I sold the Prince’s earrings to Hatshepseh to pay for that.”

“You sold the Prince’s gift?”

“Well, it’s not like I can wear the things around without people commenting on them. They don’t fit my new Mimọ style, anyway.”

“Boudi, honestly thirty aurei won’t be enough. You need to dream travel to Earth and seduce someone in their sleep. That’s what Nili is doing. We’re going to have a new gardener in the next decade or whenever he dies. Nili is visiting him on Earth to maintain her bonds on him, and then she’ll go sweep his soul from his death bed into her scented arms.”

“I don’t know how to do that, and it would take too much time.”

The carriage rolled up the hill to the palace plaza. The palace glowed in the sunlight, a shining beacon of marble against the bleak cliffs of the mountainside. The plaza was empty except for a wooden auction platform and a few limp flags. Henne stopped the carriage with a frown.

“Where is the crowd? There’s Mistress Gallinah coming out of the palace. We can ask her.” Henne cracked the whip. The carriage rolled around to intercept the portly mistress, who was carrying an empty delivery basket.

“Good morning, fledglings!” Gallinah beamed. “Or is it afternoon already? I was just delivering some new towels to Master Priapus, fresh from Isabellah’s loom and my sewing table. How is your own sewing going, Boudi-Ca?”

“Mistress Gallinah, where is the auction?”

“Oh dear, you haven’t heard? The Choshek Kishi swore the smuggler caravan was supposed to arrive last night, but it disappeared along with our new Ahyehass prospects. They were coming by the western road past the Trivium. The incident is being investigated.”

Boudi-Ca sighed. “There needs to be a way of telling everyone in the Redoubt what’s going on. We drove all the way up here for the auction.”

“Maybe when you’re a mistress you can help us with that, Boudi-Ca.”

"I really need an Ahyehass to train for my Task of Discipline, Mistress Gallinah, or I won't become a mistress. I was hoping to buy one from the Kishi."

"Untrained Ahyehasi are hard to come by in the city," Gallinah said. "The last new Ahyehasi here came from the raid on the Trivium, although that Mimọ girl Violet was the only really notable one."

Boudi-Ca bit her lip. "I'd almost forgotten about her. The last I heard; the Lady had taken her away from Prince Amanoch."

"Yes, on the grounds that Violet already has slave papers from Ambassador Lydiah. Amanoch is getting Violet back though, and so I've heard from a rumor. The Lady is trying to pressure Lydiah into revealing Lord Hades' plans, as well as why Lydiah was at the Trivium last summer. Lydiah is still a prisoner in the Lady's dungeon."

"Poor girl," Henne said. "I mean the Mimọ, not Lydiah. I've only seen the Prince once at the night of Boudi's ceremony in the palace. He looks cruel and arrogant, if you ask me."

Boudi-Ca frowned. "The Lady must be using Violet as another bargaining chip. She seems to like doing that with Mimọ girls."

"Mimọs are the sweetest Ahyehasi," Gallinah sighed. "It's too bad they're so rare. I hear Violet was captured by a Hell's army patrol and given to Lydiah as a gift, but Lydiah hasn't trained her yet. The poor girl needs to be trained. She'll feel so much better when she submits."

Boudi-Ca swallowed. "Are you hinting at something, Mistress Gallinah?"

"Am I? Well, of course I can't help you, dear Boudi-Ca, or it would break the terms of your Mistress Test." Gallinah squinted and adjusted her half-moon spectacles. "Are you wearing powder on your face, fledgling? How antique! Or is the sun playing tricks on me?"

"Yes. I'm not wearing any lip paint anymore, either. In Heaven you aren't supposed to show any blush, and your lips should be as pale as possible. Reddened lips are a sign that a young Mimọ has been kissing."

Gallinah blinked. "Surely you've been kissing, I hope?"

"Yes, mistress. Of course. I'm trying to create a complete Mimọ style, not just wear the clothes. Every fully-fledged beauty mistress has her own style. My Ahyehass Tajee is attracted to the Mimọ girl look, so I'm giving it a try. That's why I'm working on those Mimọ clothing designs."

"I think you look great, Boudi," Henne said. "You look as chaste and pale as any Mimọ I ever imagined. Your little white wings coming through your wing slits are your pièce de résistance. Your Mimọ style is really going to work."

Boudi-Ca felt a flush of pride. "Thank you, Henne. I hope so."

Gallinah shifted her basket on her thick forearm. "It's a very interesting idea, Boudi-Ca. I remember last summer you wanted to look like a vampire. So where are you two young ladies headed? Would you mind giving an old delivery girl a lift?"

Boudi-Ca eyed Gallinah's girth, and then the scant stretch of seat between her and Henne. "You want to ride with us, Mistress Gallinah?"

"Well, if you're headed back down to your house, Boudi-Ca, it would save me some walking towards the workshops. I don't ride a horse, you know, and one of the wheels on my delivery carriage broke some spokes this morning. We were delivering statuary to the vampires in the Divinity District."

Boudi-Ca shrugged. "I'll get out and walk, Henne. I need to think about what I'm going to do now."

"Nonsense," Henne said. "We don't have room, Mistress Gallinah. I'm sure you understand. Boudi's upset about the auction. She was hoping to somehow buy an Ahyehass. I'd better take her home."

"Oh, fine. Don't let me slow you girls down."

Henne swung the whip, and the carriage jolted around in a semi-circle. Soon they found the downslope out of the palace plaza. Boudi-Ca looked back at Gallinah. "That was a little rude, Henne. I didn't mind walking."

Henne gave her a look. "Gallinah deserves it for charging you for materials for your Mistress Test."

"Maybe she was also trying to help me by reminding me about Violet. Still, even if Violet is the only untrained Ahyehass in the Redoubt, she apparently belongs to the Prince again. What am I going to do? How am I going to find an Ahyehass? Maybe I could use my money to buy a good horse and go out into Meristyian hunting for one."

Henne shook her head. "From what I've heard, hunting for fallen Mimọ would take many moons, and without a skilled tracker, you'd have to get impossibly lucky."

"I could sneak up the Stairway to Heaven and grab an Mimọ from the ruins. That's how Golda got me."

"You'd have to go through the Trivium to get there. If you ran into some Old Order or a Hell's army patrol, we might never see you again. Besides, you can't just take an Mimọ Ahyehass against his or her will. It's against the laws of the Lady. The Mimọ would have to agree to leave Heaven with you."

"This is all so complicated."

Henne chuckled. "Do you want a spar to work off your frustration?"

"I practiced at blades this morning, but I'm not going to place in next spring's competition without more help. Ayelet is training Jade Turtle, and Turtle is my main competition. Minnie-Ca won last spring without Jade Turtle in the Redoubt, but Jade Turtle beat Minnie easily the spring before that. Honestly I don't think I can beat either of them."

"Don't talk like that, Boudi. You're good. You've never actually sparred with Jade Turtle, have you? So you don't know."

"That's nice of you to say, Henne. If I flashed, I might stand a chance, but use of magic is against the rules. Worse yet, some of the vampires might compete."

"Still, I don't think anyone can beat you when you flash, Boudi, unless they have incredible reflexes like Ayelet."

"Maybe." Boudi-Ca sighed. A warmth of pride flushed her throat, but she also felt a wave of despair. She kept hoping, but she was probably fooling herself. Henne patted her on the thigh.

"Let's go to my art studio."

"Alright."

Henne urged the horses faster. They made speed on the downhills through the Redoubt. They reached the Workshop District in ten minutes. Henne brought the carriage to a halt in front of Apolloniah's shop.

The inside of the shop, in stark contrast to the cold mountain air, was uncomfortably warm.

"It's warm in here." Boudi-Ca fanned herself as she followed Henne through the workshop entry room and down the adjacent hallway.

"Mistress Apolloniah must be in the smithy," Henne said over her shoulder. "She has a big furnace in the back. It feels like it's going full blast."

Boudi-Ca followed Henne deep into the workshop complex, past painting and sculpture studios, most of which were unoccupied with empty easels, dusty stools, and crates. The redheaded fledgling led her into a spacious room adjacent to a courtyard. The warm air smelled of a rich, earthy odor. A long table littered with tools and boxes lined a wall. Rags and buckets were piled under it. A wheelbarrow stood on end next to the door.

Boudi-Ca examined the odd, low wooden platform that appeared to be a turntable. "Your studio is nice, Henne. The inner courtyard reminds me of my room in Ayelet's Villa. It even has a pool. Can you bathe in it too?"

"I never bathe there. Some village humans from an Isandlwana quarry bring my sculpting clay into the city in a cart. After that, I have to keep it wet. Want to see one of my lamp designs?" Henne moved some damp rags on the worktable to reveal a lump of dark grey clay. A closer examination revealed fine carved flutes and floral curves.

"It's beautiful."

"Here's a head of a girl, too. It's supposed to be our Ahyehass, Chen. I think her lips are perfect, but I don't think her eyes are right. You've seen our housemaid, Chen. What do you think? Is there any way I could improve it?"

Boudi-Ca studied the clay image of Nili's housemaid. "You see her every day. I couldn't see anything that you couldn't. So what are we going to do?"

Henne was spreading a sheet over the low turntable in the center of the room. She sat on the platform, rooted in her purse, and removed a small candle and spoon. She struck a match, and the candle flamed. "I want to get blue-violet this afternoon."

"I didn't know you did nectar."

Henne smiled at her and dipped the small spoon into her pouch. When she withdrew it, it was filled with a purple-violet powder. "Ranavalona and I have been doing nectar recently. She has a new source, and it's cheap. Ranavalona and I used to do a lot when we saw you at parties at Isabellah's house. We always got purple before we came over. We weren't sure how Isabellah would react if we tried to include you."

Boudi-Ca sidled over to join Henne. "Where do you get the coins for it?"

"Lady Allyssia gives me coins for my work on the city. Have you ever done nectar?"

"No. Mistress Ayelet always said it was a bad habit. It slows your reflexes, and that's another reason why Golda disappointed her."

Henne smiled. "Blue-violet isn't bad. It's beautiful. This isn't from a cultivated flower like they use to grind powder down in Erebus. Blue-Violet Beauties grow wild right here in Meristyian. How bad can a wildflower be? So do you want to do it with me?"

Boudi-Ca hesitated. "I don't know if I should."

"Mistress Nili introduced it to me a long time ago when we started making love. Blue nectar makes you float, but the violet acts like an infusion of red nectar. It enhances the pleasure and makes you want sex." Henne moved the spoon over the candle, and the purple-violet powder quickly melted. "Have some. Come on. Just sip it up."

Boudi-Ca sniffed the small hot spoon that Henne offered. The spoon was only partially full. The nectar smelled flowery, like perfume. It made her slightly light-headed. She bent her head and sipped the liquid. A pleasant tingling sensation ran through her lips and the end of her tongue.

"Tilt your head back," Henne murmured.

Boudi-Ca tilted her head back. Henne slipped the spoon into her mouth and upended it. Boudi-Ca swallowed the hot contents. An intense wave of pleasure ran through her throat, her face, and her eye sockets. She closed her eyes and moaned. She was floating weightless, drifting down onto the surface of the sculpting turntable. She could see Henne over her, upside-down and smiling. Henne moved away to dip the spoon again into her pouch. Boudi-Ca took a deep breath. The nectar was stealing into her stomach, and then lower to warm her sex. Henne heated another spoonful and took it into her own mouth. The fledgling licked her lips.

"Nice," Henne said. The fledgling lifted her dress over her head and dropped it to the floor. Henne wore a silk-lined corset with thigh-high stockings, and nothing else. Boudi-Ca looked into Henne's eyes. Henne looked back. Henne was beautiful, arguably more so than Ranavalona. Boudi-Ca rose unsteadily and wormed at her own dress until it fell over her head onto the floor. When she floated back down onto the sculpting turntable, Henne had mysteriously moved beneath her, and she found herself in Henne's arms. She kissed Henne gently, then harder. She ran her hand over Henne's corset, and lower.

"Do you want this?"

"Of course," Henne murmured. "I've been wanting to, but I didn't want to seduce you and make you fail Isabellah's task."

"I've wanted you too." Boudi-Ca levered her hand between Henne's thighs from behind, and this time she opened them. Henne's shaved cleft was wet in its center. Boudi-Ca kissed Henne's neck. Henne twisted. They again met lips.

"Oh, the candle!" Henne jerked, and the candle rolled, spattering wax.

Boudi-Ca slapped and the candle went out. She picked the wax from her fingertip. She stifled Henne's giggle with a deep kiss. She felt for the freckled fledgling's hot buttock. At the same time, she felt Henne's fingers snake below the hem of her corset and insinuate themselves into her sex.

Boudi-Ca allowed the intense feelings of pleasure to rise inside her, born from Henne's agile artist fingers. She wanted to take Henne, but she didn't care in that moment who took who. She felt good, so good, drifting in the flow of the purple-violet. She bore Henne back onto the turntable. She let the weight of her body stop Henne's arm, but Henne held her sex. She surrendered and shifted her leg to allow the Henne full access. She pinched Henne's nipple and lowered her lips again to Henne's soft, lissome neck.

Finally, after long minutes of stimulation from Henne's fingers, she squirmed away. She bit Henne's nipple above the silken rim of her under-bust corset. Henne moaned. Boudi-Ca slid lower, trailing her tongue over Henne's flat belly, then lower still to taste Henne's more intimate flesh, to bury her nose there.

She cupped Henne's buttocks with one hand and inserted fingers with her other. Henne began a slow buck in rhythm. Boudi-Ca held Henne firmly, dominating her with the lashings of her tongue across her clitoris, even as she dominated the fledgling with the slashings of her sword in her basement training room. Henne spasmed and orgasmed.

"You should have fed from me," Henne murmured.

"Letting your energy go to waste is more decadent."

"Spoken like a true beauty mistress," Henne said. "Let me do you, then."

Boudi-Ca slid onto the turntable and onto her back. Henne moved over her leisurely on all fours. Henne's scent had changed. The smells of sex and sweat mingled with soap, perfume, and nectar. Boudi-Ca lifted her mouth to take Henne's mouth again. Henne's fingers found her nipple. They twisted. Boudi-Ca gasped. Henne's stockinged thigh found her crotch. She lifted and thrust against it. She felt light-headed again from the nectar pleasure.

Henne reached low. For long minutes they worked against each other. Boudi-Ca focused wholly on opening herself, to allow herself to release. Henne's tongue thrust into her mouth with a rhythmic motion that matched her fingers. Finally Henne stopped.

"Why are you stopping?"

"You need to be more purple-violet. Ranavalona was stupid for screwing things up with you. We've been sparring together now for so many weeks, and I know we were both thinking about it. I'm glad it's finally happened between us."

"I am too. I hope you can come and spend the night with me. Will Nili allow it?"

Henne hesitated. "Actually, she might be jealous. I'm the lover of my mistress, as you well know, not just her fledgling. Can we keep this a secret for as long as we can? When I first started coming over to your house, Nili kept asking me whether I was bedding you, and I always told her no. She doesn't ask anymore."

Boudi-Ca frowned. "Well, does it have to be so complicated? I don't understand why you can't just tell her. She shouldn't be jealous. You're a fledgling, not an Ahyehass. You can have whoever you want."

"Well, yes. I can, but you don't know Nili. She believes in the Old Order way of doing things when it comes to fledglings. She likes to keep me under her thumb. No matter what happens, she won't stop me from seeing you though, I promise." Henne bent and kissed her wetly, then lit the candle and prepared the second spoon of nectar.

Boudi-Ca sighed happily. She was feeling so relaxed and at ease-light and floating. Her first foray into the world of nectar with Henne had picked up her spirits, but she'd still gotten nowhere with finding an Ahyehass. In fact, she'd been saving her coins for two moons for the Kishi auction, apparently for nothing.

Was Violet still a possibility? She tried to focus on the idea in her nectar-floating head. Could she approach the Prince and work out a deal? If no other opportunities occurred to her, she would have to try the Prince, although the idea was terrifying.

At least something was happening with Henne. She'd been wondering if her tarot card love spell had fizzled with no result. Could Henne be her one true love? Allyssia's task-to sacrifice the thing closest to her heart-put her love life in an even worse situation than Isabellah's task of Discipline. If she met the perfect person and fell truly in love, she'd have to sacrifice that love to pass her test.

Boudi-Ca opened her mouth and received the second hot spoonful. The incredible wave of pleasure exploded in her very soul. The sensation of floating lifted her still higher, like she was ten feet in the air. Henne entwined with her again, and they floated together like two lotus flowers, fingering and caressing each other's petals into ecstasy.

## Chapter 15:

Ayelet perched on the edge of the precipice and looked down into the yawning abyss of the Trivium. Far below the mountain ledge, the ramparts of the old Court building were limned faintly with red light, like the cliffs above, by a raging wildfire that burned across Erebus to the north. Almost five moons had passed since the successful raid on the Trivium citadel with the assistance of Prince Amanoch and the Auerbach vampires, and during that time, the Trivium had become re-occupied. Ayelet lifted the spyglass and looked again.

Small pale shapes formed a circle in the citadel courtyard. The shapes were everywhere. Hundreds of them teamed like ants on an anthill. The new occupants of the Trivium were likely responsible for the piles of burned ash, horse carcasses, and wagon wheels that were scattered a few miles south along the road into Meristyian. The Choshek Kishi caravan had been obliterated.

"Nakah ipra thoth." Gonorrheah muttered. The blonde wizardress turned the obsidian scrying ball in her hand, rubbing her thumbs slowly over the stone, which glowed with smoky energy.

Ayelet glanced beyond Gonorrheah to where the chiropterim perched on the cliffside, a black bulk in the night. She wondered how long the well-behaved bat would sit still and silent. At the Lady's behest, she and Gonorrheah had flown through the daylight to save time, leaving the Auerbach vampires behind. She'd flown the bat herself, executing the complex control signals using the carved bone whistle that Barissianna had gifted to her.

She and Barissianna had gone on regular reconnaissance flights in Meristyian during the previous moons. They'd traded piloting duties on the bat just as they had in the bedroom. Both types of lessons had been very pleasurable, but the mutual lessons continued to be veiled under non-intimate pretexts.

She'd been thinking of Barissianna constantly on the trip, attempting to solve the problem of what she should do. The relationship couldn't continue forever as it was. The alliance between the New Order Jinni and the Auerbach vampires was a rocky one. Every moon that she and Barissianna drifted without emotional commitment was another moon closer to the end.

Gonorrheah sat back, lowered the ball, and rubbed her forehead. "Those aren't Old Order down there. They aren't Hell's army either. They're something else. They're something horrible."

"Such as?"

"I've been trying to divine their nature, but I'm not familiar enough with the branch of magic. They're powerful mysticism constructions of some kind. They're monsters-souls bound into desire-bodies, kind of like the Auerbach."

Ayelet frowned. "Every soul in Meristyian is bound somehow in a desire-body. What's so different with these creatures?"

"They aren't natural. They're engaged in a ritual of some kind, and they were born from the same ritual. Their magic is very strong. I'm concerned to probe too deeply for fear of being discovered, but that's not the worst of it."

"What's worse than a force of unknown monsters at the doorstep of Meristyian, a two-day ride from the Redoubt, a force that evidently wiped out an Choshek Kishi caravan?"

Gonorrheah shook her head. "They're practicing makumbacy, but the magic is entirely different. I've only been this close to this kind of magic once before, in the temple of the Eastern Order last year. One of the locks on the sarcophagus of Sekhmet held it. It's the Hierarchy, Ayelet. It's holy magic. I think it's the Mimọic Hierarchy."

"So they're fallen Mimọs?"

"No. They're constructions. It's hard to describe. I could talk to Prince Amanoch or Barissianna about it. They know makumbacy."

"What sort of ritual are they performing?"

"I can't see what they're doing from this distance. I'd need to see the inscriptions on the ritual circle."

"If we swing low on our way out will you be able to see?"

Gonorrheah wrapped her obsidian ball in a cloth and slipped it into her pack. "I don't want to go anywhere near those things."

"We're swinging low. We came all this way. We need to see what the Mimọic Hierarchy is doing in the Trivium."

"Just stay out of range of their spells-a hundred meters at least."

Ayelet followed Gonorrheah up the ladder onto the back of the bat. She pulled the ladder and loosed the reins. She put the whistle to her lips and blew the subsonic signal as Barissianna called it. The chiropterim went aloft. The bat would be almost invisible to the eyes of the Hierarchy below, a fleeting shadow among the dark stars of Hell's night, almost silent. Almost. Ayelet gripped the reins tightly.

The physical presence of the Mimọic Hierarchy in Meristyian was an event to be reckoned with. To her knowledge, it hadn't happened since the last full-on war between the Mimọs and Hell. She needed to know more. She steered the bat in a vertical drop down the cliff face until they reached the north end of the gap, then tugged the bat into a tight loop and dropped further. Soon the ramparts of the citadel appeared, bathed in the hellish light of the Erebus fires. They approached in a low sweep.

Barely visible forms moved through the citadel courtyard and down the ramparts. As Gonorrheah had described, they appeared to be using magic. A circle of glowing script graced the surface of the smooth stones in the center of the keep courtyard, and the sounds of chanting rose on the night air. Gonorrheah leaned over the edge of the basket with her spyglass in hand.

They passed with speed as quickly as they'd approached, and the walls of the keep fell behind. Ayelet guided the bat upwards. She hoped Gonorrheah had seen what she needed to see. Something was wrong, however. There were no more stars. A dark cloud blotted out the night. The riding basket jolted. Ayelet gasped at the searing pain and blinding light.

A boom sounded. Ayelet winced. Through her deafened ears, she could hear the giant bat keening. She struggled with the reins, trying to keep the plummeting bat in the air as long as she could. The bat swooped lower and lower. They hit the trees just past the last crags of the Trivium gap. Branches cracked. The bat rolled and hit the forest floor with a thud. Ayelet leapt from the basket into darkness. Miraculously, she missed trunks of the Isandlwana forest trees. She tumbled hard into a thicket of ferns. She hoped Gonorrheah had been so lucky.

Ayelet climbed to her feet and brushed off dirt, leaves, and twigs. Blood leaked from her wrist. Her knee hurt badly. She summoned a quick tenebris lux. The fallen bat was visible in the low magical light. It writhed and made odd chirping sounds where it lay on its side. A hole smoked in its thick hide, revealing wet blood and rib bones. One of the bat's wings smoked. The creature was still alive, but incapacitated. The bat's basket was a disaster of broken straps and slats. Gonorrheah sat on the ground nearby, struggling to unwrap her long robe from her torso.

"Are you alright, Gonorrheah?"

Gonorrheah struggled to her feet, clearly in pain. "They hit us with a spell. The priests summoned holy bolts of some kind. I felt you were flying too low, but I didn't want to make a sound by saying anything."

"We have to put as much distance as we can between us and the Trivium, and quickly. I think we went down just north of the road as it bends into Meristyian. We'll try going south away from the mountains, and if we don't hit a road, we can double back in the foothills and lose any pursuit."

Gonorrheah nodded, examining her shredded robe. "If we can get closer to the Redoubt, we can try sending messenger birds for help. Wait. Do you hear that?"

A hiss sounded, and a shriek echoed from the granite cliffs above. A wind picked up and blew through the wood. Ayelet reached for her sword hilt. She allowed the tenebris lux to wink out. "Something is coming, and I don't like the feel of it. Can you run, Gonorrheah?"

"I don't know how fast or for how long."

"Then let's find out. We'll be days on foot to make it back to the Redoubt, even on the road. Follow me. Call out if I start to lose you."

Ayelet trotted away into the darkness. They had to put distance between them and the citadel. She hoped the Mimoic Hierarchy didn't have any form of horses. She paused to make sure Gonorrheah was right behind her, then continued. She could hear the sweep of immense invisible wings high above, stirring the tops of the massive oak trees. Curiously, her thoughts were on Barissianna.

It wasn't fear that drove her forward to survive, but the desire to be with Barissianna. Barissianna had touched her deeply. She'd become too attached to Barissianna to accept losing her. For the first time in five moons, in the heat of being chased, she had to accept the fact that for the first time in centuries, she was in love, and she needed to do something. She needed to pursue Barissianna. She'd be a fool not to.

"Ayelet!"

Ayelet slowed and looked over her shoulder. Gonorrheah was laboring. Her voice betrayed her pain. The treetops of the Isandlwana Heartland thrashed. Stout oak branches cracked. A loud shriek echoed across the mountainside.

~*~

Barissianna snapped the reigns. The horse descended the wide track. She'd ridden alone into the Isandlwana night on the white mare that Ayelet had loaned her. She slowed the horse and watched for the telltale obelisk that marked the start of the Crossing Bridge. Ayelet had warned her to never ride alone, but she'd gone anyway, much to Janaka's dismay. She hadn't encountered any werewolves or Disciples of Set vampires, and she still had over an hour to get home and indoors before sunrise.

Ayelet and Gonorrheah had been gone four days on their trip to visit the Trivium-two days longer than it took to fly a bat to the Trivium and back, with still no word.

The leafy and flowery scents in the Isandlwana forest were uncanny. The trees, ferns, and other flora weren't real or earthly, much less the horse she was riding. Everything in the Lady's domain was unreal yet hyperreal, a sea of endless distracting sensations. In the case of lust with Mistress Ayelet, those sensations were proving addictive.

Barissianna sniffed the bunch of flowers that she'd picked for Janaka. She hoped they'd open and bloom with a little warmth, light, and encouragement, much like her love life had bloomed in Ayelet's arms. Barissianna sighed. She needed to stop thinking of Ayelet.

Barissianna rounded the last bend and saw the marker ahead, the marble obelisk that marked the start of the Crossing Bridge. She approached it, and the worn marble of the massive bridge shimmered magically into view. Lamp lights spangled the misty foredawn. The illusion of grey cliffs disappeared, and the high walls of the Lady's city became visible on the far side of a chasm.

She kicked her horse, and it surged forward half-heartedly, as if reluctant to return to the confines of the city walls. She crossed the bridge and passed under the portcullis, which the armored wache-sklavinnen opened for her. She urged the horse down the streets towards her house.

Her loaner house was modest, Denmark in style, with heavy stone facades and small inset windows that offered shelter from the day's sunlit brilliance. Just as she turned into the stable, she could see the thin wash of pink over the mountainside that heralded the sun's rays into the lower Earth realms.

Barissianna stalled the horse and climbed the steps into the house. The air inside was warm, thick, and smelled of incense. She shed her coat and boots and paced through the sparsely furnished interior. Iona and Ionela reclined together on one of the only furnishings in the main room-a heavy wicker divan that Ayelet had gifted to her. The two sklavinnen stirred and looked at her. Barissianna felt her Hunger stir in her belly.

"I need to feed, Ionela. Get yourself ready." Barissianna climbed the stairs. Janaka's bedchamber was on the second floor. She entered. Her lithe vampire child was asleep. She laid the flowers on his bedside table.

Her frequent blade lessons and ongoing secret affair with Ayelet had strained her relations with Janaka. Of course, he suspected her activities, although nothing had been said. The flowers were her latest attempt at a peace offering. Barissianna tiptoed back down the stairs. Vampire males could be childish. Janaka didn't own her. Nor did the Prince. With Amanoch's increasingly churlish attitude towards her, she'd begun to suspect that he knew as well, although she'd admitted nothing to anyone.

"Good morning, Barissianna."

Barissianna jumped at the sound of the male voice. Her hand twitched towards her sword hilt. Amanoch was standing in the corner of her foyer.

"Amanoch, you startled me."

The Prince sidled to the wicker divan and seated himself. "Don't let me interrupt your feeding. I was just restless. I won't sleep until I have word from Mistress Ayelet about what they've discovered at the Trivium. They've been gone now for three days and three nights. These Jinni aren't impressing me with the pace at which they handle things."

"What do you think could have happened to her and Gonorrheah?" Barissianna smoothed her hair and seated herself in front of Ionela. The sklavin finished buckling the high silver collar and leaned back. Barissianna stroked Ionela's thin arm to calm her. She sensed the tension in the sklavin's heart and blood. The presence of the Prince always made Ionela nervous.

"Something can always happen, can it not?" Amanoch muttered.

"Yes, it can." Barissianna leaned into Ionela and took a long draught from the girl. Her throat warmed with the hot life-giving blood.

"Take you and Ayelet for example," the Prince continued. "It's quite a friendship the two of you have going on, from the way Janaka talks. You're gone every other night, and you come home in the morning, or the next night, for months on end now. That old blade mistress must be a hotter lesbian cougar than I gave her credit for."

Barissianna licked the blood from her lips and avoided Amanoch's eyes. She hadn't guessed the Prince had been talking to Janaka, as much as the two disliked each other. "Ayelet is giving me extended blade lessons, and very charitably, I might add, considering she's also training Jade Turtle and maintaining her other duties. I need a lot of work with my sword."

"Barissianna, don't tell me half-truths. I'll wager your cunt hasn't done this much work since the last time you were fucking Liest. Valeriu and the men are starting to talk. You're being called names."

"They're idiots. Is that your point?"

The Prince chuckled. "You know, the amusing thing is, some of the men are almost sympathizing with Janaka. I actually heard a good word for Janaka out of the mouth of Valeriu, if you can believe it."

"Would you like Ionela? She's afraid of you, and I know you like the taste of fear in a sklavin." Barissianna bent and drew harder at the girl's neck. Ionela's arm twitched.

"Bittersweet blood is like a good Oolong tea. Oh, that reminds me." The Prince cocked his head. "I received a messenger bird from fledgling Boudi-Ca today."

"And what did she have to say?" Barissianna licked Ionela's neck and paused for the sklavin's blood pressure to re-stabilize. She always went by the feel of Ionela's heartbeat. Feeding was less optimal in Meristyian than on Earth, with no aspirin or other modern drugs to control and enhance blood flow.

"Take a guess, Barissianna."

"I'll pass. I have a feeling you're going to tell me anyway. I'm glad you brought up your Mimọ while we're on the topic of ill-advised relationships, though."

Amanoch snorted. "My father gave you Janaka because you're high maintenance, and you like to complain. That's why we performed the elaborate ritual to tote your boy toy here with you to Meristyian, too. Janaka has no other use to the clan other than to dote on you."

"You're being cruel. Liest allowed me to make Janaka because in his own way, Liest cares deeply about me. To you, a woman is a conquest. When you're frustrated by defeats, you turn to a young girl. You're doing it again. We've been beaten up recently by the Disciples and Allyssia's Jinni, and you're seeking to assuage your wounded ego by annexing a young Jinn fledgling."

The Prince's eyes flicked open momentarily to show their black depths, and then he lidded them again. "In this case, it's the young Boudi-Ca who wants to annex something. Her messenger bird humbly begged me for another gift."

"What sort of gift?"

"Boudi-Ca wants Violet. Can you believe the audacity of that little bitch? It's like asking an older wealthy man who she's never met to give her his new Porsche."

Barissianna raised her eyebrow coolly. "What is Boudi-Ca offering in return?"

"Her explanation was brief. I'm not sure how long of a soliloquy the girl can store in her little bird. Boudi-Ca wants Violet for her Mistress Test. She needs to train an untrained thrall, and Violet is the only one in the city, now that the most recent Kishi caravan disappeared. Ah, the impatience of youth."

"What did you tell her?"

"She said she'd do 'almost anything.' She must be on drugs."

Barissianna smiled wryly. "And now you're scheming how best to take advantage."

"Some Cupid kills with arrows, some with traps. That's Shakespeare, from Much Ado About Nothing. I can appreciate the irony of the title."

"I have no idea what you mean, Amanoch."

"I'm beginning to wonder who is the true victim in this equation."

"Well, given your adventures in love, I don't see how you can condemn me for my ambiguous relationship with Mistress Ayelet. In a time like this, we all need our diversions." Barissianna withdrew from Ionela's empty neck. She relaxed in her chair, feeling the sklavin's energy seeping through her body, re-sanguinating muscles that were stiff from riding.

Barissianna watched Amanoch leave the divan and inspect Ionela where she still sat in her chair. The Prince bent the sklavin's head back in her feed-collar and thumbed her cheek. He released his cock from his trousers and guided Ionela downward. The flaccid slave suckled lamely.

"Please don't rape my sklavin, Amanoch."

"You want it instead, then?" Amanoch approached. He held his cock in hand like a wand until it was inches from her face. Barissianna's stomach clenched. For a brief and terrible moment, she actually wanted to bend her head and suck it. The flicker of a smile crossed the Prince's lips. He'd seen her hesitation, and he'd seen her head move an inch downward. He'd swayed her solely with his powerful princely presence.

"Get away from me, Amanoch. I'm not a child anymore, although I'm certain you'd like me to be."

The Prince's hand left his cock to grip her hair. Pain shot through her scalp as she stiffened and resisted.

"The only thing certain is this," Amanoch replied. "Don't forget that Liest made you and Janaka. You owe him your immortality, as do all of the Auerbach. You owe our clan everything you are and everything you have. Before Liest, you were just another beggar and whore in the streets of Prague."

Barissianna snorted. "I was a whore with world-class tits and a witch's gift for spells and divination. Patriarch Liest didn't just choose me randomly, Amanoch."

"How is your research going with cirai? Liest and I are still waiting for a report. Or have you been wasting time with less important things?"

Barissianna laved her bloody teeth and swallowed. "I've been consulting with Mistress Gonorrheah, and I have a stack of tomes upstairs that I gleaned from the north palace tower and the city workshops. Unfortunately they're mostly written in English. I'm not fluent, but I'm working on them as fast as I can. I'd appreciate it if you didn't rush me."

"Sorry to distract you from your five months of steady effort." Amanoch left her and paced away, buttoning his pants. The front door slammed behind him.

The crystal panes of the window were purple with morning light. Barissianna stalked to the door and threw the heavy bolt. She half-hoped Amanoch got caught out and tortured on his way back to the Lady's palace. She returned to Ionela and detached the sklavin's feed-collar. She managed a calming smile. Both twins looked distraught.

"Come, you two. I've been alone all night, and I want some company."

Barissianna extended her hands to Iona and Ionela. She led the sklavinnen up the stairs to the second floor, glancing once through Janaka's door at his prone form. The Blue-Violet Beauties still lay on the side table. Janaka hadn't stirred. She went into her room, threw her coat on a chair, and shucked her clothes while the twins climbed into the bed ahead of her.

A thick stack of old magical tomes sat on the side table amidst her scattered, meager notes. She'd learned much about Jinn magic with the help of the magic mistress, Gonorrheah, but she'd made less progress than she'd hoped in her research into the Disciple soul-eating practice of cirai. Amanoch's accusations of self-centered laziness held a grain of truth.

A thump and a scrabble sounded at the slit above the door. The messenger bird swooped across the room to her bare shoulder and spoke with Ayelet's voice.

I'm just now coming into the city. I have a story to tell. If it's not too late, you could come to my place.

Barissianna rose quickly, slipped her pants back on, and threw on her coat. Within a few minutes, she was riding up the hill to Ayelet's Villa on the east ridge of the city. She pushed the tired horse as fast as it would carry her, racing the sunlight that tore down the stony west wall of the valley.

By the time she reached Ayelet's drive and the shelter of the front portico, her face was hot, and her hands were prickly. Instead of turning away from the light, she turned into it. Ayelet's hill was awash with dawn. Full sunlight was shining across the cypresses. Barissianna smiled into the burning light, a glorious light that made her desire-body feel even more alive.

Whatever happened with Allyssia's alliance, she would never forget her trip to Meristyian. She understood why the desire-world was a venerated vampire vacation place, a place of safety and pleasure. She also understood why Liest wanted to defend it against the Disciples of Set, who seemed Hell-bent on ruining it for everyone else. Finally she opened the door and stepped inside. She climbed the stairs to Ayelet's bedchamber.

Ayelet sat back in her favorite plush chair wearing only a skirt. Candlelight caught the hard muscles of her stomach and set her amber nipple piercings to glistening. Ayelet's skirt was hitched to her knees. She soaked her hooves in a small silver tub.

"Barissianna, I'm glad you could come. I sent the bird without realizing it was so close to sunrise. I'm so tired."

Barissianna shrugged. "I'm surprised to see you, actually. I thought I'd beat you here. It's a fair distance across the city from where the bats are stabled."

Ayelet grimaced. "Unfortunately, I didn't come back to the city on a bat. Gonorrheah and I were attacked at the Trivium. We left the bat for dead. We walked until Mistress Artemisiah and Pyrrinah found us yesterday afternoon. We just got in on horseback."

"What happened? Who attacked you?"

"Gonorrheah says it's the Mimoic Hierarchy. They appear to be building a force at the Trivium. We flew over on the bat, and they brought us down with a holy bolt of some kind. The creatures aren't Mimos, though. They're mysticism constructions."

"makumbacy? I didn't think Mimos used makumbacy."

"Gonorrheah wasn't sure. They were using Mimoic magic too, which is how she concluded that the creatures were created by the Hierarchy. She wants to talk to you. Maybe the two of you can come up with some answers. Whatever the answers are, the Mimoic Hierarchy is in Meristyian, and only a few days ride from here."

"How many were there?"

Ayelet shrugged. "It's hard to say, but Gonorrheah was afraid of them, and she doesn't frighten easily. I'm really sorry about the bat. I feel bad after you and Amanoch loaned it to me. I'm sure the New Order will repay your clan for the loss."

"I'm just glad you and Gonorrheah are safe."

"I need to feed. Will you join me?" Ayelet stepped out of the tub of water and reached for a pair of wooden batons on the side table. She tacked them together twice. The pitter-patter of footsteps sounded in the hall.

"I don't have much choice. It's morning."

"I'd love for you to sleep with me. I missed you." Ayelet shed her skirt. Barissianna winced. The cuts and bruises on Ayelet's arms looked painful. An ugly purple wound striped her thigh.

"You're hurt."

Ayelet shook her head. "Gonorrheah and I fell from about tree height when the bat pitched us. I'll heal. Gonorrheah is worse." Ayelet pulled the pearl pins in her braid to loosen it. Barissianna had the urge to move forward and help, in a gesture of intimacy, but she resisted. Ayelet's presence seemed hard and stand-offish in that moment, her aura toughened by her ordeal.

The housemaid Yenta had entered the bedchamber. Yenta was heavy of breast and hip, with a full mane of curly dark hair that fell around her shoulders. While the Ukraine dressing-girl Herzl seemed to like vampires, Ayelet's Greek housemaid was another story. Barissianna sank into the armchair that Ayelet had vacated.

"I've already fed. I'll just watch."

Ayelet nodded and pulled Yenta to the bed. Yenta raised her lips obediently, and Ayelet sealed them with her own. Ayelet reached low with no foreplay. The sklavin quivered, and within a few minutes she shuddered into a small orgasm, and then another. Ayelet rolled off of her, clearly exhausted.

"Close the bird slits, Yenta. I don't want to be disturbed by anyone for any reason. I just want to sleep."

"Yes, Mistress." Yenta went to sideboard, where she extinguished the candles. The sklavin left the bedchamber. Barissianna slipped into the bed and lay alongside Ayelet. Just as sleep threatened to steal into her limbs, and the dream world beckoned from beyond her eyelids, she was stirred by Ayelet's hand on her stomach. Ayelet's fingertips tickled her in the hollow below her hipbone. She let her arm fall to Ayelet's shoulder. She could feel the light caress of Ayelet's hot breath on the back of her hand.

"I love you Barissianna."

Ayelet's words were soft, barely audible. Barissianna turned into Ayelet and rested her head against her shoulder, as she often did with Janaka. Barissianna caressed the pinkish scab on Ayelet's chiseled bicep. One of them had finally gone there.

She'd raced Dawn and risked her skin being scorched by the sun just to see Ayelet, but in that moment, thinking of Janaka waking without her that night yet again, she wasn't sure how she felt. If anything, she felt disappointed with herself. She'd somehow presumed that Ayelet, as a Jinn, could wantonly fuck anyone, and was bereft of any human-like sense of love and commitment. She'd been wrong, and she needed to admit it.

Barissianna closed her eyes. She intended to create something meaningful with Ayelet. Someone in the clan, at least, needed to step up and represent vampire love. Meanwhile, Amanoch was flirting with the local Lolita instead of manning up with a proper courtship that could strengthen the alliance with Allyssia and the New Order. Amanoch had accused her of wasting time, but once again he was a hypocrite.

# Chapter 16:

Boudi-Ca arrived at the palace at sunset. One of the pearly front doors stood wide open to the palace plaza. Boudi-Ca strode past the silent palace guards into the great hall. She turned left towards the north tower, aware of the eyes of the guards on her. A delivery boy with a basket also ogled her as she passed.

Boudi-Ca smiled nervously. She knew her Mimo outfit looked exotic, unlike anything else in the Lady's city. She was wearing a form-fitting summer dress of modest, virginal white linen. She'd sexed up the Mimo outfit with white satin ribbons and bows of a style that would normally be placed only on underthings.

Her white gloves matched her dress, as did the white ribbon in her hair. Her shoes were also an Mimoic fashion, but jacked on three-inch stiletto heels. She was sure that her sexy Mimoic designs would be a success eventually, but designing and sewing took incredible amounts of time. She still had no expectation that she could place first or second in the visual arts competition at the Spring Festival.

She traversed the palace hallways until she arrived at the north tower. She knocked on the portal. Butterflies stirred in her belly. She pushed them away. She was determined to not let the Prince make her nervous.

She couldn't let him seduce her either-her Mistress Test depended on it. At length, she heard footsteps and the door opened. A male vampire wearing black leather armor eyed her up and down.

"The Prince is waiting for you, Boudi-Ca," the man rumbled. "I'm Bernanke. I don't think we've met."

"Thank you, sir."

Boudi-Ca strode down the corridors after Bernanke. Her pointed heels were loud in the north tower, which was otherwise silent as a tomb. While most of the vampires had moved into houses, the Prince had kept the tower as his private residence. They climbed a flight of stairs, turned right, and then left. Bernanke knocked at a massive door before leading her into a warm, lamplit room.

Prince Amanoch was waiting for her, sitting in a reclining chair in the corner of a warm room with bookshelves and maps. The Prince's long dark hair was combed and oiled. He looked older and taller than he'd seemed at the ball. He wore a black silk robe half-open at his pale chest. His eyes were dark and wrinkled around the edges. The oblique lamplight made his nose look big. He gestured at the reading chair next to him.

"Have a seat, Boudi-Ca."

"Thank you, sir."

Boudi-Ca sat on the edge of the chair next to the Prince. She tried to sit primly and virginally like an Mimo girl. She and Amanoch weren't alone in the study. The male vampire named Bernanke remained, assuming a post next to a door that led deeper into the Prince's chambers. The Prince gestured to Bernanke.

"Bring the girl from the bedroom."

Bernanke passed through the door. Words were exchanged. Bernanke returned with a petite pale girl. Violet's blue eyes were sunken and shadowed. Her faint golden halo shimmered visibly in the air above her head. Her small mouth and nose were her most attractive features. Her hair was shoulder-length, blonde, and straight. Violet was barefoot and nude from the waist up, wearing no collar or jewelry, only a short black skirt in a vampire fashion.

Boudi-Ca frowned. "I see her halo, but where are her wings?"

"She has a manufacturer's defect," the Prince answered. "I'm kidding. Ambassador Lydiah clipped her. I'm a bit ignorant about Mimọ slaves, but supposedly a clipping keeps them from ever returning to Heaven. Turn around in place, Mimọ."

Boudi-Ca felt a shiver run through her own shoulder blades when she saw the ragged pink scars on Violet's back. "Hello, Violet. I'm Boudi-Ca, a Jinn fledgling. Would you like to come and serve me, instead of the Prince? I'll take you to a nice home. You'll have your own bed and beautiful Mimọ clothes. I can't take you as my Ahyehass unless it's your own free will, though. It's the law of Lady Allyssia."

Violet nodded. "Yes, I'd like to go with you, Boudi-Ca."

The Prince smiled bemusedly. "I'm glad we've got that formality over with. So we have a deal, Boudi-Ca?"

"Agreed." Boudi-Ca kept one eye on Violet and the other on the Prince. She steeled herself. Soon she'd be walking out of the palace with her own female Ahyehass. Violet was very pretty. Meanwhile, the Prince's eyes were roaming over her.

"So how does an Mimọ become a Jinn, Boudi-Ca? I'm intrigued from a magical standpoint, although I'm not a genius with transformative magic."

"Lady Allyssia performed a ritual and a spell in the dream world. It's a long story. Would you mind if we just get on with it? Take your robe off."

Boudi-Ca caught the Prince's dark eyes, which turned from amused to stormy in a heartbeat. The Prince stood up, pulled his sash, and removed his robe, which he threw over the back of his chair. Black tattooed designs adorned the Prince's pale skin down the length of his back. The designs formed interlocking circles with strange symbols around their perimeters.

Amanoch sat back down in his chair. In front, the Prince was hairless, with a broad chest and a muscled belly. He was attractive except for the pallor of his skin. His body looked faintly wrinkled, as if pressed long against a bedsheet. His phallus was thick, pale, and formidable. The Prince reached down with his fingertips.

"Come here."

"Don't give me orders." Boudi-Ca pivoted around the Prince's knee and knelt on the floor. She took her position between his muscled legs. She looked up. The vampire's half-lowered eyelids flicked open, and she found herself riveted to the black orbs beneath them, swimming in the small whirlpools of gold flakes that pulled her into their centers.

Boudi-Ca tore her eyes fiercely away from the Prince's intense gaze and focused instead on the half-flaccid blue-veined member. The Prince's phallus stirred further, hardening until the veins bulged around its circumference. Boudi-Ca stroked with one white-gloved hand.

She bent and fit the tip of the phallus into her mouth. She swirled her tongue over the silken skin. The taste was bitter, like ashes. She took the phallus deeper, slicking it with her saliva. She pulled back, then engulfed it again. The ashen taste filled her mouth and made her stomach quiver. She worked the phallus with her hand, forming a ring with her thumb and forefinger. The Prince's phallus warmed with transferred heat. His fingers stroked gently over her head.

The Prince pushed her head downwards. Boudi-Ca gagged slightly as the phallus bounded deeper into her throat. She worked harder. She kept her mind on her goal. The sooner she could finish, the sooner she could go. She sucked with longer strokes and greater effort.

Her Jinn Hunger stirred and heated inside her, urging her harder onto the Prince's cock until the ashen taste filled not only her mouth and throat, but even her eyes and nostrils. Meanwhile, the Prince's hands wrapped around her head. Her scalp tingled. She went dizzy.

She was transported, and she wasn't in the Lady's palace anymore. She was climbing the Stairway to Heaven. She smiled and checked her watch. She was almost home. The scene shifted. She was in class. Professor Brown was explaining Earth History. She glanced at Tajee with a coquettish smile. She threw him a note when Brown wasn't looking, but Makeda Deen intercepted it. Makeda spread the note open with her pale fingertips, bent her head, stuck out her tongue, and licked sensuously.

She was in Makeda's bedroom. She crushed Makeda and showered her with kisses. She fucked Makeda with her fingers. Makeda's Mimoic face blushed with erotic bliss. Boudi-Ca blinked. Makeda was gone, and she was kneeling again on the marble floor, and the pallid, wrinkled stomach of Prince Amanoch reappeared in her view. The Prince pulled his thick phallus from her mouth.

"What beautiful dreams you have, Boudi-Ca. I've heard you prefer girls, but it's a disappointment to see it for myself."

"Those scenes in my head never happened."

"Of course, but you wanted them to. When you were wanting, you created a tiny electric potential in the dream world that remained to this day, just waiting to fill a great master of dream magic with disinterest and boredom. Let's move to my bedroom."

Boudi-Ca stood up and paced past Violet, who was standing there mutely with her blue eyes glassy and wide. The Prince's dark bedroom smelled of herbs and linens. A candle flared in the darkness, and then another. The Prince lit candles on an antique sideboard. An ancient four-poster with red bedclothes dominated the center of the room, and above it hung a gold-framed figure painting of satyrs playing with nimfas.

Boudi-Ca unbuttoned her white dress and sloughed it from her hips. She wondered if the Prince preferred her nude or in her painstakingly-made lingerie. She decided it would be best not to sully her creations with seminal fluids, or worse. She rolled down her white stockings and added her slip, panties, and gloves to the pile of Mimǫ clothes. She kept her corset. The Prince sat on the edge of the bed. She went to him, knelt, and took his phallus again.

The Prince's cock was big, cool, and silky. Her Hunger leapt yet again. She couldn't seem to help herself, as if her Hunger was especially stoked by a powerful male presence. It was a new sensation. Boudi-Ca stood up, pushed the Prince back onto the bed, and climbed on top. She slid her body sensuously over his.

He grabbed her and turned the tables, and within a second she was underneath him. The Prince centered himself and plunged his phallus deep into her sex. Boudi-Ca moaned when the pleasure flooded her belly up to her ribcage. Her inner Jinn muscles slowly submitted and relaxed to the penetration.

Chills ran down her spine when the Prince's cool lips grazed her neck. She felt the prick of his teeth, and with them a chill of horror. He lingered with his lips, kissing and nipping. His thrusts evened into a pleasurable rhythm.

Boudi-Ca contained herself and held fast against her orgasm. She had no intention of giving Prince Amanoch the satisfaction. She began her Jinn vacuum, gripping his shaft and pulling with all of her psychic strength. She rocked against the Prince, synchronizing submissively with his aggressive rhythm.

While the Prince's cock was inside of her, however, she had the control. He was in her Jinn domain, both literally and figuratively. He shuddered and weakened against her suction. His uncanny eyes flickered closed. His motions quickened, and within a few more minutes it was over. The Prince stiffened, and she worked to drain his seed completely. He was curiously bitter and stony to her Jinn taste, like limestone or charcoal.

Boudi-Ca tried to squirm away, but the Prince held her roughly, as if to re-assert his male dominance. She felt for a few moments like a caged animal on his bed, and the feeling rendered her breathless. She struggled, trying to rise until he finally let her go. She rubbed her fingers over her neck. She felt no blood. She rose from the bed, caressing the Prince's muscled arm as she went.

"I'm going now, Master Amanoch."

The Prince rolled off the bed after her. He stalked past her to his wardrobe and threw it open. "Have a nice day, Boudi-Ca," he said over his shoulder. "Feel free to send me a messenger bird anytime. You can show yourself out. Enjoy your plaything."

"Thank you, sir. This Ahyehass means a lot to me."

Boudi-Ca grabbed up her clothes. She stumbled out the door and bumped Violet forward, drying her sex with her stocking as she went. The wide-eyed Mimǫ girl allowed herself to be herded. Boudi-Ca shoved Violet, and they skittered out of the Prince's study. Relief swept over her. She'd done it. She'd paid the Prince's price, and she'd emerged with her Ahyehass.

"I can't believe you're even an Mimo," Violet murmured. The Mimo girl hugged herself. "That was so disgusting."

Boudi-Ca bit her lip. "I'm not an Mimo anymore. The Lady changed me into a Jinn. Weren't you listening?"

"Where are we going? Aren't you going to put your clothes back on?"

"I'll get dressed in a minute. I just want to get out of here." Boudi-Ca looked over her shoulder. The vampire named Bernanke had emerged from nowhere to silently escort them while Violet kept talking.

"You're really Boudi-Ca Marcus, aren't you? You were a student at the College of Sacred Moons, like Tajee was, and you joined the Conclave?"

"I haven't heard my Mimo name in a long time, Violet, and I don't really want to. From now on, you're to call me Mistress, and nothing but that. You belong to me now. I'll treat you better than the Prince. I'll teach you everything. If there is anyone here you can trust, it's me."

"Yes, Mistress," Violet whispered.

Boudi's stomach suddenly felt hollow. She hadn't known what to expect when she met Violet, or how she would feel. It felt like meeting her old Mimo girl self. Violet unnerved her, as did Violet's questions. She pulled Violet through the north tower vestibule and into the palace proper. Bernanke shut the door behind them.

Boudi-Ca finally breathed a sigh of relief. She climbed into her panties, her dress, and her stockings while Violet watched with her arms still wrapped guardedly over her bare chest. "Let's go. You're going to be living with Tajee and me. Tajee can help you too."

"Really?" Violet's eyes brightened. "Oh, that makes me happy. Tajee is sweet. He's like my hero. He was really nice when he came to visit me."

Boudi-Ca took Violet's hand and led the girl down the palace corridor towards the palace great hall. She felt a slight spark of envy at Violet's quick interest in Tajee. Violet had surely never desired to be ravished by another girl, any more than she'd desired to be ravished by a vampire. Violet would need a lot of training.

Boudi-Ca took a deep breath. She hoped it was possible. If not, she hoped she hadn't made a mistake. In Violet's case, Isabellah's task of properly training an untrained Ahyehass might be more difficult than she'd anticipated.

"From now on, Violet, you should call me Mistress. I'm your Jinn, and you're my Ahyehass. You have to do as I say. You do understand the way things work around here, don't you? You aren't completely naïve about this?"

Violet paled. "I don't know, Mistress."

"You'll desire to serve me once I've properly dominated you. You won't be sleeping with Tajee, of course, or even kissing him. Such a thing is forbidden between two Ahyehasi. I promise that I'll make you feel pleasure beyond anything you ever dreamt in Heaven, but remember there is pain too in this place. An Ahyehass can be punished if she misbehaves, just like an Mimọ."

Chapter 17:

Ayelet lounged on the couch in Barissianna's parlour. She stretched her legs, which still ached from her tumble from the chiropterim. A fire crackled in the fireplace, illuminating Barissianna flatteringly. The vampiress sat hunched at the table. Her fingers flicked over the open leaves of a thick tome. Across from the vampiress sat Mistress Gonorrheah, who puffed from a long pipe. Gonorrheah held a stout walking cane between her legs.

"So the Mimoic Hierarchy came in and took over the Trivium after we drove the Old Order out," Gonorrheah said. Faint curls of smoke rose from her lips. "And we've established that they've taken it with these 'raised crusader' things, and these things are summoning more of themselves, even as we speak."

Barissianna nodded without looking up. "They're described in a number of mysticism texts. Many of the Hierarchy's followers are so filled with religious fervor that they are willing to fall from Heaven for the Mimoic cause. They form the soldiers of Heaven's army in the war against Hell in this realm."

"What were those flying things that followed us, though? They were invisible, and they could fly. Fortunately they were so large that they couldn't fly down into the trees, but they hounded Ayelet and me for leagues."

Barissianna turned a page in her tome. "I wish I had access to my sire's archives on Earth. I think they were gloom-wraiths, another name for fallen tenshiim. I can't find any references in these texts."

"Tenshiim?" Janaka appeared in the hallway. "Aren't those pretty babies?"

Barissianna raised her head from her book. "Do you need something, darling?"

"No, I was just a bit bored upstairs. Iona and Ionela aren't feeling very entertaining, unlike you my dear, infinitely so."

Barissianna turned her eyes again to the pages. "Janaka loves to flatter me. He's good at it."

"Obviously." Gonorrheah winked at Janaka.

"Obvious are the rosettes that I've stitched in Barissianna's leather," Janaka sang. "We've been through much together, through stormy nights and snowy weather."

"Bravo." Gonorrheah clenched her pipe in her teeth and clapped her hands. "The mood in here is too gloomy. A bit of poetry is appreciated."

Ayelet rose to her feet and paced to the window. She wondered how much Gonorrheah knew of her affair with Barissianna. The Redoubt was small, and rumors of certain interracial relations were spreading, much like the rumors of an impending attack on the city. Ayelet surreptitiously eyed Janaka. He was a handsome male, clever and entertaining. He was wittier and more good-natured than herself, she had to admit, and not a bad companion for Barissianna.

Things were happening that were far more important than love affairs, anyway. Once again, the beautiful city of the Lady appeared threatened, and the threat was more dire and horrible than ever before.

The crusaders of the Mimoic Hierarchy were known to take no prisoners and accept no capitulation with evil. Whenever Heaven went to war against Hell, the Mimos burned Jinni and Djinnus alive with holy fire. They gutted nimfas, decapitated satyrs, and melted the flesh off of Seelie Kishi with their spells. Meristyian-the storied Purgatory of the Mimos-was supposed to be a de-militarized zone. Allyssia had built her city in Meristyian strategically, but had also accepted significant risks.

A grey bird scrabbled at the window slit. It swooped into the room. Ayelet received it on her shoulder. It spoke with Mistress Freyah's voice.

There has been a new development. The Lady would like you to come back to the Palace within the hour. Summer meeting room again.

Gonorrheah puffed on her pipe, sending a plume of smoke to the ceiling. "What is it, Ayelet?" Another grey bird hopped through the slit and swooped to Gonorrheah's robed shoulder. The wizardress tilted her head. "I see. Another meeting."

Barissianna pretended to pout. "I'm not invited, Ayelet?"

"I'll fill you in." Ayelet tightened her boot laces. She doubted the meeting would be closed to the ears of the Auerbach vampires, but it wasn't her place to extend invitations. "Gonorrheah, I'll take us both up to the palace."

"Nonsense," Gonorrheah said. The wizardress leaned heavily on her cane. "Why waste a perfect opportunity to practice my levitation spell? Well, alright. Fine."

Ayelet helped Gonorrheah towards the door. "Good night, Barissianna. Perhaps we'll get together another evening soon."

"We'd love to have you over, Ayelet," Barissianna said.

"Good night," Janaka added coldly.

Ayelet descended the steps from Barissianna's house. She waited for Gonorrheah to limp bleary-eyed after her. Gonorrheah reeked of herbs. They climbed into the seat of her carriage. Ayelet slid her sword between the seat and the sideboard. She snapped the reins. The horses surged into motion over the bumpy cobblestones. Ayelet rubbed her temple. The cool fall air felt good on her warm forehead.

"Thanks for taking me, Ayelet," Gonorrheah said. She awkwardly refilled her pipe, transferred it to her bandaged right hand, and clicked her fingers to produce a flame. The pipe bowl smoked. "Janaka is a handsome vampire. Care to talk about you and Barissianna?"

Ayelet shrugged. She didn't think Gonorrheah was mentally fit to discuss the social and political intricacies of her affair. "The Auerbach, like all vampire clans, are male-dominated. Barissianna was made a vampire because she whored herself to the Auerbach patriarch back in the eighteenth century. Barissianna is feeling expectations for her sex. I'm trying to help her go beyond that."

Gonorrheah tapped her pipe stem on her lips. "I do sense a hesitancy about her. She knows makumbacy, but she doesn't give herself any credit. She has more the attitude of a fledgling than a vampiress of her abilities. By the Lady, that was a wicked raven spell she threw at the Trivium."

"She's the leader of an Auerbach chantry in the New World, in a city called Vancouver. Actually, I'd prefer not to talk about Barissianna now."

"Fine by me." Gonorrheah puffed and sent a plume of smoke skyward. The carriage rolled until they reached the palace plaza. The night was clear. The stars were dimly reflected in the Lady's massive crystal bowers rising high above the palace. Ayelet helped Gonorrheah down, and then helped her wobble up the broad palace steps. The massive pearl doors were wide open, and the warmly lit interior of the great hall beckoned. Inside the palace, they turned right and climbed the long hallways to the summer meeting room.

A cluster of attendees sat in the bottom row of seats in an informal and intimate circular arrangement. Ayelet approached the ring of chairs with Gonorrheah right behind. Prince Amanoch, Matriarch Lubersky, and Mistresses Freyah, Apolloniah, Artemisiah, Pyrinnah, and Persephoneh were all there, along with a human male who she didn't recognize.

The masked Lady Allyssia sat cross-legged in an inelegant lotus position in a space between the chairs. Cupid sat in a chair beside her, also wearing his mask. Cupid's beautiful wife Psyche leaned on his shoulder with her lips at her husband's ear. There was no appearance from the divine daughter Voluptas.

Ayelet headed straight to Freyah, who was speaking with Pyrinnah. They turned to her when she approached. Freyah looked red-faced and drunk. "Hello, Ayelet. Everyone is here, and everyone is early. That's a first."

Ayelet nodded. "So what's the news? And who is the newcomer?"

"He's the news," Pyrinnah answered. "Or at least, he brings it from the east. You don't recognize him? You've met before."

"Everyone sit. Let's do this," Freyah bellowed. She lifted her drinking horn to her lips and gulped the contents.

Ayelet took a seat and stared at the tall, handsome, human male in the chair across from her. He wore leather armor and a long sword at his belt. The hilt wrapping of his well-used sword was worn. Traces of blood stained the first several inches of the scabbard, brown blotches of the kind that couldn't be expunged. The man had seen action, and a lot of it.

He caught her gaze with his dark piercing eyes. A light sheen of sweat glistened in the short grey hair of his balding forehead. A thick ring graced an equally thick finger, revealing the paw sigil of the Greybeard clan of werewolves.

"He wears a werewolf ring," Ayelet said, loud enough for the man to overhear. "So I'd guess our guest to be Prince Masad, son of Lord Hades, otherwise known as The Jackal. He is visiting from eastern Meristyian."

The man's thin lips cracked, and he nodded. "In the flesh am I."

"That's him, Ayelet," Gonorrheah said. She tapped her pipe bowl with a forefinger. "I didn't even catch on. What transpires in eastern Meristyian, Masad?"

Prince Amanoch leaned forward in his chair and straightened his dark blue coat. "I believe we should discuss first what is happening here in the west?"

"Yes," chimed Allyssia. "Tell us what your scouts have found at the Trivium, Amanoch. Then we will hear from Masad."

Amanoch nodded. "Some of you may not know that Valeriu and I took our bats back to the Trivium last night to verify what Ayelet and Gonorrheah reported. We returned this morning just before dawn. The mistresses are correct. There is a Hierarchy force occupying the Trivium outer keep. We were also attacked in the air by invisible flying creatures, but we managed to run on our faster bats."

Ayelet frowned. She wondered why a second reconnaissance mission had been necessary or even advisable, but she remained silent. She glanced at Gonorrheah, who raised her eyebrow.

"Gonorrheah, what is your opinion on these creatures," Allyssia said.

"Barissianna and I have been researching them," Gonorrheah answered. "She has a solid knowledge of-"

"The force holding the keep is comprised of raised crusaders," Prince Amanoch interrupted. "I'd estimate there were two or three hundred. They were chanting, doing some kind of magic, but we couldn't discern what it was, and we weren't willing to risk a closer look."

"Ayelet and I were willing," Gonorrheah said. The wizardress chuckled. "Or at least Ayelet was. I believe the crusaders were performing a summoning ritual. They had a circle drawn in the courtyard of the keep. I'm guessing they are summoning more of themselves. Barissianna believes the flying creatures are gloom-wraiths. Fallen tenshiim."

"Agree I with this," Masad added in his low, solemn voice. "Met I one in the east, in the Acheron Valley. Remind need I not of the last time flew gloom-wraiths in Meristyian. The twelfth century. When saw I these wraiths in the east, flew they in a Hierarchy attack on Memphis."

"The Eastern Order Jinni are under assault again?" Gonorrheah frowned. "That's terrible for Lady Sekhmet. Is that why you're here, Masad?"

"Scattered your sisters in the east have," Masad confirmed. "Disappeared Sekhmet and her priestesses. Abandoned they Memphis to the Mimos."

"What of the werewolves?" Ayelet said.

"Hunts the Mimoic Hierarchy them like dogs. Made they the wolves the first target of the purgation. Easy targets. Has the Hierarchy werewolf-hunters-"

"No one cares about the werewolves," Matriarch Lubersky interrupted. "If they are driven from Meristyian by the Hierarchy forces, then so much the better."

"This situation threatens all of us, Matriarch," Allyssia said. "We should welcome any allies we can find, including werewolves. That is why Masad has come to us. Greybeard and the Four Brothers wish to flee to the west and take up habitation in my domain. Between the Disciples of Set, the Hierarchy, and now Hell's army patrols, they are in great danger. They seek a safe haven."

"Unacceptable," Amanoch said. "The Auerbach would welcome the legendary Prince Masad at our side, but our kind cannot abide by an alliance with the werewolves, come Heaven or come Hell."

"And one, the other, or both are coming," Ayelet said darkly. "It's clear to you then, Masad, that Lord Hades and Lord Tuhan are at each other's throats?"

"Aye. See I clearly. Guess I that seeded the disaster of their previous venture much ill-will between the powers. Set against each other they be. See I the bodies in the east."

"I'm not sure if that's good for us or bad." Ayelet realized that she was thinking aloud. All eyes turned to her, but then away from her to look at Gonorrheah. Gonorrheah had opened her purple robe widely to reveal her naked breasts. The blonde wizardress grinned.

"Sorry, everyone. Maybe it's the herb I've been smoking, but it's warm, and I'm hot-blooded. I've never been in the same room with two handsome princes at the same time."

Ayelet cleared her throat. "So, Prince Masad, these raised crusaders can be sent to the void then, I take it? I'm a little unclear as to their nature."

"Can be destroyed their desire-bodies, but hardly," answered Masad. "Require a strong arm, an enchanted blade, or devil-fire. Bound the crusaders are into mysticism constructions. Chained are these Mimo souls to bodies with magic. Ripped into pieces they must be to send them to the void. Or burned by fire."

"Devil-fire I can manage," Gonorrheah said. "Ripping to pieces, not so much."

"Do we have to fight this?" Freyah muttered. "Or can we? Maybe if Heaven and Hell rage all around us, we'll be stronger."

"A wise hypothesis," lilted Allyssia.

"All the more reason not to shelter the werewolves," Amanoch said. "If the Hierarchy is after those beasts, then harboring them would bring the enemy to our doorstep."

Ayelet rubbed her sore forearm. "Why would the Hierarchy even bother with the werewolves? What would be the purpose in hunting them?"

"The strategic conflicts between the followers of Tuhan and those who oppose them have largely ceased in modern day Earth, Ayelet," Allyssia said. "Religious boundaries have been stable in the last centuries. The Hierarchy's efforts on Earth are moving backwards, if anything. The most effective way to expand their power is to carry the crusade to the dream world and Meristyian-to extinguish the root passions that sway souls from Mimoic rule, and to destroy the old gods that purvey them, until only Mimoic repression is left for the humans to turn to."

"The Lady speaks the truth," Apolloniah said. "As always. I agree with Freyah. Our only choice is to not be involved."

Allyssia nodded. "Ayelet, what do you say? I've appointed you the New Order's general. How do you view the situation, given the facts at hand?"

Ayelet took a deep breath. "I don't know if we can remain neutral even if we wanted."

"I agree," Prince Amanoch said.

"The werewolves are neutral in the greater conflict," Ayelet continued. "Masad has told us that the wolves are being hunted and killed. It seems they are part of a purgation more than a mere conquest. We might be next for targeting by the Hierarchy. They know exactly where we are, and this city would make a perfect fortified base of operations in Meristyian for any side who could take it from us. I know I'd take this city right away if I were fighting a war here, and I had an aerial force in place to take it."

"I agree with Ayelet," added Gonorrheah. "I don't see why the Redoubt wouldn't be next on the Hierarchy list after the Eastern Order and the werewolf clans."

Prince Amanoch leaned back in his chair and crossed his arms. "I'd like to say that we can try to fight the full military might of the Mimoic Hierarchy, but the problem is that I won't."

"My son speaks the truth," Matriarch Lubersky added. "If the only option is to fight, and this city is a target, then perhaps the Auerbach vampires would be best served to return to Earth. Our alliance with the New Order to keep equilibrium in Meristyian has served our purposes, but fighting the full power of both Heaven and Hell is beyond anything we can accomplish."

"Why did I have a feeling it would come to this?" Pyrinnah muttered.

"What's that supposed to mean, Jinn?" Amanoch countered. "For all you know, our presence here for the last six months has forestalled an attack on your city for this long. That was our purpose-to serve as a deterrent."

Allyssia raised her hand. "There is nothing to be gained from bickering. We will adjourn this meeting, and we will consider further what we've learned. We will think on Love. Who among the Jinni here has quarters and a good bed for Prince Masad? He has confided that he does not wish to reside inside my palace."

"He can sleep in my bed." Gonorrheah grinned. "I mean to say I was wounded when Ayelet and I fell from the bat during our trip to spy on the Trivium, so I'm sleeping on the couch in my parlour. It hurts to climb up my stairs. My second-floor bedroom is empty and available, and it has an adjoining bath."

Masad smiled. "Sounds that fine, Gonorrheah. Have you my thanks."

"That's all for this evening then," Allyssia said. "We will convene another meeting soon."

The goddess lifted her arms, and a shower of golden light dissolved her form. Ayelet rose from her seat. She watched Prince Masad shake hands with Prince Amanoch. The exchange, she noted, was cordial but cold. Masad approached her and Gonorrheah.

"Is there room in your carriage for three, Ayelet?" Gonorrheah said. "I'd like to get the Prince to my bed quickly before he changes his mind."

"Of course. Let's go. Welcome back to the Redoubt, Masad." Ayelet led the way slowly out of the Palace. Gonorrheah and the powerful son of Lord Hades made small talk behind her. She didn't listen. Her thoughts were on the events that had unfolded. Masad had brought grim news from eastern Meristyian. When they reached the palace plaza, she climbed into her carriage and took the reins. Masad settled next to her. Gonorrheah slid wincing into the rear seat. Ayelet snapped the reins and directed the carriage towards Gonorrheah's home on Laurel Row.

"So how is Mistress Golda, Masad?" Gonorrheah said. "Is she well?"

"Seems she healthy and better than ever," Masad answered. "Taught her much have I. Helps she keep the werewolves out of trouble. Ambush we can the Hierarchy soldiers in the Persium plateau. Keep we the dens secure. Avoid we the gloom-wraiths."

Ayelet eyed Masad. "Is Greybeard well? And the brothers?"

Masad looked at her. His worn face was expressionless. "Greybeard is himself, but die the brother wolves at the hands of the Mimoic Hierarchy. Think I a new great war is coming. Is well the New Order here? No more problems since the Old Order occupation?"

"We've had a year and a half of peace."

"Too quiet," added Gonorrheah. "We lost about half of our mistresses and fledglings to the Old Order during the occupation, Masad. Some mistresses went willingly and swore fealty again to Lord Hades and Lady Allyssia. Some didn't. They were punished by Hell's Court."

"Sad am I," Masad said. "Such beautiful beings are Jinni. Take you your talents for granted, but dreams many a wolf of a skilled woman in his bed. Know I the werewolf Elor misses Boudi-Ca. Asks he about her at the stronghold of the Four Brothers. Wants he to visit her in the city of the Lady. Wants he not to die to the Hierarchy."

"Ah, I remember him," Gonorrheah said. "Boudi-Ca must like red hair, I think."

Masad smiled. "Boudi-Ca is well? Benefits she from your tutelage, Ayelet?"

Ayelet looked straight ahead. She directed the carriage around a bend and onto Gonorrheah's quaint, tree-bowered street. "Boudi-Ca is no longer my fledgling."

"Learns she under another mistress?"

"She was under Mistress Isabellah, but now she's working on her Mistress Test. The Lady seems to want to make her fully fledged."

Masad looked askance at her. "Trains a Jinn fledgling for many years, even centuries, before taking her test. Before ready."

"Boudi-Ca is precocious," Gonorrheah said. "She has some difficult tasks, however, especially the one Ayelet set for her. I hope she doesn't fail and pay the Lady's price. She has potential. Her flashing ability of course is remarkable, and her healing magic could be very strong if she wanted to apply herself. It would be a pity if Boudi-Ca were made into a mere Ahyehass."

"A difficult penalty," Masad said.

Ayelet shook her head. "Boudi-Ca will not be made an Ahyehass. The Lady is merely challenging Boudi-Ca to break out of her world of girlish fantasies. If the Lady takes away Boudi-Ca's gifts and degrades her into a mere Ahyehass after all the work I've done with her, I'll pack up my blades and walk out the next day."

"You never know," Gonorrheah said. "The Lady has a history of punishing those that slight her. She's never charier and more heartless than when fighting for her survival. All of the Lady's current problems began with Boudi-Ca."

Ayelet snapped the reins, urging the horses up a low slope. The wizardress was right, and there was no rebuttal. It was difficult to divine the Lady's intentions by pure reason, however, and it might not even matter. Dark skeins were flooding the tapestry of fate, and Boudi-Ca's thread would flow with the rest of the New Order Jinni.

Ayelet eyed the sword alongside Masad' leather-clad leg. She pondered a sudden inspiration. She'd meddled in Boudi-Ca's fate once before by suggesting the fledgling should cast a love spell. Had it been her suggestion, and the subsequent casting of the love spell, that had led Boudi-Ca down a sequence of events to her Mistress Test? She couldn't dismiss the possibility. Ayelet drew the carriage to a stop in front of Gonorrheah's house. Gonorrheah exited the carriage, followed by the possessor.

"Thanks for the ride, Ayelet." Gonorrheah waved with her pipe. "I imagine I'll see you soon unless Masad sweeps me off my feet and takes me on a honeymoon."

Ayelet offered a smile. "Masad, do you plan to stay long in the Redoubt?"

"As long as I must to help the werewolves."

"Gonorrheah mentioned Boudi-Ca's most difficult test-the one I set for her. Boudi-Ca must place in an event at next year's Spring Festival. No mistress in the Redoubt can help her, but she can receive help from friends. I believe you won the Spring Festival blades event the year before last, didn't you?"

"Yes," Masad said quietly. "Won I with the Exquisite Form of the Smokeless Flames. Needs it great speed to employ. Able none of the fledglings were to match it."

"Boudi-Ca has great speed, doesn't she Ayelet?" Gonorrheah said. Gonorrheah's eyes no longer looked glazed. She'd perked up considerably. "I saw her practice once. She's really fast. She had to be fast to save us all last year at Sekhmet's temple."

Ayelet nodded. "It's sad, though, that she has no blades teacher. She doesn't do well unsupervised. Well, I bid you both good night."

Masad bowed. "Good night, Mistress Ayelet."

Ayelet watched Masad closely. She wasn't sure in the darkness, but thought she discerned a faint smile on his lips before he turned away. Ayelet prodded the carriage horses forward. It had been a long day, and the coming days would be longer. The Lady wasn't known for making quick decisions even when needed.

Apparently Barissianna wasn't fond of quick decisions either. Ayelet fingered the hilt of her sword. After visiting Barissianna in her own home and seeing her with Janaka, she wasn't sure if she could seduce Barissianna away from her husband. She needed to be relentless, cruel, and strategic.

Perhaps if Barissianna went out and socialized more, she'd make more friends among the Jinni, and the more connected Barissianna felt, the less likely she'd want to leave. Ayelet directed the carriage horses up the east hill. She looked out over the rooftops of the city and the warm glows of the recently-installed streetlights. She hadn't thrown a party in years, not since Golda had passed her Mistress Test and graduated from fledglinghood.

She summoned a bird.

I'm throwing a party tomorrow night, Barissianna. It's a unique opportunity for you to meet the legendary Prince Masad, son of Lord Hades, who is visiting the city. My door is open tonight too, of course. My home and my arms are yours.

Chapter 18:

Tajee reached into the porcelain bathtub and scrubbed the last traces of mineral discoloring with the vinegar-soaked cloth. He dipped the cloth into the water bucket and rinsed. He wiped the sweat from his brow and gazed out of the mullioned bath window. The view from Boudi's windows stirred memories and wistfulness. It was almost the same view as when he'd lived with Golda as her Ahyehass, from the vantage of fifty paces farther up the same street.

It was another autumn day in Meristyian, late afternoon judging from the little shadows marching across Mistress Hatshepseh's red roof tiles. The golden leaves of the maple trees across the street shivered in the October wind. Tajee tiptoed to breathe the fresh, crisp air that wafted from the narrow bird slit above the window. Shadow would soon come to the beautiful mountain city of the Lady, and with it his third winter.

Tajee picked up his threadbare rag and swabbed the water droplets from the floor. A small wing feather affixed itself to the linen. From the feather's whiteness, he guessed it to be his own. Violet's wings had been clipped, and Boudi's wings were changing shade to a dirty grey. He shook the feather into the water bucket and tensed his stomach against his hollowness.

Two weeks had passed since Boudi-Ca had brought Violet back from the

Palace. Violet had been happy to see him when she'd first arrived. She'd come straight to him and given him a timid hug. Boudi-Ca had immediately taken Violet up to her bedchamber for a long private discussion. Violet hadn't hugged him or touched him again.

Tajee picked up the wash bucket and walked quietly down the hall, slowing to a stop at Boudi's perpetually closed bedchamber door. He listened for the telltale sounds of Violet's pleasure.

With Violet's arrival, he'd lost some of his privileges. Boudi-Ca still invited him into her bedchamber for more menial tasks, like brushing her hair and painting her face. Those were the moments he treasured. Boudi-Ca was cunning, however. She had divined his feelings for Violet. She made sure that he never saw Violet in the nude. Boudi-Ca always closed her door, excluding him from any intimate activities. Even when the two girls took a bath together, he was required to leave the room after pumping the water.

When he'd stood for the first time outside Boudi's locked bedroom door and listened to Violet's mouse-like sighs of pleasure, he'd been afflicted with such a profound envy that he'd felt a physical pain. He was intensely angry at Boudi-Ca for manipulating Violet and training an innocent Mimọ girl to be used and abused by the Jinni. Boudi-Ca was better than the Prince, but she was still corrupted and consumed by lust. Boudi-Ca was perverting and corrupting Violet, and there was nothing he could do about it.

Tajee slipped down the hall stairs, through the foyer and the storage room, and passed on through the access door into the below-ground stable. Boudi's pony looked at him from its stall. Mary and Benedict, the resident stable mice, were nowhere to be seen, but the floor by the straw bales was clean. They'd eaten the bread crumbs that he'd left for them.

Tajee walked out of the stable and tossed the vinegary contents of his wash bucket into the grate of the sewer drain. He raised his arm to shield his eyes from the slanting sunlight. A mistress was striding up the street. Her brown linen sleeves were rolled up her thick forearms where a large wicker basket swinging. Gallinah waved cheerfully.

"Tajee, my dear! Good afternoon!"

"Good afternoon, Mistress Gallinah. It's a fine day for a walk."

"It is.  It is.  The lovely summer just won't let go."  The rotund Jinn approached him, eyeing him up and down as usual. "Is Boudi-Ca about? I need to drop off a delivery for her."

"She's here, but she's busy in the bedroom with Violet."

"As I suspected," Gallinah said, nodding sagely. "Which is why I thought to give the delivery directly to you. How is Violet? Is she adapting well to her new mistress?"

Tajee kept his face a mask. "I don't really know.  Boudi-Ca keeps the doors shut, and she doesn't tell me anything."

"Oh, you poor boy. Are you feeling neglected? Between you and me-" Gallinah closed the distance to him and lowered her voice with a wink. "You need an older mistress who appreciates you.  I might have to make some inquiries with the Lady. I could use a strong young male Ahyehass around the workshops. My Lethian doll takes a lot of maintenance, and I can only do so much."

Tajee nodded politely. Gallinah was older and more experienced, but she didn't attract him in the least. "Yes, mistress. I'm here to serve."

"Anyway, here's the delivery!  Take the things and give them to your mistress.  Boudi's design is delightful, I must say.  She's an excellent draftswoman."  Gallinah pulled a long box and a riding crop from her basket and handed them both to him. Tajee balanced the pasteboard box on his arm.

"Thank you, Mistress Gallinah. I'll give the delivery to my mistress."

"It's a nice fat end, so it won't sting too much on her rump."

Tajee picked up the empty wash bucket along with the box and riding crop.  He walked back into the stable and hung the bucket on a hook. He examined the crop more closely. He could see a bird stamped in the leather crop end. There were two possible purposes for the crop, and it was doubtful that Gallinah was worried about the rump of Boudi's pony.

Tajee weighed the ugly rod in his hand.  Boudi-Ca was truly a Jinn. Somehow, he was still struggling to accept how corrupted and transformed

Boudi-Ca had become.  He imagined Boudi-Ca snapping the crop on Violet's gentle backside. He imagined Violet crying and apologizing for a mistake. He'd witnessed the punishment of an Ahyehass once, and it hadn't been pretty. Anger and bitterness washed through his stomach.

"Tajee!"

Tajee faintly heard Boudi's call from the floor above. He eyed the pile of hay that Benedict liked to hide under. He bent and thrust the crop under the hay. He kicked hay over the crop until it was buried. The stable door opened, and Boudi-Ca looked down the stairs with her hands on her hips. She wore a white slip and a corset. Her face was powdered to go out for the evening, and her hair was already done in an Mimo girl bun. She smiled and trotted down the stable stairs when she saw the box.

"Wonderful!  It's just in time for Ayelet's party!  I'm so excited, Tajee. When did Gallinah come by?"

"Just a minute ago."

Boudi-Ca tore the box from his hands and opened it. The dress inside unfurled like a giant white flower. Boudi-Ca dropped the box and held the dress up to her body in the low light of the stable. An immodest split double ruffle was joined by satin laces. The ruffle was echoed in the long winter sleeves.

"Thank you, Tajee. Come upstairs to my bedchamber. Bring the box." Boudi-Ca dropped the box on the stable floor, swiveled, and carried the dress up the stable stairs. "This dress is extravagant. I hope Isabellah and the beauty mistresses will think so too."

Tajee bent to retrieve the box. In the bottom of it remained a white hair ribbon that matched the embroidery on the dress. The ribbon was tied to a silver collar, delicate and feminine, which was no doubt intended for Violet. Tajee followed Boudi-Ca up the stairs and through the house to her bedchamber.

Violet sat at Boudi's vanity. She wore a short skirt and a mid-bust corset that sported hinged crescent flaps in an upright position, covering Violet's nipples but enabling access. Violet's face was lightly powdered. She looked at him and smiled with her doll-like purple-painted lips.

"Hello, Tajee."

"Hello Violet," Tajee replied stiffly.

"Do Violet's hair, Tajee," Boudi-Ca ordered. "A twist and two flips. And trim her bangs. No mistakes. I've already finished her face, but you're better with haircuts than I am. Violet and I are going to a party. We need to look perfect."

"Yes, Mistress." Tajee found a pair of pins and pulled Violet's hair behind her ears. Violet tilted her head back. Her hair was silken and soft. He placed the pins for the flips and drew back the twist. He picked up the scissors from among the perfume bottles. He turned the chair and crouched in front of Violet. He leaned close to snip and straighten her bangs. Violet's liquid blue eyes were inches away from his own. He caught her gaze and stayed his hand.

Violet's eyes didn't stray from his. The look was clear, and as lustful as any look an Mimo girl could give. Tajee became acutely aware of his bent knee between Violet's legs. She moved her legs subtly to imprison it. The corners of Violet's lips curled slightly. Tajee felt his heart thump in his chest. He continued working.

"What do you think, Tajee?" Boudi-Ca said.

Tajee lowered the scissors and looked. Boudi-Ca twirled in front of the full-length mirror in her new Mimo dress. The puffs of her skirts swirled just above the hardwood floor. The design sucked close to her stomach and revealed only the merest glimpses of the ivory swell of her breasts, lifted loftily by her underlying corset. The dress bore white ribbons and buttons in all the right places.

"It's beautiful, Mistress."

"I know what you're thinking. Remember, the dress isn't supposed to be something a real Mimo would wear. It's supposed to be the idea of what an Mimo would wear, in the mind of a Jinn. I think it's incredible. Everyone at Ayelet's party is going to love it."

"It's beautiful, Mistress. Just like you."

Boudi-Ca smiled widely. "You're sweet when you flatter me, Tajee. Are you finished with my Ahyehass?"

"Yes. I could do a lot more if you gave me more time with her, though. Her hair could use a lot more trimming, and she needs more powder around her ears."

"She's fine for now. Come tie my wing-slit lacings, please."

Tajee moved behind Boudi-Ca and drew tight the wide laces that brought her dress around her small wings. Boudi-Ca was wearing a strong application of her best perfume. By the time he finished the laces and stepped back, his head was swimming with her scent. Boudi-Ca drifted in a daydream of feminine perfection to examine Violet's hair. She leaned and kissed Violet's cheek.

"Present yourself," Boudi-Ca said. Violet obediently rose and faced Boudi, wobbling slightly on her high heels, with her feet together, purple-painted lips slightly open, head down and eyes properly lowered. Tajee felt himself stir, despite himself. Violet was behaving perfectly after only two weeks of Boudi's training, and she was beautiful.

Boudi-Ca retrieved the silver collar from the box. She slid it around Violet's pale neck and snapped it shut. Boudi-Ca fastened a leather strap to the D-ring, pulled Violet close, and kissed her lightly on the cheek. Violet managed a pained smile. The petite younger Mimọ stood a few inches shorter than her mistress in her heels.

Boudi-Ca ran her hand over the upper swells of Violet's breasts and tested the folded-up nipple-flaps with her Ukraine manicured fingers. Boudi-Ca motioned, and her magical blue bird appeared. She whispered a message, and the bird flew out the open door towards the bath and the exterior bird slit.

"We're leaving Tajee. Clean up the bedchamber while we're gone. Change the linens. Wipe up the powder that spilled on the floor. Close the wardrobe. Light the lamps in the hall and the candles on my side table. We might have visitors later."

"Yes, Mistress," Tajee replied. "Is Violet really going to the party dressed just in that corset and super-short skirt with no underthings?"

Boudi-Ca glared at him. "Yes, Tajee. She'll be a little cold, but there are sacrifices to be made for beauty, especially when an Ahyehass is dressed for pleasure."

Tajee watched Boudi-Ca guide Violet out the door by her leash. Violet looked back directly into his eyes, a look that was grateful and wistful at the same time. He replied with a sympathetic nod. At the same time, his heart leapt. He'd lost favor with Boudi-Ca with his daring remark, but he'd scored a point with Violet. The two Mimo girls clattered in their heels down the stairs and across the front foyer. The door creaked open and slammed shut, and the house fell into silence.

Tajee looked around the bedroom. Shoes spilled out of Boudi's large wardrobes, which overflowed with clothes. Unused slips and corsets were piled on a chair. White powder coated the floor around the vanity, so much spillage that footprints were visible in it. Tajee sighed. He had a lot of cleaning to do.

Boudi's vanity was a wreck too-the antithesis of the orderly rows of school texts, prayer books, ink wells and writing utensils that she'd kept on her desk in her dorm room in Heaven. Eyebrow pencils, powder brushes, and mixing-mortars for lip paint lay scattered everywhere.

Tajee sat down on the edge of Boudi's soft bed. He didn't know where to start cleaning. A white satin ribbon lay at his feet. He picked it up and sniffed. It smelled like Violet's hair. He recalled how her silken strands felt in his fingers. Sadness came over him. He lay back on the bed. The sheet felt slightly damp and smelled of female sex. He closed his eyes tightly. It was torture thinking of Boudi-Ca taking Violet over and over in that bed.

His envy crested. In that moment, he felt totally alone. Violet clearly liked him, but she was an Ahyehass, and so was he. Love between them was forbidden. It couldn't be.

Living with Boudi-Ca had been his dream, but it had led to nothing, and he felt like nothing more a little assistant to Boudi's adventurous Jinn life. Since Violet had arrived, he was an afterthought to Boudi, just a tool to get her chores done around the house. She hadn't given him any sexual release in a week.

Tajee threw the white hair ribbon back onto the dirty floor. He had to admit that despite the Lady's evident acceptance of cruelty, he didn't mind serving in her domain. While he'd lived in the palace, his servicing of Persephoneh and Psyche had been bliss beyond his most lustful dreams. Boudi's arrogance, however, had become unsupportable. Boudi-Ca thought she was special, and even more since she was under consideration for a promotion.

He'd heard plenty about Boudi's Mistress Test in the previous moons. He secretly wanted Boudi-Ca to fail. If Boudi-Ca failed, she'd be degraded to the same level as him in the Jinn city-a mere Ahyehass-and then she'd learn a lesson in humility. Maybe if Boudi-Ca failed her test, she'd be more like her old humbled Mimọ self, and they could even be friends again.

Tajee gazed at Boudi's vanity, where the curious burned tarot card was wedged in the mirror frame. Boudi-Ca had bragged about her love spell in detail-how she'd cast powerful Jinn magic to draw her one true love to her. Evidently the person on the card had yet to appear, however. The figure on the card was a red-robed woman, or a man-it was hard to tell which-with two Ahyehasi at the figure's feet and a large hole burned in its chest.

Tajee felt another twinge of envy. It was completely unfair that Boudi-Ca could use magic and find her one true love, while he wasn't even allowed to touch Violet. Boudi-Ca had told him explicitly to never touch the special burned tarot card either. The card was magical and sacred. He clenched his jaw. He was tired of taking orders from Boudi.

Tajee rose from the bed and plucked the card from Boudi's mirror frame. He ripped the card in half between his fingers. He put the pieces together and ripped them again, and again, until only bits were left. He looked at the pile of little pieces in his hand. His heart thumped hard in his chest. He stalked from the bedchamber and down the hall stairs.

He hoped Boudi's special love spell would be totally broken. If he wasn't allowed to love Violet, then Boudi-Ca shouldn't be allowed to have love either. If the failure of the spell caused Boudi-Ca to fail her Mistress Test, then so much the better. Tajee descended the stairs into the stable. He felt a twinge of fear as he threw the pieces of the tarot card onto a pile of pony dung. He pushed the fear away and picked up a flat-nose shovel.

# *Chapter 19:*

Boudi-Ca sat in the corner of Ayelet's parlour. The parlour was filled with mistresses seated on every chair. Fledglings and Ahyehasi were sitting on the floor. Nili was having a heated argument with Szenes while Henne played mediator and Pyrinnah looked on with Minnie-Ca right behind.

Boudi-Ca watched the mistresses chatting in low tones. She'd hoped to test out her Mimọ fashion to see how people liked it, but not a single person had commented on her new Mimọ dress. Ranavalona had eyed her more than anyone else, but with a characteristic smirk of skepticism playing on her red-painted lips.

At least Violet was attracting glowing glances from everyone. Boudi-Ca smiled inwardly. Violet's training was going well, at least. If Violet kept progressing, Isabellah's Task of Discipline would be firmly in hand, as firmly as the leash attached to Violet's new collar.

Ayelet's Task of Mastery, however-to place in an event at the Spring Festival in less than six moons-seemed more treacherous than ever. She'd hoped to try for two contests to double her chances, but tending to Violet's training was taking a lot of her time. Despite finishing her second dress, she hadn't done enough with her clothing or blades in the previous weeks.

Violet looked over her shoulder with her sweet blue eyes. "Mistress, may

I have more wine?"

"Hand me the glass." Boudi-Ca took the glass from Violet's fingers and stalked through the foyer into the dining room, where Ayelet was standing in close conversation with a female vampire. The whispered rumors in the parlour said the vampire's name was Magistrada Barissianna, and that Barissianna was Ayelet's vampire lover.

Barissianna was beautiful, with statuesque curves, finely sculpted pale features, and straight dark hair that was almost long enough to meet the rim of her black corset, which in turn stopped short of her black skirt, revealing a sensual band of the pale skin of her stomach. The vampiress had green eyes just like Ayelet, with a hint of gold-flaked blue. Both women were observing Yenta, who was opening a fresh wine bottle.

"It's a nice party, Mistress Ayelet," Boudi-Ca said. "Violet wants more of your wine."

Ayelet took the glass from her fingers and filled it with wine. "You should be training your new Ahyehass to fetch, fledgling, not fetching for her."

"I'm just trying to keep her happy right now. She's fragile. She tosses and turns in her sleep. She's tired and weak. I'm worried the Prince did terrible things to her, but she won't tell me. I know she slept with him, and I found bite marks on her thigh, but she'll only admit that he appears in her dreams."

"That's concerning." Ayelet frowned. "You've been oiling her, I hope, to help hold her together?"

"Yes. I oil her every night after I feed from her. I think I'll have no problems passing my Task of Discipline."

Ayelet handed her the wine nonchalantly. "This wine is excellent, fledgling. Maybe a second glass will help your Ahyehass relax. It's from a vineyard north of Vegasis in Erebus. It's been aging in my cellar for thirty years. Boudi-Ca, have you met Magistrada Barissianna?"

"No, I haven't." Boudi-Ca curtseyed. "It's nice to meet you."

Barissianna smiled. "It's nice to meet you too, Boudi-Ca. That's a beautiful dress."

"Thanks. It's hand-made. You really like it?"

"I think it's delightful. It's something one might see in a Lolita fashion magazine or even on a Paris runway."

"Thank you so much. You're the first person to say anything nice. I made it myself. I was hoping to place in the arts competition at the Spring Festival with my clothing designs. At least, that's my goal for the Task of Mastery. What do you think about my dress, Mistress Ayelet? Do you think I have a chance?"

"I've forgotten the exact categories, but you're going against Isabellah's weaving, Gonorrheah's painting, Henne-Ca's sculpture, and Apolloniah's new relief friezes for the palace, just to name a few," Ayelet answered. "Is clothing design really an art form?"

"Of course, Ayelet," Barissianna said. "If Boudi-Ca took that dress to Paris, New York, or Tokyo, she could sell it for real money. You never know with the arts, though. Sometimes it takes a while for an artist to be recognized."

Boudi-Ca sighed. "Well, I don't have a while. I only have six more moons to complete my Mistress Test, or else the Lady will change me back into a plain Mimo girl again."

"Well, that complicates things," Barissianna said.

A shadow passed over Ayelet's face like a tangible thing. "Yes, it does. You know how I feel about your Task of Mastery, chérie, and I'm sure you've divined my personal bias as to how you should go about it. The whole idea of the task was to focus on only one thing."

"I know. You want me to focus on blades."

"I want you reach for your best and pass your test. Have you spoken with Masad yet, fledgling?"

"No. I think he went outside."

"Please make a point to speak with Masad." Ayelet raised her glass, moved towards the foyer, and clinked the wine glass loudly. "Ladies and gentlemen, I'd like to request that everyone walk to my training hall for a surprise. My training hall, if you recall, is the detached building in the back of the Villa on the rear lawn."

Boudi-Ca quickly fetched Violet to avoid the crowd of mistresses emerging from the rear kitchen and the parlour armchairs. She wondered what Ayelet planned, and she wondered why Ayelet wanted her to speak with Masad. The possessor son of Lord Hades was grim and intimidating. She tugged Violet out of the Villa and into the cool evening air behind Barissianna and Ayelet, who strode side by side down the driveway ahead of everyone.

Boudi-Ca sighed. Despite her bad mood over the reception of her dress, she was happy to see Ayelet with someone. Barissianna was an attractive vampiress with a near-perfect figure. Unfortunately, Barissianna was the only person at the party so far who liked her dress, which didn't bode well for her summer-long bid towards placing in the festival arts competition. She needed to get more opinions.

The night was turning cold, but Ayelet's training hall was warm with burning oil lamps mounted high on the columns. Barissianna and Ayelet strode across the polished floor towards Jade Turtle, who was already in the hall and wearing a training robe.

"Let's begin," Ayelet said once everyone had filed in. "As most of you know, I've been working with Jade Turtle over the moons since she's been back with us. She's worked very hard to regain her fighting form. As you may also know, I've worked with Magistrada Barissianna in the nights. So we're having a sparring match to ten points between my two students. No magic will be used."

"Go Turtle!" Ranavalona shouted, raising her wine glass as the mistresses and fledglings formed a wide circle around the two combatants.

"Go Barissianna!" Mistress Gonorrheah howled, pumping her herb pipe in the air. Laughter rippled through the subdued gathering. Even Masad appeared to chuckle. Boudi-Ca eyed the out-of-place human male. The mysterious possessor had appeared from nowhere to join the audience.

"Begin." Ayelet tacked a pair of wooden batons. Boudi-Ca stepped forward to watch. She was suddenly interested. She recognized the match as an opportunity to study Jade Turtle, who could be her opponent in the blade's competition at the Spring Festival, and Barissianna too if the vampiress decided to try her hand.

Barissianna held a defensive stance while Turtle circled. Finally the fledgling attacked, and the vampiress parried strongly. The clack of the wooden swords echoed in the training hall. Barissianna launched a counterattack that Turtle easily parried. Turtle was using a single long practice blade in two hands, while Barissianna dual-wielded a pair of shorter swords. Turtle again attacked, this time a side-swipe that Barissianna blocked with difficulty. Barissianna danced to the side and slashed, scoring a hit across Turtle's arm.

"Point for Barissianna," Ayelet called.

Turtle redoubled her efforts with three quick strikes, each of which rocked Barissianna back. The crowd scattered to give the fighters more room. Barissianna attempted a counterattack, but Turtle had only feigned fatigue. The fledgling surprised Barissianna with contretemps to the chest. Barissianna grunted audibly.

"Three points for Jade Turtle," called Ayelet.

The two combatants circled for long moments more. Finally Turtle, impatient, attacked again. This time Barissianna was ready for the triple strike. She parried the first blow with doubled blades, slipped close to Turtle, and batted her across the cheek and the arm. Turtle gasped. Barissianna rolled under the reverse counterattack.

"Two points for Barissianna," Ayelet called. "The match is even."

Before Ayelet had finished speaking, however, Turtle caught Barissianna off-balance, tripped her, and battered Barissianna before she managed to escape by rolling to the support of a pillar. She fended off a final attack before Turtle gave her reprieve.

"Five points for Jade Turtle," Ayelet called. "The score is eight points to three in favor of Turtle."

"Go Turtle!" Ranavalona called.

"I concede." Barissianna massaged her arm and bowed deeply. "Sorry all, but Jade Turtle is too good for me."

Boudi-Ca fidgeted. She was probably better than Barissianna, but Turtle looked very impressive. It was unfair that Ayelet was working with Turtle, while she wasn't allowed to have a mentor. Aside from Pyrrinah, who trained Minnie-Ca, and Freyah, who trained her battle-Ahyehasi, there were no other real blade mistresses left in the city except for Masad.

"I hope you all enjoyed the exhibition, however brief," Ayelet said loudly to the dispersing crowd. "My steward has a fresh round of wine for those who are staying, and my lovely dressing-girl Herzl is preparing an Ahyehass game back in the parlour."

"Delightful, Ayelet," Gonorrheah said. "Given as you never throw a party, you're certainly going all out."

"I'll stay for an Ahyehass game." Gallinah beamed.

"Are you staying, Boudi?" Henne sidled alongside her. "We could sneak away if you wanted. Ayelet's party is nice, but that parlour is too stuffy for me."

"I could leave. Do we have a carriage?"

"Yes. Mistress Nili is riding home with Szenes tonight. I say we leave together." Henne patted her small black purse.

"Could you do me a favor? Please take Violet to the carriage and wait for me. I need to talk with someone."

"Alright, but don't be long. I might take Violet and leave without you."

"Don't you dare!" Boudi-Ca handed Violet's strap to Henne and walked quickly along the walk around the Villa. Masad and Gonorrheah stood outside in the drive with smoking pipes while the rest of the party filed back through Ayelet's front door. Gonorrheah puffed and sent a plume of smoke skyward.

"Hello, Boudi-Ca," Gonorrheah said. "That's a beautiful Ahyehass you have. She's a true treasure. I think it's marvelous how well-behaved she is too, considering you've only had her for a few weeks."

Boudi-Ca felt a flush of pride warm her cheeks. "That's nice of you to say. She's very shy and difficult in bed, but I was like that too when I first arrived. She'll be ready for my test at the Spring Festival."

Gonorrheah nodded. "Just remember that Isabellah is judging her, and Isabellah is notorious for finding ways to ruin an Ahyehass' composure. So how is your blade training coming along? I hear you're practicing with Henne. How is that working out?"

Boudi-Ca gauged Masad, who was looking at her silently. "It's going fine, but I have a long way to go. It's hard to get better when I'm not allowed to let anyone teach me."

"That isn't true, fledgling. You just can't have any of the mistresses teach you." Gonorrheah smiled. "Masad, you're a renowned sword master, aren't you, if my memory serves?"

Masad nodded and fingered the hilt of the blade he wore at his belt. "Stop by I can, Boudi-Ca, if think you it would help you. Have I free time while wait I for the Lady to make a decision about the werewolves and western Meristyian."

"Thank you, Master Masad. I'm not sure when. Can I send you a bird?"

"Of course." Masad bowed gracefully. "Any time. Sure I am that Mistress Gonorrheah would like me out of her house."

"Well, that point is debatable," Gonorrheah said. "You know, a bird isn't the best way to communicate with someone who can't send one back, Boudi-Ca. Why don't you just decide on a time now? Tomorrow, for example?"

"Matters it not," murmured Masad.

Boudi-Ca hesitated. "Alright. Say around the four tomorrow, Master Masad?"

"Of course."

"Thank you." Boudi-Ca smiled, curtseyed, and swiveled as prettily as she could. She admonished herself as she ran back to the carriage where Henne waited with Violet. The last thing she needed was to flirt with another prince, but she'd done it instinctively.

"What was that about?" Henne said.

"Masad is going to help me train at blades, at least for tomorrow. So I don't need you to come over."

"Fine then, if you really prefer his help over mine. I'm teasing, Boudi. Jade Turtle is definitely making a comeback. You're going to need all the help you can get."

"So do you want to go to my place and play with me and my Ahyehass?"

"Yes." Henne grinned.

Boudi-Ca relaxed into the seat between Violet and Henne. She patted the Mimo girl's warm thigh. Henne passed her the leather strap of the leash. Nili's driver cracked the whip at the horses. The carriage jolted forward out of Ayelet's drive and down the bumpy hill.

"What do you think of my dress, Henne?" Boudi-Ca bit her lip. She was afraid of what Henne would say, but she needed to know.

"It's fine. It's fantastic, actually."

Within minutes they were rolling through the leafy streets of the neighborhood adjacent to the workshops. The carriage finally pulled up at the house. Boudi-Ca flashed Henne her bedroom eyes as she climbed out of the carriage, even as clumsily scraped her leg against mud clinging to the carriage rail. She sighed heavily. The mud would be horrible to clean from the linen. Her dress had flopped at the party anyway, and even Henne, her best friend, secretly thought it was horrible. Ayelet didn't even think it was an art form.

It was time to admit that she was wasting her time trying for the arts competition at the Spring Festival. Her best option to place in a competition at the Spring Festival, as Ayelet had known all along, was to try with swords. She'd only be competing against the fledglings and visitors in the city, not the mistresses.

Boudi-Ca escorted Violet up the house steps, followed by Henne. The front door was open. She strode into the foyer and up the stairs to the second floor ahead of Violet and Henne. She stopped in the entrance to her bedroom. A slow fury crept over her. Tajee hadn't cleaned as she'd asked. Her clothes were still strewn everywhere, powder still coated the floor, and her bedsheets hadn't been changed. Henne brushed past her, unclipping her luxurious red hair as she went.

Boudi-Ca went to the vanity to de-powder her face. She searched for a towel, but she couldn't find one, and her water bowl was empty. She sighed.

"Violet, fetch me some water from the bath and a serviette de toilette."

"Yes, Mistress." Violet took the bowl and padded away down the hall.

Boudi-Ca sat at the vanity. She watched Henne undress, a sultry reflection in her vanity mirror. A sudden feeling of horror crept over her, the melting feeling that she hadn't felt in many moons, a feeling that her life was all dire and wrong. Her eyes went glassy with queer tears. She sniffed, and her vision of Henne blurred and dimmed.

"Boudi?" Henne said. "Are you alright?"

"No."

"You're going to make it, Boudi. I have faith."

Boudi-Ca put her head in her hands and sobbed. The tears overflowed and wetted her palms. She felt Henne's hands rubbing her back and her neck. Henne's warm lips pressed to her temple, kissing her. Henne's scent was sweet.

"Mistress?" It was Violet, standing wide-eyed with the bowl of water.

"I'm fine, Violet." Boudi-Ca sniffed. "Put the bowl here, and then go and close the door. Leave me and Henne alone."

Violet placed the water bowl on the vanity, slipped out, and closed the door. Henne retrieved her purse and pulled out the nectar pouch. The redheaded fledgling struck a match and lit the vanity candle. Boudi-Ca watched Henne work. Henne loaded a small silver spoon with purple-violet nectar, and then melted it in the flame.

Boudi-Ca opened her mouth. The hot metal sizzled on her tongue. She felt the Sharp jolt of pain, but then the nectar flowed, spreading pleasure and warmth through her, assuaging the sting of the over-hot spoon. The pleasure entered her throat and filled the tissues of her face, drying her eyes and sending tingles through her nostrils. She drifted in the chair, floating by inches up in the air, as Henne filled her own spoon and consumed it.

Boudi-Ca grasped Henne's hand and stood unsteadily up. She stumbled with Henne to the bed. She fell on Henne and pressed her head into the thin fledgling's chest, searching the delicate expanses of freckled flesh for surfaces to kiss and lick. She slithered her lips over Henne's collarbone. She pulled Henne's nipple full into her mouth.

Henne groped low, but Boudi-Ca caught her hot hand and pushed it away. She worried Henne's nipple with her lips and teeth. Henne moaned and surrendered. Boudi-Ca insinuated herself bodily over the Henne and kissed her. They played back and forth, one inside the other's nectar-sweetened mouth, fencing with half-numb and tingling tongues. Boudi-Ca felt the love flowing in her head, her heart, and deep between her thighs. Even her toes were tingling.

Henne's voice drifted, close in her ears. "We're really blue-violet right now."

"Thank you for caring about me, Henne."

Boudi-Ca closed her eyes and kept kissing Henne. It was the most beautiful warm moment in the universe, and she wanted it to last forever. She didn't want to spoil things by making words. She opened her soul and surrendered to her desire to fuck her friend.

# Chapter 20:

Boudi-Ca sat at her vanity and examined her face in the mirror. Her painted lips were perfect, and her eyebrows were plucked. She'd powdered her forehead, cheeks, and hair-enough to look Mimọic but also effected. Not a single strand of hair was out of place. She wore her best leather corset with matching brown petticoats.

She'd pondered her Task of Mastery all afternoon. Despite the work she'd done on her Mimọ clothing, the arts competition was probably a dead end, and she needed to focus on blades, as Ayelet had wanted all along.

Jade Turtle was conceivably beatable with the help of Masad. She had to have faith. With Isabellah's task well in hand, that left the Lady's Task of Compassion-finding the thing closest to her heart so that she could sacrifice it for the good of another. If she could do that and also place in blades at the Spring Festival, soon she'd be a fully-fledged mistress instead of an Ahyehass like Tajee.

Unfortunately, there was also a chance that Masad could compete in the Spring Festival, so a seduction could come in handy. She needed Masad to train her but not compete, so she needed to influence him with her beauty mistress skills. Boudi-Ca opened her perfume bottle. She streaked her neck and wrists with the intoxicating scent. The clock showed a quarter before the hour. She expected Masad in fifteen minutes.

"Mistress?"

Boudi-Ca blinked. Violet's voice intruded on her reverie. The Mimọ girl had slept much of the day, sprawled on the bed like a kitten wanting to be scratched. Violet hadn't gone to bed until very late, after Henne had left to go home to Nili.

"What do you want, Violet?"

"I was just wondering about something, and I wanted to ask you."

"I'm listening."

"Do you remember how I fell from Heaven?"

"Yes. You were a student at the Crystal College of Sacred Moons. You were trying to get away from being locked up by the Conclave of Deviant Operations, and you jumped. Was the Conclave any more involved than you said? Please tell me you're not a spy for the Mimọic Hierarchy."

"I'm not a spy. I just didn't want to be locked up and punished. The Conclave does terrible things to misbehaving Mimọs."

"You're safe. You're with me." Boudi-Ca went to the bed and caressed Violet's shoulder. She'd almost forgotten about the personalized riding crop that Gallinah was supposed to deliver. She wasn't sure if Isabellah would ask her to discipline Violet, but she needed to be prepared for anything.

"Thank you, Mistress." Violet sighed. "May I ask a favor, then?"

"I'm listening."

"Well, I was remembering the day that I jumped. Professor Elliott brought a glass box into the classroom. The box was full of beautiful butterflies. I wasn't supposed to open the box, but the butterflies were so beautiful that I disobeyed the rules. I'd never seen anything so colorful in Heaven. Elliott was horrified, and she notified the Conclave that I'd been contaminated by the Isandlwana insects. That's why the Conclave was coming for me-to lock me up and purify me. I panicked and jumped into the sky."

"That must have been horrible jumping alone. I don't blame you though. When Pasteur came to take me home, I didn't want to be purified either." Boudi-Ca embraced Violet and held her close. She could feel the Ahyehass opening emotionally to her, more than ever before. She felt intuitively, as a Jinn, that she should exploit the moment. She eased back, but kept her hand on Violet's thigh. Violet smiled and lowered her head shyly.

"So I was wondering if I could see some real insects in Meristyian. I'd like to collect them in a box. Do you think it would be possible, Mistress? I'm not sure how I would do it. I wasn't sure how the insect box worked, and I'm not sure Professor Elliott knew either when she showed it in Botany class."

Boudi-Ca pondered. She was surprised more by Violet's long-windedness than by the request. Violent had never said so many words at once. "Ahyehasi aren't usually permitted such things. My house doesn't have many furnishings though, and some glass boxes might make nice displays. Mistress Isabellah has displays of hats behind glass in her hallway. Ayelet has glass cupboards in her kitchen. A display of butterflies would be nice."

Violet smiled. "So I can do it?"

"Yes. I'd like something to decorate my foyer, and it would be very special if you made something for me."

"Thank you, Mistress."

"I'll ask the mistresses about a butterfly box, and I suppose we need nets to catch them. I have to go now for my lesson with Masad."

"Is he a vampire?"

"No. He's a possessor, a hellion son of Lord Hades. He has no body of his own, that I know of, so he lives in other bodies and travels around. He's scary, but mostly nice, and he helped save the Lady. He was at Mistress Ayelet's party last night. Maybe you saw me talking to him after I gave you to Henne."

"Yes, I remember."

"I don't want you to come near him though, Violet. Just stay up here."

Violet looked at her with pleading eyes. "Can Tajee keep me company, Mistress, while you're having your lesson? I get so lonely without you. Please?"

"I suppose so, but I don't want him to see you undressed. I'm dominating

Tajee with denial, since he desperately wants to see Mimo girls naked. His boyish desire is so sweet, and it pleases me to keep it that way."

"Yes, Mistress. I won't let him see anything. I promise."

"Mistress?" Tajee's voice echoed up the stairwell. "Master Masad is here."

Boudi-Ca checked her hair again in the mirror. She looked good enough. She descended the stair at a trot. Tajee waited at the bottom. Boudi-Ca brushed past him.

"Tajee, go upstairs and take a bath, and then keep Violet company. You can sit on the bed with her and talk to her as much as you like, but you're explicitly forbidden to touch her, and she's forbidden to touch you."

"Yes, Mistress."

Boudi-Ca opened the front door just as Masad rapped again. The possessor stood outside on the step. "Good afternoon, Boudi-Ca."

"Please come in. My training hall is down the basement steps. Thank you for coming. I really have to pass my Mistress Test, Master Masad. I can't fail." Boudi-Ca ushered Masad inside and led him down the steps to the front half of the lower level.

"Looks it nice, Boudi-Ca," Masad murmured approvingly. "Small, but adequate. A high enough ceiling. Floor mats."

Boudi-Ca felt a warmth of pride. "The mats are the same ones that Ayelet has. They're woven from some sort of reeds that grow on the banks of the Acheron."

"Called they are Naiad's Solace. Know I them. Spar we will so I can see how move you, what can you do. Use you what blade, what style?"

"When I was Ayelet's fledgling, I was learning Kendo, like Turtle. When I became a beauty fledgling, Isabellah wanted me to change to lighter and smaller blades. For the last year I've learned Dervish fighting with daggers and darts, but that won't work for the blade's competition at the festival. You saw what happened to Barissianna."

"Take you a blade and begin."

Boudi-Ca donned her leather practice gloves. She selected a practice sword from the rack alongside Masad. She turned and faced Masad, who was ready for her with his practice sword extended. She circled to the left. Masad feinted, and then lunged in an obvious attempt to surprise. She blocked and carried her momentum left to weaken Masad' attacking hand. She counterattacked. Masad parried and slipped her guard to score a numbing attack against her forearm.

"Point for me," Masad said evenly. Boudi-Ca switched directions, dancing back. Masad opened his stance. She struck an overhead, and then the stab. Her Close The Lotus slipped the blade of Masad and almost touched his linen shirt, which was open at the collar showing his hairy, muscled human chest.

Masad smiled faintly. "Close enough. Two points for you."

Boudi-Ca pressed the attack. She felt a hint of anger burn into her pride. Masad was hardly trying. She battered at Masad, but his parries held like a stone wall. Masad kept slipping to the side, offering her a moving target. She angled after him with simple hard strikes, a strategy that she used against Henne. When she cornered Masad, his defenses slipped. She launched a hard attack, but Masad blocked strongly and scored a hit against her shoulder. His defensive slip had been a trick.

"Point for me. Feel you fine, Boudi-Ca?"

"I'm fine." She adjusted her hair comb and squared off again with the possessor, who was intent and expressionless.

Masad closed to attack. Boudi-Ca fell on the defensive. Her forearm still ached where Masad had struck it. She summoned energy to renew her strength. She waited for an opening. The possessor weaved his blade in front of him. She was faster than that. She danced to Masad's weak side and cleaved sidearm to strike his shoulder.

Masad tried to go under her blow, but she was ready. She dropped and kicked Masad full in the shin, but not strongly enough to send him to the mat. Masad recovered and attacked swiftly. Boudi-Ca rolled away and flipped to her feet, barely parrying a strike to her side. She circled Masad once more.

"Point for you. Score is three to two in favor of you."

Boudi-Ca continued to attack with simple thrusts, attempting to corner Masad with a good result. Masad counterattacked with surprising force.

She lost her footing. It was she who was cornered. Masad pressed the attack, landing three more gentle blows before she could regain her balance.

"Five points for me," Masad said.

Boudi-Ca feigned weakness, but Masad didn't fall for her trick. She maneuvered until she had Masad with his back to the axis of the room, summoned all of her Jinn strength, and attacked with all of her might. With each blow she beat Masad back further. On the final blow she closed the distance and kicked, sending Masad into the wall. The possessor danced away, but not before she scored again recklessly.

"Three points for you," Masad said calmly, not remotely pressed. "Score seven to six in my favor."

They danced back and forth, neither landing a blow. Boudi-Ca stabbed twice more in quick succession. On the second, Masad knocked her blade from her hand. Masad lunged for her chest, but she dropped under the practice blade. She scissor-kicked and unsteadied the possessor enough to almost knock him to the floor. She skipped to her feet with her blade again in hand, but not in time to take any advantage.

"Three points for you for near-knockdown, two points for me for disarm. Score is nine to nine. Enough."

Boudi-Ca dropped her sword and massaged her arm. "Well, what did you think, Master Masad? Can you tell me what I can do to improve?"

"Think I your techniques are fine," Masad said. "Match you might Turtle right now, defeat you her. Except not. Defeats she you easily."

Boudi-Ca frowned. "I'm sorry. I don't understand what you just said. It sounded like you contradicted yourself."

"Technically, think I you are competent. Learned you have several forms and practiced them. Move you fast. Thinks Gonorrheah right about you. An Mimoic trait. Maybe. Has been never an Mimo blade-master living in Hell. Think you when you fight, with reflexes Sharp. Require most Jinni many years to learn to discipline the passion, fuel they their strength, even if can they."

"So what's the problem, then?"

"Feel you weak inside, your body immature. Need you feed more. Arises a problem still of your will. Lack you conviction. File you your nails. Smell you good. Brush you your hair. Painted you have your lips, made you your face pretty. Fight you like a beauty mistress. Afraid are you to get dirty. Afraid are you to get hurt."

Boudi-Ca raised her hands in supplication. "I don't fight any differently than I ever did when I was with Ayelet. I'm doing exactly the same things. And I want to win just as much."

"Think I you are a different fledgling now. Noticed I. Feel you less emotional, less strong than Ayelet's fledgling. Count for everything emotions in Hell. Count for much of a Jinn strength."

"Well, what am I supposed to do?"

Masad shook his head. "Know I not, Boudi-Ca. Told you I have what you need to do. Want you to be helped? Ask you must this question."

"So you're saying that to become better at blades, I need to give up being a beauty mistress. Have you been talking with Ayelet? Did she tell you to tell me this?"

"Think I cannot on Ayelet's motives. Teach you I can new techniques. Teach you I could the Exquisite Form of the Smokeless Flames. Help you none of this with your inner weakness. Wear you the gloves why? Grip you the hilt weakly."

Boudi-Ca looked down at her worn gloves. "When I went to live with Mistress Isabellah, she wanted me to wear them when I trained with Ayelet so I wouldn't roughen my hands. I see what you're saying, Masad. Fine. I get rid of my gloves. What else can I do to get better and win? Just tell me."

Masad shook his head. "Stop you must the pretty. Only blades."

"So you agree with Ayelet. If I want to be a blade mistress, then I have to abandon the path of the beauty mistress. I like beauty, and I like being beautiful. It makes me feel good inside. I don't know if I can change, Masad, even to pass my test. I like my clothes. I like my perfume. I like my shoes. My life is who I am."

"If fail you the test, end your life will. Live you like the other Mimọs in Hell-an Ahyehass or a slave to the Djinnus and Jinni."

Boudi-Ca shuddered. "I know."

"Becomes a blade mistress one with her blade. Extends the blade she, as herself. Cuts she the illusions that surround her. Lives she hard and Sharp like her blade, no petty, no distractions. Leave I soon, Boudi-Ca, when makes the Lady her decision about my werewolf friends. If want you to abandon the path of the beauty mistress, think I no better way than leave with me. Leave you the pampered life behind."

"What? Go with you back east, you mean?"

"When the Lady makes her decision. Expect it I soon. Exists a great tradition of the travelling student and teacher. Teach I blades to you. Along the way learn you might a few things."

Boudi-Ca avoided Masad' eyes. The idea came as a complete shock. She'd need a horse. She wasn't sure if Ayelet would loan her one. How could she leave everything behind? What would happen with Violet and Tajee? Could she take Violet with her? Memories of her previous trip to the east resurfaced-cold nights in cabins, sleeping on the hard stone floor in the werewolf stronghold, and long dusty days in a saddle with no hot water or clean clothes.

"Can I think about it, Master Masad?"

"Of course. Stay you would with the werewolves. See you Golda."

"I wouldn't mind seeing Golda again."

"If decide you not to go, then suggest I work on your footwork. Flit you around like a pretty butterfly, and work that will not against Turtle. Try you should to move energy to your feet. Practice your forms slowly. Pretend you are a tree, with roots that move no man can. To practice, draw a circle on the floor and refuse to be moved. Try that you would not in a battle, but think I a useful tool."

Boudi-Ca nodded. "Thank you, sir. Ayelet did trip me up a lot when I was training with her last summer. I sincerely appreciate your time."

"Have I nothing but time. Let me know when you've made up your mind." Masad strode across the room to the stairs. Boudi-Ca followed him up to the foyer and the front door. Masad hadn't given her much of a lesson. She shadowed him out to the house steps.

"Masad, please tell the truth. Do you think I can win first or second in the blade's competition in the spring?"

Masad looked over his shoulder and smiled faintly. "As you fight today, say I can that you might, but not that you should."

"Thank you for your honesty, sir."

"Need you to be fierce. Need you to focus. Need you to kill the pretty. Makes you the pretty girl weak." Tajee gestured broadly with his hand, turned, and climbed the street with long strides of his boots over the cobblestones. He didn't look back.

Boudi-Ca took a deep breath. She felt her cheeks heating. Had Masad meant to insult her way of life to her face? A wave of depression swept over her as she closed the front door. She felt a surge of anger at the Lady. She felt unstable again, like she was going to faint. She summoned a bird. She needed Henne. She needed nectar.

"Where are you? Can I see you?" Boudi-Ca sent the bird aloft. It flew up and out through the bird slit above the front door. She tiptoed up the stairs to the second floor. Violet sat cross-legged against the pillows at the headboard in the bedchamber. Tajee was sprawled across the duvet, in a perfect position to see up Violet's skirt.

Boudi-Ca tossed her gloves on the vanity. "Tajee, could you please leave?"

"Yes, Mistress." Tajee slid off the bed and padded out of the room, avoiding her eyes. Boudi-Ca swung the door closed behind him. She climbed onto the bed and pulled Violet down. She lifted Violet's skirt perfunctorily and felt with her hand. To her relief, there were no indications of mischief. She pinched. Violet quivered. Violet was suspiciously ready and quick, however. Boudi-Ca pressed the position until a rustle of Henne's brown catbird sounded at the bird slit above the door.

I'm with Ranavalona at my workshop. You can join us if you want.

Boudi-Ca felt her heart quicken, but not from her Violet quandary. What was Henne doing at her workshop with Ranavalona? She calmed herself. She didn't want to come apart again. She sealed her mouth over Violet's lips. She rubbed faster, slipping and wriggling with her fingers. She knew just how to make Violet release quickly, and quickly she did. Boudi-Ca opened her Jinn vacuum and pulled the sweet essence of released emotional energy up through Violet's body. The Ahyehass quivered and slumped. Boudi-Ca slipped off of her.

"You're amazingly sweet, Violet, but you hold too little. You're like a cup when I need a vase. We need to work on increasing your lust and desire so I can feed better from you. I've heard an Ahyehass can be stoked, but I don't really know the way."

"Whatever pleases you, Mistress," Violet murmured without looking at her.

"Yes, whatever pleases me. You like Tajee, don't you?"

"He's nice, and he cares about me."

Boudi-Ca rose from the bed without a backward glance. She could feel it-the natural feminine energy in Violet that wanted Tajee's phallus to fill her. Violet liked Tajee more than her. It made sense. She wasn't sure how to change Violet, or whether such a thing was even desirable. It was a puzzle that needed serious attention, but her Mistress Test didn't allow her to ask for help. The situation was frustrating, and she already had a headache from trying to understand Masad' cryptic way of speaking.

"Help me get dressed, Violet."

Within minutes, she was striding out the front door in a black sack dress and sparkly silver earrings. She locked the door and trotted indecorously down the street, wobbling whenever her heels found a mossy crack in the marble flagstones. The workshops were close. She didn't need a pony. She'd walk and enjoy the beautiful cloud-spattered blue sky. A storm was threatening from the west.

Boudi-Ca descended the hill towards the workshops. As she walked, she considered what Masad had told her and the proposition he'd made, but she was distracted by thoughts of Henne, Ranavalona, and nectar. Within fifteen minutes she was striding into the warm interior halls of the sprawling workshop complex. She made her way through the halls to Henne's studio.

Ranavalona sat on the low rotating sculpting platform with her head thrown back. The ebony fledgling was nude above the waist, wearing only a loose linen cloth over one bent leg. Ranavalona glistened with oil. Henne bent with a metal tool over a large misshapen lump of clay. Henne wore nothing but a clay-smeared artist's smock.

"Good evening, Boudi," Ranavalona said. "I saw your bird, but Henne didn't tell me you were coming. I suppose I could go home and leave you two alone."

"You can join us, Ranavalona," Henne said quietly as she worked with her tool. "I won't have my two best friends not wanting to fuck each other."

"I don't mind." Boudi-Ca tried to say the words nonchalantly, but Ranavalona was the last thing she wanted. She felt a little betrayed. The night before had been the longest and closest time that she and Henne had ever spent together. She'd felt they'd reached a new level of intimacy, but Henne hadn't sent her a bird all day.

"Well then, I guess I'll stay." Ranavalona rose from the wooden platform and stretched, letting the linen wrap fall. Boudi-Ca eyed Ranavalona's sleek ebony curves and felt herself stir. She dragged her eyes towards Henne instead.

"Can I be blue-violet, Henne?"

Ranavalona arched her eyebrow. "So you're finally doing nectar, Boudi?"

"Get my purse out, Ranavalona, while I wash up," Henne said. "You look beautiful tonight, Boudi. As always."

"Delicious," Ranavalona added with a wink. Ranavalona went to the workbench where she upended Henne's leather bag. Boudi-Ca watched her move. She hadn't been with anyone other than Henne, Violet, and Tajee in several weeks. The memories of where she'd been with Ranavalona jumped back into her head-memories that she'd thought dead and buried. Ranavalona looked over her shoulder. "Where do you want it, Boudi?"

"On the floor. On the table. In the pool. On the roof."

Ranavalona lit a candle and filled a spoon. "I meant the nectar."

"I know," Boudi-Ca replied. "Should we shut the door? We aren't really supposed to be doing this, right?"

Henne chuckled lightly. "Gallinah went home hours ago. Apolloniah has mysteriously vanished on some secret project, so we're all alone, except for the Lethian doll, and he won't talk."

"Where did Mistress Apolloniah go?"

"No one seems to know. Gallinah says that even she doesn't know, and for some reason I believe her this time. Haven't I told you the super-secret Blue-Violet Beauty rule, Boudi? You can't be blue-violet if you aren't mostly nude."

Boudi-Ca offered her back to Ranavalona, who unbuttoned her dress. Henne came to her side to help, took the dress, and hung it on a hook. Ranavalona slid the spoon through the candle, heating it slowly. Boudi-Ca watched. The odor of the nectar made her nose tingle pleasantly.

"Do either of you know anything about insect collecting? My Ahyehass wants to catch butterflies and make a display for our foyer."

"Persephoneh would know," Henne said. "She collects moths and things. Good luck trying to talk to her though. You need nets and boxes and all that?"

"Yes."

Ranavalona grinned. "So how does your innocent Mimọ like punishment, Boudi?"

"That's none of your business, Ranavalona," Henne said. "Punishment is a private ritual between an Ahyehass and a mistress."

Boudi-Ca shrugged. "I haven't punished Violet. Mistress Gallinah hasn't even delivered the leather crop that I asked for."

Ranavalona surveyed the quietly fizzling nectar in the spoon. "She told us at Ayelet's party that she already gave it to you."

"You must have heard her wrong. She didn't."

"You can always trust Gallinah to gossip, and your Ahyehass was quite the topic at Ayelet's party," Ranavalona said. "After you and Henne left, I'm sure Gallinah said she delivered it to you, and she wondered if you'd used it yet.'"

"I got a dress from her and a collar, but no riding crop. Maybe it's still in the box, and I missed it?"

Ranavalona ignored her. The ebony fledgling seated herself again on the sculptor's turntable. Ranavalona reached between her legs with the heated silver nectar spoon, and then she leaned back and sighed. Her eyelids fluttered. The spoon handle remained between her thighs.

"Kiss me down there, Boudi," purred Ranavalona. "Get your nectar like a little bliss-kitten."

Boudi-Ca took a deep breath. She had a strong urge to go down there and get the nectar like Ranavalona asked. "What's a bliss-kitten?"

Ranavalona rolled her eyes. "Sometimes I can't believe how uninformed you are. They're a special type of slave owned mostly by Egyptian mistresses. They are addicted to nectar. They take nectar every day of their lives."

"They taste sweet," Henne added. "Because of the nectar in them. They're always needy though, and insanely expensive to maintain. You shouldn't take the nectar that way, Boudi. It's unmistresslike, and Ranavalona knows it."

Henne bent, reached sensuously between Ranavalona's legs, and pulled the spoon out. Henne re-filled the spoon with powder from her nectar pouch and relayed it back to the candle. Ranavalona, meanwhile, wilted onto the turntable with her eyelids half-closed.

Boudi-Ca smelled the hot nectar when Henne brought it to her-sweet and aromatic like flowers. "Can I have it like Ranavalona had it?"

Henne pursed her lips. "You don't know what you're in for, but fine. Lie down on the turntable next to her."

Boudi-Ca wriggled onto the turntable next to Ranavalona. She spread her legs for Henne. Henne's fingers pried at her most sensitive flesh. She felt the painful heat of the spoon first, and then the pleasure exploded inside her. Every muscle in her sex and thighs spasmed into flowery blooms of rhythmic contractions. The pleasure raced down her legs, filling her toes, and then spread through her belly and her chest, setting her nipples to stiffening and tingling.

"I think she likes it."

Ranavalona's voice sailed over the waves of warm pleasure. Boudi-Ca reached low with her hand, as if to contain her intense pleasure like a dam, but Henne's face was there. Boudi-Ca felt Henne licking, sending more waves of pleasure snicker-snacking around in her abdomen.

Ranavalona was grinning. Henne shifted up and kissed the ebony fledgling, who returned Henne's embrace and bore her backward onto the dirty floor. Boudi-Ca watched for long minutes as Ranavalona worked Henne. She felt hypnotized by Ranavalona's braid, which twitched to and fro over Ranavalona's dark back like a thick black snake. Henne's fingers clenched and scraped at Ranavalona's shoulder blades. Ranavalona kept her strongly pinned.

Boudi-Ca closed her eyes and re-focused on the sweet pleasure of the nectar, which still tingled in her toes and roots of her hair. Envy stirred in her belly when she heard Henne's love-sounds, but they seemed irrelevant compared to the pleasure. The hulk of dark clay lured her suddenly like a living thing, a misshapen little goddess. She stood unsteadily and went to the small table where Henne had been working. She could identify Ranavalona's semi-supine figure. She caressed the damp, dense stuff with her hand.

"Have another, Boudi," Ranavalona said. The ebony fledgling went to the workbench to retrieve the candle and nectar pouch.

Henne sighed audibly. "Leave her alone, Ranavalona. She's never had more than one spoonful." Henne had risen to sit. The redheaded fledgling looked ravished and disheveled. Ranavalona sat down again next to Henne, positioning the candle on the turntable. Ranavalona cleaned the nectar spoon crudely on the top of Henne's stocking.

Boudi-Ca watched the intimate gesture. Her heart started pounding. She was floating beautifully, like the branches of a tree, but her roots felt nauseated and rotten. Seeing Henne and Ranavalona together made her feel like she didn't really belong. She felt the urge to leave, to throw herself into her bed, to cuddle with Violet, and hide.

"I?I need to go home. I'm tired. I sparred with Masad earlier. I really didn't come here for a party."

Henne raised her eyebrow. "You sparred with Masad, then? Did you win?"

"No, but he let me tie him."

"You tied him up? Lovely." Ranavalona said. "Well, go home then, Ahyehass."

"I need to go too," Henne said. "I'm really hungering, and I can't miss the evening feeding. Put my nectar away, Ranavalona. It's too early to take a double anyway. Did you walk here, Boudi, or ride?"

"I walked."

"I'll drive you home. Ranavalona, do you want to come?"

"I'll come," Ranavalona said with a grin. "But only if you stop being such a nice, sweet, helpful fledgling, Henne."

Henne smirked. "For you, never."

Boudi-Ca retrieved her dress while Henne extinguished the studio lamps. She didn't bother getting her dress back on. She floated after Henne and Ranavalona down the dark workshop hall to the street. The nectar was so pleasant and happy in her body. The bows on her shoes were like butterflies lifting her feet. The west wind buffeted her bare skin like a sky god wanting some Jinn play. The gusts down the mountain carried cool rain.

Henne urged the horses to speed ahead of the storm. The carriage came to a stop within minutes, even as heavier raindrops began to fall. Boudi-Ca took a deep breath to say goodnight, but Henne's quick kiss rendered her silent. She clumsily returned the kiss and went into her house. She climbed the stairs up to her bedchamber.

Violet lay asleep in bed, in the single light of a guttering candle. Boudi-Ca found the box that her Mimọ dress had come in. There was no crop inside. She descended the stairs, still floaty, like she would ascend off the stairs with every step. She took each step slowly and deliberately until she reached the foyer.

A flash of lightning lit the bird slit above the front door. A rumble sounded, and the window frames rattled. The storm outside was increasing in intensity. Tajee lay in his storage room bed in the light of a flickering oil lamp. He stirred and looked up at her. Boudi-Ca steadied herself.

"Tajee, did Gallinah give you a riding crop? Ranavalona said Gallinah delivered it."

Tajee looked at her with his eyes guarded. "Yes, Mistress. Gallinah gave it to me, but I didn't want Violet to get hurt. So I hid it in the stable. I won't lie to you. Punish me if you want."

Boudi-Ca blinked. "You stole from me, Tajee? Of course you'll get a punishment. I've never given you a punishment before, but I'm going to give you one."

"As you wish, Mistress."

"I want my crop on my vanity in the morning."

"Yes, Mistress."

Boudi-Ca turned back into the hall. She almost jumped out of her shoes when the front door swung open, and a dark form that looked like a vampire slipped into the foyer, carrying a fierce gust of wind. White teeth grinned in the gloom.

"You forgot to lock it." Ranavalona brushed droplets of rain from her face and closed the door behind her. She stepped wordlessly across the foyer. Boudi-Ca gasped. Inside of a second, Ranavalona was pressing against her with practiced fingers under her dress, fishing into her sex like hooks, pushing her onto tiptoe. Boudi-Ca moaned. A pervasive pleasure waxed in her belly, and she was one with Ranavalona and a feeling of wetness.

The lightning crashed again outside. Boudi-Ca felt the thunder shake the wall behind her buttocks, where Ranavalona had pressed her. Boudi-Ca moaned. From the corner of her eye, she glimpsed Tajee in the frame of the storage room entryway.

"Tajee, don't look! Go away!"

"Yes, Mistress," Tajee mumbled.

Boudi-Ca gritted her teeth, even as the pleasure mounted in her belly. "What are you doing Ranavalona? I'm with Henne now, not you."

"No you're not. You still want me, and you just can't admit it."

"No," Boudi-Ca groaned. Another of Ranavalona's fingers pushed into her intense wetness. The fledgling's thumb rubbed rhythmically against her wet, sensitive button.

"Where's your bed?" Ranavalona growled. "Answer me."

"Upstairs."

Ranavalona released her, only to seize her by her hair and pull her towards the stairs. Boudi-Ca whimpered. She couldn't bring herself to resist. Wetness slicked her inner thighs, and her sex tingled from where Ranavalona's fingers had claimed her. They climbed the steps one by one with Ranavalona pulling her hair the entire way. When they reached the top, Boudi-Ca fell to her knees. When they reached the bedchamber, she was crawling. Ranavalona dragged her up onto the bed.

"That's a good pet."

Boudi-Ca lay back with her heart pounding. Her head, she realized, had fallen on Violet's leg. Violet stirred and shifted under the covers. "Mistress?"

"Please leave, Violet." Boudi-Ca put her hands over her face. She couldn't face Violet in that moment. She was floating on purple-violet nectar, lying on her bed with her legs spread open, and Ranavalona was pulling a nectar pouch from her purse, and a spoon. Ranavalona filled the spoon and transferred it to the candle. Ranavalona licked her lips.

"Just give me a minute."

"Ranavalona, I don't want Henne to know about this. Please promise me. This is just between us, and you aren't to touch Violet."

Ranavalona's eyebrow arched in the candlelight. "You really care what Henne thinks? The mistresses talk about you, and when they laugh, Henne laughs too. That's all I'm going to say."

"I don't believe you."

"You're going deeper into the purple-violet with me. You need to."

Boudi-Ca felt Ranavalona's fingers prying on her thighs, and then the hot spoon nosed her pink. The incredible wave hit her again, and she was flying even higher. She twisted and bucked against the spoon, but Ranavalona only pushed it deeper. The pleasure was so intense that her muscles knotted up. Boudi-Ca let out a scream. She heard Violet, distant as if through water. Violet was standing in the half-open bedchamber door.

"What are you doing? What are you doing to my Mistress?"

"Silence, Ahyehass," Ranavalona admonished. "Unless you're asking me to punish you, in which case you'd better be serious. Your little Mimo ass wants a hard spanking?"

"No. I'm sorry."

Boudi-Ca heard the door shut. She was alone with Ranavalona, and completely at Ranavalona's mercy. Waves of pleasure lapped inside her, as if she were a boat, rocking on the sea that was her bed. Ranavalona's warm hands were her only ropes, the only moorings that kept her from losing herself permanently. Ranavalona's hot body pressed against hers, and she welcomed it, her safeness and stability. She clutched Ranavalona and felt wet tears in her eyes.

She felt a familiar pressure then against her nether place, her forbidden place. Ranavalona's bone phallus pressed deep and lodged itself inside once again, just as it had the previous summer. Boudi-Ca groaned and whimpered. She felt her wetness welling instantly her sex.

Ranavalona kissed her, licked her, rubbed her, and stroked her. She felt waves again overtaking her, and she was exploding, inundating her bed with wetness. Ranavalona fucked her for long minutes, continuing on and on, until she seized, gripped the sheets, and entered another timeless, breathless climax. She went limp and delirious. The bedchamber descended into a deafening silence. Boudi-Ca shuddered. She didn't think she could possibly release again. Mercifully, Ranavalona's fingers stopped and lifted. Ranavalona leaned over her, smiling gleefully with her dark visage silhouetted against the candlelit ceiling.

"You're mine, Boudi. Tell me."

Boudi-Ca took a deep breath. "Yes. I'm yours."

"I own you. Tell me."

"Yes."

"That's right, because I just seduced you. You just failed Isabellah's Task of Discipline, which means you failed your Mistress Test, which means you're going to be an Ahyehass. That is, if I tell anyone what just happened."

Boudi-Ca frowned in her purple-violet sea, struggling to comprehend the ramifications of what Ranavalona had just said. She was physically devastated and ravished, but Ranavalona's words were slowly sinking in. "No, Ranavalona. You didn't seduce me. That's not how it happened."

"Who is Isabellah going to believe, you or me? Besides, both of your

Ahyehasi saw me dominating you. The Lady and the mistresses will get the truth if I tell them."

"What do you want from me?"

"I want full access to your bed. Maybe if you get a taste of what it's like to be an Ahyehass with me, you'll be even more motivated to pass your Mistress Test."

"I hate you."

Ranavalona laughed. "You love me, Boudi. Your body doesn't lie. By the way, I know where I can get some butterfly nets. I'll bring them down here tomorrow. We'll take your Ahyehass to catch some butterflies."

*Chapter 21:*

Tajee watched Violet swing the long-handled butterfly net. The butterflies fluttered weakly around the magical street lights in the east side city plaza. The insects were searching for warmth in the cool air of the October day, oblivious to Violet's attempts to capture them.

Tajee carefully held two glass jars full of insect prisoners. A handful of beetles lumbered about in the bottom of one of the jars-bizarre black creatures with shiny carapaces. Five butterflies of different sizes and colors fluttered in the second jar. He could feel them hitting the sides of the jar, trying in vain to escape.

Tink. Tink. Tink. Tink.

Hatshepseh's strong Ahyehass girl was splitting firewood in the nearby backyard, with her head-wrapped Mistress assisting. The girl swung her axe, and the sound echoed in counterpoint with the butterflies.

Ker-chunk. Ker-chunk.

Another day had passed in the Lady's domain. Another sunset was purpling the tiled roofs, and another October storm threatened the city. The yellow and grey thunderheads loomed over the just-visible parapets of the city's gatehouse towers. An occasional thump of thunder rumbled in the distance, but there was no rain. Not yet.

Tajee gazed surreptitiously at Boudi. Boudi-Ca sat on the sidewalk bench nearby, talking in low tones with her girlfriend, whose name was Ranavalona-Ca. He'd placed the riding crop on Boudi's vanity as she'd asked. Boudi-Ca hadn't punished him yet. Nothing had happened yet either as a consequence of ripping apart Boudi's special tarot card. Boudi-Ca was obsessed with her own face when she looked in the mirror. She hadn't even noticed the missing card.

Ranavalona looked at him with a smile. Tajee looked down. Ranavalona had caught him looking at her a number of times. Ranavalona's eyes were like butterfly nets. They grabbed and hypnotized. Ranavalona had stirred him to arousal when she'd ravished Boudi-Ca in the dark foyer the night before. Boudi's cries of pleasure behind her closed bedroom door still haunted his memory. Ranavalona was a calculating feminine force, like a black queen on a chess board.

"Careful, Violet." Ranavalona cautioned from where she sat. "Don't trip. Stay under it and be patient. It's bound to come closer to the ground."

Violet swung her net at an elusive high-flying butterfly. Her clumsy attempt to capture the flitting insect was comical, but her enthusiasm was infectious. Violet stretched on tiptoe. Her dress swirled with her energetic efforts. The wind from the coming storm complicated the butterfly's flight, making Violet's task difficult.

"You can do it, Violet," Boudi-Ca encouraged.

Violet jumped and swung. Still the net was empty. She grunted in frustration and looked towards Boudi. "Mistress, can you please catch it? It's a big one, and I want it."

"I'll help," Boudi-Ca answered.

The large blue butterfly had wandered away from the street light towards a tree. Ranavalona stood up and followed it, and after her went Boudi. Boudi-Ca took the handle of the net from Violet and appeared to focus. She scrunched her nose, disappeared, and re-appeared under the butterfly. With a flash and single deft swing of the net, she had it. Tajee felt a warmth of envy. Neither he nor Violet had evidently kept the ability to flash like an Mimọ in Heaven.

"Quickly, Tajee." Ranavalona beckoned. "What are you doing back there?"

"I'm coming." Tajee set down the beetle jar and carried the butterfly jar to Boudi. Boudi-Ca bent and pressed the net to the surface of the street. The butterfly struggled in the threads. She reached under and pinned the creature with her finger.

"I wonder if the big one's bite?" Boudi-Ca extracted the butterfly slowly from the prison of the net.

Tajee opened the jar to receive the butterfly. He quickly clamped the lid back on. The butterfly fluttered to the bottom of the jar and stilled. It didn't flutter madly like the others, as if sensing its fate. Violet leaned in and studied the noble creature closely.

"It's dead, Mistress," Violet said sadly.

Boudi-Ca shrugged. "We have to kill them anyway to display them. I sent a bird to Mistress Gallinah. She's trying to find a glass case for us. Speaking of Gallinah, I think it's time for punishments. Let's all go inside."

Tajee felt a warmth of fear tingle in his limbs. Ranavalona grinned at him. He dropped the butterfly jar then. He wasn't sure how it slipped. He winced and waited for it to shatter on the street stones, but it didn't. Boudi-Ca flashed again in the blink of an eye to kneel at his side. She snatched the bottle from disaster and tucked it under her arm.

"It's going to be cold tonight," Boudi-Ca said. "I'm glad I started the fire in the basement before we left." Ranavalona kissed Boudi's cheek. Boudi-Ca took Violet's hand. The three women trooped silently towards the house.

Tajee followed. The mood had turned dark, like the clouds. Violet was no longer skipping happily. Instead, she was dragging her net. Thunder cracked above the city. The storm was approaching over the palace. Lightning lit up the crystal towers of Allyssia's bower. The wind had an unusual direction and smell to it, a pungent scent of sulfur, unlike the usual updraft of flowery Isandlwana scents.

When they entered the house, Tajee felt Boudi's fingers wrap around his bicep. She escorted him and Violet down into the basement training room where a fire burned low in the hearth. Tajee stood still while Boudi-Ca unfastened his pants and stripped him, and then locked his wrists into cuffs.

Meanwhile, Ranavalona added wood to the fire. Tajee eyed the riding crop, which lay on the hearth. He went to his knees on the rough training mat in response to Boudi's pointed finger, and then Boudi-Ca left him to help Ranavalona attend to Violet. The two Jinni guided the Mimọ girl to all fours. Boudi-Ca grabbed the riding crop and readied it.

Boudi-Ca nodded at Ranavalona. "Lift her dress up for me. Violet gets a practice punishment for my Mistress Test, and Tajee gets the real thing."

Ranavalona lifted Violet's dress from under her stockinged knees and bunched it up over her back. Tajee shifted his weight on his knees, forming a tripod with his cuffed hands. He felt anger bloom in his chest. He suddenly liked Ranavalona much less.

"It won't hurt," Ranavalona added. "It's a small suffering compared to Tajee's."

Tajee watched Boudi-Ca turn Violet around so that her backside was towards the fire. Boudi-Ca positioned the crop and swung. Violet winced when the crop hit. Boudi-Ca swung again and again.

"And eight, nine, and ten." Boudi-Ca stilled the crop. Violet's whimper was achingly loud in the silent basement. Tajee bowed his head. He couldn't watch. He heard footsteps. The two Jinni stood directly in front of him.

"It's your turn, Tajee," Boudi-Ca said. "I can't bring myself to hit you really hard though, so Ranavalona agreed to it for me."

Boudi-Ca reached into her hair and tugged loose her ribbon. She reached under him and insinuated it around his phallus and testicles. Tajee felt his phallus stiffen as Boudi's fingers tied the ribbon in place. Meanwhile, Ranavalona shucked her dress. The ebony fledgling went to the sword rack clad only in her corset. She produced a long wand that appeared to be a piece of the training mat-one of the reeds that had worked loose where the mat was unraveling at the foot of the basement stairway.

Tajee craned his neck to follow the line of Ranavalona's dark thighs. The cleft below the edge of Ranavalona's corset was a magnet for his Ahyehass desire. Ranavalona had a dark thatch, unlike Boudi, who was shaved to look like an Mimọ. His head swam. His phallus throbbed between his legs, tied tightly within the prison of Boudi's hair ribbon.

Ranavalona stalked behind him. Tajee caught Violet's eyes. She was watching with intense curiosity. Her blue eyes were barely visible in the shadows cast by the firelight behind her. Boudi-Ca was watching him too.

"You have a beautiful body Tajee," Boudi-Ca said. "You're so young and strong."

Ranavalona cleared her throat. "It's true. He has beautiful brown skin too, but we're here to punish Tajee for stealing, not to make him feel good about himself. Apologize to Boudi-Ca for hiding that riding crop, Tajee."

"No. I won't feel sorry for not wanting Violet to suffer."

"Your punishment just doubled," Ranavalona said. The cane fell. Tajee gasped. Pain laced through his buttocks. Ranavalona struck again, and a third time. The pain was intense, more than he'd ever felt. He caught Violet's glassy eyes. Her pale eyebrows were scrunched. She looked as if on the verge of crying.

"Ranavalona," Boudi-Ca said, fidgeting. "Please don't hit him so hard."

Ranavalona swished the cane. "Sit up with your hands behind your head, Tajee."

Tajee complied. He rocked back onto his knees and clasped his hands behind his head. Ranavalona kicked him forward. He fell face forward onto his chest. Ranavalona's shoe lodged hard between his buttocks, grinding him into the mat. His phallus and testicles protested painfully, swollen and pinned under him.

"So do you love Violet, Tajee?" Ranavalona asked. "Why did you hide that riding crop? It's such a strange thing for an Ahyehass to do, especially one as well-behaved as you. Boudi-Ca and I want an explanation. The more quickly you answer, the more quickly this will end."

Tajee instinctively tried to think of an answer that wouldn't betray his feelings about Violet to the Jinni, but his thoughts failed him. His phallus was in pain. Ranavalona was grinding and poking at his most sensitive places with the pointed heel of her shoe.

"I hid it because I wanted the attention of my mistress. I wanted to be punished. I was jealous of Violet."

"You're lying," Ranavalona said. "You look and act like such a sweet

Mimọ boy, but deep down, you're just a lying little Ahyehass." Ranavalona removed her foot. The cane fell twice more, then three times, then silence. At that moment, a distant thumping sounded in the house, different from the thunder of the storm, which had grown distant.

"Someone's knocking on the door," Boudi-Ca said, her voice hesitant. "I'll go see who it is. Maybe it's Henne."

Tajee took deep breaths. He was relieved for the small reprieve, but Boudi-Ca was leaving to climb the basement steps. He was wary of what Ranavalona might do. He could see Ranavalona out of the corner of his eye. She stepped forward and settled onto his back. She wore no underthings, and her intense feminine heat warmed his skin.

"I personally like lies," Ranavalona said. "They make life worth living. Why is a beauty mistress the most beautiful of all? She's the most skilled of all liars. I love it when an Ahyehass plays games with me. You're in love with her, Tajee, aren't you? Boudi-Ca isn't here. You can tell me. I won't use it against you."

Tajee wasn't sure how to respond. Ranavalona's thighs tightened around his torso. The ebony fledgling's fingers insinuated into his hair, tightening around his head. She pressed the side of his face to the mat and bumped up and down on his lower back. Each impact ground his phallus into the rough reed mat underneath him, eliciting waves of pain from the abrasion.

"Please let me venerate you," Tajee grunted.

"What? Say that again."

"I want to venerate you. Please."

"It's a gift." Boudi's voice echoed in the stairwell, loud and excited. She came running back down the stairs from the foyer. "It's another gift from the Prince, Ranavalona-a purple crystal on a gold chain. The Prince himself just delivered it. Look. The crystal is huge! It has some kind of writing on the side of it."

"Is the Prince still here, or did he leave?"

"He left." Boudi-Ca shrugged. "He smiled kind of funny at me, handed me the box, and got back on his horse. He was all wet from the storm, and he seemed to be in a big hurry."

"I'm going to allow Tajee to release, and then you can show me the crystal."

Tajee gasped. Ranavalona's weight left him, jarring his phallus yet again into the mat. She grabbed his arm and turned him over onto his back. Ranavalona climbed on top of him. Her wet pumpum enveloped his aching phallus with one swift stroke. She wasted little time in applying her Jinn pressure. She rode him like a horse in front of Violet and Boudi.

Tajee clenched, queerly embarrassed that everyone was watching. Within scarcely a minute, his pleasure exploded. His testicles collapsed under Ranavalona's suction, and he groaned and spurted. Ranavalona milked him for several seconds with her inner muscles. Tajee lay still, surrendering to the familiar emptiness-the relief and after-pleasure of a Jinn draining.

Ranavalona stood and strode to Boudi-Ca by the stairs. The two fledglings spoke in whispered tones as they examined a large crystal on a chain. Boudi-Ca held it cautiously. She finally slid it back into the box at Ranavalona's encouragement. She pulled Ranavalona by the sleeve up towards the foyer. A whispered argument ascended the stairwell.

Tajee breathed with relief. He wasn't sure what the argument was about, but at least his punishment appeared to be over. He was alone with Violet. Violet lay curled in the firelight of the hearth. Her blonde hair lay loose and tangled, and her bangs were in disarray. In her simple dress, she looked like a wilted flower. She was still watching him. Tajee dared to slither across the mat and settle next to her.

"Are you alright, Violet?"

Violet sniffed. "Yes. I'll be fine. I'm sorry about what they did to you."

"It felt good at the end."

Violet looked closely at him. "Do you like Ranavalona-Ca?"

"She isn't half as beautiful or amazing as you are."

"Thank you, Tajee," Violet smiled and lowered her eyes shyly. "Would you ever want to kiss me?"

"It's forbidden for two Ahyehasi to be together, unless the Mistress permits it. I'd probably kiss you anyway."

"Boudi-Ca is so perverted, you know? For a woman to lie with a woman, or a man with a man, is the worst of the worst. It's unthinkably sinful.

Does anyone get properly married in this place, or do they just have sex forever?"

Tajee swallowed. "I've heard that a few Jinni here are married to each other, and all the Jinni down in Haawiyah must marry men by law. Mostly everything is just lust and sin. The Jinni keep pushing you into it, and you can't resist. The pleasure is just too much. Boudi-Ca used to be like you, but she became one of them."

"Have you, have you ever thought about escaping?"

Tajee eyed the stairway and lowered his voice. "I used to. Do you?"

"Yes. They say I can't go back because of my wings, but for all I know, the Jinni are lying to me. I was such a fool to let those women in red get me. I had no idea."

"They captured you, right? After you jumped from Heaven?"

Violet wiped her eye. "Yes. I woke up in a strange place. There was sand and water, but no Mimos. I couldn't find anyone to help me. I started walking and walking. I was crying and hopeless, but then I found a road. I saw some horses and women riding them. The women were wearing red uniforms of some sort."

"I'm sorry, Violet."

Violet choked a laugh. "I was so happy to see someone! I ran up to them smiling, and they just started laughing at me, like I was a complete idiot! One of them started hitting me with a cord, and my body went numb. And then she got off of her horse and hit me some more on my legs and in my face. She tied my hands together and threw me over the back of her horse. I wanted to scream, but-"

"They severed your wings?"

"They took me to that castle with the howling winds, and they gave me to Ambassador Lydiah. Her creepy silver eyes were so delighted when she saw me. I didn't realize that I was just a toy for her to play with. At the time, I had no idea such cruelty even existed. Lydiah cut off my wings." Violet stopped speaking. Footsteps sounded again on the stair. Boudi-Ca appeared alone in the candlelight. She glared at them for a second before she spoke.

"There's something wrong, Tajee. Something is wrong in the Redoubt."

"What is it, Mistress?"

"Ranavalona and I don't know much. We just received birds from Freyah telling us to stay home and lock our doors. And then Ranavalona and I finished our argument, and I threw her out of the house. Go down and close the stable doors, Tajee. If you need help throwing the bars to lock it, let me know."

# Chapter 22:

Ayelet lay submerged in her upstairs tub. She eyed the sword propped against the wall, her blade waiting within an arm's reach. Through the unshattered window, she could see faint patches of purple through the clouds where lightning still played. It was almost morning. She heard a scratch at the window. The bird had finally come. It scrabbled through the slit, landed on her bare shoulder, and spoke with Freyah's voice.

Ayelet, we need you at the palace this morning for a critical meeting with Lady Allyssia. Come immediately, or as soon as possible. I also have the new sword you ordered.

Ayelet climbed from the tub and toweled herself dry. She was glad Barissianna's surprise gift was ready-the replacement sword for the one broken at the Trivium-but it was of little importance compared to everything else. She summoned a messenger bird.

Yenta, get the carriage ready. No, make that a horse. Saddle my brown stallion.

Within fifteen minutes she was dressed and strapping a blade to her waist. Herzl stood on a chair to slip pearl pins into her braid. The dressing-girl handed her a leather tricorne hat as she swept out of the bedchamber door.

Yenta waited in the dawn light outside the stable with a horse at the ready. Ayelet leapt into the saddle, urged the horse down the drive and into the street, and then gave rein. She made the palace within minutes. She tethered her horse and trotted up the steps. An Ahyehass directed her towards the fall meeting room. She strode down the hallways, keeping pace with the other mistresses who were also hastening on the way.

The cozy fall meeting room in the west wing of the palace was warm with the flames of a few hundred candles that sat on decorative half-columns. Several mistresses were already seated in the concentric circles of chairs.

Allyssia lounged in the throne in the center of the room. Her golden skin shone with oil in the candlelight. Instead of the Lady's customary mask of ivory, she wore a mask of leaden grey. Cupid flanked her with a matching leaden mask. The young daughter Voluptas hid her tearful round face against the love god's hip.

Ayelet took a seat in the highest occupied row. Masad was there. He nodded at her in a gesture of silent respect with his face expressionless. For several minutes, mistresses continued to trickle in-Nili, then Persephoneh, who also appeared damp from a bath, and Pyrinnah. Mistress Gallinah and the divine daughter Harmoniah chatted in terse tones with Mistress Yuliah as they entered the meeting room as a trio. Gonorrheah ambled in after all the others with the help of her cane. Her unlit pipe dangled from her fingers. She rubbed her eyes.

"Gonorrheah and Charlaineh are here. Let's begin," Allyssia said. The Lady's voice was barely audible. The goddess looked almost weary in her mask, although it was impossible to believe. "I'll be brief. The vampires have left the city by mutual agreement. Our alliance with the Auerbach vampires has ended."

Ayelet frowned. "All of them, my Lady? We aren't keeping any ties to the Auerbach through our alliance?"

"No," replied the goddess softly. "If there are no further questions on this issue, I will continue."

"No, my Lady," Ayelet said.

"Good. As for the werewolf clans, I have made my decision. I appreciate the aid they gave us in freeing Sekhmet and saving our city from occupation by the Old Order, but their request for permission to come live here in western Meristyian is denied. They would be ill-served by doing so, Masad."

"Very well, milady," Masad said. "But with the vampires gone, and no invitation to the werewolves, how plan you to defend your Redoubt?"

The goddess was silent, then stood and spread her arms in a gesture of benevolence. "My Jinni, a tragic moment has come upon the New Order. A new war is dawning between Heaven and Hell, and this age-old strife has burst into flame in my beloved corner of Meristyian. Both factions are knocking on my door. Both factions want this beautiful city for a military base. One side brings violence and death, and the other brings an offer of recapitulation. It was a difficult and unwelcome decision, but one that I had to make."

"My Lady?" Gallinah said with her eyes wide. The shocked tone of the jovial rotund mistress spoke the feeling in the room.

"This war of the Mimoic Hierarchy is a war against all Jinni, my daughters, both New Order and Old Older," the goddess continued. "You know that I no longer have the resources to protect you from what comes. Lord Hades himself arrived at my palace last night with Archduke Yitzhak. I stand before you defeated. It is no surprise, now, that I can no longer resist Him."

"Oh, dear," Gallinah whispered audibly.

Ayelet felt her stomach drop in empathy with the wave of sadness that passed through the room, as if all passion to live had left her. She'd never heard such silence, such stillness as in that moment. No one in the chamber moved.

"Negotiations are currently in progress with Lord Hades," Allyssia continued. "The esteemed Ambassador Lydiah is now free, and she will be our liaison to negotiate with Lady Allyssia. These negotiations will reach a swift conclusion. My Redoubt will become a citadel for Hell's army against the Mimos. Above all, Meristyian and its peoples must be defended against a new purgation by the Mimoic Hierarchy, which continues its endless campaign to destroy love, lust, and all things we hold sacred. This threat is greater than our differences with Lord Hades, so sacrifices must be made."

"Lady Allyssia, I beg you." Gonorrheah looked aghast. "There has to be a better way."

"If this deal will save the city, then we would do well to take it," Szenes said in counterpoint. "It's better than the Mimoic Hierarchy invading."

"Who will be in charge of the city?" Freyah asked.

"The Redoubt will be occupied by the military forces of Hell's Army," Allyssia answered. "Archduke Yitzhak will come and take command of defending this citadel. Freyah's battle Ahyehasi will relinquish their current duties, and will instead serve Hell's troops in every capacity. Mistress Freyah will oversee their new duties as their steward, and work closely with the Smokeless Flames commanders on strategic deployment of Hell's soldiers to defend the city against an attack."

"Is the Smokeless Flames coming, as well as Hell's army?" Gallinah asked.

"Yes. It's my understanding that the Smokeless Flames will be sending a small division. They will be the chief local organizers working with us. Ambassador Lydiah will organize the re-integration of the New Order Jinni into the Old Order. Commander Befanah of the Smokeless Flames will oversee local city security in Freyah's place and work with Freyah and her battle Ahyehasi to make the city run smoothly."

"I don't understand," interjected Pyrinnah. "What laws will we follow, and whose implementation of them?"

"We have faith in you, my Lady," Freyah added. "There are so many questions raised."

The Lady inclined her leaden-masked head. "There will be a transition time, Mistress Freyah, and there will be confusion until we can pass the city to the full control of the Smokeless Flames and Hell's army, again for the express purpose of defending Meristyian against a purgation by the Mimos. This decision is also for the Seelie Kishi, who have many nimfas and satyrs living in the Heartland. I know we will have Nankariders patrolling our skies to defend against the Hierarchy gloom-wraiths. We will have Djinnus soldiers occupying our gatehouse. We will have squads of soldiers in the streets at all hours."

"What will happen to the New Order mistresses?" Pyrinnah persisted. "Will we be punished like the others? Will we be hauled off to Hell's Court, sentenced, and sent to the Merian dungeons?"

"No. Of course I would not accept such terms. There will no ebon control collars for any more New-Order-mistresses. You will all retain your Ahyehasi, your homes here, and your possessions. You need only be willing to recognize Lady Allyssia again as your queen, mother, and leader. If you do not wish this, then the city gates are open. You are free to leave."

"And how long will the transition be," Szenes said. "Before anyone might return to Haawiyah, if we wished it?"

"I can say that an official Registry will be made listing all of the residents of the Redoubt-all masters, mistresses, fledglings, and their Ahyehasi," Allyssia answered. "Freyah will assist in completing this list for Ambassador Lydiah, who will scribe copies and deliver them to the necessary parties for pardons, among other things. All of your devoted Ahyehasi must be properly registered with slave papers with Hell's Court in the coming months. I would also recommend branding them as per Old Order tradition, but that is an individual choice. I will assume that none of my Jinni will start mistreating their humans."

"When will the Nanka arrive?" Ayelet said. "And the Smokeless Flames?"

"Hell's army Nankariders are in flight from Mer and might arrive at any time," Allyssia answered. "Please note that there is no such thing anymore as the Old Order or New Order. From this moment forward, we are all Jinni united against the Mimoic Hierarchy. The Smokeless Flames mistresses who arrive should be politely invited to parties. I'm expecting our resident beauty mistresses to play a key role as hosts."

"Hosts? Can they really be considered invited guests?" Gallinah clucked. "I'm sorry, Lady Allyssia. I don't mean to be rude."

"All Jinni are one, and we should welcome the Smokeless Flames," Allyssia said with an even tone. "It was not so many centuries ago when you all lived side by side. You might even know some of them by name, like Ambassador Lydiah and Commander Befanah. Perhaps you will even re-find old friends. This flies in the face of everything that we have believed in, I know, but the circumstances are extreme. Heaven's forces are at our doorstep with the will to destroy us."

"At least the vampires are gone," Szenes said. "I prefer the devil I know to the devil I don't."

"At least make an effort to contain your excitement Szenes," Gonorrheah said. "I rather liked the vampires. Barissianna had a few of my books, actually. She didn't return them."

Allyssia gestured with her open hand. "Are there any more questions? Love must be mentioned. For many of you, the freedom to love other women was the main reason you came to Meristyian with me after the schism. I regret the need to realign with Lord Hades, but I will do everything in my power to fight Hell's Court for your freedoms to love who you want."

"Thank you, my Lady," Nili muttered. "I won't expect much."

"Keep in mind that love between two Jinni is still considered treason by Lord Hades, and will now become forbidden to openly practice this city. You should refrain from any public lesbian activities, as if you were living again in the capital city of Mer. Yes, I expect this to be a problem. The arriving Smokeless Flames and Lord Hades' soldiers will be all too knowledgeable that my city is a different color. Many of them will be prejudiced against you, and I may not be able to defend every indiscretion."

The room was somber and silent. Gallinah bowed her head and looked at her feet. Ayelet relaxed her hands. She'd been clenching the arms of her chair with a force almost strong enough to break them. She cleared her throat.

"Thank you, my Lady. For everything."

Allyssia nodded her leaden mask. "And thank you, Ayelet. All of you have my thanks for your service over these past peaceful centuries in my city. May you all walk with Love and hold me in your hearts in these terrible times." The goddess waved her hand and disappeared in a column of golden dust that floated upwards towards the ceiling.

Ayelet slipped quickly out of the aisle and strode upwards and out of the chamber. She felt so heavy with emotion that she could hardly move her feet. The Redoubt would soon be ruled by Archduke Yitzhak, assisted by Commander Befanah and Ambassador Lydiah-two high-ranking members of Allyssia's Smokeless Flames.

Nanka would soon fly overhead, and Djinnus soldiers would soon prowl the streets of the Lady's city. Worst of all, the laws of Hell's Court would be instituted. Her relationship with Barissianna was illegal and treasonous. She would also be exposed to arrest, and not just for lesbianism. She was a criminal in the eyes of Hell's Court with a massive bounty, payable in gold aurei to less scrupulous soldiers that might make a try for her well-known head.

Ayelet quickened to a trot ahead of the other somber mistresses. She exited the palace alone and stopped, gazing at the ledge on the west mountainside where the Auerbach had been keeping their bats. The ledge appeared empty in the light of morning. She had to see for herself. She had to be sure Barissianna was gone before she allowed herself to grieve.

She turned right towards the end of the palace steps and descended the small path that led behind the stables. She found the trail at the base of the mountain and climbed upwards along the steep rock for several minutes until she reached the ledge where the Auerbach chiropterim had been kept. The wide, guano-painted ledge was indeed empty of bats, except for a single sickly bat that huddled at the end.

Ayelet stood for long minutes. Her life had come crashing down around her, just like the Lady's Redoubt itself. The vampires must have left in haste, along with Barissianna. A curt male voice at her shoulder surprised her.

"Look you for something?"

Ayelet whirled and pulled her blade from her sheath. Masad stood right behind her, looking along the stony ledge, oblivious to the sword aimed at his face. Ayelet slowly lowered her guard. "Masad, you shouldn't surprise people like that."

"Fear me should you not. Better with a blade are you, anyway."

Ayelet shrugged. "When a legendary assassin stalks a legendary blade master, history shows that the assassin wins. Care to tell me why you're following me? These are dangerous times. Where do your loyalties lie?"

"With my adopted people in the east. My werewolves. Wanted I only to ask you of Boudi-Ca, but rushed you out of the palace."

"I'm sorry, Masad. I'm jumpy. My lover is gone. Hell's army is coming. I've killed many times for the Lady. I've got a long list of Hell's Court bounties on my head."

"Close to long is mine."

"Touché. What did you want with Boudi-Ca?"

"Wondered I if spoke she to you of going with me into the east. If wished she to take me as her teacher of blades. Have I no plans to be here in the coming days when arrives Hell's army. Asked I Boudi-Ca to let me know, but has she not, and wanted I not to go knocking and put her on the spot."

Ayelet frowned. "I didn't know about your offer. That's kind of you Masad, but I'm a little concerned. I have a vested interest in that fledgling. Given your track record of abandoning things, how serious are you in this? You'd really take your time to teach her properly?"

"Mentored I recently another Jinn. Liked it I did."

Ayelet arched her eyebrow. "Masad, if any harm comes to Boudi-Ca, I shall be very put out. On the other hand, I don't know which would be worse for her-going away with you into the east, or staying here under the aegis of Lord Hades."

"Insult you me so much?"

"I'm sorry. I'm a bit distraught right now, and I don't know what to say. According to the rules of Boudi-Ca's test, I'm not supposed to be helping her. Honestly, I have no idea if her test will even be valid when the next Spring Festival happens in six months, if it happens."

"Have you a point."

"I'm sorry I can't help you, Masad. Right now, I have other things on my mind, like Barissianna. Can you track her in the tapestry? Can you confirm that she really left me without saying goodbye?"

"Yes. Left the vampires with their bats. Feels that one ill?" Masad pointed at the sickly bat, which was missing its basket. Its heavy leather harness was still strapped around its torso, however.

Ayelet eyed the bat. "It might be the one that was shot down by the Hierarchy when Gonorrheah and I did our surveillance of the Trivium citadel. I think the vampires dragged it back here from the forest to try to save it, even though the basket was destroyed. Apparently they left it behind."

Masad scratched his stubbly chin. "Yes, looks it poorly to fly."

"I'm going to go, Masad. I need to keep moving so I don't feel anything. Thank you for everything you've done for the Lady. Maybe I'll see you sometime in the east."

Masad lowered his eyes. "Yes. Hope I will for peace."

Ayelet strode back down the path. She leapt onto her horse at the stables and made pace across the city. When she arrived back at her Villa, the last vestiges of the morning storm had passed over. Wet, frost-browned flowers stirred limply in their beds with the dying sulfuric gusts. Winter had come.

Ayelet pushed through the unlocked front door. Her habit of not locking doors, she realized, would have to change greatly. She didn't trust the Smokeless Flames or Hell's soldiers any farther than she could throw them. Turtle was seated on the first step of the stairs in the front foyer of the Villa, waiting for the morning blades lesson.

"Mistress, what's happening?"

Ayelet regarded Turtle silently. How could she tell the lesbian fledgling, who had suffered horribly under the Old Order, that the enemy was coming to take over? Yenta and Herzl had heard her enter and rustled down the stairs in their robes and slippers. Ayelet forced a smile.

"I have news, everyone. The Auerbach vampires have left us."

Turtle raised her eyebrow. "What about Magistrada Barissianna?"

"She left too without a word. Worse yet, Hell's army and the Smokeless Flames are coming to take the place of the Auerbach. Lord Hades and Lady Allyssia will help defend this city from the Hierarchy army that is invading Meristyian. The occupation will come at a price. We will come under their jurisdiction, at least for a time. For now, western Meristyian will become a front for another war between Heaven and Hell."

Turtle's jaw dropped. "This is horrible."

"I know it's terrible news, Turtle. You'll still be my fledgling. I'll have your back. There will be troops in the streets, but there will be no ebon collars or black nectar used to control us. Turtle, go get into your training robe. We'll practice at blades. With the coming of hard times, we need to focus. We need to be strong."

"Y-yes, Mistress."

Ayelet pressed forward and hugged Yenta and Herzl, who were silent and wide-eyed. She climbed to her bedroom to get her training robe. Why hadn't Barissianna said goodbye? What was Boudi-Ca planning to do about Masad' offer to take her into the east for blades training? Would Boudi-Ca even have a Mistress Test? Everything had gone to Hell in one morning, literally and figuratively.

# Chapter 23:

"Eyes down. Chin up. Feet apart. Hands open. Lips parted. Stomach tucked." Boudi-Ca swung her riding crop and smacked Violet's pale buttocks. Violet squeaked. "Very good, Violet. If you fail to measure up to Isabellah's inspection, I'll fail my test. All of my blade practice will be for nothing."

"Yes, Mistress."

Boudi-Ca swung a third time. Violet remained poised, rocking forward slightly onto her toes to soften the blows. Boudi-Ca pinched and firmed Violet's nipples before swinging the crop twice more, enough to make Violet squeak again. Boudi-Ca smiled inwardly. The very best Ahyehasi in the city had characteristics that made them special. Violet's cute squeak was her secret weapon for the presentation at the Spring Festival.

"You're beautiful, Violet. I'm so lucky to have you. Go ahead and put your clothes back on and help me with my dress."

"Yes, Mistress," Violet said with her eyes properly lowered. "Thank you, Mistress."

"Well, thank you for the insect box. It's beautiful. I want you to make another one soon as a little gift for Mistress Isabellah."

"Yes, Mistress."

Boudi-Ca slumped in front of the vanity. She examined her face. Her eyebrows seemed to always need more plucking. She wanted to look perfect for the most important party that she'd ever attended-a party for the reunification of the Jinni. She'd received so many birds during the previous week from Henne and Ranavalona about the Hell's army occupation that it was all starting to melt together. It was all happening so fast.

Gone were the days of peace in Allyssia's city. Within a single week, hundreds of Djinnus soldiers had flown into the city on the backs of Nanka, ready to fight the Mimoic Hierarchy. The streets echoed with the heavy march of their boots and the clatter of their armor and weapons. The adjacent empty house of Mistress Golda had been converted into a barracks. Music, coarse laughter, and loud voices could be heard at all hours, mostly in male tones, but occasionally female.

The Djinnus weren't the only soldiers employed by Hell's army. The Old Order Jinni had arrived in notable numbers. Their blade mistresses and sorceresses all wore red robes and sashes. According to Henne, they were the Smokeless Flames-the assassins of Lady Allyssia, who was the real queen and mother of all Jinni, not Lady Allyssia.

Violet had an Mimo dress ready. Boudi-Ca climbed into it. Violet drew the wing-slit laces tight. Boudi-Ca kissed Violet goodbye and swept down the stairs. Tajee had her pony ready outside the stable. She climbed astride. She prodded it up the alley and down the street, ignoring the lusty gazes of the Djinnus soldiers who were lounging outside the barracks.

Boudi-Ca felt her belly twinge with Hunger. Ranavalona's intimate attentions were weakening her strength. She and Ranavalona had been together twice since the fateful night that Ranavalona had seduced her, and she always got the short end of the energy exchanges, of course. She'd fought with Ranavalona, however, and hadn't seen her for a week. Meanwhile, she was worried that Ranavalona could cause her to fail her Task of Discipline.

Ranavalona's wicked attentions had made her miss Henne. Her secret agenda at the party was twofold. She wanted to talk with Henne about Ranavalona, and she wanted to talk with Gonorrheah about the Prince's sudden, mysterious gift. The purple crystal necklace was tucked away in the cup of her corset. She hadn't put it on for fear of a curse or a spell.

It took her thirty minutes to ride through the city to Nili's home. Carriages lined both sides of the street. Guests milled through Nili's gardens. Boudi-Ca hitched her pony and strode boldly through the front door. Nili's foyer was warm and smelled of incense. A green messenger bird whizzed up and out of the bird slit. A brown bird flew past in the other direction. Ahyehasi bustled in and out of the parlour, where several mistresses lounged, including Gallinah, Nili, and the piano teacher, old Mistress Melkeh.

There were two guests in the parlour who were clearly from Hell's army- an older woman in a red uniform with greying brown hair and a sword at her waist, and a tall male in black leather armor. The Djinnus sat in an armchair, talking with Nili. Henne sat folded at Nili's feet as per tradition, looking up at the Djinnus with her glorious red mane stark against the poofs of Nili's voluminous black sateen dress.

Boudi-Ca bit her lip nervously. Everyone in the parlour was wearing Old Order blacks. Her white Mimọ dress made her stand out, and she felt like a white swan at a black swan party. Henne saw her then. Henne rose, swept out of the parlour, and hugged her.

"Hi, Boudi-Ca," she whispered. "I haven't seen you in a while."

"Are they from Hell's army?" Boudi-Ca nodded at the parlour guests.

"Yes. The mistress is Commander Befanah," Henne replied solemnly. "She's in charge of the Serpent Sisters in the city. The Djinnus is a Wyrm-rider in Hell's army. It's really stuffy in here with them, Boudi. I'm supposed to be a host, but this whole thing is horrible. Everyone is depressed and afraid, but we're pretending to be nice to these people. I was thinking of getting out of here and going up to the palace. Commander Befanah said the Hell's army Nanka are nesting in the Lady's great hall. Would you be interested in seeing them?"

"That's horrible."

Henne grimaced. "I know."

"I'll go. Can you drive? I only have my pony."

"Nili's carriage is blocked in, but maybe we could take Szenes's carriage. Try to find Ranavalona. I'll press on for a little longer."

"Alright." Boudi-Ca leaned to kiss Henne, but Henne pushed her back. Over Henne's shoulder, Nili glared daggers at her, and Gallinah's hand was poised in horror over her lips. All heads in the parlour turned to look.

"Lesbianism is illegal in public now, Boudi," Henne whispered quickly. "That was almost a disaster. Don't forget."

"I'm so sorry Henne."

"Just try to remember next time." Henne swept her hair over her shoulder, painted a smile on her face, and returned to the parlour. Boudi-Ca pivoted and stalked down the hall. Her cheeks felt hot, and a gloom crept over her tepid enthusiasm. She nearly bumped into Gonorrheah, who limped around the corner while lighting her pipe with a cane under one arm.

The wizardress held the end of a leather leash, which was attached to a small creature. The creature was four-legged, in the shape of a miniature horse, but with a beak and small wings, and a feathered neck and head that rose almost as high as Gonorrheah's thigh. Boudi-Ca skittered to avoid bumping into the thing.

"What is that, Mistress Gonorrheah?"

Gonorrheah lit her pipe with a flick of her fingers. Fire sparked, and she puffed, sending up a plume of sweet-smelling smoke. "It's a hippogryph, my dear beauty fledgling. A travelling merchant was selling the eggs the year before last at the Spring Festival. Several mistresses bought one, but mine was the only one that hatched. Ha. I know things about magical animals that others don't."

"Like what?"

"Hippogriffs prefer wet climates. Their eggs thrive in soggy nests that overlook bogs and whatnot. Did anyone listen to me? No. They did what the Gypsy told them."

"Mistress Gonorrheah, I know you're amazingly knowledgeable about magical things. In fact, I was wondering if you could look at this for me. It was a gift." Boudi-Ca removed Amanoch's purple crystal from her corset and handed it to Gonorrheah. The wizardress rubbed it between her finger and thumb.

"Fascinating, fledgling. This is dream magic."

Boudi-Ca bit her lip. "So it's a spell, then. What should I do with it?"

"If I were you, I'd see if I could use it. It's dream magic of a divinatory nature. If you'll let me have it, I could do some research, but it might take a while."

"Fine. Thank you so much, Mistress Gonorrheah. Have you seen Ranavalona?"

"She's upstairs in a bedroom," Gonorrheah said breezily. "She and some other fledglings are playing a game, and I'm too old and dotty to get an invite inside."

"Thank you again, Mistress Gonorrheah."

Boudi-Ca climbed the stairs into the upstairs hallway. Henne's bedchamber door was closed. She tested the locked handle. She knocked. After a minute, the handle clicked and the door opened. Ranavalona smiled with her eyes hooded.

"Why if it isn't Boudi-Ca. One spoon of purple-violet is the price of entry to our private party." Ranavalona stretched a spoon with a dollop of dark liquid in it. Boudi-Ca opened her mouth to decline the offer, but the nectar smell made her quiver with a sudden profound urge.

"Fine." Boudi-Ca bent and took the spoon in her mouth. Ranavalona tipped it up. Boudi-Ca sucked the thick liquid down, and a deep pleasure coursed from his throat to her arms, her chest, her breasts, and her sex. Ranavalona's hot hand grabbed hers and pulled her through the door.

Henne's bedroom was bathed in candlelight. A row of five Jinni bent over one side of Henne's bed with their bare rumps in the air and their dresses and slips pushed over their backs and heads, obscuring their identities. A tall, muscled Djinnus soldier slowly worked the row with his impressive phallus.

"What's going on?" Boudi-Ca felt her head swimming deliriously with the nectar's initial effects. Ranavalona pecked her on the ear.

"We're playing a Jinn game. That's Captain Kordrag. He's a wyrm-rider. He's taking three of us on a moonlight ride on his Nanka tonight-the three who can make him come. I won the first round, but Persephoneh must have let me. I think she isn't trying. Have you met Lieutenant Nefra of the Smokeless Flames?" Ranavalona gestured at a lanky Jinn sitting in the chair next to Henne's mirror. "She isn't playing with us."

"It's nice to meet you, Lieutenant." Boudi-Ca nodded at the Old Order Jinn. Nefra looked strong, even stronger than Ayelet. She wore red military garb, similar to Commander Befanah's in the parlour but less extravagant. Nefra had long brown hair and matching eyes, with solid shoulders over a modest chest.

Nefra nodded back with a smile. "Likewise."

"You look beautiful this afternoon, Boudi-Ca." Ranavalona leaned close to sniff. "What do you think, Nefra? Is Boudi-Ca not the most lovely and desirable Mimọ fledgling you've ever met? She's the only Mimọ fledgling you've ever seen, really. She's a creation of the Lady. See her little wings?"

Nefra looked askance at Ranavalona. "I've heard brief mention of Boudi-Ca. It's interesting to see her in person. You and Boudi-Ca seem to have some chemistry, Ranavalona. Are you two lesbians?"

"Boudi-Ca and I? Never," Ranavalona answered. "Why would I fuck an exotic Mimọ fledgling with shy umber eyes who licks up nectar like a pit hellion and orgasms like a banshee? I could get arrested."

Nefra's eyes were veiled. "I have no intention of reporting any lesbians. This city was created by Allyssia as an homage to all forms of Love. I understand that. Officially I'm supposed to enforce the illegality of it, but unofficially I sympathize."

Boudi-Ca eyed the long-sheathed sword propped by Nefra's knee. Nefra had evidently worn her blade to the party. "That's a nice sword, Lieutenant Nefra. Are you a blade mistress?"

"Of course. And you're a beauty fledgling, I assume?"

"Boudi-Ca is both blades and beauty." Ranavalona gave an exasperated sigh. "Underneath her pretty little exterior, she's very talented. She's so talented it's boring, really. She only studies blades though so she can pass her Mistress Test. Her task is to win first or second in a competition at next year's Spring Festival."

Nefra looked surprised. "I didn't even consider that Lady Allyssia would have that tradition here. I suppose it will be something to look forward to in the spring, assuming we can hold this city against the Mimoic Hierarchy."

Boudi-Ca eyed Nefra's worn, capable-looking hands. "You'd compete, then?"

"I usually do. If you need to place to pass your Test, then I'm sorry. It's been a long time since I've been defeated."

"You have some stiff competition, Boudi-Ca," Kordrag said suddenly, looking over his shoulder from where he fucked at the edge of the bed. "Nefra is one of the best blade mistresses in all of Hell. She's tougher than most of our best men, and she's studied for centuries with Commander Befanah."

"Boudi-Ca has studied with Mistress Ayelet," Ranavalona said quickly. "Ayelet is the best blade mistress in the history of the Jinni."

Kordrag refocused on the rump of the Jinn in front of him. His muscled buttocks were thrusting in an easy, machine-like rhythm. "Yes, I heard the Butcher of Mer was living in this city. I wonder how Ayelet will reconcile with the Hell's Court devils."

"Master Masad offered to train Boudi-Ca too," Ranavalona added.

Nefra blinked. A shocked look froze her weather-worn face. "Masad? Surely you don't mean Prince Masad?"

"Yes. The Prince." Ranavalona threw her arm over her forehead and pretended to swoon. "Prince Masad, legendary assassin and son of Lord Hades, wants to train Boudi-Ca. He's just another of Boudi-Ca's many princely admirers."

Nefra nodded slowly. "Would you care to spar sometime, Boudi-Ca? I'd love to have a friendly match with you, just to see your techniques."

"Maybe," Boudi-Ca answered. "I think you might lose."

"Haha!" Ranavalona guffawed. "Boudi-Ca has finally gone mad. She's cracked under the pressure. If she doesn't place at the festival and fails her test, Lady Allyssia will turn her into an Ahyehass. Since there's no New Order anymore, an Ahyehass pretty much means she'll be a slave girl with an owner, a brand on her backside, and Court papers to seal her fate."

Nefra tapped her sword hilt pensively. "That's a shocking price for failure. I've heard of Jinni becoming slaves for extreme reasons, like a punishment from Hell's Court, or if their husband wants such a thing. Well, I usually compete in the festival. I enjoy it, and it's sacred to Lady Allyssia. At least, with the help of my blade, this city will still be standing in the spring to have a festival in the first place."

The room lapsed into silence. Ranavalona swiveled into Kordrag. She massaged his buttocks to stimulate him. He grunted his appreciation. Boudi-Ca avoided Nefra's hawk-like brown eyes. She realized that her chances to pass her Task of Mastery decreased hugely if the new city regime was participating. She'd have to win not only against Turtle, but also against the Smokeless Flames Jinni and the Hell's army soldiers.

Boudi-Ca eyed the nearby side table. Silver spoons glinted in the light of the wax candles. Spilled nectar covered the table top. She stepped to the table and swabbed the spilled powder with her fingertip. She transferred it to her tongue. She swabbed up more nectar, strafing her wet finger to gather a bunch of it. A hand grabbed her hand and held it fast.

"Don't."

Boudi-Ca gazed down at the hand that held hers. Lieutenant Nefra had leaned forward in her chair. Nefra had a long reach and a very strong grip. Nefra's bent fingers were warm. Boudi-Ca licked the remnants of sweet pleasure from her lips. "Why not?"

"It isn't healthy for you."

Boudi-Ca straightened. "Let go of my hand. Why do you even care?"

Nefra released her and leaned back. "I care because I've seen too many blade fledglings use nectar and quit the Smokeless Flames. I care because I've seen too many mistresses use nectar and stop caring about their fledglings. We train every day to fight and defend Hell. We live on the edge, literally. It's easy to use nectar to blunt that edge, but nectar slows our reflexes. Nectar slows our minds. We have to stay Sharp. We have to ask ourselves what we're fighting for."

"To live and love who we want," Boudi-Ca answered immediately. She glared into Nefra's brown eyes, which widened, but didn't flinch. She was acutely aware of the space between her and the lieutenant, as if the air itself had thickened.

"Yes, I suppose," Yellen said softly. "We also fight to win, and you'll never win against me if you're doing nectar."

Boudi-Ca sucked her nectared finger. She heard a male grunt. She turned her floating head. The buttocks of the Djinnus jerked as he hammered and released his seed. His anonymous feminine receptacle wriggled her rear end, rose up, and pivoted to reveal her identity in victory. A tight smile painted Minnie-Ca's face. Captain Kordrag dried his phallus on the side of her skirt.

"At ease, ladies," Kordrag drawled. "I'll take five before the third round."

The voices were distant. Boudi-Ca steadied herself on her heels. The nectar was really starting to hit her. She was floating like a leaf on a pond, or like a butterfly on an updraft. She focused on the door and took a step, but she felt a tug on her arm, and she found herself in Ranavalona's arms. The ebony fledgling met her with a kiss.

Boudi-Ca opened her mouth to take Ranavalona's hot wet tongue. Desire raced through her soul. Everyone in the room was suddenly watching, including Lieutenant Nefra. Boudi-Ca felt herself being guided towards the bed. She struggled to get away, but she was falling onto her face. She was easy, she knew. She knew that Ranavalona knew.

"Boudi, are we going to see the Nanka, or not?" Henne's voice came as if through a tub of water. Boudi-Ca turned. Henne's face glowed above her. Henne's red hair sparkled as if on fire. "What have you done to her, Ranavalona? Did you give her some of my black stash?"

"No," Ranavalona said. "Not unless it got mixed in. How did you get in here?"

Henne stuck out her tongue. "I have the key to my own bedchamber. Boudi-Ca is coming with me."

"Boudi-Ca stays," Ranavalona countered. "She's joining the game for the final spot on the midnight Nanka ride with us."

Boudi-Ca struggled to get up. "I'll go with Henne."

Ranavalona sighed audibly. "Boudi, you're such a coward. I give you these opportunities to become a bona fide beauty mistress, and you let them go by. Fine."

Boudi-Ca allowed Henne to help her from the bedchamber. They descended the stairs to the foyer where, surprisingly, Ayelet was waiting. Boudi-Ca blinked. Her head was swimming, and the stripes on Ayelet's black dress seemed to sway like little yellow snakes. Despite Ayelet's abnormally elegant appearance, her visage looked typically grim.

"Would you mind driving, Henne?" Ayelet said.

"Of course not."

They left the house. Ayelet's carriage was parked down the street at the end. Boudi-Ca climbed unsteadily into the rear seat with Ayelet. Henne climbed into the front and snapped the reins. The horses surged forward. Boudi-Ca felt Ayelet's hand clasp her knee briefly before retreating.

"You look a bit out of sorts, chérie."

Boudi-Ca glanced at Ayelet. The hazel eyes of the blade mistress were like a hawk, piercing her. Henne half-turned her head, as if unsure whether to join the conversation. Boudi-Ca steadied herself against the carriage seat. The swaying trees over the road drew her attention, yet only succeeded in making her dizzy.

"You seem out of sorts too, Mistress Ayelet. With all the changes going on, I'm sure you have a lot more to worry about than I do."

Ayelet tilted her head, as if experiencing a painful memory. "I've lost a certain someone who was special to me."

"You mean your vampire lover?"

"Yes," Ayelet answered. "Barissianna is gone, fledgling, and I didn't get to say goodbye. That vexes me. I fear for Barissianna's happiness. And there is something else. Over the past months, I was having a sword made for Barissianna, a special blade to replace one that broke during our attack on the Trivium last summer. Unfortunately, I didn't have a chance to give it to her. I would like to. In fact, I intend to."

"You mean you're going after her?"

"Yes. Something such. I've made up my mind. The Auerbach left one bat that had been wounded, but I've patched it up. I'm going to try to fly it. It doesn't have a basket any more, but I've rigged something to stay on its back."

"How will you find Barissianna? Do you know where to go?"

"Barissianna showed me the location of one of their chantries on a map. I'll start there. If Barissianna isn't there, then I hope the Auerbach vampires will help me find her. If not, I might have to crack some skulls."

"Do you want me to go with you?"

Ayelet looked surprised. "No, of course not, fledgling. I mean, I'd be delighted to have your company, but I'm taking Jade Turtle. It will be good for her to get out and get her mind off of everything. I'd prefer that you stayed and focused on your blades. I did want to ask you something, however."

"What's that?"

"The wounded bat needs healing. If I can't get it off the ground, I can't fly. If I can't fly, I can't try to find Barissianna. I was wondering if you might try to heal the bat for me with your Mimọ magic."

"I'll try my best."

Ayelet smiled. "That's all anyone can ask. We'll go up there to the landing after we see the Nanka, and you can take a look. By the way, have you spoken with Masad lately?"

"No."

"You aren't going into the east with him then? I assume he's already left the Redoubt, anyway. If anyone is less loved by Hell's court than me, it's him. He gave secrets to the Mimọs and disowned his own father."

"I didn't go with him."

"Well, if that's what you want, fledgling, then so be it. The illusions and seductions of beauty can be intense. Someday you'll grow beyond such things as your wisdom deepens. Masad and I can only offer you the bread. It's your choice to eat it or cast it aside."

"Mistress, please understand. What about Violet? And besides, I think I'm in love with Henne." Boudi-Ca felt herself warming with the embarrassment of what she'd just said under the influence of the nectar. Henne was listening to the conversation.

Ayelet nodded. "Fine. Those are your choices."

"Violet can't ride a horse. She wants to write in her diary and catch butterflies, not go on the road with me and Masad."

"Did you learn anything from Masad when he visited you?"

Boudi-Ca shifted uncomfortably in the carriage seat. They were passing Isabellah's house, riding up the last street to the palace plaza. She looked up at her old bedroom window, where she'd lived for many moons with few troubles and fewer cares other than love and beauty. She looked at Henne, trying to gauge how Henne felt about her sudden declaration of love.

"Masad said that I need to choose between being a beauty mistress and a blade mistress. He said I float like a butterfly, and I don't have my feet on the ground."

Ayelet looked askance at her. "Forgive me for saying so, but your tone sounds defeated, Boudi-Ca. Do you still plan to try to complete your Mistress Test, or are you giving up?"

"I haven't given up. I'm still training almost every day with blades. I'm just not going to be able to learn from Masad. Whatever happens, happens. Masad did give me a few things to work on. I'm truly tired of worrying about it. I'm doing my best, and the rest is up to the Lady."

"Perhaps."

"Are you even coming back, Mistress Ayelet? Because if you didn't, and you took Jade Turtle with you, then maybe some of my competition-"

"I plan to come back after I see Barissianna. The Lady needs me. Jade Turtle is no longer your main competition, anyway. Lady Allyssia created the Spring Festival in times long past. It's sacred, and it's celebrated every year among the Jinni in all of Hell's biggest cities. The Hell's army soldiers won't compete, but you can expect the Smokeless Flames to dominate us in the military competitions. They don't limit the competitions to only fledglings and guests. They compete for real."

"That's bad, then."

Ayelet cleared her throat and brushed a stray strand of greying hair over her ear. "Yes. With the arrival of the Serpent Sisters, your Task of

Mastery has become ten times harder, and completely impossible if you keep wasting your days doing nectar."

Boudi-Ca felt the flush on her cheeks deepen. Ayelet spoke to her like a child. Ayelet made her feel ashamed. Ayelet had always had high hopes for her. Of all the New Order mistresses, Ayelet alone had believed that she could become something special as a Jinn.

Boudi-Ca looked away over the carriage seat. On the other hand, no amount of talent ever seemed good enough for Ayelet. She sifted through her fears as the carriage rumbled across the palace plaza. She wasn't giving up on her Mistress Test. Why did Ayelet think she was giving up?

Soon Ayelet's carriage rolled to a stop at the palace. Boudi-Ca climbed out and walked in Henne's shadow up the wide marble steps. Henne was unusually mute and solemn with her eyes lowered. They passed through the palace doors and down the short-arched entry hall to where Master Priapus stood with a stable boy.

The two males were looking at the five scaly green Nanka that lounged in Allyssia's great hall. Each creature was almost as large as a house. The Nanka were chained to the massive marble columns that supported the circular balcony of the second floor. Like their smaller bat cousins, the Nanka wore sturdy riding baskets where their long necks met their backs.

Ayelet walked forward past Henne, right up to the tail of the nearest Nanka. She stretched out her hand and touched a large scale on the Nanka's tail. Her eyes were distant, as if remembering far off places and times. Boudi-Ca crinkled her nose. She didn't want to go closer. The Nanka gave off a horrible sulfuric smell.

"Be careful, Mistress Ayelet," Henne said.

"If it tries to nibble on me," Ayelet said calmly. "It will get my blade rammed up its big nose. I'm no feed cow."

Henne nodded. "They've got all those cows out there that they brought in from the Isandlwana villages. I wonder when they feed it."

"They eat at dusk," the stable boy said from his position at the palace doors. His nervous voice sounded a pitch higher than it should have been.

"It's his job," added Master Priapus, patting the boy on the shoulder. "He helps herd five cows up the steps every morning, and he helps to clean up the messes after."

The closest Nanka snorted, apparently having ascertained that Ayelet wasn't a threat. The beast lowered its head to the marble floor. Boudi-Ca advanced a few more steps until she was side by side with Henne near a marble column. The huge ugly beasts seemed all wrong in the beautiful and peaceful palace interior. Straw had been strewn across the floor, not so much to provide comfort, but to soak up the abundance of reptilian excrement. The whole chamber smelled unpleasant.

Henne retreated from the Nanka. "It's nice to see Haawiyah Nanka again, but once you've seen them, you've seen them. I just hope they can stop the Hierarchy gloom-wraiths if those self-righteous Mimos try to attack."

"All Mimos aren't-"

Boudi-Ca gasped. Henne turned suddenly and embraced her with a daring forbidden kiss right on her lips. She held Henne for long seconds. She didn't want to let go. She could feel the warmth and energy leaping between her breasts and Henne's through the fabric of their dresses. She caught Ayelet's eyes over Henne's shoulder. Ayelet seemed pained for a second, and then the elder mistress smiled faintly and looked away.

"Boudi! I've been looking everywhere for you!" Tajee's voice broke the stillness of the moment. He was panting as he trotted into the shadows of the great hall from the bright light outside the palace. Boudi-Ca untangled herself from Henne. She felt an itch of anger. It was just like Tajee to ruin a moment.

"Tajee? What in the name of the Lady are you even doing here?"

Tajee leaned and put his hands on his knees to rest. "I've been running all the way from the house. I found the party, but Mistress Gonorrheah said you left. I was coming up here to find Master Priapus."

"Well what is it?" Priapus strode forward. "This should be interesting. What could be so important that an Ahyehass would run all over the Lady's city like a fool?"

"They took Violet," Tajee continued. "Ambassador Lydiah came to the house. She had some official-looking papers and a bunch of soldiers. She said Violet belonged to her!"

"By the Lady," Ayelet muttered. "And so it begins. The whore of Babylon rivals Allyssia herself as a bitch."

Tajee sniffed and wiped his eyes. "Ambassador Lydiah said something about the 'rules of the reunification' and stolen property. She grabbed Violet, put her in a carriage, and took her away. Violet was crying and crying!"

# Chapter 24:

Ayelet tugged the reins of the chiropterim and guided it lower. Early morning glowed over eastern Meristyian, revealing a rugged highland dotted with snow-covered peaks. The lake was visible just below. Odors of moss, algae, and fish mingled with the smell of stone. Steep basalt walls reflected black across the waters. Ayelet looked over her shoulder. Turtle was behind her, holding fast on the back of the bat.

They'd flown through the night after leaving the confines of the Redoubt far behind, and then through the day and through the night again, guided by the dim morning star on the eastern horizon and the stormy thunderheads of Erebus over the mountains to the north. They'd flown basketless, lashed to the bat's stout woven harness with leather straps.

They'd followed the line of the northern Isandlwana mountains east over the Alpacians. They'd flown over the rugged lake regions of the northern Tuskan plain and into the vampire country of the Carpathian uplands. They'd flown past the shores of the Black Sea towards the place that Barissianna had shown her one night on an old Auerbach clan map.

Ayelet clenched the reins. Her arms and hands were profoundly fatigued. She could only hope the Auerbach would prove to be willing hosts. She hungered, desperate like Turtle for an Ahyehass, tired from emotions spent through so many anxieties. It had taken hours of sustained effort to stay on the bat and hold fast against the fierce and chilling winds.

The bat, at least, seemed fine thanks to Boudi-Ca's magical healing. The healing had taken a heavy toll on the fledgling, however, who had already been devastated by the loss of her Ahyehass. Ayelet guided the bat lower with a warmth of anger at Ambassador Lydiah and the Smokeless Flames.

She almost couldn't blame the Ambassador for re-taking her Mimọ slave, but Lydiah could have restrained herself from such a cruel act for the sake of relations. Why had the Lady even permitted such a thing? Had the Lady no power left whatsoever over her own city?

Ayelet gritted her teeth. She just needed things to be resolved. She needed to know that Barissianna was safe. She needed to deliver the gift blade, and then she would return to the Redoubt, despite her personal risk as a wanted criminal, because Allyssia and Boudi-Ca needed her more than Barissianna.

The bat continued to descend in the damp pre-dawn air. Barissianna had mentioned that the chantry was in the middle of a lake, accessible only by air, and a chantry soon appeared at the place Barissianna had indicated. Hidden in a bay at one end of the great dark lake, a tower of stout black basalt rose on a stony island. A long causeway of mossy stones stretched to the tower from the base of a sheer basalt bluff at the water's edge, essentially fortifying it from a ground assault, unless the enemy brought very long ropes.

Ayelet guided the bat in a long circle around the bay, scanning for any sign of danger. Nothing moved below. The top of the tower appeared to give a trapdoor entrance, but also a very precarious landing for the tired bat. The chiropterim had barely flown even without the weight of a basket. Its wing beats were slowing, and it labored to rise.

The bat completed its circuit around the bay. The morning light revealed deep recesses under the basalt overhangs. The causeway connected the vampire tower not just to the cliffs, but also to a hidden bat landing. Ayelet guided the bat into the dark shelter of the towering rocks. A leveled area of dirt and gravel revealed itself-a bat landing under the cliff where a few other chiropterim were already parked. Ayelet drew the bat down. It dropped rapidly to a jarring stop. The bat stumbled and lowered itself to the ground, exhausted.

"This looks like the place," Turtle said nervously.

Ayelet nodded. "I just hope they aren't all asleep this morning."

The landing appeared to be deserted of vampires. Ayelet winced as she unfastened her buckles. Her legs were terribly stiff. She climbed off of the bat and paused to catch Turtle, who tiredly followed her down. The bat landing, on closer inspection, was littered with trash. Burned remnants of baskets were scattered across the sands along with piles of charred bones and bits of fur.

Ayelet rested her hand on the hilt of her blade. Her skin pricked. Amidst the charred refuse lay broken swords and muddy pieces of paper. Had the Auerbach repelled an attack? The scene almost looked like a battle had taken place, and the disturbed earth suggested the conflict had been recent. She had no answers, but she suspected she'd find some in the tower.

The causeway across the water was constructed of the same stone as the cliffs around it-black and volcanic, wide enough for two to walk abreast. Ayelet led the way to the base of the tower, which looked much larger from the ground, a monolith of defensibility. The Auerbach had done well in building it. Narrow archer slits cut the stone above the shadowed entrance, but otherwise the forbidding edifice was featureless and infenestrated.

As they approached, the heavy iron-bound portcullis went into motion with a scream of gears. Ayelet stepped back cautiously, keeping Turtle at her side. Dark figures appeared from within.

The vampires were at ease with their blades sheathed. They ducked under the rising gate and stopped just inside the shadow of the archway. Ayelet raised a hand in greeting. The vampires that faced them weren't Auerbach, she realized. The dark skin and swarthy, desiccated visages revealed them to be Disciples of Set.

Ayelet lowered her hand and slowly grasped her sword hilt. Her blood lust bubbled up on the vortex of her whirling mind. She hadn't felt her blood lust for a long time, not since her last battle with Disciple vampires.

Her blood lust was a distinct feeling. The energy welled up unbidden from her elder depths, urging her to deliver pain to the enemies of the Lady. She had to negotiate, but she had no intention of sparing any of them.

"Greetings. I'm Mistress Ayelet, representing Lady Allyssia and the Smokeless Flames. We're looking to deliver a peaceful message to Magistrada Barissianna and the Auerbach clan, but I'm perfectly willing to kill all of you instead if necessary."

One vampire inched ahead of the rest. His wrinkled visage was inscrutable. His eyes were lidded. The vampire glanced at the bright line of sunlight that traced the tops of the basalt cliffs. "Come inside, out of the light." He motioned. "We can tell you where to find the Auerbach."

Ayelet hesitated, but nothing about those rank-and-file vampires threatened her skills, even in a dark room and outnumbered. She could take them all and torture them as necessary. She stepped forward into the gloom. The lower level of the tower had once been splendorous, but now was dark and gutted. The smell of ash and charred wood was heavy on the air. Piles of debris ornamented a polished wooden floor. The vampires fanned out to face her.

"Where are the Auerbach?" Ayelet slid her sword from its sheath. "I would strongly suggest telling me immediately." The vampires looked at her and grinned. Only a slight shiver in her legs alerted her to the trap. The floor gave way. Ayelet flailed for purchase and found none. She dropped several feet into black water. She sank, but didn't find a bottom-the water pit under the tower floor was deep and cold.

Ayelet stroked strongly for the surface, but her sword weighed her. When she reached air, the lid of the pit above was closing. She heard gears grinding, accompanied by the ring of swords. The guttural death-cry of a Disciple split the air. Steel clanged on steel. Turtle had evaded the trap. She was fighting the vampires. Ayelet smiled grimly.

"Take them, Turtle! You can do it!" Her yell echoed on the pit walls, and then the trap was completely closed. Ayelet kicked her feet to tread water in the total darkness. Her hands kept hitting solid objects in the water, and a stench invaded her nostrils. The pit's former victims were keeping her company. The ringing sounds of swords went muffled, and then faded away.

Ayelet exerted an effort with one arm, summoning a small tenebris lux that lit up the mossy pit walls. She followed with a bird intended for Turtle. The bird seemed to flicker and disappear not far from her fingers. Ayelet's throat clutched. There was either no exit whatsoever from the pit, or Turtle was dead. The lid of the pit was several feet up. It was strongly bound with rusty iron and heavy wood planks. The lid was well out of reach.

She felt along the wall as she swam, searching for handholds, but she found few. She prayed silently for Turtle. She let the lux fade to conserve her strength. She treaded water in the pit for long minutes, and longer. The fatigue of the long ride heightened in her tired limbs. Finally she tried to jam her sword into the stones of the pit wall. She struck repeatedly until the sword sank into a seam of mortar. She held onto the blade to buoy herself, spitting foul water from her lips.

After a while, she relinquished the weight of her pants, her boots, and her shirt until she wore nothing but her corset. No one came, and she still heard no sound other than the lapping waves. The water was cold. Hunger gnawed at her belly. Weariness crept ever deeper into her limbs.

Ayelet held onto her sword for what seemed like an hour, then two, then three, then forever, until her corded arms felt like lead and Hunger wracked her belly. Finally she heard a sound. At first she thought she was hallucinating in some way. The dull thumps resonated in her head. With a squeal, the pit began to open. A red light sparked on high, revealing a face.

Ayelet felt her stomach knot. It was a devil, judging from the mottled, putrid color of his skin. She heard a rattle, and then a splash.

"Climb," the devil said. His voice was harsh and emotionless. "Or tie it around yourself and we'll pull you out. You can leave your sword down there. You won't be using it where we're going."

Ayelet looped the rope under her armpits. If she had to fight, even without a blade, she would need all of her remaining strength. She tied a hitch while the devil looked on.

"I'm ready."

"Pull her." The devil signaled behind him, and the rope tightened and lifted her, inch by inch, until she reached the lip of the pit. Ayelet drew herself out. She attempted to rise on shaking legs, but a strong hand on her shoulder kept her on her knees. She gathered herself, dripping water on the floor. Behind her, the valves of the pit reversed again and began to close.

Ayelet recognized the handsome bearded male who smirked at her in the low light of a red tenebris lux. He was no ordinary devil. He was Archduke Yitzhak himself, a general in Hell's army, one of the most powerful sons of the dread Lord Hades.

Yitzhak wore a long black robe and a blade in a gilded, rubied sheath. He was accompanied by a half dozen Smokeless Flames assassins in their customary red robes and wide sashes striped with gold and black bars. A Disciple of Set vampire rounded out the assembly. Ayelet tried to hide her feeling of disgust.

"Archduke Yitzhak. It's a pleasure to see you."

The archdevil peered at her and stroked his beard. "Mistress Ayelet, you're rather wet and bedraggled, but I never forget a face."

"Where is my fledgling? Where is Jade Turtle?"

"She's fine, but she's a quiet type, unfortunately for her. Perhaps you'll be more forthcoming. What you doing here? You expected to see the Auerbach. What did you want with them? Are you carrying a message to your old allies, perhaps? Is this a secret plan carried out by Lady Allyssia? Is this plotting and skullduggery?"

"I came to visit a friend. That's all. Where are the Auerbach?"

The Archduke smoothed his robe nonchalantly. "They are not here. I ask you again, why did you come looking for them, Mistress Ayelet?"

"I told you. I'm on a personal mission to visit Magistrada Barissianna, a close female friend of mine."

Yitzhak pursed his lips with an air of annoyance. "Sadly for you, this chantry was captured a few days ago after the Auerbach left the Lady's city in western Meristyian. The Auerbach were tracked here and defeated by a well-organized force of Jinni and Djinnus led by myself and assisted by the Disciples of Set. The Auerbach clan leadership was wiped from Meristyian. We've had forces in Meristyian secretly for some time now, and a pair of trackers have been watching the Redoubt for the last year since we determined its location. All of that boiled down to the destruction of another vampire clan that refuses to properly recognize the rule of Lord Hades in this place."

"Well, good for you." Ayelet gritted her cold jaw. She couldn't believe Yitzhak's words. It was unlikely that even Archduke Yitzhak could wipe out Prince Amanoch and his small legion of vampires, unless they were tired, hungering, and taken by surprise.

"So I ask again, Mistress Ayelet," Yitzhak continued. "With the reunification, you serve Lady Allyssia once again. Why not tell me everything, in good faith, and I might let you go home."

"I'll consider it." Ayelet gathered her feet under her. She gauged the distance to the open door and the night beyond. Six Serpent Sisters stood ready to stop her. Even if she'd had her weapons and full strength, she wouldn't be able to get past them before Yitzhak unleashed the full power of his devil magic. She wished in that moment for Boudi's flashing ability.

Yitzhak motioned with his mottled hand. "Please get back on your knees, Ayelet. If you won't cooperate willingly, I'm going to have you cuffed. These are difficult times, and I'm sure you understand." He motioned to the vampire. "Nazim? A double cuff please. She's very strong."

"With pleasure, Archduke Yitzhak." The vampire produced a pair of heavy manacles.

Ayelet stood up and backed away over the closed lid of the pit. She had no intention of getting cuffed. "The Jinni are reunified as you said, Yitzhak. We are allies against Heaven, not enemies. Our treaty agreed that all prisoners will be released and exchanged. That implies that no more should be taken."

Yitzhak smiled. "Come now, Ayelet. You're a murderer. You killed three of your own sisters during the separatist movement so many years ago. Or was it four? You've also killed a fair number of devils. Hell's Court isn't happy about that."

"My count stands at seven Jinn deaths on my hands, twice as many devils, and four times as many Disciples of Set. You haven't considered the skirmish at the Temple of Sekhmet, where Mistress Enneamiah was presiding. I'll seek forgiveness from Lord Hades when the time is proper. It's my belief that the agreement of the Jinn reunification should render those crimes unpunishable."

Yitzhak shook his head. "Nonetheless, I'm afraid you'll have to be held for the time being, along with your fledgling. Now please get back down on your knees, unless you want to fight us without a weapon."

"I want to see my fledgling." Ayelet clasped her hands behind her back. She had no choice. The vampire named Nazim approached and cuffed her.

"You'll see your fledgling," Yitzhak murmured coldly. "I'm taking you to her. Nazim, lead us to the bat. Sisters, please take the rear."

Ayelet tested the manacles on her wrists. They were solid steel. She watched the key disappear into the vampire's pouch. The vampire Nazim, she noted, didn't appear overly excited about taking directions from the Archduke. She filed the knowledge away for future reference.

She padded barefoot through the open portcullis with Yitzhak's hand pressed against her back. The devil's red tenebris lux illuminated a floor stained with sticky fresh bloodstains, and then they were walking down the causeway in the night. Two bats with ladders waited at the end of the causeway. Ayelet eyed the nearest ladder.

"Sorry Yitzhak, but I can't climb cuffed like this."

"Yes. Nazim, if you please?"

Ayelet felt the vampire's cold hands fumble with her wrists. One cuff came free. She gripped the chain in her hand and swung. Yitzhak was taken by surprise. The heavy iron ring thudded into his temple. Ayelet backpedaled, but the vampire Nazim was quick, seizing her by her wet corset. She sent an elbow into his midsection, a vicious blow that elicited not even a grunt from the undead. She escaped the vampire with a drop and roll. She was free. The vampire's sword hadn't even cleared its sheath.

Ayelet dove headfirst towards the dark waters, but she jerked sickeningly short. A Flames-Sisterhood narcabyss whip had snagged around her ankle.

She kicked, trying to free it, but numbness filled her calf, and then her foot. The whip dragged her back onto the gravel of the causeway. Another whip snapped around her leg, and a third around her arm. The Serpent Sisters braced themselves. Ayelet groaned as the numbness spread through every inch of her flesh. She surrendered against the horrible cords, and the Smokeless-Flames Sisters reeled her in like a fish, chuckling amongst each other.

"And this after I tried to be civil," Yitzhak said, examining his fingernails. "I expected better from you, Ayelet. I assume you've heard of an ebon collar? I brought one in case things got out of hand. Hold her."

"We have her, Archduke," growled one of the Smokeless-Flame Sisters. "She's weak."

Ayelet numbly kneed Yitzhak's groin, but he only grinned, as if he'd actually enjoyed the painful impact. Ayelet spat as the cold metal collar closed around her neck. She immediately felt strange, constricted, and pacified when the collar locked. It was a strange and hopeless feeling, and she suddenly knew how Turtle had felt.

A stubby ebon wand appeared in Yitzhak's hand. Ayelet clutched at the collar, which became hot. Her head went buzzing, then painful. She could scarcely think, much less resist. She felt herself being pulled to her feet. Yitzhak directed the ebon wand at the ladder.

"Disobey me and you'll feel the real pain, Ayelet," the devil said. "One flick of the wand in your direction will incapacitate you. I'm giving you fair warning. Now get onto the bat, bitch."

Ayelet focused and climbed the ladder slowly. Nazim guided her into the rear seat, where he settled next to her. Yitzhak took the reins. Ayelet shook her head to clear the cobwebs. The ebon collar didn't affect her when the matching ebon wand wasn't close to it. The bat flapped its wings, and soon it was gliding over the lake, swooping above the cliffs towards the mountains beyond. The crescent moon was bright in the sky. The bat wheeled around a peak, and the stars tipped.

Ayelet struggled to remain alert. The air was frigid on her bare skin, and soon she was shivering uncontrollably. The vampire cast sidelong glances at the swells of her breasts over the rim of her corset. She leaned back to put them on display. Her eyes kept straying, despite herself, to the vampire's pants. She was so hollow, so desperate to feed. How many days had she been without an Ahyehass?

After some hours, the bat dipped into a descent, increasing its speed until the wind whistled through the woven basket. The beast swooped over open country, then barreled down a steep-walled valley. Low cliffs rose on both sides. At the end of the valley, the bat flew straight at a cliff wall. A hidden cave entrance revealed itself at the last second. The bat shuddered to a stop inside the cave under a clump of broken stalactites. The second bat, which had been following them, swooped in carrying the group of Smokeless-Flame Sisters. The air in the cave was warmer with the light of several burning torches.

"Home sweet home, Ayelet," Archduke Yitzhak said jovially.

"Where are we?" Ayelet managed. "Is this northern Persium? Is this a Disciples of Set stronghold?"

"We are in Dead Sedde," the devil answered. "It's a very ancient place. Nazim, please help Mistress Ayelet down, if you will."

Ayelet allowed the vampire to guide her to the ladder and down. Her legs wobbled as the Disciple guided her across the uneven cave floor, followed by Yitzhak. A set of worn steps led down into the bowls of the living rock. The air warmed still further as they descended. The passage opened into a smooth-hewn underground chamber with a table. Another vampire greeted them from a chair.

"Is this the other, Archduke?" the vampire croaked.

"What does she look like to you, Harmud?" Yitzhak answered. "A dinner guest? Where is Mistress Astaarteh?"

"She's down below, still interrogating the other one. I imagine she has cracked, but she hadn't when I went to check last."

"Or maybe she is stupid and just doesn't know anything," Yitzhak said with a roll of his eyes. "Why must I always do everything myself? I'll take Ayelet down. She's ebon collared, so I'm perfectly safe."

"That's good, Archduke. We were so worried for you." The vampire named Harmud snickered. "The keys are on the hook."

Ayelet felt Yitzhak's gloved hand on the back of her neck, applying pressure on the rim of her collar. She stumbled forward down a long flight of stone steps under a low barrel-vaulted ceiling. The hall widened at the bottom to allow a row of large barred cells to either side. Jade Turtle knelt nude in one cell, chained to a ring in the center of the floor by her ebon collar. Ayelet swallowed. She recognized Mistress Astaarteh. The ancient elder daughter of Allyssia sat on a low stool with her long legs and slender hooves splayed commandingly around Turtle's bent, naked figure.

Jade Turtle raised her head. "Mistress Ayelet! Mistress!"

"Gag her, Astaarteh," Yitzhak said coldly. "She's done."

Astaarteh smiled. "Of course, Archduke. I'll find something suitable."

Ayelet clenched her fists, but she could do nothing. Both of her captors were sorcerers, older and more powerful than her. Yitzhak led her to the corner cell and pushed her inside. Beyond, the hall widened into a larger chamber. Peculiar odors of herbs and chemicals wafted on the air.

"Yitzhak?" Astaarteh approached. "The fledgling is gagged. Do you need help?"

"Yes. Get me cords and a long bar. I want two phalluses and a pair of scarab clamps. I'm going to break Ayelet. I tried to be nice, but Ayelet will need some persuading."

Ayelet clenched her manacled fists together with an effort to strike, but Yitzhak was ready with the ebon wand. The collar burned around her neck and her head blanked. She collapsed immediately to the floor. She was weak. She was so weak.

"Don't do this. Please."

"Consider it done," the archdevil replied. He kicked her in the stomach. Ayelet grunted. The pain shocked her abdomen, and she fell to her elbows. Yitzhak crouched, reached under her, and raised the floor chain to lock her collar, holding her poised with her face inches away from the dirty stones. Yitzhak had produced a knife. Ayelet felt the cool blade run up her spine, cutting her corset laces. The devil pulled the corset away.

"Very nice," Yitzhak said with obvious pleasure. "I'm looking forward to working with your flesh, Ayelet. I'm glad to have you here so much sooner than I expected. You saved my Nankariders a trip."

"What do you mean? You planned this for me all along? A swift justice, a quick run through a hastily made court, and a dire punishment decided for my crimes?"

"Nothing that elaborate." Yitzhak chuckled. "The plan is to evacuate the Redoubt of all New Order Jinni. I need the houses for my soldiers."

"That wasn't the agreement."

Yitzhak reached under her and pinched her nipples firm. His long fingernails bit. "There's no harm in telling you now. You see, my father has decided that He doesn't really want the New Order Jinni back in Allyssia's fold. They're more trouble than they're worth-a lot of paperwork in the Court, ill will, and bickering over their assets in both Mer and Meristyian. Of course all of the New Order mistresses are criminals. Meanwhile, my father and I have a special project that needs strong subjects for experimentation."

Ayelet grunted. Yitzhak's pinches had found the undersides of her breasts. His cruel fingers worried at her skin, digging and probing back and forth, as if testing and mapping the sensitivity of her tissues. "Experiments? What are you talking about?"

Yitzhak leaned so close that she could smell his sulfurous breath. "cirai, my dear Ayelet. cirai. We've taken the secret from the Disciples of Set, as was our plan all along when we drew up the alliances with them. My father wants this for himself. It's the knowledge of my father's father after all-Kronos. Astaarteh and I have task of unravelling the working procedures for cirai-learning to use it on all types of beings, not just vampires. We might like to use it on Jinni, for example."

Astaarteh approached the cell with a tray. Yitzhak sat back and accepted it. Ayelet struggled to summon what Barissianna had told her about cirai. It was the art of soul-stealing, of extinguishing the essence of one soul and infusing it into another. Horror welled in her belly, even Yitzhak dumped warm oil over her buttocks and her sex.

The length of a metal bar slid across her calves, followed by cords. Her legs were pulled apart to form a tripod. Hands reached under to apply the clamps to her nipples, which forming an electrical circuit with her sex, where Yitzhak's fingers had begun to probe.

The fingers of the devil stroked her, pulling forth pleasure from her hollow, numb depths. Her Jinn Hunger burned still hotter in her belly. Her yearning to be filled was moving to an animal place, a place beyond words. Through the many sets of cell bars, she could see Jade Turtle watching with a gag in her mouth.

"You're going to do cirai on Jinni?" Ayelet managed. "You're going to experiment on the New Order?"

"You told her, Yitzhak?" Astaarteh said Sharply.

"I couldn't resist, dear," the devil replied. "She won't escape to tell anyone, and it's better if she knows what's happening. She'll suffer so much more."

"The Lady will find out," Ayelet growled.

"Not likely," Yitzhak said. "Ambassador Lydiah and Commander Befanah themselves don't even know. No one knows except me, my father, Allyssia and Astaarteh. The Nanka riders will fly the New Order mistresses out of the Redoubt with the supposed plan of taking them to their new homes in Haawiyah. They'll land at an intermediary camp where I will divert them here. They'll be confused. We'll arrange long delays so they're weak from their Hunger, just like you."

"And you call the New Order Jinni betrayers," Ayelet spat. "The Lady will stop you and your lies. She will stop you!"

"She will stop no one. I'm not called the Great Deceiver for nothing, Ayelet." Yitzhak chuckled. "Give me some credit. Once the registry of New Order mistresses and fledglings has been made, the Redoubt will be declared too dangerous for the New Order to stay, and then the abductions will unfold."

Ayelet winced. Yitzhak was working her harder. His filed fingernails bit into her innermost flesh. She turned her head to the limits of the chain on her neck. She tried to catch Astaarteh's eye. "You're in favor of this, Astaarteh? Allyssia will subject her own Jinni to this? What of the reunification and joining the two orders together again in good faith?"

Astaarteh didn't answer. Ayelet winced when Astaarteh's hand slapped her face. Astaarteh swung again. Ayelet felt her legs tremble when a blunt implement nosed at her anus. Yitzhak pushed it in. She felt the inevitable wave of intense weakness, followed by the wetness. Astaarteh continued to slap her face back and forth, raining cruel blows. Ayelet blinked and tried to hold back the tears, but her eyes were wetting like her nethers.

She could no longer contain her desperation when Yitzhak penetrated her. She closed her eyes and moaned open-mouthed. He worked her slowly at first, then pressed his thrusts deeper and deeper, tearing her tissues with every backstroke. His thick barbed cock slowly conducted her body into a protracted orgasm of both pleasure and pain-a roaring blackness, an unstoppable wave.

Chapter 25:

Tajee quietly eavesdropped on the dark basement stairs. The heat from the fire that smoldered in the training room drifted up the warm stairwell. He could clearly hear the discussion between the three fledglings.

"They're taking over everything," Boudi-Ca said. "I hate them! Mistress Gallinah sent me a bird to warn me to lock my doors. The soldiers snuck into Hatshepseh's house across the street and raped her, and Mistress Juliah was raped too. I can only imagine what horrible things Lydiah is doing with Violet."

Tajee put his hands on his head. More than two weeks had passed since Violet had been taken away, and Boudi-Ca was still crying on the shoulder of anyone who would listen. He couldn't blame her. He felt more or less the same way. He heard Ranavalona's sultry, edgy voice.

"It could be a lot worse, Boudi. Ambassador Lydiah is a high-ranking official in Hell's Court. Violet has a good chance for a nice, pampered slave life."

Henne's lilting, more pacifying voice followed. "She's right. Violet will be living in style. She'll have the best of everything."

"She'll have the best nectar," Ranavalona added. "She'll have the highest quality slave cage and whips for that soft skin. And then there is Lydiah's husband, Archduke Fennel. Violet might be intended as a fresh gift of flesh for him."

"By the Lady, Ranavalona, stop being cruel!" Henne's voice was Sharp. "I've had it with you. Just because Boudi-Ca isn't crying today doesn't mean she's ready for twisted humor."

"I was just telling the truth."

"It's worse that Lydiah is a beauty mistress," Boudi-Ca said with her voice muffled. "It makes it personal, like she's so much better than me. And she is, of course."

"Just let it go, Boudi," Henne said. "To survive, you have to adapt. You have to turn every situation to best advantage. You have to move on."

"Nonsense, Henne." Ranavalona said. "She needs to keep fighting and clawing."

"I'm going to fail anyway and become a slave." Boudi's voice broke into a sob. Tajee took a deep breath and hugged himself on the step. In all of the time that he'd known Boudi, both in Heaven and in Meristyian, he'd never seen her so sad. In the two weeks that had passed since that fateful afternoon, Boudi-Ca had been inconsolable. He'd tried to comfort her, but she'd pushed him away. When she took him to her bed out of Jinn necessity, she hardly spoke to him.

Boudi's sadness had reawaken the depths of his love for her. She was afraid, vulnerable, and uncertain, just like in Heaven. Even her emotional rejections also reminded him of Heaven again. The voices had begun anew in the training room below, in lower tones. Tajee crept a few more steps towards the bottom of the stair, just out of sight of the three fledglings.

"Why won't you talk with Isabellah, Boudi?" Henne was saying. "Maybe she could use some of her influence. Maybe if we all move to Haawiyah, Isabellah could petition the Court for you to-"

"I can't talk to her," Boudi-Ca snapped. "I'm humiliated enough as it is. Isabellah told me all along the Prince was bad news, and she was right. If I'd never gone to the ball and caught the Prince's eyes, none of this would have happened. Now my chances of passing my Mistress Test have gone from small to nothing. Violet is probably on her knees right now in Lydiah's bedchamber, and soon I'll be on my knees too when the Lady makes me into a slave."

"So what?" Ranavalona drawled. "Go back to Isabellah and admit you were wrong. At least have the guts to do that much."

"She's too proud to go to Isabellah," Henne said. "Boudi's fate is in the hands of the Lady anyway, not Isabellah."

Boudi-Ca sighed audibly. "I wish Ayelet were here."

"Ayelet isn't here," Ranavalona said.

"Maybe someone should go and try to find her. She wasn't supposed to be gone for weeks. I'm worried."

"Ayelet fled the city because she's afraid. She assassinated a few people for the Lady during the schism of the Jinn orders," Henne said. "She also slaughtered a bunch of devils who tried to apprehend her while she was recruiting for the New Order down in Mer. The Hell's Court devils never forgive or forget. No one talks about it, but everyone knows it. Ayelet claimed it was love, but she had other motives for getting out of this city-the huge bounties on her head."

"Ayelet wouldn't lie to me. She went to find Barissianna, not to hide from anything. She told me she'd be back."

"Well, she'll come back then."

"Maybe I should go ask Masad for help. At least I could get my training and still try to place in blades at the festival, even if I fail every other part of my test."

"Boudi," Ranavalona said. "There are only four moons left before the Festival. There isn't much time left to go into the east, and you don't even know where Masad is."

"I think I do," Boudi-Ca said breezily. "I'm going to do it. I'm going into the east to find Prince Masad, and I'm going alone. And he'll either help me, or he won't. If he will, then I'll be in his debt. If he won't, then it will be a nice trip on one of Ayelet's horses into werewolf territory. I don't have Violet anymore, so why not."

"Sure. You should do that." Ranavalona laughed.

Henne sighed audibly. "The Redoubt is closed, and the gates are heavily guarded. The soldiers aren't letting anyone leave the city. Please don't try to leave, Boudi."

"Do you have any idea what it's been like the last two weeks without Violet, Henne? I have nothing here, except you. I don't have a mistress. I don't have an Ahyehass. There's no way I can pass my Mistress Test. The Old Order and Hell's soldiers have taken over the Redoubt, and I hate them. The soldiers stare at me everywhere I go. When I go outside my door, I'm afraid I'm going to get raped like Mistress Hatshepseh. They're coming for me next. I can't stand it anymore. I have to do something."

"Boudi, you're distraught," Henne said. "You aren't thinking straight. If you're lonely, I'll ask Nili if you can come stay with us. What do you think of that? We can make a spare room for you, at least until they ship us back to Haawiyah, if they decide to."

"What do you mean? Who is going to Haawiyah?"

"There is a rumor that the city might be too dangerous for civilians to stay here," Ranavalona said. "The forces of Heaven are expected to attack. The Smokeless Flames has a list of everyone in the Redoubt, and they are talking about flying us all back to Haawiyah. That's what I heard from Szenes, who heard it from Master Priapus."

"Nili is furious," Henne said. "The Old Order promised we could stay, and now they might force us out of our homes. There's nothing we can do. Nili sent a bird to the Lady, but the Lady hasn't answered yet."

"Well, if this doesn't happen until spring, then we'll still have a Spring Festival," Boudi-Ca said. "I could ride over the mountains to Masad, train, and get back in plenty of time to at least try at blades."

"The gates are watched at all hours by Djinnus and Smokeless-Flame Sisters," Ranavalona said. "Sorry, but Henne is right. You can't leave. Henne and I would miss you, too."

"Well, I don't think either of you is my Hierophant."

"Hiero-huh-what?" Ranavalona said.

"Her Hierophant," Henne said. "Remember the love spell she cast last summer? Boudi-Ca is still waiting for him or her to show up."

Tajee shifted on the step. His heart thumped uncomfortably in his chest.

He could hear Ranavalona muttering. "Let's get the purple-violet out. Come over by the fire, Boudi."

"You know, I think I just want to be alone," Boudi-Ca said tensely. "You two go ahead and enjoy yourselves with each other like I know you want to."

"Boudi-"

Tajee heard footsteps, accompanied by a stifled sob that sounded like Boudi. He leapt to his feet and tiptoed up the stairs. He started into the storage room, but he veered at the last second and sprinted up to Boudi's bedchamber instead. A single candle guttered on the nightstand. Boudi's bedclothes were rumpled and unkempt. Tajee slipped into the bed as Boudi's footsteps ascended the stairs.

He pretended to be asleep, waiting for her. She entered, flopped down, and lay alongside him as if dead. Her eyes were closed, and strands of her fine honey-Brunette hair were stuck to the dampness of the tears on her cheeks. Tajee dared to touch her shoulder.

"I love you, Boudi. Please don't be sad."

Boudi-Ca opened her eyes a fraction. "We've come a long way together, Tajee. I'm glad you're still here with me. You're the only one who has always been loyal to me, no matter what. It looks like it's all going to end in a few moons though. My Mistress Test is hopeless. I've failed every task, really, or I'm going to."

"Surely there's something you can do?"

"I went to the palace and argued with Ambassador Lydiah. She was rude. She wouldn't even listen to me. I sent her some birds, asking her to reconsider, but she ignored me. I have to have an Ahyehass to pass my Mistress Test, Tajee."

"I wish I could be your Ahyehass."

"You were already trained by Golda. There isn't a single untrained Ahyehass in this city, and I can't leave the city to look for one because of the soldiers. I have no clue what to do. I should have left with Masad. I should have taken his offer to train me. I thought I'd just be fighting Turtle. I didn't realize that I'd be competing against Lieutenant Nefra and all of the Smokeless Flames assassins."

"Tell him you changed your mind."

"Masad left, like Ayelet. He went back to the east. He's living with the werewolves. I could go find him and take him up on his offer, but I can't leave the city. Everything is sealed by the soldiers. None of the New Order Jinni are allowed to leave."

Tajee grimaced. "I might know a secret way out."

"You're imagining things, Tajee."

"No, I'm not. I don't know about getting a horse down there, but when Herpessenia stole me from Golda the year before last, we left the Redoubt with Mistress Ivanka through a secret passage."

"A passage? Where?"

"It starts in a house and goes underground to a trail in the chasm outside the Redoubt. It was night by the time we got outside, and I was kind of terrified, so I wasn't paying too much attention. They had a huge Nanka waiting with a riding basket on its back. We all climbed in, and off we went, flying away from the city."

"Where is this house?"

"I'm not exactly sure. The house was at the end of a twisty street, and it was big, dark and empty. The houses were really tall and close together, and they were three stories, not two like yours. There were sculptures and balconies."

Boudi's silver-umber eyes brightened. "That's probably the Divinity District. The District is up on the edge of the city, so I guess it makes sense. Would you know the house if I took you to it?"

"Maybe."

"And you think someone could take a horse through?"

"Maybe."

"Well think, Tajee! Yes, or no? Can a horse fit into the passage?"

"There are stairs. Can horses go down stairs?"

Boudi-Ca stared into space for long minutes. Tajee watched her. Boudi-Ca was next to him, close on her bed with her leg against his. He loved her, and she was finally talking to him. Everything was perfect in that moment.

He wasn't sure if he should have told her about the passage, but he wanted to help.

"I don't know what to do, Tajee. I've thought about going and seeking out Masad, and taking him up on his offer after all, but I was never really serious. With the city closed down by the occupation, it was impossible. If I could go into the east and find Masad, then I might be able to find an Ahyehass too. My Mistress Test could still be saved. I could also visit Golda. What do you think?"

"I know you'll do what's right for you, Boudi. And I want you to be happy. I love you. I'd kind of like to see Golda too." Tajee looked at her, and she looked back at him. Her eyes glistened in the shadow cast across her face by her honey-Brunette hair.

Boudi-Ca leaned and kissed him. Her breath was heavy. Tajee shifted closer to her, and she let him. In that moment, he'd never felt closer to Boudi. He'd come so far to be lying with her on her Jinn bed. Deep in the house, down in the basement, Henne cried out with sounds of pleasure. Boudi-Ca closed her eyes tightly, as if feeling pain, and rolled away.

"I'm going to pack. Get dressed, Tajee. Take your heaviest hat and coat. Go to the stable and saddle the pony. We're going to find your secret passage with a quick stop at Ayelet's stable to switch my pony for a real horse."

Tajee quickly slipped into his trousers and shirt. He found his hat and coat in the storage room. He descended into the cold stable. He could hear Ranavalona-Ca and Henne-Ca in the adjacent basement room through the thin walls of the metal ash chute. The two fledglings were still enjoying each other. He worked to saddle the pony.

Boudi-Ca entered the stable within minutes. She handed him a large bundle of fabric in which she'd hidden her travel pack, including her sword and fighting knife. He followed her on foot with the bundle as she drove the pony up the hill to Ayelet's Villa in the moonlight.

Tajee waited while Boudi-Ca worked in Ayelet's stable, bathed in the glow of her magical Jinn light. She transferred her clothes, diary, and other belongings into the saddlebags of a great stallion. He followed again on foot as Boudi-Ca led the way down the opposite side of Ayelet's hill into the heart of the city. They met an Djinnus patrol that eyed them but said nothing. They met a second patrol as the road turned through a pair of massive open gates.

"Where are you going?" grunted one of the armored Djinnus soldiers.

"It's a delivery from the workshops," Boudi-Ca said sweetly. "We just finished these curtains and appurtenances. I know it's late, but we're working hard to get the Divinity District refurnished for more barracks for you boys."

The Djinnus nodded and drank in Boudi's body with his silvery eyes. "On your way then, sweet thing. I'll hope to see you later at the Pandocheion, or maybe in a dark and lonely street. Either way works for me."

Tajee kept his eyes carefully lowered in front of the Djinnus. He was impressed by Boudi's deception. Her lie had passed as smoothly as silk. He followed Boudi-Ca up a steeply climbing street with extravagant houses that looked familiar.

As they climbed, the memory of that fateful night with Herpessenia returned to him, and when he drew up to the house near the end of the street, he felt almost certain it was the one. He remembered the wide walk where Herpessenia had stood and where Mistress Artemisiah had levelled her bow and launched lightning bolts. Boudi-Ca was gazing at him closely.

"Is this the house?"

"I think so," Tajee answered.

Boudi-Ca peered into the dark, unadorned windows. Her breath steamed the elevated mountain air. "It looks like it's still empty, thankfully. The hedges haven't been tended in forever. You say the passage is inside, Tajee?"

"Yes. We went straight down the front hall into a large square room. There was a big opening in the floor. I can show you."

"No. If the soldiers know about this, they have guards."

Boudi-Ca slipped off of her horse, handed him the reins, and went to the front door. She tested the handle. It didn't turn. Boudi-Ca disappeared suddenly, leaving an empty patio bathed in moonlight. A few minutes later, the door opened, and Boudi-Ca emerged with a smile.

"Give me the stallion, Tajee. Thank you so much for showing me. You're sweet."

Tajee frowned. Conflicting emotions roiled in his chest. Boudi-Ca was about to leap again into the unknown, just like when she'd joined the Conclave, only to be abducted from Heaven. On that occasion, she'd gotten herself into trouble so deep that she'd never gotten out of it.

"Please, Boudi. Take me with you."

"I'm not taking you with me, Tajee. You'll slow me down. When I'm gone, I'll expect you to not tell anyone. Go back to the house, and if anyone comes to the door, tell them I'm still very upset about Violet, and I don't want to see anyone. That's the truth, so you won't be lying. Can I count on you?"

"Boudi-Ca I-"

"If you love me, and you're still devoted to me, then you'll do as I ask."

"Yes, Mistress. When will you come back?"

"I don't know. I could be back soon if I can't get my werewolf-friend whistle to work. I didn't hear anything when I blew it a while ago in my room. First I have to get over the Alpacian mountains somehow in this cold. Hand me my sword and knife, Tajee. I can't stand here talking with you. A patrol might come up the road."

Tajee unwrapped the bundle of cloth. He handed the blades with their sheaths and straps to Boudi. "You're going to be cold in just a dress."

"No, I won't. I'll be wearing your warm hat and your coat, Tajee. Hand me those too. You'll run back past the Djinnus and say we forgot something at the workshops. Then you'll lock yourself in my house and hide."

Tajee felt a faint warmth of anger, but he did as Boudi-Ca asked. Boudi-Ca leaned and gave him a last lingering kiss on his lips, and then she stole his coat and transferred his hat to her head. "I'm not leaving for good. I'll be back in March for the Spring Festival to complete my Test. This is just something I have to do. I'm going to miss you."

"What about Henne-Ca and Ranavalona-Ca?"

For a moment, sadness crossed Boudi's face. "Henne won't fall in love with me because she thinks I'm going to fail and become a slave. I'll show her, and I'll show Ranavalona. I'll show everyone. I'll pass my test. If I can't, then I'll just have to leave the Lady forever and live in exile like Masad."

"Boudi-"

Tajee watched Boudi-Ca disappear into the dark house with her horse and gear. The tip of her sword clinked on the marble doorframe. She closed the door behind her without another word. He had the urge to run after her. He wanted to beg her to take him with her. He couldn't bear the possibility of never seeing her again. He finally hugged himself against the cold, turned, and walked alone down the steep twisting street.

He ran into another patrol of Djinnus soldiers, but they left him alone, to his relief. He made his way quickly down the eastern side of the city back to Boudi's house. He re-entered through the stable. He peeked down the basement stairs. Henne and Ranavalona had left, leaving the training room empty. He locked the doors, descended into the basement, and curled up on the warm reed mats in front of the dying fire. He slept.

~*~

Tajee awoke to a pounding on the house door. He ignored it, hoping it would go away. Morning light shone through the basement half-windows, which gave onto sunken wells at street level. The pounding at the front door continued. A bird swooped into the room then and landed on his shoulder. At first his heart leapt, but the bird wasn't Boudi's. It was Henne's voice that spoke.

Tajee, where are you?

Another bird swept into the room. The bird spoke with Ranavalona's voice.

We know you're in there. Open the door, Tajee, or else.

Tajee ascended to the foyer. He slid back the bolts on the front door and pulled it open. Henne and Ranavalona stood on the step. He put on his best innocent face. "Boudi-Ca is sad about Violet and doesn't want to come out."

Henne looked sternly at him. "You're lying, Tajee. Boudi-Ca isn't here. If she was, my messenger birds to her wouldn't be fizzling. What happened? Where is she?"

"I can't believe you dragged me out of bed for this nonsense, Henne." Ranavalona looked tired and annoyed. "Tell us where Boudi-Ca is, Ahyehass."

Tajee quailed. "I?I can't tell you. I promised her I wouldn't tell."

"So she's alright, at least? Tell us details, Tajee. Where is she?" Ranavalona pushed past him into the foyer. Henne followed with a faint pleasant wave of flowery perfume. Henne closed the door, and the two fledglings stared him down in the half-light and silence.

"Fine, but you have to promise not to tell anyone. Boudi-Ca left the Redoubt. There's a secret passage that I know about. I showed her. She had a horse and her sword. She was talking about Masad and werewolves."

Henne put her fists to her temples. "Oh, no. Lady help us."

"Tajee," Ranavalona said. "If Commander Befanah and Yitzhak's brute brigade find out that Boudi-Ca left the Redoubt against the rules, and even worse if they think Boudi-Ca went looking for Masad or Ayelet, Boudi-Ca could be in big trouble. Huge big trouble."

"Bigger than big," Henne said. "I was thinking last month when Boudi-Ca was talking about Ayelet that I was glad Boudi-Ca wasn't Ayelet's fledgling anymore, because it would be bad for her. If they think Boudi-Ca is in league with Ayelet somehow-"

"This is probably worse," Ranavalona added. "I wonder how long it will take them to catch on to her being gone. Does Boudi-Ca get birds from anyone but us, Tajee?"

"Mistress Gallinah sends Boudi-Ca birds about her Mimo clothes and things, but not much lately, and not every day."

Ranavalona shook her head. "Gallinah will sniff this out right quick, Henne. Gallinah is the biggest gossip in the city, and probably in all of Meristyian."

Henne pursed her lips, and her perfectly plucked red-gold eyebrows scrunched. "We need to throw Gallinah off the scent. What if we went to the workshops and mentioned to Gallinah that Boudi-Ca is so deeply depressed about Violet that she's closed down all of her messenger bird slits to mourn. She doesn't want to see a soul. It's the only way to explain to Gallinah why her birds aren't getting answered."

Ranavalona grinned mischievously. "I like the direction you're thinking, Henne, but surely we can do better. Let's spread some serious misleading rumors around this screwed up little city. Meanwhile, Tajee will close the slits and lock the house up, and not answer the door. Can you even handle that, boy? If you're answering the door already and blurting out where Boudi-Ca went, without us even torturing you, I'm worried about Boudi's future."

## Chapter 26:

Ambassador Lydiah knelt before Archduke Yitzhak with her eyes lowered to the folds of his black cloak. She thrust one hand down into the cold Isandlwana snow. In all of her centuries as a Jinn in Hell, she'd never knelt in snow. She needed to focus. Her conversation with the archdevil was one of the most important of her career. The stressful months of winter had worn her down, but she couldn't allow fatigue to get in the way of her ambitions. She couldn't make any mistakes.

"You may rise, Ambassador." Yitzhak's devil voice was silken, sibilant.

Lydiah rose and brushed the snow from her sleeve. She could feel the power of Yitzhak in her every pore, although his power seemed diluted in the rarified Isandlwana sunlight and altitude. She couldn't help but feel aroused by the archdevil. He was alluring despite his urine-yellow skin, which was blotched like her husband's with the burgundy stains of his devil-magic. She knew well how the devil aspects of Lord Hades could turn a Jinn into a week-kneed female. Her husband, Archduke Fennel, was very much like his brother.

Archduke Yitzhak examined his black nails, aware of his effect on her, but uncaring. He had no intention of planting his sister-in-law's ass on the rocky crown of a mountaintop. Yitzhak had taken her on wyrmback away from the city not for the beautiful view, but because he had something important to say, away from Allyssia's eavesdropping ears.

"Is everything ready?" Yitzhak asked. "Are we ready to transport the first group of New Order out of the city this morning?"

"Yes, sir. Mistress Melkeh, Mistress Szenes, and her fledgling Ranavalona-Ca are ready with their five so-called Ahyehasi in accordance with the schedule."

"The humans are slaves. We will refer to them that way."

"As you wish, sir. Were you planning to attend the seeing-off ceremony in the palace plaza? I understand that many of the New Order Jinni will be there. They might appreciate the gesture."

"I will attend," the archdevil answered. "Only because I'll escort the transport group in a third Nanka. It's a slight alteration of the process approved by our Lord."

Lydiah nodded respectfully and tried not to betray her concern. She'd worked for three months to set up every detail to re-integrate the New Order Jinni back into Haawiyah, negotiating the vast and treacherous terrain of legal complications with Hell's Court.

She'd made numerous trips on wyrmback from the Redoubt to the capital city to ensure political and Court immunity for the New Order mistresses, as had been promised to Lady Allyssia. She'd checked and re-checked every piece of paperwork and every step in the chain of re-integration. She'd even met with Lady Allyssia herself in Haawiyah.

"I thought we had the entire process set up, my Lord, with a welcoming ceremony in Mer in three days, along with temporary housing while Court records are revised and existing criminal records are expunged-"

"There's a last-minute change of plans," Yitzhak interrupted, reaching up and smoothing his trimmed black beard. "The first New Order mistresses will leave this morning, but they'll be diverted into the care of Hell's army at our base outside of Vegasis. I've already apprised the Nankariders. You'll need take no special action, Ambassador. We wouldn't wish to upset the New Order mistresses unnecessarily. Only you, Commander Befanah, and my two most trusted Nankariders will know of this."

"Of course, my Lord. As you desire, so shall it be."

"Any questions then?"

Lydiah pushed the gears in her head to turn, trying to understand the politics of what was happening. She'd been an ambassador for Hell for almost two centuries, and a beauty mistress for far longer than that. She knew a lie when she saw one, and a disaster in the New Order re-integration could have significant repercussions. Worst of all, she was in the perfect position to take the blame for any failures.

"If I might ask, my Lord, how long will I be staying here?" Lydiah smiled sweetly. "Now that the plans are in place, and the Lady's city is in full occupation, my skills might have uses elsewhere. You've clearly taken things into your hands and out of mine."

"You're still needed here, Ambassador Lydiah," Yitzhak said summarily, as if he'd not only expected questions, but he'd expected that one.

"Very well, my Lord. I can cope with a need-to-know situation. What else did you need me for, then?"

"I'll be away overseeing this special arrangement for the New Order mistresses. In the meantime, there remains a small issue that needs tending to-a loose end."

"You mean the missing Mistress Ayelet?"

Yitzhak cracked a small smile on his discolored lips. "Ambassador, I can inform you in confidence that we apprehended Ayelet three months ago in the east. She is a completely broken toy. Ayelet will never kill again, or even raise a blade."

"Ah, that's wonderful to hear, my Lord." Lydiah smiled with relief, not because the murderous Butcher of Mer had been apprehended, but because Yitzhak was finally confiding in her. He wasn't done yet. His baleful yellow eyes registered more on his mind.

"I understand there is another New Order Jinn missing, however, who is not yet accounted for."

"Who do you mean?"

"I mean the Jinn Mimọ named Boudi-Ca. I mean the fledgling whose slave you took by force. We've spoken of this once before."

Lydiah formed her best mask of apology and contrition. "My Lord, you know that Violet was my slave, gifted to me by a scouting party not far from the Trivium. I already prepared slave papers for her and sent them to Hell's Court-"

"Some things are more important than your prized collection of Mimo slaves, Ambassador Lydiah. I asked you to pacify the New Order Jinni, not rile them."

"Of course, my Lord." Lydiah conceded. "Perhaps I was tactless, but Violet is of no consequence, and she was my stolen property. I didn't think to bother you with something so trivial."

"As I understand it, resentment has grown among Allyssia's Jinni over the winter months. There are rumors of anger and ill-will over your handling of Boudi-Ca."

"Yes, my Lord. I've heard this too from Lieutenant Nefra, who is mingling with the New Order Jinni at parties, pretending to play the role of a lesbian sympathizer. Some rumors in the city say that we arrested Boudi-Ca and sent her to a terrible fate because she protested too much about her slave. She's disappeared from the city, which gives the rumor credence."

"Was something done that I don't know about?" Yitzhak stepped closer, adjusting his cloak. "When you reported to me some months ago that Boudi-Ca was harassing you, I instructed you to ignore her."

"I ignored her, my Lord. She went away, but Allyssia's Jinni seem to think that we made her so. They're making noise for Boudi-Ca's release from imprisonment. The rumors are lies, of course, spread by dissidents in the city, but Boudi-Ca's poor, sad story has become a rallying banner for anyone who wants to listen."

Yitzhak looked away across the sky and the clouds gathering over Meristyian. "This is an unfortunate distraction from my father's strategy, Ambassador. The orderly relocation of Allyssia's Jinni must proceed calmly and according to the plan."

"You mean according to your modified plan."

Yitzhak smiled with his eyes half-lidded. "Exactly. I'm tasking you with finding Boudi-Ca, Ambassador. Silence the voices of the dissidents so that we don't provoke the Lady and her allies until it's too late."

Lydiah raised her hands in supplication. "We've had the Lady's city sealed like a wine cask all winter with heavy patrols at every gate, tower, and wall, as you've asked, my Lord. I don't know how Boudi-Ca could have left the city unless your soldiers failed at their duties."

"The fledgling may have unexpected resources and a will to resist us. Please recall that she is Mistress Ayelet's former fledgling."

"You think their disappearances are connected, my Lord?"

"I deal with facts," Yitzhak answered. "Find the facts. Find Boudi-Ca."

"And then?"

"Interrogate. Conciliate. Use whatever means necessary to pacify the malcontents in the city. Ensure that the relocation plan proceeds according to schedule."

"I hope you don't mean that I should give my slave back. I've spent the last three months reconstructing Violet's training, undoing everything Boudi-Ca did with her, from the way Violet looks at me, to the way she squeaks annoyingly-"

"No. Giving the slave back would send the wrong message. Perhaps Boudi-Ca should make a public statement exposing the falsehood of the rumors that we imprisoned her. Perhaps, in exchange, you should apologize for taking her slave."

Lydiah nodded. "I'll do anything necessary to achieve your objectives, my Lord. I could also note that if you desire to pacify the former New Order Jinni in the city, then maybe your soldiers should refrain from raping them whenever they can corner one in a dark alleyway. I'm receiving one or two complaints every week. Perhaps these lesbian Jinni deserve punishment, but the soldiers aren't the judges. So is there anything else, my Lord?"

"Yes. I expect the Spring Festival next month to be a grand homage to Lady Allyssia and centuries of Jinn tradition. I'll expect this to be viewed as a goodwill event in the reunification of the Jinni, something that looks good in the eyes of the Kishi and all other factions in Meristyian."

"We're still inviting the Gypsies and Kishi to the Festival, correct?"

"I want you to work with the Gypsies and Kishi personally, assuring them that they will be safe from Mimǫic Hierarchy forces on the Isandlwana roads, and that everything will be orderly by the time of Allyssia's traditional festival. Our Lord has the safety of Meristyian well in hand."

"You're not afraid of the Gypsies spreading more dissent in the city?"

Yitzhak smiled faintly. "To the contrary. When they leave, we hope they'll spread news to the vampires, the werewolves, and the Kishi that abandoning neutrality and pledging renewed fealty to our Lord and Hell's Court is good and desirable. That's why we need the dissent in the city over Boudi-Ca defused."

"Understood. Our Lord must wear a benevolent face."

Yitzhak's eyes darkened. "No. Our Lord must wear an invincible, protective face. Therefore the Smokeless Flames should win every possible event in the festival. Everyone who attends should leave impressed and intimidated by our strength. The weakness of Allyssia's Jinni gives us an opportunity to impress."

"Of course. Why take only one bird in hand when we can lure two or three with the same protection scheme from this grave and deadly Mimǫic threat."

Yitzhak smiled thinly with a glimmer of amusement in his yellow eyes. "Yes. The Mimǫs are dangerous, Ambassador Lydiah, and in times of fear and uncertainty, the weak must seek the shelter of those who have strength."

"Understood, my Lord."

"In fact, my father may undertake discussions with the Seelie Court about renegotiating our treaties. Without the special protection of Hell's army, many of Oberon's nimfas and naiads in Meristyian might die."

"Who did our Lord send to see Oberon?"

Yitzhak arched his charcoal eyebrow. "Are you interested in a trip to the Blessed Isles, Ambassador?"

Lydiah snorted. "I'm interested in any climate with less snow and ice. Allyssia is clearly influencing the weather in Her domain, making all of us miserable out of spite."

"If you do well in the coming months, Ambassador, a more comfortable position for you should open up. For now, let's get back to the city so you can prepare for the departure, and so I can escort the New Order Jinni to their final destination."

Yitzhak strode through the snow back towards the great scaly Nanka. The Nanka sent gouts of sulfuric breath steaming across the mountaintop. Lydiah followed, lost in thought. Whether a new war with Heaven was brewing or not, a position at the Blessed Isles would be far more pleasurable and less dangerous than Allyssia's city. According to reports, the Mimọic Hierarchy had developed a force of three thousand in the Trivium over the Isandlwana winter, but no one knew if they intended to march. The Mimọs so far had refused diplomacy.

Lydiah climbed up the rope ladder and pulled it after her. She settled into the front seat of the Nanka basket alongside Yitzhak. She watched Yitzhak manipulate the reigns with his black-gloved hands. Lydiah licked her lips. She wished her husband's brother would manipulate her with the same skill and intimacy. She twisted the diamond wedding ring on her finger.

The Nanka launched into the sky amidst a cloud of blowing snow. The beast swept down the mountainside. Within short minutes the magical veils of the city of Allyssia shimmered away. The jumble of snow-laden rooftops came into view, interspersed with a spiderweb of plazas and leafless oak trees. The Nanka veered towards the Lady's magnificent palace and crystal spires.

The two transport Nanka for Szenes and Melkeh were positioned at the bottom of the palace steps. The Nanka were freshly washed. Their scales gleamed stark coppery green in the morning Isandlwana sunlight. Small figures moved like ants on the palace plaza. The slaves were hoisting crates of belongings into the baskets with ropes while the mistresses supervised. Yitzhak brought the Nanka around over a rooftop, then down to a hard landing.

Lydiah threw the ladder over the edge of the riding basket. She climbed down. She couldn't know what Yitzhak truly planned for Mistress Szenes and Mistress Melkeh, but whatever was coming for those rebel lesbians, they deserved their fates.

She couldn't second-guess the will of Lord Hades either, but the events of the next few months could either boost her career in Hell's Court or deal her a major setback. She could not fail. She felt confident that she could handle both the Spring Festival and the troublesome fledgling named Boudi-Ca. She'd manipulate Boudi-Ca like a puppet on a string, but first she needed to find the crying little bitch.

# *Chapter 27:*

Good morning, Boudi. Could you come to the great hall? The messenger bird spoke with Golda's sultry, purring voice. Boudi-Ca rinsed her ink pen and wiped it clean. Golda often sent birds in the werewolf stronghold, but this one sounded urgent.

Boudi-Ca pinned her hair, bent over her small bedside mirror, and drew a pencil over her eyebrows. She took up a boar-bristle brush and powdered her imperfections. Her face seemed different-more weathered since her long two-week trip to eastern Meristyian the previous fall. She looked a little more like an experienced Jinn and less like an Mimọ.

She dropped the pen, wriggled her feet into her tight shoes, and tip-toed out of the bedchamber, taking care not to wake Elor. The shaggy red-haired werewolf still slumbered after his night patrol.

The sleepy hallways of the Stronghold of the Four Brothers were silent. Boudi-Ca strode boldly. She was proud of the click of her three-inch heels on those old stone floors. Her clicking was her hallmark, heralding her passage wherever she went. She wasn't the only Jinn in the stronghold, but she was the only one who wore heels. Golda went barefoot or wore boots.

Four figures sat around the massive oak table at the end of the great hall. Masad was dressed in his customary leather armor with his sword at his hip. As usual, the balding head of his human host was sweaty, reflecting the light of the fire in the hearth behind him. Brother Marcus, the oldest of the four werewolf brothers, towered at the head of the table. His hairy brow was squirreled with concern, and his furry ears were twitching. Marcus wore a leather vest that revealed the tattoo on his shoulder, and he held an ale stein in his massive hand.

The third attendee at the meeting was Golda, who lounged easily next to Masad on the bench, dressed like a man in pants and a vest. Her wild red hair hung low over her forehead, half-obscuring her brooding and tired eye sockets. The fourth person at the table was a warrior woman in exquisite white armor. Boudi-Ca stared as she approached. It was Mistress Artemisiah.

"Have a seat, Boudi-Ca," Golda said. "We have a visitor this morning. She came in last night."

Boudi-Ca sat at the table, which was so werewolf-sized that her corseted chest barely cleared the edge. Golda poured her a cup of tea from a battered silver pot. Boudi-Ca received the hot drink gratefully. "Thank you. I thought you disappeared during the attack on the Trivium last year, Mistress Artemisiah, or were the rumors wrong?"

Artemisiah nodded. "I was lost, but I was not taken prisoner by Archduke Fennel. He transported me to a different place, so as to better battle me on his own terms. This allowed me to resist and flee before his father, Lord Hades, could arrive to assist him. Unfortunately, the place to which Fennel took me existed in the future."

Golda smiled wryly. "Let's start over. Boudi-Ca, apparently Lady Allyssia at first refused to allow the Redoubt to be used as a base by Hell's army. She didn't intend to sell out the New Order at all, and she was ready to fight with the help of the Auerbach. Her brother Hades wasn't happy with that."

"Yes," Artemisiah added. "So Archduke Fennel used the Ebon Timepiece, a thing of Lord Hades' own invention. He went back in time to our attack on the Trivium. There, he phased me into a private pocket of the dream world, creating a future timeline where the Lady didn't have me. His scheme worked. Fennel was able to change the events and create a new reality. I eventually escaped from that trap and returned to Meristyian, only to find the Lady had surrendered in the different timeline, and the Redoubt was occupied by the Smokeless Flames and Hell's army."

Masad stroked his chin. "Playing with time is like yanking the weave out of the hands of the Fates as work they. Appreciate this the Fates they will not. Recoils the weave must at some point."

Artemisiah nodded. "I could have revealed myself and exposed what Lord Hades had done, but even if a council of gods were convened over the issue, it would only buy Lord Hades more time to wreak havoc on the Lady's creation. And so the Lady sent me away, to come here with this message-the city of the New Order will be surrendered in western Meristyian, but we will reform elsewhere."

"Tell Boudi-Ca the rest," Golda said, running her long fingers over the carvings and doodles on the worn werewolf tabletop.

Artemisiah nodded solemnly. "Mistress Ayelet has been missing all winter, as well. The Lady doesn't know her whereabouts. She wants Ayelet found."

Boudi-Ca bit her lip. "Ayelet told me last fall that she was going to go look for Barissianna in the east. Barissianna was her vampire lover. When I left the Redoubt, people were saying Ayelet left for other reasons. They think Ayelet and Jade Turtle fled from the Old Order and the judgment of Hell's Court."

"Yes, fledgling," Artemisiah answered sagely. "Yet the Lady wants to find Ayelet nonetheless, so we need to find the Auerbach chantries."

Brother Marcus cleared his throat. "I hope our maps can help you locate those chantries. We haven't been up north much lately because it's too dangerous. Our last scouting reports are years old now."

"Well, at least we have something to go on," Golda said. "We have a track to follow, and sitting here at this table are two of the greatest trackers in all of the realms between Heaven and Earth."

"Three, Golda," Artemisiah murmured. "Modesty doesn't become your talents, any more than for Boudi-Ca."

Boudi-Ca felt a flush of pride. "Am I going to help?"

Artemisiah smiled. "Of course. We aren't asking the werewolves to stick their necks out any more than they already have by harboring us. You're an able blade fledgling, Boudi-Ca. You'll come with us on the hunt for Ayelet. We're starting out tomorrow."

Brother Marcus stood up to his full height. "I have some things to do, ladies and gentlemen. Let me know if you need anything else."

"Thank you, Marcus," Masad said. "Boudi-Ca, like you to practice?"

"That's fine."

"I'll join you two," Golda said. "I really need to warm up my fighting skills. Eastern Meristyian is crawling with the Mimoic Hierarchy, Hell's army, Smokeless-Flame Sisters, and Disciples of Set."

Boudi-Ca followed Golda and Masad down one of the many halls that adjoined the great hall of the werewolf stronghold. She could feel Golda's tension, and the tension was infectious. It seemed unlikely that Ayelet was in trouble. Ayelet was probably living with Barissianna, hiding away with Jade Turtle. She wondered how long the hunt would take.

It was the first week of February, according to the werewolf calendar. She had four weeks left before she had to trek back to the west to participate in the Spring Festival for her Task of Mastery-if she went back. She hurried to keep up with Golda and Masad, who were striding ahead of her on longer legs.

The werewolf training hall was on the south-facing cliff of the stronghold. The room was cold in the morning from exposure to the open air and light shafts. The military hall was rudimentary. Ramshackle racks of old, battered weapons lined one wall. There were no reed mats-only a dirty and worn stone floor.

"Rapiers," Masad declared.

Boudi-Ca pulled on a protective mask and selected one of the thin, blunt-tipped weapons. The leather grip felt comfortable and familiar. She'd trained blades with Golda several times over the winter, but they'd never sparred. They'd sparred instead with their tongues in Golda's bedchamber during a three-month dance of intimacy. The cat-shifter was twice as chary and unpredictable as Henne, but also brought twice the energy to the bed.

Boudi-Ca admired the muscles that rippled in Golda's back and shoulders as she flexed, strode to the center of the room, and positioned herself en garde. Boudi-Ca felt a ping of nervousness. Golda was stronger and taller than her by nearly a head, and had long, powerful arms. She really didn't want to fight Golda. Boudi-Ca took a deep breath and launched a tentative attack. Golda parried and counter-attacked, and then they sparred in earnest.

Boudi-Ca concentrated. Sparring with Golda was almost like sparring with Ayelet. Golda, like her, had also been Ayelet's pupil. Conscious of Masad scrutinizing her every move, she focused especially on her footwork, which she'd been working on all winter. It was easy that morning for her to stay low to the earth, not floaty and butterfly-like.

She parried a move from Golda that she'd never seen before, then scored a point on the contretemps with her speed. Golda growled. Boudi-Ca suppressed a smile. A flush of pride warmed her breasts. She scored another point on a counterattack. Quick counterattacks were her forte. Golda was skilled, but a little slow. Golda finally called for time and pulled off her mask.

"You're good, Boudi. You're flexible and fluid like a willow tree."

"Look good you do, Boudi-Ca," Masad said. "Switch to me while rests Golda."

Boudi-Ca faced the blade master. He engaged her slowly, building up speed, and then they were dancing around the floor. Boudi-Ca focused. At first Masad used moves that she knew, but then he changed styles, and she was forced to improvise. He scored a point, then another. She tried a contretemps, but it was ill-timed. She wasn't sure if her shot to his shoulder had been a point or not.

"Good," Masad said. "Again."

They practiced for an hour. She made little headway, as usual, against the indefatigable Masad. Finally he stepped aside and Golda took over for him. Boudi-Ca pushed on, scoring point after point against her taller and stronger lover until Golda yielded again.

"That's enough for me," Golda muttered. "I'm going to head out on an afternoon patrol soon. Will I see you at the party later, Boudi-Ca?"

"There's really a party? I'm still a beauty fledgling after all. When is it?"

"It's at sunset. It's a full-blown werewolf fête in Lady Artemisiah's honor. I guess we forgot to mention it to you earlier. Until then."

"Bye." Boudi-Ca accepted Golda's kiss on her cheek, and then she was alone in the room with Masad, who was watching her closely, as always. She felt unusually happy inside at having beaten Golda. Her chest felt warm with pride. "Do you think I've improved while studying with you, Master Masad?"

Masad gave a smile, a rare gesture from the possessor. "Fight you better than months past. Have you joy. Have you passion."

"What do you mean?"

"Seen and felt you much. Loss of your Ahyehass. Arrival of Hell's army at your home. Decision to leave home and come here among the werewolves. Have heated you the flames, the fire of your journey."

"I think you're right, Master Masad. Do you think I'll escape the flames, or will they consume me? Will I pass my Task of Mastery? Will I win first or second at the Spring Festival if I go back?"

A cloud passed over Masad' face. "Advise I not to go back. View they will your disappearance like Ayelet-a vote of no confidence against the reunification."

"I told Tajee to lock up the house until I got back. I can go into the city by the same secret passage. There are a lot of people in the Redoubt now. There are soldiers everywhere. They're too busy to notice a little fledgling like me. I have to go back, Master Masad."

Masad pondered. "Understand I the consequences if fail you the tasks of your Test. Compete the Smokeless Flames in the competition, think you?"

"Yes. There is one Smokeless-Flame Sister, at least, who said she'd compete. I met her at a party. Her name is Lieutenant Nefra. She's supposed to be really good, or at least she arrogantly says so."

Masad shook his head. "Teach I to you the Exquisite Form of the Smokeless Flames, because works it against Jade Turtle and the competition in the New Order. Know you that the Smokeless-Flame Sisters are masters of this. If fights Nefra against you, becomes a liability the Exquisite Form, not an asset. Wins Nefra against you with your own technique."

"If you say so. I just have to do my best."

Masad approached and patted her on the shoulder. "Try you do, Boudi-Ca. Took you a brave step for a beauty fledgling. Please you would Ayelet, if knew she."

"Do you think we'll find her?"

Masad grimaced. "Talk I will with Artemisiah. Form we will a plan. Creep we quietly, like mice. Understand you? If intends Lady Allyssia to escape and create another Jinn order, betray we cannot her hand. Extract the Lady's enemies persuasively their information."

Boudi-Ca sighed. "If that's true, then I'm even more afraid. If the Lady is re-forming the New Order, I can't just keeping hiding out here hoping the Lady will forget about turning me into an Ahyehass. I have to pass my test, or I'll face the consequences eventually."

"Think I the Alpacian snow worse now than in November. Think I the mountains can you not pass. Advise a return to the west I cannot."

"I don't know what else to do."

Masad squeezed her shoulder, but his face was emotionless. "Make I cannot your decisions, Boudi-Ca. Teach I blades to you. Well done today. Pressed you not Golda, but when attacked she, defended you well. Based all warfare is on deception. Come naturally this to you."

"Thank you, Master Masad." Boudi-Ca felt the tension relax a bit from her shoulders. Masad was being nicer to her than ever before. She put away her rapier and followed him back down into the depths of the werewolf stronghold. She diverged in the lower passages towards the room she Shared with Elor.

All warfare is based on deception. The words of Masad echoed in her head. If true, then her beauty fledgling skills could prove more useful than Ayelet was willing to admit. She needed to write down the things that Masad told her. Unfortunately, she was way behind in her diary. In fact, she'd hardly written at all since she'd arrived at the werewolf stronghold.

She'd use that afternoon, she decided, to catch up on documenting her adventures before she left again on another adventure with Masad, Golda, and Artemisiah.

Boudi-Ca quietly entered her room, tiptoed back past the still-sleeping Elor, and extracted her diary, pen, and ink from her bags. She poured a small saucer of water and dampened a rag, lit a candle, and climbed into her bed. She wrapped her blanket around herself with her diary open.

Boudi-Ca nibbled on the end of her ink pen. In truth, her journey across Meristyian the previous November had been so harrowing that she didn't want to remember it, but she wanted to summarize at least. She dipped her pen in the ink and put the nib to the paper. She wrote the first thing that came to her mind.

If it wasn't for Ayelet's valiant stallion, I might have collapsed on that snowy road in the Alpacians. I might have gone to the void. When I finally descended onto the Tuskan Plain, I was bad off. I had to rest for two days. My Hunger was intense, and I was cold, but a nimfa came into my camp. She was curious and worried about the stranger in her wood. I revealed that I was a New Order Jinn, loyal to the Lady.

The nimfa took me to her grotto. She gave me a warm place to sleep. She gave me what I needed. I briefly considered making her my Ahyehass, but I wasn't sure if such a thing was allowed. She would have been too stupid to pass my Task of Discipline anyway, and I would have felt bad about collaring her after she'd been so nice to me and saving my life.

After I said farewell to the nimfa and the snow of the Alpacians, the traverse to the Tuskan Plain was uneventful. The stallion surged on tirelessly. I was lonely during that time. The nimfa, I realized, hadn't been satisfying company. I regretted not bringing Tajee with me.

Boudi-Ca sighed and wiped her ink pen. Her old Conclave pen wasn't in the best condition. She focused, trying to remember those long, fateful days in the saddle on her way into the east from the flowered fields of western Meristyian.

The beginning of the Persium Plateau was almost as difficult as the Alpacians, but it was emotional, not physical. I had no idea where to find the werewolves. I wasn't sure of the road. I only had the werewolf-friend whistle that Elor had given me, and I couldn't make it work.

The whistle was a small tube with rounded ends, in all appearances a shell from the Sea of Desire. No matter how hard I blew in each end, I couldn't make a sound. I didn't realize at the time that the whistle was working, but I just couldn't hear it.

My progress was slow. The plateau was a maze of canyons and mesas. My body ached from nights spent sleeping on the hard ground. I was sad. If it wasn't for the coming of winter, and the snowy road through the Alpacians, I might have turned back.

I held onto my desire. I had to find Masad, and I had to find a new Ahyehass somewhere, or I would become one myself. I rode doggedly on.

Boudi-Ca rinsed and wiped the pen again. She was hungering just thinking about the effort of her journey. She eyed the big red-haired werewolf in his bed. She and Elor were on different schedules-he patrolled during the long hours of the winter night, and she was awake during the day like Golda. Elor didn't mind her waking him for feeding. She'd write one more page, and then wake and take.

The werewolves found me in the middle of the night, finally, and took me to the Stronghold of the Four Brothers. Everything went well. Marcus and Elor welcomed me. I took the bed of Elor's roommate, who was killed by the Mimoic Hierarchy. Masad agreed to give me lessons as he'd offered, although he was worried I could be tracked by the Smokeless Flames.

Golda had come to live with the werewolves too after the Eastern Order had been scattered again by a Hierarchy attack. After only a few days of talking, dancing, and flirting, she invited me to her bedroom. As the winter snows fell, and the Persium Plateau grew cold and desolate, our relationship bloomed. Is Golda my Hierophant card? I don't know. I don't think so.

It's now almost the first of February. If I want to be back to participate in the Spring Festival in March, I have to leave soon. I don't think Golda or Masad want me to, but I have to pass Ayelet's test.

I still have no idea what I need to sacrifice for the Lady's task. As for Isabellah's task, I still haven't found another untrained Ahyehass to replace Violet, but I have until June for that, when my test ends after one year. I can't even think about Violet and what she's going through. I hate Ambassador Lydiah.

I hope Tajee is surviving. I feel very sorry for leaving him alone. I hope he can forgive me when I see him again. I owe him kindness.

# Chapter 28:

Tajee idly stirred the fire with the brass-handled poker. He added another log. The basement room was warm and cozy. He'd trucked his bed from the storage room down to the lower level. He was camping in the middle of Boudi's training mats, which were warmer than the upper floors.

The snowy winter had been long and uneventful. The soldiers marched in the streets during the day, and at night they made noise in the barracks next door. Ranavalona visited occasionally to check on him, and he'd welcomed her desire to use him for her Jinn needs. Otherwise, he'd kept the doors locked and the windows and bird slits closed.

He'd ignored the occasional unannounced knocks from Gallinah and another mistress who he hadn't recognized. Gallinah's visits had thankfully stopped some weeks after Boudi-Ca had disappeared, when the snows fell in earnest on the little city. The house had been silent except for the patter of little mouse feet.

Benedict and Mary had moved inside with the weather. Even Ranavalona wasn't sure why mice lived in Hell and not in Heaven. Hell was the default, Ranavalona said. Lord Tuhan picked and chose the souls to serve Him, and Tuhan had no use for rodents. He'd informed Ranavalona that some cats lived in Heaven. Ranavalona had only laughed. She was more interested in his cock than talking four-legged philosophy.

Tajee yawned and stretched. Without a mistress, he felt a desperate ache every day. He longed to be taken as the Jinni had trained him. He wished his dark-skinned Mimo would come again, but he hadn't become attached to Ranavalona, or she in particular to him. She simply used him, said a few words of encouragement, and left.

He often worried about Violet in Ambassador Lydiah's hands. Lydiah was cruel, but at least she was beautiful-a regal white-blonde Jinn with grey-silver eyes and a shapely, well-endowed, middle-aged female figure. He sometimes fantasized about Lydiah and Violet together. It was wicked, and he felt horrible for it, but when his lust was high he couldn't help himself.

Tajee heard a knock on the door then. The knock came again, harder and more insistent. The knock didn't sound like the ones that had come before. It was heavier and echoed in the upstairs hall. Tajee closed his eyes. He lay back on his bed on the floor of the basement, waiting for the interloper to go away.

He heard clicks, thumps, and creaks-the bolts sliding back and the front door opening. The sounds were loud in the deadness of the house. Tajee climbed to his feet and tiptoed towards the basement stairs that led up to the foyer. Boot steps sounded above, and then faded as they climbed up the stairs to the second floor and Boudi's bedchamber.

Tajee's heart leapt. Was Boudi-Ca home? He climbed the stairway to the foyer. A Jinn in a red uniform looked straight at him from where she stood in the light pouring through the front door. She was taller than him by a head. She beckoned him forward with a crooked finger. Her silvery brown eyes glimmered from the darkness of her silhouette. A tarnished silver ring dangled from her long fingers, a ring that bristled with dozens of house keys.

"Come out, slave," she commanded. "I'm Lieutenant Nefra. What's your name?"

"My name is Tajee." Tajee stepped forward and presented himself. The Lieutenant was a strong woman, much like Mistress Freyah but less muscled and more lithe. Nefra's brown hair was done up in a loose bun, a feminine counterpoint to her military presence.

"No one is up here," a voice called from the floor above. "From the dust on her vanity, Boudi-Ca has been gone for quite a while." Boot steps sounded again on the staircase. Tajee pivoted, and his mouth went instantly dry. Ambassador Lydiah descended the steps into the foyer to glare at him.

"His name is Tajee," Nefra offered. "He's quite a handsome Mimọ boy. Where is your mistress, slave? Where is Boudi-Ca?"

"She isn't here."

Lydiah advanced. She was dressed in a long black coat, in contrast to her platinum blonde hair. She removed her black gloves as she approached. Lydiah's hand was lightning-quick. Tajee blinked and gasped. The hard leathery slap stung his cheekbone. "Where in the hells did she go, boy? Tell me immediately."

Tajee almost answered, but he caught himself. He'd sworn to Henne and Ranavalona that he'd say nothing. He loved Boudi. He wouldn't be responsible for getting her into any deeper trouble than she already was. He stood still as Lydiah reached behind him and examined his wings. He shivered viscerally. Her cold fingers probed and stroked his skin.

"Just tell us where she went, Tajee," Nefra said. "Stories are running rampant in the Redoubt. Some stories say Boudi-Ca is holed up in her house, but most say the fledgling was abducted and tortured by the Smokeless Flames. We had nothing to do with her disappearance. We're trying to find the truth."

"Tell us, Tajee," Lydiah said. Her tone changed from steely to silken. She caressed his neck. "You're such a beautiful Mimọ boy, aren't you? You know, I'm a highly distinguished collector of Mimọ slaves."

Tajee looked at the floor and tried to not betray his increasing fury. He'd almost forgotten how much he loathed Ambassador Lydiah for taking Violet away. "I'm not a slave. I'm an Ahyehass. How did you get in here, anyway? How did you get Boudi's key?"

"We're the ones asking the questions," Lydiah countered. "Where is Boudi-Ca? Like Nefra said, we are trying to smooth over this little misunderstanding. Just be a good little boy and tell us everything."

Tajee bit his lip. The two mistresses were staring at him. Lydiah's steel grey-silver orbs were cold and unflinching under her black-lined lashes. He glared back at her. "Forget it. I'm not telling you anything. Go away."

Lydiah beckoned to Nefra. "Take this slave and lock him in Allyssia's dungeon. I'll search Boudi-Ca's house further, and then I'll come and interrogate him."

Tajee felt his heart pound when Nefra produced a pair of cuffs from her belt pouch. For a moment his resolution wavered, but he held his tongue. He couldn't be responsible for getting Boudi-Ca in big trouble. He would never forgive himself. He knew that only too well. The cold bands clicked around his wrists.

"Come along," Nefra said matter-of-factly. "Why aren't you wearing a collar?"

Tajee didn't answer. The Jinn in the red uniform guided him by the shoulder and helped him onto a great black horse. Nefra had strong hands. She climbed onto her saddle behind him, and then they were off through the streets at a leisurely pace. They took at least twenty minutes to reach the palace, where Nefra dismounted at the Lady's stable. She guided him up the palace steps, past the Hell's army guards, past the scaly Nanka in the great hall, and past the bloody carcasses of two half-devoured cows.

Tajee looked around, hoping Master Priapus might see what was happening, but he saw no one except the armored soldiers of Hell's army and a few collared Ahyehasi. The Lady's palace seemed different than when he'd served there the previous fall-darker somehow and more foreboding. The scurrying, tired-looking Ahyehasi kept their eyes glued to the floor.

He knew the palace well. He knew the door to the palace dungeons, although he'd never gone through it. Nefra guided him firmly through the door and down a steep stairway with her strong hand on his shoulder. They passed down a stone corridor and more stairs that led deep into a maze of torchlit catacombs. They finally passed through another door into a large dark-walled room of pitted volcanic stone.

Several free-standing silvered cages lined one wall of the dungeon room.

Nefra dragged him easily by the arm to one of the cages, but she didn't throw him inside. She locked one of his handcuffs to an inch-thick cage bar. The Lieutenant turned and exited the dungeon. Her footsteps echoed and faded up the passageway.

Tajee slumped against the cage. A gnawing fear began to creep through his mute resolution. Jinn toys of all shapes and sizes adorned the walls of the palace dungeon. Some of the toys were simple phalluses. Others were more elaborate and multi-pronged. Some of the toys were whips and straps, and others bore shiny, wicked blades and long, needle-like points. Tajee felt queasy. He'd suspected that Lady Allyssia had a dark side. The secret dungeon room proved the theory, unless the room was a recent addition.

He waited for what felt like an hour, then two. Finally he heard footsteps. The heavy door swung open. Ambassador Lydiah entered alone. Without her long coat, Lydiah's short red skirt and half-top accentuated her perfect frame from her full breasts to her taught rear end. She'd coiffed her long white-blonde hair up behind her head, revealing glittering diamond earrings. She carried a leather bag, which she laid on the work table. She smiled at him, and the recurve of her painted black lips turned subtly cruel.

Tajee tried to steady his nerves. He had to stay strong for Boudi. Lydiah approached him and slid a gloved hand down the cage bar that he was cuffed to, as if testing its strength. The expression on Lydiah's face appeared pained.

"Tajee, I don't think you understand," Lydiah began. "This missing fledgling is causing problems for this regime, and therefore for me. The former New Order mistresses are angry, and Boudi-Ca has ignited a tinder box. This is nonsense. Neither Hell's army nor the Flames has wronged Boudi-Ca. In fact, we're worried about her well-being. Please help us, Tajee. Where is she?"

"I don't know."

Lydiah sighed deeply. "Stop this charade immediately. I'm an expert on Mimo psychology, and I know when an Mimo is lying. I've seen all of the well-meaning lies that Mimos tell when they try to cover for each other.

Just tell the truth and make it easy on yourself. Did Boudi-Ca leave the Redoubt? Or is she hiding somewhere? If so, why?"

"I don't know."

Lydiah went suddenly playful and conspiratorial, like the sun appearing from behind a cloud. "I'm not a cruel mistress, to be honest, Tajee. Do you find me desirable? Come now. At least confess that much for me."

"I, yes, Mistress."

Lydiah reached down and stroked his cheek. "I like you. You're such a beautiful, sweet, devoted slave. Am I right?"

"Yes. I suppose."

"You give every impression to me of a boy who has been told by his mistress not to tell anyone anything. Am I right? You can tell me that much."

Tajee hesitated. "Yes, Mistress."

"Good. I thought so. Let's go ahead and get you up." Lydiah produced a key in her fingers. "I confess that I had an ulterior motive for telling Nefra to bring you down here. I can feel your need. I want you to take your clothes off."

"Yes, Mistress."

Lydiah removed his cuffs and helped him stand up. Tajee felt his head tingle and his phallus stir. Lydiah's intoxicating perfume was overwhelming and pleasant. His lust slowly ignited unbidden in his loins. He removed his shirt and dropped his trousers. Lydiah wrapped her warm hand around his neck and guided him across the room to the work table that dominated the center. The table's wooden surface was worn and scarred.

"You don't have a brand, either," Lydiah murmured. "How interesting. Why don't you have a brand Tajee?"

"I'm not sure what you mean." Tajee sniffed. Lydiah's perfume was an intense cloud of pleasure. She smelled of flowers, skies, furs, bones, sex, shoes, and the most intimate possibilities of feminine skin. He'd never smelled such an alluring complexity. She pressed him slowly against the table from behind. The table was low-slung and met the tops of his thighs. His exposed phallus and testicles just cleared the edge.

The fabric of Lydiah's skirt was soft where the fronts of her thighs pressed into the backs of his. Tajee felt the urge to reach back and touch her. As he moved his hand, however, Lydiah gripped his wrist. The cuff clicked and connected to his other wrist. She locked his hands behind him.

Lydiah trapped his cuffed hands between her thighs and reached around his body. She tugged his phallus while at the same time grinding into him, rubbing the edges of his cuffed hands against her heated, fabric-covered mound. Tajee stretched and suppressed a moan. His arousal was rising higher and higher. He couldn't help himself.

Lydiah whispered as she stroked him, and he strained to listen, but the words in his ear were queer and incomprehensible. She was hard against him from behind, yet soft-firm yet feminine. Lydiah's touch and voice were art forms. She stirred deeper into his depths like a constricting serpent, leaving him breathless and unbearably sexual.

"What kind of mistress would leave a beautiful slave like you alone?" Lydiah teased suddenly. "Boudi-Ca was a fool to leave you, wasn't she?"

"Yes, Mistress," Tajee answered. Lydiah's hand kept stroking his phallus, evoking more pleasure. He felt the depth of his need-that inexorable need that Golda, Boudi, and Persephoneh had cultivated in him over the previous two years.

Lydiah kept stroking him. She pressed rhythmically into his buttocks, as if fucking him from behind with her hips. She removed her hand from his phallus for a moment, only to wet it with her mouth. When her hand returned, it was wet and slippery. Tajee moaned.

"That feels good, doesn't it, boy, and you're going to-" Lydiah whispered, and her voice trailed off into more inaudible syllables before strengthening again. "Yes, tell me it does, darling."

"Yes, Mistress."

"Did Boudi-Ca leave the Redoubt?"

Tajee clenched his throat, but the words emerged. "Yes, Mistress."

"Did she go looking for someone?"

"Yes, Mistress."

"Who did Boudi-Ca go to see? Where did she go?"

"I can't say, Mistress. I can't-"

Tajee wrenched and gasped. Agony splintered into pure pain, and the pain laced hard through his testicles. His vision blurred momentarily, and his legs shivered. He braced himself against the table edge, and the pain lessened only slightly.

He looked down, and his stomach clenched with horror. Lydiah had thrust two golden bodkins like nails through the loose skin of his testicles. His testicles were pinned to the top of the wooden worktable, even while his phallus kept straining upwards, unphased. Lydiah patted his back.

"You need to breathe for me, Tajee. Whenever you're ready to tell me where Boudi-Ca went, feel free, darling. Are you ready yet?"

"No." Tajee clenched his fists in his handcuffs. All of the anger he'd ever felt towards the Jinni and their evil ways surged in his chest. "Never."

"Good," Lydiah lilted. "This could get interesting. Your hate is impressive, boy. If Boudi-Ca stoked you to such delicious bitter passion, I admit I'm impressed." Lydiah leaned and licked his ear. "You're too devoted a slave for your own good. Just talk to me. Where did Boudi-Ca go?"

Tajee gasped. A paddle cracked against his buttocks, jolting him forward. New daggers of pain laced his testicles and radiated into his phallus. The paddle cracked again-a third time and a fourth. The paddle cracked again, and again, and again at his tenderized flesh. Tajee jerked, and he felt tears overflowing his cheeks. He tried to move his cuffed hands to protect himself, but the paddle kept dodging his attempts to block.

"Please stop. Stop!"

Lydiah laughed. "Begging is excellent progress, Tajee."

Tajee tried to relax, so as not to give Lydiah any more satisfaction. Lydiah was kneeling behind him, he realized. Her hand wrapped around the back of his ankle. He felt more pricks of pain, and shocks of agony raced up his leg. Tajee glimpsed movement across the room. The dungeon door opened, and Master Priapus strode through with a scowl like a storm cloud.

"Excuse me, Ambassador Lydiah. What in the name of the Lady are you doing with that Ahyehass?"

"I'm interrogating him." Lydiah's tone was cold and silken. "This is the

Ahyehass of fledgling Boudi-Ca. I found him in alone in Boudi-Ca's house."

Priapus drew himself up to full height. "I demand that you release Nina immediately, under the Lady's laws pertaining to the punishment of the Ahyehasi of others."

"The boy has two names? Fine. I want to see a copy of his Hell's Court ownership papers to prove this ownership that you're implying."

Priapus hesitated. "We don't have papers here in the Redoubt as you well know, Lydiah. We've always used an honor system to keep track of our humans. Please let me return Nina immediately to his palace duties until Boudi-Ca is found. We need all the help we can get to host you and your officers."

"This slave is withholding information critical to the safety of the city, Master Priapus," Lydiah countered. "I have every right to question him as part of my official duties, but I'll release him to you on the condition that he doesn't leave the palace."

Tajee felt Lydiah reach around his waist and pull the pins free from his testicles. The agony lessened to a throbbing, burning ache. He found his clothes on the floor and quickly slipped into them. He avoided Lydiah's eyes and hurried out of the dungeon room. Master Priapus was waiting for him in the hall.

"Thank you so much, Master," Tajee said.

Priapus rubbed his shoulder and directed him up the long stairs to the palace. When they reached the great hall, Priapus pulled him quickly into the shadowed side gallery under the second-floor colonnades. "What did the Ambassador want with you, Nina?"

"She wanted to know where Boudi-Ca went. I wouldn't tell her."

Priapus nodded. "Good. Good, Nina. There is a lot of dissent in the city over the Boudi-Ca situation, and the Ambassador wants the poor girl's head. Do you know where she is, Nina? Perhaps you should tell me. Maybe I can help."

Tajee hesitated. He'd sworn that he would tell no one, but he felt he could trust Master Priapus. He looked over his shoulder across the great hall, but none of the guards or even the sleeping Nanka were in hearing distance.

"Boudi-Ca left the Redoubt to go find Masad and the werewolves."

"Really? How did she get out?"

"She went through a secret passage in a place called the Divinity District. It's in an empty house near the end."

Priapus nodded sagely. "Yes. I see. She knows where Masad went?"

"Yes. I think so. Boudi-Ca made me promise not to tell anyone. So did Henne-Ca and Ranavalona-Ca, but maybe the rumors are worse than the truth. Is Boudi-Ca really in trouble?"

"I couldn't say what the Ambassador is planning. Let's get you settled back into your old quarters, Nina. Things aren't quite like they were when you left last summer, with the Nanka living in the great hall and the squads of Djinnus soldiers roaming the corridors, but there are still plenty of chores."

Tajee frowned. "So I get tortured, and now I have to do chores?"

The master's hand came to rest on his shoulder. "Down in Haawiyah, a severe punishment is common for a lying slave. Are you angry at Lydiah?"

"Yes. If I see her again, I might try to kill her."

Priapus grimaced. "No. The Ambassador is a very powerful elder Jinn. If you see her in one of the hallways, don't even look at her. She could throw you headfirst into a wall with a flick of her wrist. All she needs is an excuse."

"Yes, sir."

"And don't feed your anger either, Nina. Come to think of it, your anger may well have been what Lydiah wanted from you."

"Why would she want me to be angry?"

"So she can drink it from you. It's a very powerful emotion that is most enjoyed by the most powerful and wicked Jinni."

"Great. That's all I need-another Jinn after me."

"You need to adapt to the crueler ways of the Old Order, Nina. We all do. You need re-learn how to serve a Jinn. You're not stupid. You know things are changing. Sometimes it can be painful if a slave doesn't behave, and you didn't behave. Now go on back to your room. Your quarters should be as you left them. I'll try to find some balm for your aches. I'll be there momentarily."

"Yes, sir. Thank you, sir."


~*~


Lydiah sat on the edge of the torture table. She faced the dungeon door with her legs elegantly poised and her skirt hitched to reveal almost everything. She casually cleaned the bloody shafts of her bodkins on a white handkerchief while she scanned the impressive rack of toys and tools on the wall.

Allyssia's dungeon was her favorite place in the entire palace. She desired in that moment to find another other slave to punish to the sweet ending, a slave less well-protected by the palace steward. She heard the heavy footsteps within a few minutes. Lydiah stowed her bodkins in her purse. It boded well that Priapus hadn't made her wait. The overly-endowed master pushed through the dungeon door.

"Boudi-Ca left the city, Ambassador," Priapus said. "Apparently the young Mimọ fledgling knows where Prince Masad is hiding, and intends to join him."

Lydiah smiled. "Didn't I tell you my tactic would open Tajee up? If you slap Mimọs mercilessly, they look for the closest strong shoulder for succor and sympathy. It's the nature of how they serve Lord Tuhan. So where did Boudi-Ca go?"

"Boudi-Ca didn't tell Nina. The fledgling left the Redoubt via a secret passage in the Divinity District. Nina said something about werewolves. Unfortunately, that's all. I'm very familiar with Nina from the months he spent working for me in the palace. I'd know if he were holding anything back."

"Thank you, Master Priapus. I expected as much, but it's unfortunate."

Priapus cleared his throat. "So about our agreement? We'll have no more soldier patrols in the east wing? We need a safe, quiet, calm environment for the smooth functioning of the palace. There have been too many violent incidents with the soldiers. These problems have lowered the morale of my palace Ahyehasi."

"It's surprising to me that Tajee has no papers or brand, Priapus. He's a stunning slave, and his anger is overwhelming coming from an Mimọ boy. I've met many young fallen Mimọs, and I've never felt the like. I love how Allyssia makes him dress as a girl, as well. I keep the same rule for my boys. At first they're humiliated, but slowly they're more submissive and vulnerable to my influence before they even know."

"I know you're a brilliant mistress, Ambassador. I should read your books."

"I'll find one for you." Lydiah smiled coquettishly. Males were ever-predictable, and Priapus' phallus was imperceptibly stirring under his skirt. Priapus cared for Tajee, but less than for his own pleasure and the second part of the agreement at hand. "So would you say Tajee belongs to Boudi-Ca?"

"Not exactly," Priapus answered. "He belongs to Lady Allyssia. Everyone knows that, and that should be good enough for anyone."

"Far be it from me to accuse you of equivocating, Priapus, but I do my research. I went to a number of sources asking about Tajee."

"I'm not sure what you mean to say."

"Well, I suppose if Tajee is a palace slave now, then he's fair game for anyone staying at the palace, like myself. Now that I've tasted the Mimọ boy, I'd like to requisition him properly."

"For what?"

"I want his services, although we might chat a bit about certain secret passages during our rest breaks. We might trade passages, so to speak."

Lydiah eyed Priapus. The palace steward looked truly tense and uncertain for the first time since she'd opened negotiations with him. His enormous phallus stirred still more at its moorings. Priapus lowered his eyes submissively and stepped still closer to her.

"I feel a bit envious, but I'll send in the request. I'll see that Nina comes. If you hurt him again, however, you can forget it. He'll tell me."

Lydiah looked away and nonchalantly rubbed her thigh, spreading her leg and hitching her skirt a bit more to her hip, escalating the force of her influence on Priapus. She was feeling dangerous in that moment. Boudi-Ca was turning into a serious problem-perhaps more of a problem than Yitzhak realized.

Based on Tajee's testimony connecting Boudi-Ca with the traitorous Prince Masad and the treacherous, rebellious werewolves, a gentle capitulation with the fledgling was no longer advisable, much less a public apology as Yitzhak requested. Boudi-Ca needed to be tortured and interrogated for every ounce of information that she possessed in her dumb little Mimo brain, and then she needed to be locked away.

"Thank you, Priapus. So let's move on to our other things, things impossible in real flesh, but lovely through the world of an illusionist."

"I'm eager to see your skills, as you can see."

Lydiah summoned the energy from her sex and transformed herself. She willed the changes in her arms, her legs, her breasts, and her face. She knew what Priapus wanted. Like most men, Priapus wanted the thing he could never have. Priapus' enormous size was a great blessing, but also an emotionally painful curse, preventing him from pleasure through many normal orifices. Even desire-realm flesh and bone had its physical limitations. Her point of view shifted and lowered. When she pulled Priapus' cock from his skirt, she employed the hand of a young girl.

"So beautiful," Priapus murmured. He stepped back and held her at arm's length to admire her work. "Ginger hair suits you. Are you sure this won't hurt?"

"How sweet." Lydiah gripped Priapus' still-stiffening cock and pulled him close. She planted little kisses on his big hairy chest. She opened her psychic vacuum and drank a morsel of Priapus' heated lust for her, siphoning it with effort through his ribcage. "You're going to stretch me, but no. Your eyes will see a young girl with a budding figure, but I'm no innocent virgin. Your cock will have a whore."

*Chapter 29:*

Boudi-Ca twirled on the dance floor and shook to the beat of the drum. The party in the stronghold was in full swing, and she was an epicenter of femininity among all of the hairy half-men.

She'd taken a warm bath thanks to Elor's efforts at heating the water for her. She'd taken a long nap. She'd painted and primped for the party, although her old lizard-stoppered perfume bottle, sadly, was empty. Her dress was her one complete Mimo dress that she'd brought all the way across Meristyian with her, replete with ribbons and bows. Her corset exaggerated her silhouette of youthful beauty. Elor was a clumsy dressing-boy, but neither Tajee nor Violet could tie a corset more tightly.

Boudi-Ca changed partners to a brown-snouted werewolf who she didn't recognize. It felt good to dance and forget for a while her worries about Ayelet, Tajee, and her Mistress Test. When the song was almost over, she came face to face with Golda. Golda took her by the hand and twirled her around. Golda's hand was warm, and her nude body, tanned from the many hours that she spent patrolling outside the stronghold, bore a soft sheen of oil in the firelight.

Golda was beautiful. Her thick auburn hair and lightly freckled face were reminiscent of Henne, but there the comparison stopped. Whereas Henne was waifish and diminishing, Golda was bold and energetic. While Henne kept herself shaved, Golda wore her red-brown hair wild in the wildest places.

Golda seemed to have grown hairier since the shifter had been living in eastern Meristyian. She was furry around her ears, her armpits, her lower stomach, and her sex. Golda said her hirsuteness was from shifting so frequently into cat form. Either that, or the hair of the werewolves was rubbing off on her.

Boudi-Ca took a quick breath when Golda pulled her close, body against body, then released her to arm's length. Golda's presence was magnetic. Boudi-Ca matched Golda's movements, conscious of all the werewolves watching them. Then the song stopped and changed, and Golda moved on her own, going solo.

Boudi-Ca made her way off of the dance floor. She didn't feel like dancing more anyway. Elor caught her eye from where he lounged with his friends, Deuce and Martin. The werewolves were relaxing on mats and cushions. Boudi-Ca joined them. Martin offered her a pipe. She puffed.

The werewolf herbs made her feel good, but they were nothing like nectar. Of all of the things she missed from the Redoubt besides Violet, nectar came to her mind the most, even more so than Henne. Boudi-Ca gazed at the dance floor where Golda slow-danced with brother Marcus, who had taken the floor with brother Paulus.

"Looks like the evening meeting is over," Elor said. "Any idea if we're going on the warpath, Boudi-Ca?"

"I don't know," she said. "I don't think so." She took the proffered pipe again from the werewolf Deuce, who caught her eyes and grinned. Deuce was handsome as werewolves went. Deuce had flirted with her all winter, but she'd stayed loyal to only Elor and Golda. Elor had stayed loyal to her too, of course, in the absence of other women. Golda, on the other hand, took werewolves by the dozens to her well-traveled bed.

Boudi-Ca handed the pipe back. She'd been feeling more and more over-accoutered as the weeks and months among the werewolves passed. At first she'd been ogled in her Mimọ dress, but after a while she'd become a pretty fixture around the stronghold and little more. It hadn't helped her popularity that she'd refused the many overtures from everyone but Elor, and moreover that she'd begun a relationship with Golda, which upset many of the werewolves, who felt envy and even contempt at the concept of two women together.

Boudi-Ca smoothed her dress. As quickly as her body had relaxed, her mood had darkened and become depressed again. She felt like leaving the party.

"Elor-" she began, but at that moment a small gold and green bird swooped low and landed on her shoulder. Come to my room if you want to. It was Golda's voice. Golda was striding from the dance floor towards the hallway to her bedchamber on the far side.

Boudi-Ca rose to her feet and crossed the dance floor. She followed Golda down the dark, close hallway. The werewolves watched her go. They'd seen Golda's bird. They always watched for it, like a game. They'd come to know what it meant for the lucky recipient. That night, apparently, it was the Mimọ girl's turn again to visit Golda's bed.

Boudi-Ca arrived at Golda's bedchamber, where Golda was lighting a fresh candle. The bed was dirty and overworn but still cozy, piled with an array of pillows, all of tired silk and bearing the curious artistic designs of the Eastern Order Jinni.

Golda's bedchamber was a modest oblong stone room with sloping walls up to an arched ceiling-a room cut from the raw rock like the rest of the werewolf stronghold. A pair of sheathed swords sat in one corner, and several staves stood in another. A curious painting of a spiral hung on one wall. The bed and side table were the only real furnishings. Golda's clothes were folded and stacked neatly in three old crates.

Golda stood at the edge of the bed with a faint smile on her face. "I decided I'm in the mood for a quiet, gentle evening before the trip. We're leaving first thing in the morning, I think. Masad is still in the meeting chamber with Artemisiah. He'll let us know."

Boudi-Ca nodded. She slipped close to Golda, touched the shape-shifter's arm and stroked upward to her strong shoulder. Golda returned her caress.

Boudi-Ca shivered. Golda's touch always had an undefinable Jinn intensity, the emotiveness of a female, a depth of feline feeling and passion that no mere werewolf could match.

"You're beautiful, Boudi," Golda murmured. "I'm glad I've been able to spend time with you this winter."

"Help me with my dress." Boudi-Ca turned and offered her buttons to Golda's fingers. Golda fumbled in the candlelight for long moments before helping her lift the voluminous Mimọ-style dress over her head. Boudi-Ca unfastened her garters and pushed down her stockings along with her panties. Golda's warm fingers on her hips steadied her as she undressed.

Boudi-Ca straightened and pressed her corseted breasts against Golda's larger unrestrained offerings. Boudi-Ca tilted her mouth up, but Golda didn't lower her lips across the inches. Boudi-Ca felt Golda's fingers at the nape of her neck, thrilling her again, and then rising to the tie that held her hair in place. Golda shook it free and tousled her hair in her fingers.

Boudi-Ca gazed into Golda's blue eyes, framed by her red mane. She found Golda's chin with her hand and pressed forward with her lips again, insistent. Golda pulled her back and off balance, and they fell together onto the bed.

Golda's lower fur was bristly. Her tongue was like Ranavalona's-thick and strong. Boudi-Ca hitched. Golda's hand slipped over her thigh to her sex. She thrust, but Golda's fingers only teased and stroked. She bounced slightly, inviting entry, but still Golda teased her. She slid away and down to Golda's voluptuous breasts, where she licked wide curves and tongued at the nubs.

Golda turned the tables then. The stronger mistress rolled and took control. Golda assaulted her with lips, tongue, and teeth around her collarbone and down to her breasts like a kitten, or like a tide of kittens. Golda's mouth roamed everywhere, then lower. Boudi-Ca moaned at the hot kisses on her mons and clitoris. She clutched her fingers into Golda's hair. Golda lapped and sucked, drenching her cleft with wetness.

Golda produced a phallus from a hidden place. The phallus was double-ended. Boudi-Ca shifted her hips to allow one of the ends to slip inside her. She watched as Golda swallowed the other end, and then they both lay on the bed, enveloping the phallus together with their nethers meeting in the middle.

Golda began to rock her hips to the rhythm of the dance that could faintly be heard through the stone of the stronghold. Boudi-Ca met her rhythm as best she could. She worked her softer thighs against Golda's thicker, stronger ones. Golda's hot furry sex bumped against her own, crotch against crotch with a pleasurable sensation.

Boudi-Ca lay back into the pillows and danced with Golda horizontally, legs against legs, hands against hands, pumpum against pumpum for several minutes until they both had achieved gentle climaxes. They lay together entwined on the bed until Golda sat and removed the phallus that joined them. Boudi-Ca smiled as she fell again against the hot skin of the wild cat-mistress. She lay like a sated kitten against Golda's breasts, which rose and fell visibly in the candlelight with her every abundant breath.

"This is what we're fighting for, Boudi," Golda murmured.

Boudi-Ca sighed. "You're right. This is nice. I feel like we're different, but you bring the wildness out of me. It's like magic."

"This is magical, and so few understand it." Golda turned and kissed her head. "You're beautiful, Boudi. I think I could love you."

Boudi-Ca bit her lip. "I could love you too. Thank you so much."

"For what? Loving you?"

"For accepting me for who I am, and letting me be who I am. For not judging me, and for not trying to tell me what to do." Boudi-Ca kissed Golda full on the lips. She licked and met tongue against tongue. It was cool in the room. Golda's welcoming, loving, unjudging warmth felt wonderful.

"Hello in there?"

Boudi-Ca froze against Golda's chest. Masad' voice came from the hall beyond the patterned door hanging.

"We're in here," Golda called. "You can come in."

Masad stepped into the room. The possessor gazed down at them with his face expressionless and unsurprised. "Provided us Brother Marcus has with possible locations of the Auerbach vampires. Bases he the information on past werewolf reconnaissance. Take we will a divide approach to find where Ayelet might be hiding, the better to help avoid trackers. Get we lucky maybe. Or not. Plan we will to leave in the morning, if gets everyone ready."

"We'll be ready," Golda said. "So we're splitting up to cover more ground and move silently? I hope Boudi-Ca will be with me?"

"No. Comes she with me," Masad answered. "Needs she to feed. Feed a young Jinn can I. Go you will with Artemisiah. Feed you can from what friends you find in the wild. Good night."

Boudi-Ca frowned and watched Masad leave. She'd never been with Masad in a sexual way, and she felt a little resentful, assuming she'd understood him correctly that he would be feeding her Hunger on the trip. She didn't like the plan, but she couldn't refute it either. Meanwhile, Masad' departure had left a residual tension in Golda's bedroom, as well as a cool draft. Boudi-Ca hugged herself.

"Will we find Ayelet, Golda? Eastern Meristyian is really big."

Golda shrugged. "Well, like we were saying this morning at the table- Masad, Artemisiah and I are all in the ranks of the best trackers in Hell. If anyone can find Ayelet, we can. It might seem like Hell's army is taking over everything in order to stop the Hierarchy from further encroachment on Lord Hades domain, but the Lady still has a few aces in the hole."

"Um. What are aces, and what hole are they in?"

Golda chuckled. "Never-mind. It's a werewolf expression from a card game they play. Speaking of werewolves, I just realized we should both feed well tonight. Sleeping together will leave us weak. You know what I mean?"

"Right. So I guess good night."

"Good night." Golda lifted her hand and sent a messenger bird flying off through the stronghold, no doubt to call an adoring werewolf. Boudi-Ca bent and gave Golda a kiss. She was being dismissed. It saddened her that Golda never wanted her to spend the night. They could have Shared a werewolf. They could have called Elor. She'd learned not to argue with the way Golda wanted things. She rose and collected her clothes.

Despite the fact that she and Golda had been sleeping together all winter, they weren't in love. Golda, like Henne, didn't want to commit to an amorous relationship.

Boudi-Ca stalked out of Golda's bedchamber. She was beginning to wonder if true love among the Jinni was a childish fantasy, a myth. She hadn't pushed Golda any more than Henne, despite her desire for real committed love with another woman. She was still waiting for her Hierophant. She was ready to give up. Strangely the card had been misplaced anyway. In her haste to pack for her trip, she'd looked to take it, but the Hierophant card had been missing from its place on her mirror.

She didn't bother putting her clothes back on. She passed Golda's burly brown-haired lover, who was already hurrying down the hallway with a stupid grin on his toothy face. Boudi-Ca stalked across the dance hall. She strode in the nude through all of the werewolves back to her room, where she pulled her saddlebags from the corner and began to pack.

## Chapter 30:

Boudi-Ca rode behind Masad up the steep mountain trail. They'd ridden fast from the Persium Plateau. The difficult and maze-like terrain had given way to increasingly steep mountains as they'd traveled north from the werewolf stronghold through eastern Meristyian, on a route paralleling the canyons of the vast Acheron valley.

They'd headed towards two old known locations of possible Auerbach chantries. On the fifth day they'd reached the first-a chantry tower at the top of a steep volcanic canyon. They'd found the tower fortified by Hell's army and not under Auerbach control. The reconnaissance notes of the werewolves had been outdated. With Masad' skilled direction, they'd managed to escape detection and ride on. Three days later, they were approaching their second objective in their search for Ayelet-a stone tower on a remote lake.

The morning sun felt good at the cold Isandlwana altitude. The sun lit up the trees below in the valley. Boudi-Ca followed close behind Masad along an exposed ridgeline towards a lake that could be seen down through the trees. The possessor led the way on a grassy animal trail through boulders of black stone.

She felt tired, although she'd been feeding acceptably from Masad. He gave her his cock every evening when they pitched their bedrolls and lay down to rest-gently, perfunctorily, and from behind, without kissing her or even removing her clothes.

She didn't mind Masad' dispassion. The possessor filled her well enough through the human body he wore, and it was hard not to be grateful for a male phallus when she was feeling her Jinn Hunger. Her curious gratefulness, in turn, concerned her. She had no desire to get comfortable in a relationship with another emotionally unavailable Prince.

Masad slowed and stopped ahead. Boudi-Ca drew abreast. The animal track they'd been following bent to the top of a cliff. They looked down at the shore of a large icy lake. A little island graced the edge of a gloomy bay below, and from the island rose a squat tower of black stone. The island was reached by a causeway from the lakeshore below the cliffs.

"Arrived we have," Masad said. "Must find we a way down."

The possessor spurred his horse along the cliff line, through a field of old broken rock spangled with green lichens. They made a painstaking circle halfway around the bay, with Masad making frequent detours to the cliffs to look for a descent, until finally he stopped at the edge for long moments. Boudi-Ca drove her horse forward. Masad had dismounted and kneeled on one knee to look over the edge. The drop was only fifty meters to a sandy beach that met the beginning of the causeway that led to the tower.

"Is there a way, Master Masad?"

"Climb I will. Wait you here with the horses."

Boudi-Ca frowned. "I can just flash down. I don't need to climb."

Masad smiled faintly. "Fine. If can you, meet me there. Tether the horses to one of these trees. If find we nothing here, go we back empty-handed to the meeting point. Hope we Golda and Artemisiah fared better."

"Do you sense anything yet?"

"Stinks this place of vampires. Think I there are some inside, but protected the place is by heavy enchantment. Obfuscation vampire magic. If stumbled a few wolves not directly on it, know we not that it exists. See I bats hiding below. Think I a landing."

Boudi-Ca watched Masad slide over the edge of the precipice and climb in the sunlight, lowering his body hand over hand down the steep rock until he disappeared. She tied off the two horses, crept to the edge, and looked over. She felt a Sharp twinge of nervousness. In truth, she'd never flashed downwards.

She summoned all of her courage and flashed. The familiar grey ribbon uncoiled before her, and she slid down it. She emerged on the damp black sand of the beach, stumbling and unnerved, but unharmed.

Masad was only a fraction of the way down the cliff. Several giant bats were sheltered in the shadows of the stony overhangs. Riding baskets sat strapped to their backs. They seemed to be sleeping. Boudi-Ca walked to the causeway, where the treacherous ice of the lake met crushed and broken rock that had been built into a path that led to the island tower. The tower appeared larger from lake level, and larger still as she neared it. The wind from the icy waters was cold. She wrapped her cloak around her body for warmth.

At length, Masad reached the ground and joined her. She followed him down the causeway towards the tower. The front of the tower was constructed of sheer stone blocks with thin slits giving way to darkness. The tower was ancient and worn. Pale blue-green lichens spangled its vertical facade. Masad rapped on the massive portal with the hilt of his blade. The possessor waited, then rapped again.

"Sleeping the vampires are," Masad said. "Wonder I if need we wait."

As Masad spoke, an uncanny scream sounded from the tower. Boudi-Ca jumped back, her heart pounding, but the scream was only the massive door rising on the rusty mechanisms that drew it upwards. When the door reached its apex, dark forms moved in the interior. Boudi-Ca peered closely, hoping to see Ayelet or Barissianna, but the vampires were all darker-skinned, not anything like the pale Auerbach.

"Looking we for the Auerbach, not the Disciples of Set," Masad said to the vampires. "Can you to tell us?"

"Come. Inside. We talk," answered one of the vampires. He stepped closer to the sunlight. "You stink of dogs, Gypsy. You stink of big dogs."

Boudi-Ca summoned a bird, whispered, and thought of Ayelet. The bird fizzled on her fingertips. Her heart sank. "She isn't here, Master Masad. The bird should have gone to her."

"Masad? This is the Jackal?" The vampire's visage contorted with fear and loathing.

Masad drew his blade and leapt to attack. The crowd of vampires met him with bitter fury. Swords clashed and rang. One vampire howled, and its body flopped back with a spray of blood. Boudi-Ca pulled her Oya-blade quickly from its sheath and advanced to assist Masad.

The interior of the tower was dark. Masad was engaged with three vampires at once, and two more were descending the inner tower stairs. A vampire in the back was aiming a crossbow. Boudi-Ca slipped a dart from her cuff and flung it. It found the creature's face. The vampire snarled, shouted a guttural word, and reached for a nearby lever. A crash sounded. Boudi-Ca gasped. The floor just inside the tower door gave way. She was falling in mid-air alongside Masad and one other vampire.

She flashed instinctively. Time froze. The ribbon curled up to the edge of the yawning pit. She teetered on the edge, then flashed again right behind the vampire who had pulled the lever. She spun and swung. She connected. The vampire's head lolled on its neck and toppled, spraying its lifeblood across the stone wall. Boudi-Ca tightened her grip on her blade. The rest of the vampires had seen her, and they were coming.

She readied an aggressive stance. Her survival instincts took over-the wildness that Golda sometimes evoked in her. She flashed forward and impaled the first vampire on her blade. He made a croaking sound when she withdrew. Masad, she realized, was trapped in the pit. She was alone and beset from all sides. She spun and parried, ducked and executed a hateful kin-hex. A vampire stumbled when his feet flew from under him.

She rolled across the lid of the pit, which had fully closed again. The three remaining vampires followed her. She parried and slashed with a whirlwind attack. The vampires were slow. She outpaced them easily. She slashed one across the throat. Its wicked curved blade fell from twitching fingers.

Boudi-Ca parried twice and danced to the side. The vampires circled.

The one she'd impaled had risen to re-enter the fray. She flashed again and spun with a cut. This time she focused and made no mistake. Another head rolled to the floor.

"Damned Jinn devil," one of the two remaining vampires growled. The vampires fled, heading for the nearby spiraling stairway. Boudi-Ca pursued them. She speared an ugly buttock. The vampire roared and stumbled. She slashed ferociously across an arm raised in defense. The loose clothing of the vampires was like paper under the edge of her Oya-blade. The vampire regained its footing and fenced with her.

She parried and tried a contretemps that left the vampire again on the defensive. Within seconds she found the vampire's neck with the tip of her sword. It clenched and doubled over. She cracked its head, and it fell, quivering, down the tower stairway. She left it there. The last vampire had disappeared up the stairs with a patter of footsteps.

Boudi-Ca surveyed the bloody scene. The two vampires that she'd felled were still moving. She strode across the floor and beheaded them both. More blood spurted across the stone floor, mingling with the spreading pools from the others. She went to the lever and pulled it to re-engage the trap mechanism. Again the pit lid swung open to the distant rattle of chains and massive counterweights. She went to the edge of the pit. Masad treaded water, looking up at her.

"Can you do anything, Boudi-Ca? Killed I have the vampire that fell."

"Wait."

Boudi-Ca searched and found what she needed among some barrels under the stairs-several lengths of rope. Within minutes Masad was climbing over the edge of the pit. Boudi-Ca crinkled her nose. The pit emanated an awful stench, and Masad was drenched with it. A nasty cut scored his forehead. Masad dropped a blade on the stone floor.

"Think I Ayelet was here. Fell she in the pit. Found I this blade in the wall."

Boudi-Ca examined the blade. It looked like Ayelet's favorite sword. She suddenly felt sick. "You think she's still in the pit, Masad?"

"Know I do not. Lives still a vampire?"

"Yes."

"Let us find him. Perhaps answer can he."

Boudi-Ca watched Masad strip his soaked clothes and replace them with a borrowed vampire outfit. She looked over the edge of the pit and saw no signs of Ayelet-only fetid black water. She summoned a small tenebris lux, but the light from the spell only illumined slimy, slanting pit walls.

Her legs felt heavy like her belly, not just from the possibility that Ayelet had sunk into the depths of that horrible pit. She'd spent a lot of effort with her flashes and nervous energy in the battle. She'd emerged victorious, but her feeling of pride was hollow.

She helped Masad scour the tower for more evidence of Ayelet. The place had once been lavish, but had been burned, gutted, and stripped. Crusty bloodstains of all shapes and sizes dotted the walls and floors. Two feed-slaves were locked in one room. They were poor and abused. Their necks were adorned with masses of purple bruises. Boudi-Ca felt her Jinn Hunger rise nonetheless at the sight of the near-naked, vulnerable humans. At the top of the tower, a heavy door resisted entry. It was barred from the other side. Masad scratched his head.

"Find a key need we."

"I can flash through," Boudi-Ca offered. "But I prefer to see where I'm going."

"Find I something here in my pockets." Masad fished in the pockets of his vampire clothes and produced a key ring. A key turned in the lock, and the door swung open. The vampire was waiting in a combat stance in the center of the room. When he saw them, his curved blade dropped from his fingers and clanged on the floor.

"Just take my head. Take it," he muttered with his thick accent. "I surrender. I don't have the balls to die fighting against the Jackal."

Masad approached him with his sword at the ready. "Give me your name, Disciple."

"I am Nazim."

"Fell a Jinn into the pit. Was some time ago, this. Know you her?"

"Why should I tell you?"

"Say you something of not having balls? Kill you we will to find our friend."

The vampire eyed him. "If I tell you, will you let me go? You're a betrayer of your father Set all-knowing, a betrayer of the great one I serve. You've left a path of dead vampire bodies ten centuries long. Why should I be any more than dead to you?"

"Tell you us of Ayelet. Live you may."

The vampire's lips pinched. "Archduke Yitzhak came to visit. He was with Smokeless-Flame Sisters. They took Mistress Ayelet to a place named Dead Sedde. This was three, four months past."

"What did they want with Mistress Ayelet?" Boudi-Ca interjected. She held her Oya-blade at the ready. Intense emotions were welling in her chest. She wanted to kill the awful Disciple of Set then and there.

"We took this place before she came. We killed the Auerbach. They landed on their way back from the west. We were ready for them with a trap. After that, I was left with my men to clean up the mess. Then the Jinn comes. We caught her in the pit, and we got her fledgling too."

"Friend?" Boudi-Ca bit her lip. "You mean Jade Turtle?"

"I don't remember," Nazim answered. "It was months ago. The fledgling hurt three of us before we took her down. She wasn't a murderous little monster like you have as your pretty friend, Prince Masad."

"Monster?" Boudi-Ca felt her cheeks warming. "I'm not a monster!"

"Destroyed you the Auerbach all?" Masad said. "Left you none living?"

The vampire shrugged. "Archduke Yitzhak was here and Mistress Astaarteh, many Smokeless-Flame Sisters and a legion of Djinnus with Nanka, and some Disciples. The Auerbach hungered from their trip. They were weak. The Auerbach Matriarch and others were burned by Yitzhak and Astaarteh. The whole side of the lake was on fire."

Masad nodded slowly. "Think I you tell the truth."

The vampire Nazim nodded. "Yes. We killed them. When Ayelet came, we captured her. We went and got the Archduke at Dead Sedde. He came and took Ayelet away. So you will let me free? I am no threat. I promise I can just leave. Please?"

Masad hefted his blade. "Can leave Boudi-Ca."

"Thank you, Master Masad. I'll go see the vampire slaves." Boudi-Ca turned and descended the stairs. She felt trembly. Ayelet had been captured by the enemy. She recognized the name of Archduke Yitzhak. He was the devil avatar of Lord Hades, designated to command the Redoubt. In the chamber above, a guttural cry of pain was cut short.

Boudi-Ca returned to the dank room where the two slaves sat. She summoned a tenebris lux to examine them more closely. The vampire slaves were hollow-eyed, pale, and chained to metal chairs. One was a young male close to Tajee's age, and the other was a somewhat older-looking girl. The boy was nude. The girl wore only a dirty skirt. Boudi-Ca examined the girl's manacles.

"What's your name?"

The human girl didn't answer her. Both sides of her neck were grim gardens of purple punctures. Hundreds of scars were also evident on her forearms, thighs, and wrists. Boudi-Ca tugged at the manacles. They were securely fastened. At the same time, her Hunger rose at the proximity. She eyed the boy, who looked back at her sullenly.

She sidled over to him and kissed his cheek gently. His skin was ravaged almost as much as the girl-slave. Boudi-Ca shivered thinking of such a thing happening to Tajee. She could heal the vampire slaves with her magic, but the effort would exhaust her precious energy reserves. She faintly heard Masad' footsteps on the stair. The possessor entered.

"Look they not healthy," Masad remarked.

"We have to get them free. We can't just leave them."

The possessor looked skeptical. "Think I that we leave them."

"Sitting here chained?" Boudi-Ca felt a warmth of anger. "No. I'm sorry Master Masad, but I don't think so. Maybe I can work on them with my magic and heal them."

"Linger here we cannot. Think I can we take them. Have we new rides-the vampire bats. Hope I you have not grown too attached to your horse."

Boudi-Ca sighed. "I've learned not to become attached to things in this world. I need to feed soon, though. The battle took a lot out of me. I can't believe I did that. I killed four of them, Master Masad. They weren't so bad."

"Gain you confidence, Boudi-Ca. Good. Still. Feeding you I have been for the past several days. When feeds a Jinn from a god, or even a hellion prince like me, take power she can, beyond what is normal. Refer we to such powers as siddhi."

"Well, if that's what happened, and you gave me the siddhi to help fight the vampires, then thank you, Master Masad. So let's free these slaves like real heroes."

"Here. Have I more keys. Try them."

Boudi-Ca took the keys and bent to work on the chains. The third key worked. The manacles came free. The girl slumped and rubbed her wrists. Boudi-Ca shifted to the boy, who gazed at her gratefully with his brown eyes.

"So it's alright if we take them on the bat, Master Masad?"

Masad scratched his chin "If yes, then think I you must learn to fly."

"You mean fly a bat by myself? I can't fly!"

"Know I not the Disciple signals, but know I that a control whistle is simple. Blow one time. Blow two time. Decipher we will together."

"Great. Just what I always wanted." Boudi-Ca unchained the boy. Flying one of those giant bats was absolutely terrifying. She tried to think of an excuse-any excuse-for why she couldn't do it.

"Far faster than horses," Masad continued. "Go we could all on one bat, but weighed in the sky we would be, like the Auerbach. If split we on two bats, have we a better chance to run if find we trouble."

"You mean you would have a better chance to run."

Masad shrugged. "Take you the slaves is your decision, Boudi-Ca. Need them I do not. Go they with us, then ride they can with you. If take them you want, then fly you must a bat. That, or leave them. Defeated I will not be to save two human souls who have nothing to offer me."

"Fine, if you're like that. I'll try for their sakes. I'm not just going to leave these slaves here for who knows what sort of monster to rape them some more. What about Ayelet? I've never heard of a place called Dead Sedde.

Do you know where to go?"

"Go we will to the meeting place with Artemisiah and Golda. Discuss we will how to proceed." Masad turned abruptly on his heel.

Boudi-Ca motioned to the slaves. "Come. Hurry."

The humans stood and wobbled on their shaky legs. Boudi-Ca slowed and waited for them. Neither of poor, abused humans would serve for her Mistress Test, or even serve well to feed from, but her Hunger in that moment wasn't discriminating.

She herded the humans down the tower stairs after Masad, who was moving quickly. At the bottom of the stairs, Masad worked the pit lever again, and the lid valves of the pit closed with a rumble and screech of rusty gears, allowing passage across it and out of the tower.

Boudi-Ca followed Masad down the stony causeway with the slaves. It was terrible to imagine Ayelet being defeated and captured by a pit trap. Her heart pained just to think about it. The day had clouded outside, and a cold wind was blowing. The towering black basalt cliffs around the icy lake emanated a feeling of foreboding and dread.

## Chapter 31:

❦

Barissianna submerged herself deeper into the warm womb of the bathtub. She listened to the hollow sounds of the water lapping on the tub walls. The water evoked memories of that fateful day when Hell's army had launched an aerial attack on the fleet of Auerbach bats as they'd approached the Blackrock chantry.

Like Amanoch, she'd barely survived the fire and Nanka talons. She'd crashed in the lead bat, so she'd been back onto her feet and leaping away when the storm of fire had hit the landing. She'd dove into water while everyone else was getting charcoaled, including Janaka.

She'd swum the entire bay underwater through the cold and dark to emerge on the other side, where she'd hidden amidst the rocks and watched from a distance as an entire division of Hell's army, a devil general, and half a dozen Smokeless Flames sorceresses had decimated most of her clan's Isandlwana presence in one pitched battle.

She'd found her way on foot during the following days to the last remaining chantry of the Auerbach-the Rubicund Cliffs tower commanded by Magistrada Beign. She'd lost everything she owned in Meristyian, including all of her important research on the soul-stealing art of cirai.

Janaka was also missing. She hadn't dared return to look for his remains, and he hadn't re-appeared. She, Amanoch, and Bernanke were apparently the only survivors. While Amanoch and Bernanke had already gone through the ritual to transfer their souls back to their entombed bodies on Earth, she'd chosen to remain and wait for more survivors, in the off-chance that Janaka might be among them.

After four long winter months of staying in the Rubicund Cliff chantry, however, she was ready to accept that Janaka gone to the void, as well as Iona and Ionela, Matriarch Lubersky, Valeriu, and everyone else.

Barissianna slid out of the water and sat on the edge of the tub. She wrung her hair into the warm water. She grabbed a towel and dried herself. Her research into cirai had come to a grinding halt with the loss of her materials, even though she'd started a new notebook, recording what she remembered. She'd made less progress than she'd hoped with the scattered selection of old tomes in the city of Allyssia. She'd been distracted from her task by her affair with Ayelet, as well as Janaka's jealousy.

She regretted her decision to stay the winter in Meristyian and not to go home sooner. She could have been in New York with Liest at that very moment, consoling him over Matriarch Lubersky. Supposedly Liest was already drowning his sorrow with younger girlfriends, including Magistrada Minette from the chantry in Colorado. Liest was looking for a replacement wife, a new clan Matriarch. Barissianna sighed. Was she even on the list? Did she want to be? Her future, and the future of the winnowed Auerbach clan, had been on her mind all winter.

Vancouver provided enough diversions for her with its underground night life, her BMW, her clothes, her boy toys, the internet, and other amenities of modern society. Likely she would be home soon. Beign had said that he expected Liest to pull the plug on the last Auerbach chantry and completely abandon their presence in Meristyian. The alliance with Lady Allyssia had been a definitive disaster.

Barissianna stood and wrapped herself in a unisex clan robe. At least she'd had time to make peace with the loss of Janaka, albeit not with Ayelet. There had been no time to say goodbye to Ayelet when they'd left Allyssia's city, or so Amanoch had insisted at the time. The double loss of both Ayelet and Janaka had sent her into a depression the likes of which she hadn't felt in a long time in her vampire life.

She'd tried to travel through the dream world to visit Ayelet in her sleep, but she'd been turned back by the Lady's dream defenses-the immense black bastions that surrounded the hidden city. No amount of effort had helped her-an accomplished dream-walker-to penetrate the multiple barriers, which had been reinforced by the efforts of Amanoch's own interlaced spells.

She'd seen the Mimoic Hierarchy outside the Lady's walls too, or sensed them-the presences of Mimoic watchers, dangerous holy crusaders that would prey on a lone vampire. She'd tried twice to get through to Ayelet in the dream world. She hadn't tried a third time.

Barissianna tossed her hair over her shoulder and faced the doorway. Quick footsteps alerted her to the presence of Magistrada Beign. Beign thrust his head inside the bath. The chantry figurehead was overdressed as usual in his pinstripe waistcoat, like a paunchy penguin peeking around the corner. Beign normally wore cosmetic reading glasses in his chantry in Baton Rouge, but not in Meristyian. His gold-flaked eyes were wide with tension under his finely waxed eyebrows.

"It's possible this chantry has been compromised, Barissianna. We may need to begin the rituals immediately to transport our souls back to Earth. This isn't good."

"What? Slow down, Beign. What's going on?"

"Two Jinni are here," Beign answered quickly. "I thought since we're both of the same rank, we could speak to them together. You're more experienced with this Jinn bullshit."

"Were these Jinni caught by a night patrol?"

"No, they just showed up in front of the tower this morning. I talked with the Jinni through the gate, and then I left them without letting them inside. The one who talked to me has moon-silver in her eyes. Her clothes didn't show any affiliation with Hell's army or with the Smokeless Flames though."

"A couple of Jinni wouldn't just wander here for no reason."

"Right. They asked for you, Barissianna."

"What? Why didn't you say so, Beign?" Barissianna threw off her robe and climbed into a sack dress. Could Ayelet be knocking at the front door? Her heart quickened. She could think of no other explanation. She grimaced at her image in the mirror. She looked awfully dead. She'd looked hideous all winter, but she'd felt queer about asking Beign for some of his makeup. She had no lipstick, no powder, no creams, no nothing.

She slipped into her shoes and ran down the flights of stairs as quickly as her feet would take her, through the entry hall to the front door, which stood open. She pressed past Beign and his gaggle of armed guards in the shadowy entry room. She stopped and scrutinized the two cloaked Jinni who stood outside the front gate bars. Neither of them was Ayelet, and both were armed-one with an ivory white longbow and the other with a sword strapped at her hip.

The redheaded Jinn stepped closer to the chantry gate and spoke through it. "I'm Mistress Golda of the New Order, ambassador in Eastern Meristyian for Lady Allyssia. My companion is Mistress Artemisiah. Are you Magistrada Barissianna of the Auerbach?"

"Yes. I'm Barissianna. I recognize Artemisiah."

Artemisiah smiled benevolently. "We're looking for Mistress Ayelet, who came this way. Have you seen her?"

"Please come inside." Barissianna reached past the guards and pulled the lever that raised the chantry portcullis. Beign protested behind her, but she ignored him. She escorted Artemisiah and Golda through the chantry hallways into the first-floor parlour. The roaring fire in the hearth spread heat and light across the tartan armchairs and antique oak bookcases.

Magistrada Beign was right behind. He closed the door, sealing the four of them in the parlor's warmth. Tension was etched on Beign's face.

"Barissianna, are you sure you know what you're-"

"Yes, Beign. These are friends. Artemisiah, this is Magistrada Beign, the commander of this chantry, which is the last operating Auerbach chantry in Meristyian."

"It's nice to meet you, Magistrada," Artemisiah said with a smile of condolence. "Thank you for your hospitality."

Beign frowned. "How did you find this place?"

"We have our sources," Artemisiah answered. "And we're also trackers. Rest reassured that we're New Order Jinni, and we're only searching for Mistress Ayelet. If Ayelet isn't here, we'll be on our way, and we won't trouble the Auerbach further. If she's here, however, we'd like to see her, in good faith."

"Well, that's just the problem isn't it," Beign said. "Lady Allyssia betrayed us once, and she will again. The last I heard, the New Order Jinni have returned to serve Lord Hades-"

"We've done no such thing," Golda said heatedly. "Or at least some of us haven't."

Barissianna cleared her throat. "Beign-"

"What, Barissianna?" Beign paced back and forth, never removing his eyes from the two female visitors, who sat stiffly in their seats. "Allyssia severed all ties with our clan. She threw our clan out of her city, conveniently leading to an ambush by Hell's army. Matriarch Lubersky and your husband went to the void, along with a lot of our men. How can we welcome these Jinni as guests?"

"I'm sorry you feel the way you do, Magistrada," Artemisiah said. "I can assure you that the Lady had nothing to do with the disaster that befell your clan. I myself am only just learning of it. What happened, Barissianna?"

Barissianna cleared her throat. "It was a disaster. We'd flown across Meristyian over three straight nights. We were all tired, and Hell's army was waiting for us at the Blackrock chantry. Do you know of the place?"

"No, but we have friends who may have gone there."

"They'll find trouble, or nothing. This chantry here is all we have left. Why are you looking for Ayelet?"

"She came into the east looking for you, Barissianna," Artemisiah said. "You haven't seen her?"

"She's not here. Which means-"

"That she never arrived," Golda finished. Her gloomy blue eyes grew still stormier under her windswept red hair.

"And for that I'm grateful," Beign added. "We don't want Jinni coming here, or anyone for that matter. We do have obfuscation spells, but anything that goes in and out of this chantry could potentially be tracked. Can I speak with you in the hall, Barissianna? Please?"

"Fine." Barissianna followed Beign into the hall, where most of the occupants of the chantry had gathered to listen-a dozen armed vampire men ready to attack or defend.

"We should try to reach Liest and tell him about this," Beign whispered, once he'd pushed the parlour door closed.

Barissianna rolled her eyes. "Why?"

"We don't know the loyalties of our visitors, and someone out there obviously has my chantry pinpointed on a map. This is bad, Barissianna. This is very bad."

"Everything is fine, Beign. I promise you we're in no danger, or at least not much danger. It's minimal. Or at least, I hope."

"Right, Barissianna. Maybe you've been compromised too, letting your personal life get in the way of clan business. Yes, Amanoch told me about your affair, having a relationship with a Jinn behind your husband's back. You've clearly been seduced by the minions of Allyssia. They have a lock on your mind."

"Beign, please not in front of everyone-"

"So this Ayelet was your Jinn lover?" Beign persisted. "She came out here searching for you? Tell me the truth."

Barissianna licked her dry lips. "Yes. That appears to be true."

"Well, I don't have a problem with you fucking a Jinn, but I can't trust you to be objective in this, Barissianna. Jinni can't be trusted. Cupid kills some with arrows, and some with traps. The Jinni lay traps."

"Where did you hear that quote, Beign?"

Beign hesitated for long moments. He straightened and plucked at his waistcoat. "Amanoch. I shouldn't tell you if he didn't, but just about everyone knows except you. The whole thing is bullshit."

"Tell me. What the hell are you talking about?"

Beign fluttered his hands. "Amanoch told me something when he arrived here after the attack. He said Lady Allyssia's son cast a spell on him to make him fall in love with a Jinn fledgling. Amanoch said that he confronted Cupid personally. A disagreement ensued. A rift in the alliance formed. The bats were packed and everyone left the city of Lady Allyssia."

"What? That wasn't the story Amanoch told me."

"Maybe he feels embarrassed. Maybe he feels threatened. Liest chose you to lead the all-important research into cirai, not him."

"Please don't tell me that my husband, Lubersky, and all of our men went to the void because Amanoch's male ego got in the way of our alliance with Allyssia."

Beign pivoted and swept past the men. He headed for the tower stairs. "Love becomes more and more dangerous the closer you get to her bosom. This conversation is over, Barissianna. You're being too emotional. I'm going to summon Liest and speak with him about this. Men, guard the door and allow neither of those Jinni to leave."

Barissianna sighed and followed Beign up the long flights of spiraling stairs to the fourth level tower ritual room, which was stuffy and warmer than the levels below and smelled faintly of frankincense. She watched Beign ascend the ritual dais and transfer a match to the candles around the flat-topped altar.

"Beign, let me speak to the Jinni alone. They prefer to deal with women. Maybe if I can be persuasive, they'll confide more. Amanoch never meshed with the New Order Jinni. That's apparently why the alliance failed. It wasn't the fault of the Jinni. The love spell was probably just in Amanoch's head, and I don't mean the head on his neck."

Beign shrugged. "Let's talk to the Patriarch. It's been a few weeks since we spoke to Liest. The arrival of these Jinni is a good excuse to pester him about letting us return to Earth. I'm tired of waiting here commanding this chantry, just waiting to be attacked by Hell's army or the Mimoic Hierarchy. I just want to go home to Baton Rouge, hang with my boys, and forget about this Meristyian bullshit. Unlike the rest of you, I came here for a straight-up pleasure cruise in the emotional realm. I wasn't supposed to deal with any of this."

"This isn't a crisis, Beign. Please calm down. If these Jinni can help me connect with Ayelet-"

"Like I said, you're being too emotional. Step inside and close the door."

"You're really pissing me off, Beign." Barissianna closed the door behind her. She stood at the edge of the dais and watched Beign work. He paced a circle around the pentagram-inscribed dais, making piles of salt at the loci of the elements. He removed the night-crystal from around his neck. Liest's night-crystal was a smoky quartz. The power of the silver latticing glowed visibly. Beign placed the night-crystal in the center of the altar, closed his eyes, and began the complex spell that would enable Liest's magic gem to find a channel across the planes.

Harbat Solomon Ussishkin Elicit

Thrice times nine Beign uttered the words. Smoke from the braziers swirled into a circle, and power crackled above the altar.

"Patriarch, I'm so sorry to disturb you from your sleep, but we have an event here at Rubicund Cliffs. Two Jinni have arrived. Yes. They're looking for Mistress Ayelet, a Jinn who apparently came out this way from Lady Allyssia's occupied city. Exactly. Ayelet was looking for her lover, Barissianna-"

Barissianna shifted uncomfortably while she listened to the one-sided conversation. What did Liest think of her lesbian fling? She'd spoken to Liest through his night-crystal earlier in the winter, but Liest had only wanted an update on cirai. He'd wanted progress on the research that could help defend the clan against the Disciple vampires. She'd offered the patriarch only bad news. Beign was giving Liest worse news.

"-yes sir, the two Jinni are sitting right now down in my parlour-"

Barissianna crossed her arms and waited for the verdict. She felt ready to end it and return to the comfortable confines of Vancouver without her husband. Still, it was flattering that Ayelet had come looking for her. Ayelet was a sudden smoldering ember in the coldness of her losses. Beign was moving. He withdrew slowly from the altar.

"-thank you sir, we'll begin preparations immediately."

Barissianna gritted her teeth. "We're leaving then?"

"Yes," Beign answered. "Liest says we can close up our presence in Meristyian completely. I'll perform the ritual on everyone to extinguish their desire-bodies and send them back to their Earth vessels, and then I'll transport myself."

"I'm not going to like this ritual."

"You'll be fine." Beign's mood had visibly improved. "I haven't lost a single person in an Isandlwana transfer. You can go first if you want. That way you won't see everyone else's blood running down the floor grooves."

"I've wanted this, but now I'm worried about Ayelet."

"This isn't optional, Barissianna. This is an order from the Patriarch. None of our clan will be in Meristyian until this new war between Heaven and Hell blows over, and that could take a century or more. Let's get the Hell out of this bullshit and go home. Earth gets tiresome, but there's far less risk of final death."

"What about Artemisiah and Mistress Golda?"

"Liest says to dump them into the front hall pit and shut the lid."

Barissianna blinked. "What? No. That's ridiculous. They came in peace, and I wanted to talk to them more about what's going on with Ayelet."

Beign shook his head. "We're all leaving the tower now, and Liest says we can't leave with these Jinni knowing the location of our clan's last safe haven in Meristyian. Period. If we ever come back, Rubicund Cliffs will be our re-entry point, so we need it sealed up, warded like our holiest of holies, and one hundred percent safe. The Jinni have sent many of our people to worse fates lately anyway."

"Not these Jinni. Did Liest say anything about wanting to talk to me, or wanting my opinion?"

"No." Beign slipped past her and opened the door. "This is the plan, Barissianna. Just stay up here and out of the way. I'll discuss the routine with my most trusted men. We'll show the Jinni to the door. The floor drops them into the pit. We lower the compression blocks in the front room and create a sealed tomb, and then we all retreat to the top floor and transport home. God, I hope we've kept the trap hinges oiled though. If it fails and those Jinni get loose on us-"

Barissianna watched Beign descend the stairs, muttering to himself. Did Beign or Liest even know what Artemisiah was capable of? It was possible that the pit lid wouldn't hold against the power of her lightning bolts. But then, Artemisiah might not be able to fire her lightning after she fell. There was no water in Beign's pit like in the Blackrock chantry. Beign's pit sported an array of nasty steel spikes instead.

Barissianna descended to the second level and entered the silence of her personal quarters. She had to admit that Vancouver was beckoning her back. In her chantry on Earth, she'd have her books, her DVD collection, and her laptop. She'd have Victoria's Secret underwear and the best California wines. She could snort cocaine, lie on the chantry roof, and watch the stars spin by. She could take a break from her magical studies and everything else if Liest would let her forget about cirai.

Of course, she wouldn't have Janaka. She'd have friends and drugs, but the drugs barely compensated for blunted earthly sense endings. Even the best drugs couldn't equal her mind-blowing experiences when she'd been entwined with Ayelet. The incredible Jinn vacuum had loosened her hold on her soul, and she'd surrendered totally. She hadn't even cared in those moments when pleasure was everything. Despite all of the material comforts of Earth, the physical world was a dull and thick dream compared to the addictive desire-world.

Had Ayelet really seduced her? Had Amanoch really been influenced by a love spell from Cupid? One thing was certain. In any minute, the Rubicund Cliff pit mechanism would spring, and the visitors in the parlour would go to the void, and any connection she had left to Ayelet would be severed, despite the fact that Ayelet had apparently risked life and limb to traverse Meristyian to see her.

Barissianna swallowed. She couldn't believe what Liest was doing. It was just like a male to be spiteful. Liest was like Amanoch-childish in his need for conquest, and childish in his need to lash out if he didn't win. Liest was a great dream sorcerer, a near-demigod. It was sad that he'd lost his heart after the second world war. There was only one thing that stirred Liest, and that was the power of cirai-the mysterious mysticism magic possessed by the Disciples of Set, a magic that had transformed the Egyptians into the most powerful vampire clan in existence.

Meanwhile, she'd failed in the quest that Liest had given her to find cirai's secrets. Liest had long been sure that the clues to the mystery were somewhere in Hell, in the environs of the last resting place of Kronos and the old titans.

Barissianna examined her scant replacement notes, recalling the many hours she'd spent combing Allyssia's book collections for clues. No. She wasn't ready to go home yet. She wasn't ready to give up on Ayelet, nor on her cirai quest. She'd be in big trouble disobeying Liest's orders, but all would be forgiven if she could find the secrets of cirai.

She had only seconds to make the decision. She stuffed her notes into a satchel with her writing implements. She grabbed a cloak and hat from the wardrobe. She skittered out of the door. She quickly descended the stairs to the first floor in time to see Beign escorting Ayelet and Artemisiah towards the chantry entryway. Beyond them, the entry was cleared of men. The trap was ready.

"Wait." Barissianna shouldered her satchel and advanced past Beign, pushing forward to join the two Jinni as they stepped out onto the pit lid. She clasped Mistress Artemisiah's shoulder. "I would like to humbly beg to join your search for Ayelet. Ayelet isn't here at this chantry, but if there is anything I can do, I've decided that I want to help you."

Artemisiah nodded slowly, as if considering. A twinkle glimmered in her eyes. Barissianna felt her face flush slowly with embarrassment. A girlish blush was another thing that she never felt in her dead cold vampire body in the Earth realm.

"You may come with us," Artemisiah said finally. "We'd be delighted."

"Barissianna?" Beign said. The kommissar stood at the opening of the entry room with his hand on an old nimfa statue in its niche. The pit lever was hiding behind the statue, a few inches from Beign's fingertips. "You dare to defy Liest? You know what this means?"

Barissianna nodded. "I'm not sure what Liest will think, but if he exiles me, demotes me, or has me killed, then so be it. Whatever he does, the punishment will be his to decide for his blood daughter, not yours." Barissianna stared Beign down meaningfully, and as she did, a shiver went down her spine. From the look in Beign's eyes, he was actually considering dropping her along with the Jinni onto the steel spikes.

She turned, put her hand on Golda's back, and guided the two Jinni to the chantry exit. With every step, she felt better. Beign wasn't so much of a brute as some of the other chantry leaders. He could talk tough, but he wasn't so hardcore. When she reached the archway to the outside, she felt tears coming to her eyes. She wiped them curiously. She wasn't sure if the tears were from her decision, or from narrowly escaping death as a traitor to the Patriarch, but either way she'd made the biggest decision in her life as a vampire since she'd made Janaka.

"Shall we?" Artemisiah stepped ahead into the light. Her white armor was blinding even in the shade of late morning.

Barissianna squinted and pulled her hat lower over her eyes. Two horses were hitched in front of the tower-one white and one black. "You know, I?I don't have a horse, and I didn't realize we were riding."

"You can ride my horse," Golda said solemnly, as if she were offering a heartfelt gift.

"That's very kind of you, Mistress Golda, but I wouldn't have you walking. I forgot to bring gloves as well. I won't turn to ash in direct Isandlwana sunlight, but my skin will still burn."

Artemisiah shrugged. "That's fine. We're only on our way to rendezvous with the other search party. They travelled farther than we did, so we have some extra time. Would like to go back inside and get gloves?"

"No. That wouldn't be advisable." Barissianna glanced back at Beign, then out into the brightness. "Maybe this is a big mistake. I'm more trouble to you than I'm worth. I can't even offer a chiropterim. There's no bat landing here. That's a reason Beign's chantry has stayed secret for all these years."

"No worries." Golda grinned. "I'll poke around for a bit. You can have my horse when we leave at dusk. We'll find somewhere to get you some gloves."

Barissianna stared at the redheaded Jinn, who was stripping off her pants and shirt, leaving herself fully nude. Golda was wearing no underthings. She strode to her horse and stuffed her equipment into her saddlebags. Golda looked over her shoulder and smiled at Beign and his boys, who were still watching from beyond the chantry gate.

When she was naked, Golda transformed. Her nose elongated, and fur raced from her red mane down her arms. Her chest bulged, and her legs thickened. Within moments a massive lioness, sleek and red-brown, loped away through the trees of the forested valley.

"Let's make ourselves comfortable in the shadows," Artemisiah said pleasantly, as if nothing unusual had just happened. The blonde mistress walked into the shade along the base of the chantry wall. "It's a fine day. We can relax here and chat a bit."

# Chapter 32:

Meristyian was beautiful from the sky, even if the scene kept tipping dizzily. Boudi-Ca kept a death grip on the reigns of the giant bat. She clenched the bat whistle between her teeth. Masad swooped lower ahead. She sucked air to whistle, but the bat automatically followed the leading bat down.

The brilliant orange orb of the sun was setting over the western horizon-cutting into the distant blue saw that looked like the Alpacian range. Boudi-Ca gave more rein to the bat. She prayed that Masad would land before dark. Her stomach and leg muscles ached from the prolonged effort of holding herself steady in the crazy basket.

Masad had taught her in an hour how to fly the great beast, but she still felt nervous controlling the thing. In the rear seat of the basket, the two human slaves huddled and held on for their lives. She couldn't communicate with them-at least not in English, English, or Aramaic. They seemed grateful nonetheless that she'd saved them from the vampires.

Masad drifted still lower, and the bat again made the adjustment to stay in the possessor's wake. They'd been flying for half the day. They'd set out in morning from their camp while the grey mists of night had still shrouded the mountains. They'd taken a number of breaks. Masad had said they would soon reach the mountain fastness where they'd meet Golda and Artemisiah instead of taking days on horseback to traverse the same rugged terrain.

Masad dipped again and veered low over a piney forest. Boudi-Ca could see the sinuous black course of a stream below the leafless trees. Masad followed the valley for a few seconds, then swooped precipitously towards a snowy meadow. Boudi-Ca whistled the bat down, trusting the massive animal to make the stop, and it did, with a skidding, hopping, shuddering jolt that made her spine shiver. It was over. Boudi-Ca grabbed for the edge of the basket as the bat swayed and steadied itself.

Masad threw his basket ladder and climbed down. Boudi-Ca threw her own ladder over the edge of her basket and descended on shaky legs. She motioned for the two Ahyehasi to follow. She was glad to hit the snow, even though her tired feet were cold. Masad was there with a rare smile.

"Found I Golda's track in the tapestry. Coming they this way. Flew we over them, so finds us Golda soon. Save we a few days of waiting. Rest in an abandoned werewolf camp under the cliff, the edge of old Greybeard territory."

"I'll find some firewood." Boudi-Ca followed Masad to the cliffs with the two humans right behind her. As Masad had suggested, there was a grotto at the base of the cliff where a shallow cave coughed up jumbles of rock to form a sheltered space between giant boulders. A blackened ring of rocks marked an old fire pit.

Boudi-Ca dropped her bags and indicated the slaves should wait. She strode out again into the snow, returned with an armful of wood, and then set out for more. She'd nearly gathered a second armful of dead half-frozen hemlock when she was startled by a brown lioness loping towards her through the gathering gloom. Golda changed shape and rose from the ground in a fluid motion to stride over the snow in the nude.

"Boudi, it's good to see you. A week was too long."

Boudi-Ca returned the warm hug and kiss. Golda's lips and skin were cold, and she smelled of pine needles and fur. Shapes moved behind Golda through the trees, accompanied by a clomp-clomp of horse hooves. Mistress Artemisiah approached, and behind her rode a woman who was swathed in a long grey cloak. Boudi-Ca studied the woman's pale face and long dark hair.

"Is that Magistrada Barissianna?"

Golda looked over her shoulder. "Yes. We found Barissianna, but we didn't find Ayelet. I guess you and Masad didn't find her either, or you would have already told me."

"Come to our camp." Boudi-Ca led Golda back to the little camp among the boulders while Barissianna and Artemisiah hitched their horses. Masad already had the fire going from the first load of wood. Golda rummaged in her bags and dressed herself. They all settled around on the ground. Boudi-Ca nudged shoulders with Golda. Her mood lifted a little bit. She hadn't realized how dour she'd been, or how much she'd missed Golda after only a week. Golda, as if sensing her sentiment, leaned and kissed her on the cheek.

"So what have you two come up with, Boudi? Artemisiah and I found the Auerbach vampires, although the welcome wasn't as warm as we expected. Barissianna came to help us. I'm not sure if you all have met. Barissianna, this is Boudi-Ca and Prince Masad, son of Lord Hades."

Masad bowed his human head in solemn greeting. "Found Boudi-Ca and I the Disciples of Set at an Auerbach chantry on the great black lake. Said they that the Auerbach were slaughtered. All dead."

"Not all," Barissianna muttered grimly. "More than ninety percent. So you visited the Blackrock chantry and lived? You did better than my clan, but I suppose you didn't face a legion of Hell's army. The Disciples have a garrison there?"

Boudi-Ca took a deep breath. "Not any more. We killed them all, but not until the last one told us where to find Ayelet."

"What?" Golda raised her eyebrow. "Why didn't you say so?"

"I just did. Well, we know, but we don't know."

"Said a Disciple that interrogated we," Masad said. "Holding her are they in a place called Dead Sedde. Said the vampire that Ayelet was captured, then taken to Dead Sedde by Archduke Yitzhak and the Smokeless Flames."

"Then we just have to find this place," Golda said.

"No." Masad' voice was curt. "Think I that find it we will not."

"You don't think we can track them?"

"Think I that go we should not," Masad answered. "Risk we too much. Risk we a fight with Yitzhak, my father's most powerful avatar. Advise I not to face him. Need we to rethink what do we. Claim we can the assets back at the destroyed Auerbach chantry. Bats. Weapons. Found Boudi-Ca these slaves. Think I that the New Order Jinni must stop hunting."

Boudi-Ca felt heat rising inside her. Masad hadn't confided his opinion until that minute. "We can't just leave Ayelet to her fate, right? We're going to go find her."

"Think I not to negate your opinion, fledgling," Masad said without meeting her eyes. "Advise I not to try. Think you of your own lives. Wishes the Lady to risk all of this? Prepared you are to sacrifice all for Ayelet? Even if find you Dead Sedde, prepared you are to accept death and the void?"

"Inclined I am to agree, Masad," Artemisiah murmured. "We should retreat to the werewolf stronghold with the new information and formulate a plan. I don't know where or what this Dead Sedde place is."

"I know what it is," Barissianna said. Her face was pale in the flickering firelight, and her voice was scarcely a whisper.

"Go on, Barissianna," Golda said.

"Dead Sedde is said to be the place where the titan Kronos took his children to swallow each of them after his consort Rhea gave birth. Everyone knows the story of how the Olympians were born."

"I don't," Boudi-Ca said. "They didn't teach us these things in Heaven. Who is Kronos? I've sort of heard of the Olympians."

"Kronos was the father of Lord Tuhan and Lord Hades," Barissianna replied. "Kronos impregnated his titan consort Rhea six times, and six times she gave birth, but each time Kronos took the child and ate it, except the last. Only Tuhan, who is now lord of the Mimoic Hierarchy, escaped Kronos through trickery. With Rhea's help, Tuhan caused Kronos to vomit up his previous five children, releasing Lord Hades, Demeter, Poseidon, and a few others. Kronos was then cast down into Haawiyah in an event called the Titanomachy. This is in the Greek myths."

"The old Greek myths aren't entirely accurate," Artemisiah added. "The titans all came to Earth to feed from the humans, either by worship or from taking energy from them directly, like Allyssia and her Jinn daughters. All of the children eaten by Kronos were really the avatars of titans, not the titans themselves. My sister Demetriah is an avatar of Allyssia like I am. Kronos swallowed my sister back then for the same reasons that Lord Hades has captured her and imprisoned her now-to gain power at the expense of a rival titan."

"That I didn't know," Barissianna said. "If Kronos swallows parts of other gods and not only his children, that supports my theories even more. He wanted to rule over all of Earth, just like Tuhan and Hades rule over a divided Earth now."

"Yes, just like his father Uranus before him." Artemisiah smiled faintly. "Masad is also a grandchild of Kronos, and he's older than I. Have you anything more to add, cousin?"

"Perhaps," Masad said. "From whence comes your knowledge of Dead Sedde, Magistrada Barissianna?"

"It comes from my research into cirai. It's a project that I've been working on for some years now. The Disciples are using cirai to consume the souls of other vampires, including my clan. That's how they've become the most powerful clan on Earth. The reference to Dead Sedde was in a mysticism grimoire. So my theory is that the Disciples are using the same sort of makumbacy used by Kronos to swallow the avatars of the rival titans so long ago."

"I can't argue against that theory," Artemisiah said.

Masad gazed at Barissianna intently. "Know you where is Dead Sedde?"

"No. For a long time, I never thought the eating was literal. So I never thought there was a literal cave either. Lately since I've come to understand the nature of Meristyian and the structure of energy forms here, I wonder if Dead Sedde is real. Many things are real here in the desire-world, but they are only symbols or words on Earth. Maybe the energy moves back and forth, changing things just like with the Isandlwana mountains and plains."

"Still know you not where it is," Masad said. "Think I too dangerous an undertaking, even to attempt to rescue Ayelet. Lose you may too much. Consider you that Ayelet was lost months ago. Know you not if she is still there."

"Do we have more allies we can call on?" Golda said.

Masad shrugged. "Ask we not the werewolves to take such a risk. Ask we could Sekhmet and the Eastern Order, but scattered they went when the Hierarchy assaulted again in Memphis at Ptah's old temple."

Boudi-Ca put her hand on the pommel of the Oya-blade at her hip, the sword that had been a gift from Ayelet. "I have to try to rescue Ayelet. Anything else is unacceptable."

"This might be bigger than Ayelet," Barissianna said. The dark flaked eyes of the vampiress sparkled almost golden in the half-dark. "It's too great a coincidence that Lord Hades would have a secret base in Dead Sedde, which is supposedly the occult birthplace of cirai, and this base is connected to the Disciple vampires you found at Blackrock."

"I hope you are wrong, Barissianna," Artemisiah said.

"What if I'm right? What if the Disciples of Set and Lord Hades are working together on cirai? The Disciples have been consuming the souls of other vampires, but Kronos consumed gods. What could Lord Hades do if he developed his father's titanic powers to eat his enemies and grow stronger?"

Golda's eyebrows furrowed. "Lord Hades could consume the avatars of the Lady. He could take all of that power and finally win the war against his brother, Lord Tuhan."

"And he has the Lady fragmented," Artemisiah added. "He has Demetriah imprisoned under Mer. He now has Persephoneh under his thumb since the Lady's city was taken. Ivanka has been missing for many moons. No one knows where she is. Lord Hades also tried for me at the Trivium. I was lucky to escape from his devil avatar, Archduke Fennel."

"Like little morsels," Golda said. "This isn't good, Barissianna. Are you sure about all of this? Masad, if you're worried about the future of the New

Order, I'd say this is pretty worrying."

"I was wondering why the Mimoic Hierarchy went after Memphis as soon as they developed a force in Meristyian," Barissianna continued. "We know that the Old Order and the Disciples went out of their way to take Memphis a year and a half ago, where they imprisoned Sekhmet and occupied her temple. Why does everyone want that ruined little city? Maybe there is knowledge in Memphis. Maybe the Hierarchy knows about cirai too, so they are escalating things."

"Speculate you greatly, Barissianna," Masad said.

"So we have to go," Boudi-Ca said. "We have to find out what's going on in Dead Sedde and save Ayelet if we can."

Masad shook his head. "Think I perhaps some truth in Barissianna's ideas. Still talk you of fighting an avatar of my father in Archduke Yitzhak. Go I not against my father. Eat me he could and would, if thinks the Magistrada correctly."

"The titanic history of cirai is all about the son defeating the father, Prince Masad," Barissianna said. "Lord Tuhan and Lord Hades defeated Kronos together, and that's why Kronos is imprisoned down in Haawiyah to this day."

"You've fought a lot of battles, Masad," Golda said. "Have you ever lost one?"

"Live I today because know I when to run," Masad answered. "And so name me the werewolves 'The Jackal'. Comes war in Meristyian between big dogs-Lord Tuhan and the Hierarchy, and Lord Hades and Hell's army. Run the little dogs must. If plan we to preserve the remnants of the New Order Jinni, remains it our plan. Have I the Clan of the Four Brothers to think of. Need me the werewolves more than you. Have they not another god to help them."

Boudi-Ca felt tears coming to her eyes. She wiped them. She couldn't believe what she was hearing, especially from Masad. "I'll find this place and walk in by myself with a Sharpened stick if I have to. I refuse to go home without Ayelet."

"I am committed to finding the secrets of cirai," Barissianna added. "So

I'll go to Dead Sedde."

"I think it's interesting, Masad, that everyone who loves Ayelet is sitting right here by this fire." Artemisiah's voice was unusually loud and strong in the shelter of the boulders. "Ayelet's lover and both of her most recent fledglings are here. Have you considered the unlikelihood of us all sitting here, somehow at every turn knowing exactly where we needed to go? Have you considered the possibility that the old Fates themselves have stirred in this time of unbalance? You've always been an agent of the Fates, Masad."

Masad remained silent and looked away into the gathering darkness.

"Well," Golda said. "It's true that I love Ayelet, even though we never saw eye to eye."

"I was Ayelet's lover," Barissianna said. "I don't know how much you all know about it, or even the right words to say among the Jinni. She's still special to me, and I hope that I'm still special to her. I'll fight to help save her."

Boudi-Ca took a deep breath. "I thought Archduke Yitzhak was supposed to be commanding Hell's army in western Meristyian. He might not even be in Dead Sedde. Would you help us then, Masad? Would you help if your father's avatar wasn't there?"

Masad nodded with his face expressionless. "Yes, help I would then. Very well, convinced me you all have. Feed you all should from the slaves. Leave we will by midnight and travel fast on the two bats. Shelter us darkness will."

"I might be able to remember some clues about Dead Sedde's location," Barissianna said, shaking her head. "I lost all of my old notebooks in the attack on my people. I think it's here in Meristyian, but the Acheron river basin is a vast and unforgiving place to try to find one cave. We're facing mountain ranges and thousands of Earth-miles of treacherous terrain occupied by our enemies."

"Trouble yourself not, Barissianna," Masad said. "Know I, more or less, where this Dead Sedde should be. Five or six hours more of flying." The shelter among the rocks fell silent, except for the crackle of the fire. Boudi-

Ca stared at the possessor.

"I thought you said you didn't know where it was."

Masad tilted his head. "Never said I this. Said I that you did not."

Artemisiah rose and paced towards her horse. "Get some rest and feed, fledgling. Prince Masad has never owed us or the Lady anything, and he still doesn't. We should be grateful for any assistance he gives."

Boudi-Ca shrugged off the sense that Masad had insulted her. She'd almost come to trust Masad and feel like he cared about Ayelet, but maybe she'd only deluded herself. Maybe princes just weren't trustworthy. Boudi-Ca felt a slow surge of fear suck at her stomach. On the other hand, if Masad was afraid to go to Dead Sedde, it was surely a most horrible place, far worse than the gloomy vampire tower on the lake.

"Boudi-Ca, are your humans available?" Golda spoke low in her ear.

"Yes. You can have one, or both."

"For Barissianna too?"

"I suppose that's the feeding they know." Boudi-Ca nodded at Barissianna, who nodded back almost imperceptibly. The vampiress had shed her cloak with the waning light. She tossed her long black hair over her shoulders as she approached the two Ahyehasi, who sat quietly one beside the other at the base of a nearby boulder.

Barissianna settled herself next to the boy and bent. The gasp of the male was audible. His face turned up, registering pleasure and pain. Barissianna's tousled dark head tottered as she buried her face in his ravaged neck.

Boudi-Ca beckoned to the female human in turn. The girl obediently rose and approached. Boudi-Ca drew the girl's frail body close between her and Golda. She reached low under the girl's dirty skirt. Golda leaned with a kiss. Boudi-Ca massaged and stimulated the girl for Golda's benefit. As Ayelet had once explained, vampire feeding had rendered the girl weak, breaking her desire-structure and eroding the walls of her reservoir of love energy. Neither of the vampire slaves held much sustenance for a Jinn.

Finally the girl gave up her orgasm, and Golda sucked the energy from her. Boudi-Ca turned the slave's mouth for her own kiss, and she and Golda changed positions. It took nearly an hour to procure two more feeble releases from the girl, and then from the dregs of the boy, who sported fresh red punctures from Barissianna's use of him. Meanwhile, Masad and Artemisiah spoke in low tones until everyone had fed and was resting.

"Is everyone ready?" Artemisiah finally said. The moon had risen in the late evening, and the last of the firewood spat and smoldered. "We've decided that Masad and I will fly in one bat. The rest of you will follow with Barissianna flying. The Ahyehasi will stay here and rest with the horses."

Boudi-Ca stood and strapped on her Oya-blade. She'd worked hard at her blades for over two years. She hoped she could use her skills to pay back Ayelet for those uncountable training sessions. She strode to the bat, climbed the ladder, and settled next to Golda in the back while Barissianna took up the reins and the whistle. Soon they were flying through the night in the wake of Artemisiah and Masad.

The moon rose cold and full over Meristyian, bright enough to illuminate the mountain peaks. Boudi-Ca hunkered into Golda's warmth when the cold began to bite. They flew for hours without stopping. The bat began to labor, coasting and beating its wings more heavily. The faintest pink of morning daylight shone on the horizon when they finally began their descent into a wide valley. They landed with a thud and shudder in a grassy meadow. Boudi-Ca followed Barissianna and Golda down the ladder. Masad and Artemisiah waited for them.

"Dared I only to go this close," Masad said. "Waits the cave at the bottom of the gorge. Know I not the way, so track we must. Find the threads of the vampires in the tapestry. Stay close. Follow in the rear, Golda."

"You got it, boss," Golda said.

Then they were off, filing behind the possessor. The snow was thick and frozen. Boudi-Ca stepped quickly, trying not to slip. They came to a steep drop, and she carefully picked her way down the rocks to where Barissianna and Artemisiah waited for her at the bottom. They slowly clambered down the valley over the course of an hour as the dim grey of morning light washed through the trees. Barissianna pulled her cloak tightly over her head.

A steep cliffside finally loomed.  A glow shone through the trees-the warm light of flickering torches at the cave entrance. Masad had stopped in the shelter of a pair of massive rocks that bordered a frozen stream. "Feel I presences," he said.

"As can I," Artemisiah said.  "Jinni.  I sense two women guarding the entrance, but nothing more. The deeper parts of the cave are shrouded in protective spells as ancient as time."

"Possess I will the weaker Jinn to help us gain entrance," Masad said. "Feel I that she might be a fledgling.  Help us a distraction will."

"Wait. The stronger one is moving away," Artemisiah said. "You may now have your chance, Masad. I hope the mistress isn't an excellent tracker. If she is, she already knows we're here."

Golda sniffed. "Why waste a good tracker on guard duty?"

"Maybe if you're guarding something really important?" Barissianna offered. "I'd just like to get out of the coming sunlight, so let's do this."

"Give me three minutes," Masad said. "Signal I will from the entrance when possessed her I have successfully. Call I will."

"Go," Artemisiah said. Masad stalked off across the snow towards in the entrance of the cave. Boudi-Ca fondled the hilt of her Oya-blade. She was nervous, more so even than at her Mistress Test ceremony or the first time she'd slept with Henne. The cold night had cut through the leather of her boots to numb her toes. She tried to imagine Ayelet inside the cave as a prisoner.

"Watch out for their whips," Golda said quietly.

"Let's go," Artemisiah said. "I hear his dove call."

Boudi-Ca followed the other women along Masad' tracks.  The cave entrance appeared to be barricaded with great blocks of stone, leaving only the upper half of the cave entryway open. An unpleasant smell drifted on the air as they neared. A torch flickered, held high by a figure over the massive stones. Artemisiah darted forward quickly towards the entrance, bounding over the snow like a white rabbit.

Boudi-Ca ran as quickly as she could to keep up. She was the slowest of the bunch. She resisted the urge to flash. She hadn't fed well. She needed to save her energy. The maw of the cave was even grander up close. The cave was mammoth. She climbed after the others up worn rocky ground and under the vaulted overhang. Golda scaled the difficult stones like they were simple stair steps. Boudi-Ca picked her way until she reached the top and hopped down behind the natural barrier where the others waited.

The male form of the Masad lay dead on the floor in a pool of his own blood, beheaded, by all indication, by the young Old Order fledgling in the red robe who was evidently Masad' new host. The attractive brunette fledgling wiped her sword and brandished it.

Boudi-Ca looked away. The possessor suddenly made her skin crawl, even more so thinking of him feeding and fucking her for the previous days. She wouldn't feed from him anymore, or at least she hoped.

"Ambush I will the mistress next," said the dark-haired Masad in his young, lilting, female voice. "Wait for my lead." Masad stalked swiftly down the corridor. Boudi-Ca followed behind Barissianna and Golda, who in turn followed Artemisiah. The stench kept getting stronger deeper in the cave.

"This guano stinks," Golda whispered. "I can't smell anything over it. They must have a lot of bats coming in and out of this place."

"Or they've never cleaned," Barissianna offered. "That would be typical of the Disciples."

A brief, strangled cry sounded ahead and cut short. Again Artemisiah sprinted, this time pulling her ivory white longbow from her shoulder. Boudi-Ca drew her sword and followed. The giant-sized tunnel widened into a cavern dimly lit by torches. A pair of great bats with riding baskets rested beneath massive stalactites near one wall. Masad bent over a woman in a red uniform. He slashed, finishing off the mistress, who twisted and fell motionless. Blood spurted. Her head lolled.

Footsteps sounded further down the passage, accompanied by a coarse voice. A leather-armored vampire emerged and stopped short at the sight of Masad. "What in the hells? What's happening here?"

Artemisiah drew her bow and let fly. The vampire ducked. The lightning bolt bounced off of the vampire's shoulder and thundered into the wall, shattering stone. The vampire tumbled to the floor, grabbing at his head. A second vampire emerged, then disappeared back into the passage. He angled and ran away from Artemisiah's line of sight.

"Help!" The vampire's shout echoed. Boudi-Ca flashed. The ribbon slid under her feet. She slipped through time along the uneven cavern floor, past the fallen vampire who was frozen in the act of getting back up, into the passage, to emerge at the back of the second vampire.

She swung her blade. The tip cracked into the fleeing creature's spine, but he was too fast, flying ahead of her. She executed a hateful kin-hex. He stumbled and toppled like a rag doll, but not before he reached a second well-lit cave room.

Boudi-Ca leapt and stabbed again as the vampire tried to rise, this time impaling him. He gurgled blood and slumped. She planted her feet and descended with an executioner's strike that nearly severed his neck. The vampire guard sprayed more blood, and the deep cave descended into silence.

Boudi-Ca held her blade at the ready. She'd ended up well ahead of the others. She stood at the entrance of a gloomy room lit by torches. A thick book and writing implements sat on a heavy, pitted desk. Behind the desk sat a pair of chairs, and nearby was a stack of old iron-bound barrels. She sensed a presence in the room just as the pulpous Old Order narcabyss whip snapped around her wrist. Agony shot up her arm, and numbness came with it. Her Oya-blade clattered from her suddenly useless fingers.

The whip jerked. Boudi-Ca toppled hard to the floor at the feet of a regal and powerful-looking Old Order Jinn, who had been standing out of sight along the near wall. A second Jinn in a red robe entered the room from a connecting passageway. She appeared to be a fledgling.

"What's happening, Mistress Astaarteh?" the fledgling in red said. "By the balls of Cerberus! She has wings! Is the Mimoic Hierarchy here?"

"We have intruders," Astaarteh barked. "Get ready to fight."

Boudi-Ca reached for her sword with her left hand, but the mistress with the whip waved her hand and muttered. The room went pitch black. Boudi-Ca grunted. A boot collided hard with her head. She yelped and saw stars in the darkness, but at the same time she heard the passage of large paws and felt a heavy weight pass over her. Golda roared.

A shriek sounded in the inky darkness, followed by the sound of ripping fabric. Boudi-Ca rolled away from the sounds of struggle. Her right arm was mostly numb, but she was free. She climbed to her feet. She massaged feeling into her wrist and fingers. She couldn't see anything. The darkness in the room was an unnatural, magical creation.

Boudi-Ca summoned a tenebris lux, but it sputtered on her fingers. She willed the magical light more fiercely into being with all of her inner strength. It finally flared above her head. The darkness fled and the room again resolved in the light of the torches on the walls.

"Be careful, Golda," Artemisiah cried out from the hallway. "It's Astaarteh!"

Golda still tore at the Old Order mistress, who barked another spell. Golda's tawny feline frame burst into flame. The smell of burning hair filled the room. Golda roared and skittered away, pawing at her eyes. Boudi-Ca reached low and re-took the hilt of her Oya-blade. Out of the corner of her eye, she saw Astaarteh aim a crooked finger at her.

Boudi-Ca flashed to the first shelter that caught her eye-the heavy oak desk. Flames inundated the floor where she'd stood a second previously, sending up a gout of acrid smoke. She'd emerged from her flash unscathed. Barissianna uttered a spell then, and arcane harpy eagles streamed across the room to pile into Astaarteh. The harpy eagles cawed and ripped into flesh.

Astaarteh muttered and a wind tore through the room, blowing the harpy eagles away, but a lightning bolt from Artemisiah's bow struck Astaarteh full on the chest, rocking her backwards. Boudi-Ca felt another presence behind her. The fledgling in red had leapt to attack with a blade in hand. Boudi-Ca raised her Oya-blade and blocked in the nick of time.

Boudi-Ca engaged the fledgling in the red robe, who smiled arrogantly, but the fledgling's smile quickly changed to frown. Boudi-Ca slashed, attacked, parried, and parried again. She was faster than the fledgling, but the fledgling was cunning. Boudi-Ca saw an opening. She attacked. It was a trick. She overextended, and the fledgling flipped a dart from her sleeve that struck her full in the throat. Boudi-Ca tore the dart away.

The fledgling lunged in her moment of unbalance, stabbing at her unprotected chest. Boudi-Ca twisted, and the blade scored only a glancing hit. Boudi-Ca flashed, dancing through time and space behind the fledgling in red. The fledgling whirled with a look of shock on her face. Boudi-Ca raised her sword for the killing blow, but Golda was faster. The fledgling went down with Golda's jaws on her neck. Golda's furry cat chin dripped with blood.

Boudi-Ca shook her head and blinked away tears. Her throat was burning where the dart had struck her. Her breast burned too where the tip of the blade of the red-robed fledgling had nicked her sensitive skin. Her head swam, and her mouth went dry. She turned nonetheless and advanced past Golda, who was finishing off the fledgling, and surveyed the scene in the room.

A new enemy had entered the chamber-a tall man in a dark robe. His beard was perfectly trimmed, and gold rings glinted on his long bony fingers. He raised his hand, palm facing upwards, and Artemisiah cried out. A black coil had stretched forth to strike Artemisiah in the chest. The coil hung in mid-air, lifting Artemisiah in a grip of darkness.

Artemisiah managed to draw an arrow to her bow and leveled it, despite the spell that held her. On the far side of the room, Barissianna was engaged with Astaarteh. Barissianna's sword flashed, but Astaarteh parried with her whip, slipping the blow and catching the vampiress with her whip to the neck. Barissianna squirmed to the side. Astaarteh raised her hand, and a stream of fire poured onto Barissianna, who screamed with pain.

Boudi-Ca flashed. The ribbon uncoiled across the room. She almost didn't make it. Her vision of the room was strangely dark and hazy. She appeared behind Astaarteh and stabbed backwards. She connected. Her blade drove clean through Astaarteh's ribcage. Barissianna's clothes were on fire, but the vampiress lurched into Astaarteh and embraced her. The Old Order mistress groaned and flailed, sending gouts of fire from her fingertips, but Barissianna held fast, ravaging with her fangs.

Boudi-Ca felt her legs wobble. The room was spinning around her. She fell inexplicably to her buttocks. Her throat burned. Her breast ached. Warm fire raced up her limbs to congeal heavily in her chest.

Artemisiah's brightness caught her eyes. Artemisiah was shedding sparks of white light through the room. She was suspended in air, unleashing lightning bolt after lightning bolt, which flew in slow motion across the room to strike the chest of the tall man in black, who seemed to only shrug them off.

The man's left arm was still raised, and the smoky black coil from his fingertips enveloped the white-armored mistress. The smoke seemed to be squeezing her. With his right arm, the man traced a circle in the air, and a hellion-a winged creature half as tall as a man and twice as ugly-congealed into being.

Boudi-Ca closed her eyes. She was in a dark plain under a blue-violet sky. She was crawling, trying to escape the thing that slithered towards her through the red umbers. Thorns tore at her arms, her legs, and her breasts. She couldn't crawl fast enough. The thing was at her legs, slithering over her feet and her bare buttocks. The thing wrapped around her torso. She couldn't get away. She couldn't move another inch.

The Viper King wrapped her entire body and began to slowly squeeze. Boudi-Ca struggled, but the King was far stronger than her pathetic attempts to escape from him. He crushed the breath out of her. He constricted her neck, and she could feel his tongue flicking at her ear. The King whispered, imparting wisdom both ancient and forbidden in a sibilant, hissing speech.

*Chapter 33:*

Barissianna kept her death-grip on Astaarteh, one of the two eldest of all Jinni, one of the First Fledglings of Allyssia herself. Astaarteh shrieked another spell. Barissianna felt the hex hit her belly and chest with such force that her teeth were ripped free from Astaarteh's neck. Barissianna spat blood and flesh. She rose unsteadily to her feet. Astaarteh was nowhere to be seen.

Meanwhile, Archduke Yitzhak, for that was who he surely was, was engaged in mortal combat with Artemisiah. Across the room, Golda leapt to try to intervene, but was intercepted by the hideous imp, who rebuffed Golda's attack with a power and energy that belied its small size. Golda circled the ugly little creature.

Barissianna raised her blade and stepped forward, sifting through her memories for any spells she dared try against Yitzhak. As she considered her options, the Archduke noticed her coming. He snapped his black wand and muttered, even while he kept Artemisiah held fast in magical black coils.

Barissianna raised her hand. The fairy counter-charm to the mysticism drain occurred to her in a heartbeat. Yitzhak's spell was cancelled, and she countered with her own. Yitzhak muttered his own counter and bounced her spell back in turn.

Barissianna hiccupped. Her follow-up curse was caught her mouth, as if a demonic finger had poked her there, leaving her breathless. The imp squealed with a high-pitched keening sound as Golda ripped off one of its wings. Yitzhak uttered syllables again. Two serpents dripped from his wand. The first slithered towards Golda, growing in size with every sinuous movement. The second serpent slithered towards Artemisiah's legs.

Barissianna raised her blade and stepped closer. She tried to form words and a spell, but she still couldn't speak. The first serpent struck at Golda. Golda roared in pain. Artemisiah lurched and lowered her bow. She waved her hand with a spell instead.

White rabbits dripped from Artemisiah's fingers. The snake under her feet ate the rabbits one by one, only to swell and finally burst. Dead white rabbits spilled from the snake's belly. The mingled mass of scales and fur dissipated. Yitzhak growled audibly as he looked down at Golda, who skirmished with both the imp and the snake. Her cat fur was spattered with a mess of minor injuries, but she still stood. Yitzhak leveled his wand at Golda. Barissianna wanted to yell, to do anything to stop Yitzhak from killing Golda, but she was still crippled by silence. She suddenly glimpsed Astaarteh again, who had re-appeared directly behind Artemisiah. Astaarteh threw her arm around Artemisiah's throat. A blade flashed.

In that moment Artemisiah cried out and levelled her bow. She unleashed a final bolt of bright light, brighter than any of the others. The bolt exploded into Yitzhak, raining down stony debris from the ceiling. A torch bounced loose from its sconce and rolled. Golda mashed the imp's head and batted the creature against the wall like a toy, where it collapsed in a quivering heap. Golda shifted then. Her form flowed, and she became a nude red-headed Jinn. She climbed unsteadily from her knees to her feet.

Barissianna cleared her throat. The curse was gone. She'd regained her voice. The battle appeared to be over. Only she and Golda still stood. Boudi-Ca and a red-robed fledgling lay dead or dying on the floor. Artemisiah, Astaarteh, and Yitzhak had all disappeared, and so had Masad. Barissianna nudged Boudi-Ca with her toe. The fledgling appeared pale and cold. Golda warily scanned the adjacent passageways.

"Where in the Hells did they go?"

Barissianna shook her head. "I don't know. Maybe they went to another dimension, and they took Artemisiah with them. This seems like déjà vu."

"By the Lady, not Boudi." Golda knelt, touched Boudi's temple, and stroked her cheek down to her flushed neck. She slapped Boudi's cheek gently. "Boudi? She's unconscious. I don't see any real wounds, just a few nicks on her neck and breast. And where in the hells did Masad go? Did we lose him too?"

"I don't know," Barissianna replied. "Artemisiah followed Boudi-Ca into the passage, and I followed her. Masad was in the body of that red-robed fledgling. I figured he was right behind me. Are you alright, Golda?"

"I feel very burned and cut up, but my change heals me. My arm bone might be cracked. You're looking a little singed yourself. Astaarteh must not have liked your outfit."

"I'll survive. I know she has better fire spells, but maybe she couldn't use them in this small room. So it's just the two of us left then. What are we doing? Are we going farther in, which could be suicidal, or are we getting out while we're still alive?"

Golda's blue eyes returned to Boudi. "I'm a little distraught right now, Barissianna. I'm not thinking right. There are more presences in here somewhere, but I can't make them out. The ancient magical shrouds over this place dampen my tracking senses. Are you still fit?"

Barissianna nodded. She felt incredible. "I just drained an elder Jinn. I was so giddy a few minutes ago that felt like I could burn the place down myself. If I hadn't been a fool to let Yitzhak silence me, I was ready to duel him."

"Then let's go deeper in. We've come this far. The way behind us is open. We can run if we get any more resistance."

"What about Boudi-Ca?"

"She wouldn't want us to turn back now." Golda paced to the hallway to pick through her split-open clothing. She retrieved her sword. "Come on.

I feel presences down here, and I'm going to trust my instincts on this one."

Barissianna followed Golda, who led the way down the most promising passage. The passage was wide and slanted deeper into the rock. They didn't go far before the hall opened into a low, sprawling chamber.

Rows of tarnished silver cages lined the room in double rows. The cages were occupied by several prisoners. A hunched figure sat in the closest one-a nude woman with her hair undone around her shoulders and her hands clasped together in the embrace of sleek black cuffs. The woman looked up wanly. Golda approached the cage.

"Mistress Szenes? Is that you?"

The Jinn leaned forward. A chain rattled on the floor. "Golda? Mistress Golda?"

"Szenes?" Golda moved to the next cage. "And Ranavalona-Ca? What are you two doing here? Are you here voluntarily?"

"By the Lady, no," Szenes answered. "It was a trick. We were supposed to go back to Haawiyah. We had all of our clothes, jewelry and things on the back of one Nanka, and Ranavalona and I were riding on another with our Ahyehasi. The Nanka stopped at a camp in the mountains. We could see the storms of Erebus ahead, and then they surprised us. They chained us and hooded us. When they took our hoods off, we were in this place. Where are we?"

Golda scowled. "You're in a cave in northeastern Meristyian. They didn't let you feed?"

"No," Szenes answered. "They're starving us. We haven't fed the entire time. Ranavalona and I hunger terribly, but we still have our wits about us, if only barely. Please get me and my fledgling out of here before we go to the void."

"I'll look for a key. Do you know where some keys might be?"

"I think Mistress Astaarteh has them."

Golda grimaced. "Maybe there is something on that desk. I'll be right back. Wait for me here, Barissianna."

Barissianna acknowledged Golda's request, even as her blood sense was rushing in her head. She recognized Szenes and Ranavalona-Ca from casual acquaintance at the Lady's Redoubt, but her thoughts were on someone else entirely.

She stalked through the cages. At the end, in the black shadow of a corner, the form of a woman lay chained to the floor in the center of a cage. The woman lay on her back, unmoving. Barissianna pressed her face to the bars. The figure in the cage was familiar. Amber pendants still hung from her exposed nipples.

Barissianna shuddered, and she felt a sudden urge to vomit up the rich blood in her belly. Ayelet lay on the floor, gaunt and motionless as if in a coma. Ayelet was all wrong. Ayelet's body was missing both of her arms at the shoulders.

"Ayelet!" Barissianna felt her shout choke in her throat. Ayelet didn't stir, but her eyes cracked open, and a faint glimmer of recognition was just visible.

"Mmph," Ayelet murmured.

"Barissianna, I've got them. The keys." Golda re-entered the cell area. She turned the keys in the cages, releasing Szenes and Ranavalona-Ca. Golda's face betrayed her horror when she came to Ayelet's cell door. Her hand trembled as she unlocked it.

Barissianna thrust her way inside. She wrapped Ayelet in an embrace. Ayelet's skin was cold, and her head was slack on her neck. Her shoulders were mere stumps of hideous, stitched-together flesh.

"Ayelet!" Szenes gasped as she approached, looking down. "I saw something hunched over here, but it never moved. I had no idea who it was, or even if it was still alive. Oh my, by the Lady! Oh my! Don't look at her, Ranavalona."

Ayelet opened her mouth. "Barissianna? Is this the void?"

"No, Ayelet. We're both alive. We came to rescue you."

"Rescue? You're real?" Ayelet's lips quivered. "Turtle. They took her into the laboratory. cirai-"

"cirai? Here?"

Ayelet nodded vaguely. "Experiments. Who else is with you?"

"It's just me and Golda now," Barissianna answered. "Mistress Artemisiah and Yitzhak seemed to have neutralized each other. Boudi-Ca and I took down Mistress Astaarteh, but Boudi-Ca is in a bad way. She's unconscious, and we don't know what's wrong with her."

Ayelet's eyebrows twitched to a frown. "How did Boudi-Ca fall?"

"She was fighting a Smokeless Flames fledgling," Golda said. "She got some minor cuts, but that's all."

Ayelet closed her eyes. Her head lolled. "Poison. Antidote."

"What should we do, Barissianna?" Golda said, averting her eyes from Ayelet. "Should we try to get Ayelet and the others out of here, such as they are? I checked the cages. We have Szenes, Mistress Nenneh, Ranavalona-Ca, a few others, and half a dozen Ahyehasi."

Barissianna frowned. "We need to find an antidote for Boudi-Ca. Ayelet said her fledgling Turtle is here too. They took her to a laboratory. It must be nearby."

Golda nodded. "A laboratory sounds like a good place to start looking for a poison antidote."

"I've heard noises coming from that hallway over there," Szenes said, pointing. "I think that's where Yitzhak spends his time when he's here. They took Mistress Melkeh down there, but she never came back. Where are we going to go? We can't go back to the Redoubt. Lydiah and Yitzhak have betrayed the Lady and broken their promises to us."

Golda's visage darkened further. "Let's go to this laboratory and see what we're dealing with."

Barissianna followed Golda and Szenes down the hallway. The ebony fledgling named Ranavalona-Ca lingered to look down at the crumpled, severed form of Ayelet. Barissianna steeled herself. All of the hatred she'd ever felt for Lord Hades and the powers of Hell were boiling over in that moment. Her love for Ayelet had gone leaden in her sour stomach, along with the memories of wonderful Jinn pleasure.

The laboratory was a ritual chamber with an ancient work table in the center surrounded by candelabra and canopic jars. Barissianna sniffed. The room smelled like bittersweet nightshade and other sundry herbs and chemicals. Rows of shelves held vials, bones, and various leather and metal implements of restraint. She stalked to the heavy wooden table, which was adorned with manacles attached by chains to its four corners. At the end of the table sat a hide-bound book with yellowed pages.

Barissianna turned to the first page and leafed through the devilish English script. The book was labeled clearly as an exegesis on cirai, with a brief technical opening followed by a series of instructions accompanied by handwritten notes.

"What is it Barissianna?" Golda said.

Barissianna held up the book. "This room and this book might be the last pieces of the puzzle that I've been researching. This might be a place where cirai rituals are performed."

"And it isn't a safe place to hang out and chat," Szenes said, wrapping her arms around herself. "Shouldn't we be trying to escape? I don't mean to sound like a coward, but I'm really, really weak. Ranavalona-Ca and I need to feed."

"Szenes is right," Golda said. "We need to get everyone out of here as soon as possible. I have no idea what an antidote to poison might look like, or even what poison afflicts Boudi-Ca. Do you, Barissianna?"

"Ask Ayelet. Maybe she can say more. I'll stay here." Barissianna felt a shiver at her own words. "When we leave, I have to take cirai with me."

Barissianna examined the table. Faint brown discolorations stained most of its surface. She knew well the ferrous colors of blood scrubbed from old wood. She sniffed the contents of one of the jars near the dais. She discerned the acrid odor of ammonia. The elements of the ritual appeared similar to the ancient Egyptian methods of preservation.

She leafed deeper into the cirai book, scanning dates and entries. The book detailed experiments on various unwilling subjects-failures and partial successes, notes and procedural corrections. The shelves and jars appeared to hold all of the needed ingredients.

Another small tunnel sloped down into the rock from the ritual chamber. The floor of the chamber was worn and stained red at the entrance. Barissianna tucked the heavy book under her arm and crept along the tunnel alone, deeper and deeper into the stone.

The air grew warmer. The tunnel widened and belched the smells of rot, sulfur, and ages of decay. It smelled like a vent, perhaps a passage down to Erebus or a backdoor to the cave complex. Barissianna advanced until the tunnel ended abruptly. It was no secret exit-only a precipice lit by guttering oil lamps. Barissianna leaned to look a hundred feet or more into blackness.

She widened her eyes to see with her night vision. She could make out the dim outlines of bones in the depths of Hell's crust, many bones thousands of years old perhaps, and the crumpled forms of what appeared to be many bodies, warmer than their surroundings. The rotting corpses were the gaseous hosts to a horde of scavenging insects. Barissianna backed away from the edge of the pit and strode back up the tunnel towards the ritual chamber.

"Barissianna!"

She heard the faint distant voice of Golda calling her. She quickened her pace up the tunnel. When she arrived at the ritual chamber, the Jinn cat shifter was waiting for her. Golda had carried Boudi-Ca's body to the ritual chamber and placed her on the work table. Boudi-Ca lay unmoving with her eyes closed, appearing feverish and deathly.

Barissianna grimaced. The fledgling was beautiful-a credit to the Jinni. It was a pity to see her near death. "Does Ayelet need something to feed from, Golda? I could offer myself-"

Golda shook her head. "Szenes got her an Ahyehass. I think she'll make it. Ayelet still has enough strength left to feed, although just barely. Her willpower is unbelievable. Where did you go? What's down that lower passage?"

"Nothing but a lot of bones. I'd guess they were victims of the cirai experiments."

Golda held up a second book. "When I went up to the first chamber to retrieve Boudi-Ca, I found this book in the desk. It's a list of mistresses and fledglings who live in the Lady's city. I can't believe it, but apparently they plan to bring them all here. That would match Szenes's story."

Barissianna nodded. "They're bringing them here for cirai. Yitzhak and

Astaarteh planned to consume their souls, or at least experiment with them
."

Footsteps sounded in the passage to the cells. Ayelet appeared with
Ranavalona and Szenes on each side, supporting her. Barissianna felt her
stomach sink again. She could hardly look at her former lover. Ayelet
wobbled back and forth, armless and unbalanced, but made it into the
chamber to gaze down at the unconscious Boudi-Ca on the wooden table.

"Anyone find Turtle?" Ayelet whispered.

Barissianna gestured at the far tunnel. "There are a lot of bodies down
there that I couldn't identify. It's kind of far to walk."

Ayelet leaned and sniffed at the blackening blotch on Boudi-Ca's swollen
neck. When she drew back with effort, a trace of a scowl was etched on
her gaunt face. "Boudi-Ca is poisoned with Nokian viper venom. The
potentized version is a sacred elixir of the Smokeless Flames, a concoction
bestowed by Lady Allyssia for use on their weapons."

"I've heard of it," Golda said. "I haven't heard of a cure."

"It can be resisted by a very strong soul with the help of a good healer,"
Ayelet said. "No ordinary herbs or magic will cure the poison because it's
combined with a powerful curse. I have no idea of the resistance of Mimos
to poison. Otherwise without a healer, I'd expect Boudi-Ca to go to the
void within a few hours."

Golda sniffed and wiped her eye. "By the Lady. Boudi-Ca didn't deserve
to go like this. Are you sure, Ayelet?"

"Yes," Ayelet answered. "I was once a fledgling in the Smokeless Flames.
I've dealt with this poison intimately. Part of the Flames training is to parlay
with the Viper King and gain a resistance. I completed the resistance ritual.
I assume I'm still immune."

"What about a werewolf shaman?" Golda said. "We have bats waiting
outside the cave. We could take Boudi-Ca to the Stronghold of the Four
Brothers."

"Perhaps," Ayelet said.

"Sounds good to me," Ranavalona interjected. "Let's get out of here and
take Boudi-Ca with us."

"What about the others?" Barissianna said. "There's a whole list of New Order mistresses that they're still bringing here."

Ayelet's brow furrowed. "Are you serious?"

"We found some kind of manifest in the front room." Golda lifted the book. "It's a list of New Order mistresses and fledglings. Only the first four are marked off-Mistress Melkeh, Mistress Szenes, Mistress Nenneh, and Ranavalona-Ca. It looks like they plan to experiment on all of them, or kill them, or whatever. Something needs to be done. Where in the Hells is Masad?"

"By the Lady," Szenes said, exasperated. "Get me and Ranavalona-Ca out of here please, and then consider your careers as epic heroes. The Sisters and vampires come and go from this place all the time. Reinforcements could arrive."

"Agreed," Ranavalona-Ca muttered. "I feel sorry for Boudi-Ca, but I'm running for the exit in ten more seconds. I don't care where I end up, as long as it's not at the end of a narcabyss whip."

Barissianna fingered the tome in her hands. "I've only had a few minutes to look at this place. I need more time. If I can find a way to prevent or counter cirai, it could stop the Disciples and save my clan."

"Szenes and Barissianna are both right," Ayelet said with a sigh. "I suggest that Golda guide Szenes, Ranavalona-Ca, and the other prisoners to safety. Barissianna can bide her time. This work is very important to her."

"Alright," Golda said. "So we'll take Boudi-Ca to a werewolf shaman, Ayelet?"

"Boudi-Ca has only a few hours before the Viper King whispers her soul to the void, and perhaps less, considering she looks weak and underfed. How long is the journey to the werewolf stronghold?"

"Masad guided us up here on bats, but now he's gone with Artemisiah. I can't fly those things. Even on the bats, I'd think at least eight hours. The stronghold is far away."

Ayelet nodded. "Take Szenes and get out of here. I'll take care of Boudi-Ca and keep Barissianna company until she's ready. Go."

Golda's face was a mask of resolution. She sniffed and wiped tears from her eyes. She leaned and softly kissed Boudi's forehead and lips. Ranavalona-Ca also bent over the table and kissed Boudi-Ca on the lips, then followed Szenes and Golda from the room. Barissianna fingered the tome of cirai. She was alone with Ayelet. She gently touched Ayelet's shoulder.

"What happened to you, Ayelet? Do you want to talk about it?"

Ayelet shrugged. "I was looking for you, of course. I had a gift for you. Freyah made you a new sword. I'm sorry. At least I have a chance to say good bye."

"I'm sorry too, Ayelet. I'm so, so sorry. Amanoch wouldn't let me go see you. We left that very night. When we arrived at the Blackrock chantry, we were attacked on top of that. It was the worst night of my life. I lost Janaka and everything. The Auerbach clan here in Meristyian was destroyed, and I was lucky not to go to the void with the rest of them."

"I feel your pain, Barissianna."

"My problems are nothing compared to yours, of course. I'm glad you at least tried to come and look for me. I came for you in the dream world, but the Lady's bastions around her city turned me back. So you went to the Blackrock Chantry?"

"Yes. The Disciples occupied it. They caught me in a trap. Archduke Yitzhak brought me here. They took pleasure in breaking me. I thought that would be all, but Astaarteh and Yitzhak brought me in here. They said they needed parts of me for unique experiments. They heated a fire in the furnace. Yitzhak brought a saw. I don't remember anything else except for the pain. A week later, when I was mostly conscious again, they brought me back in and took my other arm using the same procedure."

"I'm so sorry, Ayelet."

Ayelet half-laughed, half-sobbed. "It sounds crazy, but I was almost hoping to find my arms lying around in here somewhere. I think I've gone mad. I've been floating in and out of delirium and hopelessness for an eternity."

Barissianna felt her throat clutch. What could she say? She had the urge to hug Ayelet, to pull her close, but she couldn't bring herself to do it. The vibrant, hazel-eyed elder Jinn who she'd once known seemed to be closed and far away, in a distant time and place.

Barissianna leafed through the tome in her hands, examining the devil writings. She could feel the darkness and power of cirai in the pages. She needed to take the book someplace safe. She needed to contact Liest and somehow transcribe the book to the Earth plane. Most of all, she needed to complete her quest before Lord Hades and the Disciples tracked her and made her pay for thieving their unholy research. Ayelet's voice intruded on her consciousness.

"Is that book a recipe for cirai?"

Barissianna looked up. "Yes, I think so."

"Can you do it?"

"cirai? I have no idea. I need to know the practice and theory. I have no real intention of stealing anyone's soul. It looks like the ritual described here is performed by a third party anyway, not for oneself."

Ayelet cleared her throat. "Is there any chance that you could attempt cirai for a charitable cause, right here and right now? I've had a lot of time to think during my imprisonment, and I've come to realize that Boudi-Ca and Golda are all that I have left in this world, all that matter to me. I will never fight again, so my students must fight for me. Unless we find a poison antidote somewhere in these caves, which I can't even bring to Boudi-Ca without arms, your cirai might still save her from the void."

"What do you mean?" Barissianna felt a chill run up her spine. She knew what Ayelet meant, although she couldn't believe what she was hearing.

Ayelet's hazel eyes were far away in distant memories. "As I said, I was once a Flames fledgling. I have a resistance to the poison. I was told long ago that the resistance to the curse-poison was not physical but spiritual. I know the words to whisper. I know how to entreat and pacify the Viper King. I've lived through him and survived. If Boudi-Ca were to absorb my soul, then she would know how to do this too. Isn't that how cirai is supposed to go?"

"It's just a theory, Ayelet. Your soul is not worth sacrificing-"

"Yes, it's worth it. For her, it is. To me."

Barissianna felt her heart shrink at the mere thought of attempting such dark magic. The walls of the cave seemed to close in around her. Ayelet had indeed gone mad. "There may be a way, Ayelet, to take your soul to Earth. Liest is a very powerful makumbacer. It's possible, if we brought cirai to him together, that he would help you as a reward. We could put your soul into a new body on Earth. You could live among the vampires. You could maybe live with me in my chantry."

Ayelet shook her head in the negative. "I don't belong amongst the Auerbach any more than you belong amongst the Jinni, Barissianna. Either tell me this is possible, or tell me another way to save Boudi-Ca. That's all I am asking."

"It might be possible. But-"

"Look at me, Barissianna." Ayelet drew herself up to full height. "Look at me. I know you can't even look at my body right now. Archduke Yitzhak and Astaarteh have taken everything except my favorite fledgling, who I raised from the day of her initiation. I fed her with my own hands. They won't take my protégé from me. They won't."

Ayelet was sobbing openly, unable to wipe the tears streaking her cheeks. Barissianna felt her own tears forming as well. She leaned heavily on the table. The fledgling Boudi-Ca lay pale and still. The chest of the young, pretty blonde Jinn rose and fell in an abbreviated, barely perceptible fashion. Her breaths ran low and fast.

"I don't think I can do this, Ayelet. I don't know what my chances are, but they can't be good. I refuse to kill you."

"You must try! You must do this for me, and then you must take that book away from this place. You must destroy it. If the evil inside the book won't let you destroy it, then you must hide it in the most cunning way you can devise."

"I will." Barissianna nodded, although she knew she was telling a lie. She would find a way to deliver cirai to Patriarch Liest. It was her personal ticket to forgiveness, and it could potentially save her clan's existence.

"We are wasting valuable time." Ayelet's visage was grim. "I wish to volunteer myself for your research, Barissianna. Study the book. I'll try to help you locate the reagents for the ritual. We must do this quickly."

## Chapter 34:

"-Voulez vous jouer les cartes?" The aunt was old and stuffy with a powdered wig. Her teeth were white like sugar candies. "Et cette carte, la carte de La Hierophante-" The Hierophant card was old and worn. The figure on the card was blood red and inscrutable. The aunt held it between two manicured fingers.

She was dead. Her fingers dropped the crucifix that she'd clutched in vain. She waited by the road until the dark carriage came. The shiny black door opened. "Portia," the shadowed woman said. "Welcome to Hell."

A pair of torches burned at the altar. The chapel was packed with Smokeless-Flame Sisters. They lifted her and deposited her bodily on the altar. The ropes cut into her flesh. Above her rose the statue of a hooded snake-Allyssia the mother goddess, the great lady Smokeless-Flame.

"Remember the teachings, fledgling, remember the words, or you will not survive this night-"

Pricks came, and then pain. Her throat swelled, and panic seized her. She lay in the grass. Something came from the blackness. The serpent slid over her legs, seized her, and began to whisper. Boudi-Ca drifted away from the stream of queer memories. She could feel the coils of the Viper King around her body, still crushing her.

He owned her neck. Her every breath was his, and he whispered foul words with it. She remembered the teachings. She whispered back. The Viper King released her. The world congealed. She slowly awoke on the slab of stone.

She could feel the weight of everything above her head. She could hear the silence. Her heart quickened as the memories of the place came back into her groggy mind-the battle with the Old Order Jinni and the poison. She'd been poisoned, but somehow she'd survived. She needed to leave.

Boudi-Ca slipped off the slab table. The room tipped, but she landed on her feet. Her foot brushed against her Oya-blade in its sheath. Someone had neatly folded her clothes with her sword belt. She climbed into her pants, her shirt, and her padded brown coat. She tied her boots and strapped her sword around her waist, and then she advanced from the room through a cave passage sloping upwards. She passed a room with several old metal cages, all empty.

She climbed another tunnel into a chamber scorched with fire and smeared with bloodstains. The body of a red-robed fledgling lay dead. Dead, decapitated vampires lay amidst still-damp rivers of blood in the far hallway. Boudi-Ca hesitated. Memories came like dull, throbbing pains in her skull, mingling with the stew of her confusion. What had happened? Where were the others? Had they found Ayelet?

She made her way to the lone bat in the great entry cave. She climbed slowly up to the basket while her head steadied. Daylight bloomed outside the cave. She glimpsed a patch of blue sky. She took up the whistle that hung in the basket. She snapped the reins, and then she was flying out of the cave, darting under the stumps of old broken stalactites.

She scanned the rising slopes of the remote valley for any trace of Golda or Masad. She saw nothing but snow, ice, twisted trees, and stones. She realized that she was lost, and she didn't have her werewolf whistle. Navigating Meristyian from the air seemed hopeless. She flew for several minutes. She eliminated the possibilities in her head, all while her Jinn Hunger mounted in her belly. Finally, she steered the great bat towards the pale burning disc of the Isandlwana sun.

She flew for hours until the sun tipped into darkness over the looming Alpacian mountains. She flew on, trusting the bat to avoid the high peaks in the night. The morning sunlight cast the Isandlwana Fields into a vast plain of undulating pinks and purples. It was the most beautiful thing that she'd ever seen. She alit and rested amidst the millions of flowers. The bat surged to and fro of its own accord, hopping and snapping up mouthfuls of butterflies. When the well-trained bat came back to her, she went aloft again.

Sunset was approaching when she left the Isandlwana Fields behind and reached the familiar mountains that sheltered the Redoubt. At first she couldn't see the city through the magical veils, but she could see the black crevice of the gorge, and above it the familiar stony valley. She'd found her way home, and her heart leapt, borne on the tide of her overwhelming, soul-sucking Hunger. She was desperate to feed-in fact, she was ravenous.

Boudi-Ca whistled and directed the bat down the gorge. The bat swooped low over the trees, coming in from the dark eastern sky where it might go unseen by Hell's soldiers. She landed at the ravine bottom, exited the bat and looked at the cliffs to re-find the secret passage. After much deliberation, she finally began to climb, following faint animal trails up the steep slopes and ledges. When darkness crept over the chasm, she summoned a tenebris lux. Her Hunger drove her relentlessly to find the passage into the Lady's hidden city.

Finally she found the familiar rock formations, and she plunged into the dark tunnel. After another twenty minutes, she climbed the stairs into the first floor of the abandoned house in the Divinity District. She slipped out of the heavy front door, through the hedge, and down the narrow, twisting street. The crisp mountain air was wonderfully pungent with wood smoke.

She hoped and prayed to the Lady that Tajee was still where she'd left him several weeks previously-safe and sound in her house, waiting to be taken. After she'd fed, she planned to send a bird to Henne and catch up on current events. She realized that she had no idea of the month and day. Was the Spring Festival over, or did she still have a chance to take up a practice blade and try for her Task of Mastery?

At the gates of the Divinity District, she flashed past the Hell's army guards. She took the little-used hill road past Ayelet's Villa. She descended again towards the workshop district and reached her house without being seen by any soldier patrols.

At her house, she slipped carefully around the corner and along the wall. She hopped up the front steps. A pair of Hell's army soldiers stood in the street outside of Golda's old home, smoking and chatting with a blonde Smokeless Flames fledgling in a red robe.

Boudi-Ca tested the front door handle. The door was properly locked. She eyed the soldiers next door. She didn't want to make a commotion by knocking. She flashed. She summoned a tenebris lux in the darkness of her front foyer. Violet's butterfly box still sat on the hall table with the insects mounted inside, dead and dry. The box was dusty.

"Tajee?" Boudi-Ca kept her voice hushed in the stillness of the house. She hungered so much. She desperately needed Tajee. He wasn't in the storage room. She ascended the stairs to the second level. Her heart leapt when she saw the wash of candlelight under the crack of her bedroom door. She opened the door with a smile. The warm candlelight illuminated two nude women on her bed.

Henne's legs and arms were splayed to accommodate the long body of a lover, who lifted her head from where she was kissing Henne's neck. Boudi-Ca clenched her fingers around the hilt of her sword. The memory came slowly-a dim recollection of the reunification party at Nili's house. The woman had shoulder-length brown hair and a sandy, weathered complexion. Her hard, silver-brown eyes were careworn around the edges. The Jinn who embraced Henne was Lieutenant Nefra of the Smokeless Flames.

"Boudi! By the Lady, you're back!" Henne extricated herself with a look of shock. Nefra sat up and reached quickly for her red uniform, which lay in a jumble on the floor. Boudi-Ca felt her heart pounding. Her face went burning hot.

"Yes. I'm back, finally. I've been on a long adventure. I'm sorry if I'm interrupting something, but you two are in my bed. You seem to like taking other people into my bed, Henne."

"I'm so sorry, Boudi. You were away for a long time, and we needed a secret place to be together. No one has been arrested yet, but after Nili pecked me on the cheek at a party in the Divinity District last month, Ambassador Lydiah made an example of us. We were officially humiliated in a public statement warning everyone to cease and desist with lesbian activities. Now the soldiers are watching Nili's house. I think Nefra likes the thrill of the forbidden." Henne smiled sweetly at Nefra, who half-smiled back as she climbed into her uniform pants.

Boudi-Ca crossed her arms to suppress the flush of anger that mixed with envy in her chest. "Well, I'm glad my home could give you the opportunity for a romp. How did you get in here, Henne? Where is Tajee? He was supposed to lock himself in my house until I came home."

Henne paled. "The Smokeless Flames has copies of keys to a lot of houses in the city. Nefra has access to those keys. Tajee is back at the palace."

"So where have you been, Boudi-Ca?" Nefra said smoothly as she pulled on her boots. "We've been looking for you."

"Who is 'we'?"

Nefra shrugged. "You're wanted for questioning. Lydiah posted a reward in gold aurei for anyone who finds you, in addition to your bounty posted by Hell's court."

Boudi-Ca frowned. "I guess my disappearance didn't stay a secret then."

Henne shook her head. "Not recently, Boudi. It's hard to explain. Ranavalona and I couldn't tell the truth, or you'd be in worse trouble."

"Truth? What's the truth?" Nefra interjected, reaching for her sword belt. "You said you had no idea where she went, Henne."

Henne looked sheepish. "Please don't be mad. Boudi-Ca is my best friend. I had to protect her. Surely you can understand that."

Nefra hefted her blade. "I have to take you to the palace, Boudi-Ca. It's my duty. You're a person of interest, and the Ambassador wants to talk with you."

"I'm not going anywhere."

Nefra shrugged. "We can do this the hard way."

"Bring it." Boudi-Ca reached for her belt and pulled her Oya-blade. The weight of the steel felt good in her hand. She was dangerously weak from a need to feed, but her Hunger fueled a mood to hurt someone, a strong desire to cut and see blood. It was a queer, disturbing urge that she'd never felt before. Nefra matched her move, putting her blade en garde.

"Yellen, please don't," Henne pleaded. "Couldn't you just forget you saw Boudi-Ca? Please? Do it for me."

Nefra shook her head. "You know I can't do that, Henne. I have to do my duty."

Boudi-Ca snorted at the sword pointed at her chest. "Your duty doesn't include breaking into my house and fucking my girlfriend on my bed. You deserve a punishment."

"No!" Henne interposed herself. "Stop, you two! Boudi, why are you even here? Why did you even come back?"

"I was hoping to not get arrested."

Henne palmed her forehead. "There are signs on the barracks all over the city with your printed portrait. Well, sort of. Mistress Gonorrheah made the printer's blocks for them, and she screwed them up on purpose. They don't look anything like you."

"You're not a traitor for having left the city," Nefra said. "It may not amount to more than breaking curfew. I just know they want to question you. You're Henne's friend and I respect that, Boudi-Ca. I don't have any ill will against you personally, so don't make me hurt you."

Boudi-Ca snorted. "What makes you think you can hurt me, you hypocritical tramp? Since when was an Old Order Jinn supposed to be a lesbian, anyway? Maybe I should take you to the palace for a good questioning."

"Are you sure you want to do that?" Nefra smiled, but her eyes betrayed her nervousness. "That would get Henne in trouble too. On the other hand, maybe if I just kill you because you resisted arrest, I'll be commended and no one will know anything."

Nefra burst into motion. Her blade darted like a cobra. Boudi-Ca countered. Nefra closed, testing her with a flurry of blows. Boudi-Ca parried them all and countered with a contretemps. Nefra barely managed the parry. Her face registered surprise.

"Please stop!" Henne pleaded.

Boudi-Ca forced a smile, but she was in trouble. She hungered far too much. She had little energy left after flying for two days and a night across Meristyian. Nefra attacked her again with a feint followed by a hateful kin-hex. Boudi-Ca felt her skin prick. She hadn't fallen for the trick, but Nefra had pushed her into the bedroom corner. Her senses were strangely heightened in that moment, as if she knew everything that was coming, if she only tuned to it.

Nefra pressed the attack again. Boudi-Ca parried, locked Nefra at the wrist, and turned them both, allowing her to dance a side-step back to the opening of the bedroom door. Nefra twisted free, leveled her sword, and met her eyes. "Not bad. I'm impressed."

"Catch me if you can."

"You're going to get caught." Nefra raised her hand and summoned a messenger bird. "I have the fledgling Boudi-Ca cornered here. She's at her house."

"Yellen?" Henne said quickly. "How are you going to explain why you're here, and more importantly, why I'm here with you?"

"Get dressed and go home, Henne. Quickly. If you aren't here, no one will question you. I'll send you a bird later."

Boudi-Ca didn't wait to hear the rest of the exchange between Nefra and Henne. She turned and ran down the hallway, down the steps, and through the foyer. She flung open the front door and ran outside. Stars twinkled in the sky over the Lady's city. The sky was a deep purple, not yet swathed in full night. The Lady's crystal palace bowers were silhouetted at the head of the city against the orange sunset glow that still limned the high mountainsides.

Boudi-Ca eyed the soldiers in the street in front of the house next door. There was no point in being a fugitive in the city. If they really wanted her for questioning, Hell's army could have all of the soldiers combing every street and home. She needed to leave by the way she came. She needed a new plan.

Pain lashed across her back, accompanied by snapping sounds.

Boudi-Ca groaned as numbness filled her back, shoulder, and buttocks. Two Smokeless-Flame Sisters darted around each corner of the house. Within a split second, she was surrounded. Another narcabyss whip snapped. She felt the impact, and more numbness coursed into her limbs. Boudi-Ca collapsed to the cobblestones. Her sword clattered. She heard footsteps, and yet another whip snapped into her. She raised her hands in surrender as the lashes found her legs. Pain and numbness bloomed all the way up through her empty belly.

"Excellent job, ladies." Nefra trotted down the steps of the house and into the street. "You got here fast."

"We were already on her track," said one of the Sisters. "Our lookout spied this little rebel coming through the secret passage, just as Lydiah predicted."

Nefra nodded. "Cuff her. I'll take Boudi-Ca to the palace dungeon and apprise Lydiah of the capture."

"Right away, Lieutenant."

Boudi-Ca tried to struggle, but she was numb. She couldn't believe what was happening. Flashing away was pointless-she had no use of her legs. The Smokeless-Flame Sisters rolled her over and caressed her legs and arms further with the narcabyss whips to make sure she was thoroughly helpless. The military Jinni smelled like cigar smoke and ale. They relieved her of her Oya-blade.

Boudi-Ca felt a wet tear tickle her cheek; a feeling even more acute than the metal cuffs that snapped around her numb wrists. She glimpsed Henne watching from the shadows. Henne's face was a mask. Boudi-Ca hardened her own face and looked away. Henne was a traitor. She was fucking the enemy.

Nefra, meanwhile, had re-appeared with a horse. Boudi-Ca attempted to kick and struggle, but the strong lieutenant lifted her up, tossed her like a sack onto the back of the horse, and then tied her in place with straps like an animal.

The horse surged into motion. Nefra directed the horse through the streets of the Redoubt, escorted by a cadre of Sisters and accompanied by occasional catcalls from passing soldier patrols. Boudi-Ca clenched her hollow belly against her fear and embarrassment. She rode in utter indignity with her rump in the air, but she wasn't yet defeated.

By the time the horse reached the palace, her numbness had worn off just enough that she could walk. The Sisters pulled her roughly. Boudi-Ca struggled to clear her head. She realized that the numbness had evened out through her body almost like nectar, affecting her thinking as much as her limbs. She needed to flash away and escape, but she knew the moment needed to be perfect, even as the moments were ticking away.

In the palace, the Smokeless-Flame Sisters led her through the great hall into a side gallery, through a large doorway, and down a stairway into the palace bowels. They passed through another thick door into a lamplit room with a heavy, low wood worktable in the center and rows of tarnished silver cages lining the walls.

The Smokeless-Flame Sisters thrust her into one of the cages and locked it, then filed out cheerfully. The dungeon plunged into silence except for the murmur of voices outside the outer door. Apparently the Smokeless-Flame Sisters had posted guards.

Boudi-Ca tested the silver bars. They were solid, even if they were useless to hold her. Her body and mind were almost cleared of numbness. She bent and stretched to help work her energy through her limbs. She scanned the room for other exits than the guarded door, but there was no other apparent egress.

She eyed the long table and the many implements of pleasure and pain that hung from the hooks all over the stone walls. Lieutenant Nefra had suggested that she might not be considered to be a criminal. She hoped that was true. She'd soon know the truth.

Within minutes, quick footsteps sounded on the stair, followed by muffled exchanges of words. The dungeon door pushed open. Boudi-Ca felt fury at the sight of the cruel Old Order mistress who had taken Violet away from her.

Ambassador Lydiah wore her white-blonde hair done up in a silver clip. A curve-fitting red dress hugged her shapely feminine figure to mid-thigh. Diamond earrings glittered in the shadows of her ears. In stark contrast to the colors of red and bone, Lydiah's thin lips were painted black under her narrow nose, and she wore black leather gloves.

Lydiah laid a coiled narcabyss whip on the wood table in the center of the room before striding closer to the cage. Her silver-grey eyes were bright and seemed to glow with power in the lamplight. Lydiah's perfume was strong and nectary too, adding another dimension to her intense aura. Boudi-Ca turned her eyes away with difficulty. Under any other circumstances, she might have been impressed and even captivated by Lydiah's breathtaking beauty. In that moment, she hated Lydiah. The ambassador's black lips curved slowly into a smile.

"And so we meet again, Boudi-Ca. What do you have to say for yourself?"

"Did I do something wrong?"

"Well, you were once an Mimọ girl, and now you're a Jinn in Hell, so yes. By that singular description you've done some things very wrong. Of course, your story is also quite interesting. I have to admit."

"Whatever I did, and whatever you think I've done, I didn't mean to do anything wrong."

Lydiah laughed. "So we have the standard Mimọ girl excuse-a pretense of meek innocence with a refusal to take responsibility for yourself. You're disappointing me, Boudi-Ca. I was hoping for more."

"Get used to disappointment."

"Yes, I see a typical mixture of Mimọic humility, lust, and indignation. I see a typical confusion, too. You feel alone. You feel vulnerable."

"That much is true."

"Do you ever get tired of it-being confused?"

Boudi-Ca lowered her eyes to pretend to think, but she surreptitiously glanced at the closed dungeon door. She wasn't sure if the Smokeless-Flame Sisters were still out there or not. She gauged the possibility of flashing fast enough to get past the range of their whips. Unfortunately, just thinking about flashing made her Hunger leap in her belly. If she expended great effort trying to escape, she had to admit the possibility that she might run out of energy long before she flashed her way out of the city. Even if she did make it out of the city, another long flight on the bat without feeding first was unthinkable.

"Sometimes I do feel confused, Ambassador Lydiah."

"Look at me, Boudi-Ca."

Boudi-Ca looked at Lydiah's silver-grey eyes, which were hard and cold like the surfaces of gemstones. Lydiah was very close to the bars, and the ambassador's black-painted lips looked very kissable. Boudi-Ca felt her stomach lurch. Even after two and a half years as a young Jinn, it was hard to tell the difference between her Hunger and real attraction.

"What do you want from me?"

Lydiah pivoted and went to the heavy table in the center of the room. She seated herself sensuously on the table's edge. "I want answers, Boudi-Ca. The New Order Jinni aren't allowed to leave the Redoubt without an escort, but you went anyway. Where did you go, and why was it so important?"

"I went to study blades with Master Masad. That's all. I went to stay with the werewolves for a little while. If that's illegal, then I didn't know."

Lydiah arched her eyebrow. "So you know the current location of Prince Masad? He's in a hidden werewolf stronghold?"

"Maybe."

"I'll take that as a yes. You also know the location of Mistress Ayelet?"

"No."

Lydiah drummed her fingers pensively on the surface of the wooden table. She caressed the coils of her whip. "There are many ways to extract information, my darling Boudi-Ca. After nine centuries of interrogating Mimọs, no Mimọ has ever been able to withhold information from me. Take Tajee, for example."

Boudi-Ca felt her heart pound. "What have you done with him?"

"Let's just say that he's very vocal in bed. He's a handsome boy, eager to please. I finally got him to confide in me. He likes me, even though it took him a while to admit it. Yes, he and Violet are two fine Mimọ slaves. I've enjoyed using both of them, and I know they've enjoyed it too. You must miss your friends, don't you Boudi-Ca? I can see how much you're hungering. You're so empty and weak."

"You're just like all of the Old Order. You're cruel and heartless."

Lydiah ran her gloved hand across her impressive breasts with mock indignation. "Cruel? I'm not being cruel yet. I like you, Boudi-Ca, except for the unfortunate things I've heard about your lesbianism, which is illegal and pathetic. Jinni were created by our Lord to serve men and cocks. Have you never felt an Djinnus inside you?"

"If you liked me, you wouldn't have stolen both of my Ahyehasi from me."

Lydiah's black lips curled again into a smile. "I'm sorry you're hurting, but our good Lord didn't make me an ambassador for Hell because I'm sentimental. Yes, I think you're very confused. You're an Mimọ caught between dominance and submission-between a rock and a soft place. I've talked to a lot of people about you actually, Boudi-Ca. I've learned that you're trying to pass your Mistress Test, and you only have a few months left. How is that going?"

"Not very well."

Lydiah nodded. "I spoke to Mistress Gallinah, and she described your tasks to me. You're quite popular among the New Order Jinni. Will I need to use harsh methods to get the information I need from you? Tell me. Where is the werewolf stronghold? Where is Ayelet? Where is the traitor Masad?"

"The last time I saw Masad, he had taken the body of a Smokeless Flames fledgling in the halls of Dead Sedde."

"Interesting. What about Ayelet and the werewolves?"

"I really don't know."

Lydiah clucked. "I hear more innocence, this time twisted into lies. Tajee was the same way. He took some convincing. I had him pinned right here on this table."

Boudi-Ca scanned the racks of toys and torture implements on the dungeon walls. She gauged her chances of flashing, grabbing something pointy, and somehow driving it through Lydiah's wicked black heart. "Go ahead and torture me. I know you want to, and I know you're going to. We might as well get it over with."

"You don't just 'get over' torture, Boudi-Ca. Proper torture, when properly applied, lasts a long time and leaves scars. The Hell's Court devils will tell you that's an important part of it. If that's what you want, then you're right. We might as well get started. The Spring Festival is next week. If I start torturing you now, I might be finished by then so I can go and enjoy myself at the celebration."

"Fine. Let's get started."

"I'd like to start by removing your wings like Violet. It's tradition."

Boudi-Ca shrugged nonchalantly. "They get in my way anyway."

Lydiah slipped off the table and approached the cell with her whip. Boudi-Ca eyed the whip as Lydiah uncoiled it. She gathered herself. She'd run out of moments to escape. Lydiah was going to paralyze her. She had to try to flash, despite her weakness. She could flash to the wall and get a poker, and then she could flash behind Lydiah and ram the poker into the ambassador's ribcage just like a sword. Lydiah stopped and surveyed her from a safe distance.

"I was just teasing you, Boudi-Ca. I like to play. I don't want to hurt you. I want to help you, but you have to be willing to work with me." Lydiah paced in front of the cage, trailing the whip over the stone floor.

Boudi-Ca felt like she might faint. She hadn't ever been so nervous, not even when she'd received her Mistress Test. "How do you want to help me, exactly?"

"I understand that you're attempting to place first or second in an event at the Spring Festival. That's one of your tasks for your Mistress Test. Is that correct?"

"Yes."

Lydiah nodded sagely. "And if you fail, according to Mistress Gallinah, Lady Allyssia has promised to undo your transformation and make you into an ordinary Mimo slave. Despite your failings, I think that would be a waste."

"I agree completely."

Lydiah circled the whip lazily in the air with her black-gloved hand, as if pondering. "The Mistress Test is sacred, and the Spring Festival is a sacred celebration of Lady Allyssia and the first fledglings. Therefore your task at the Spring Festival is doubly sacred. So I ask-are you still wanting to fight in the blade's competition, even against our Smokeless-Flame Sisters?"

"Yes, I would like to fight. Please."

"Good. Good. I'll allow you, but on one condition. Are you aware of the vicious rumors in the city? The rumors say you never left the city at all, and instead you were abducted by me and the Smokeless Flames, and that we cruelly imprisoned you and tortured you all winter."

"No. I didn't hear that."

"My superiors want me to smooth over the relations with Allyssia's Jinni and assure them that we did no harm to their golden girl. We want a peaceful reunification of the Jinni with none of this ill-will, for the benefit of everyone. I want you to make a public announcement that I've done nothing terrible to you, Boudi-Ca, and that all of the rumors are lies. You'll make a statement of apology for breaking the rules of the reunification. You broke the rules and left the city of your own free will."

"Fine. I'll do all that after I fight."

"Excellent." Lydiah smiled widely. "I think I'm being gracious in this, and I hope you appreciate it. You'll have your chance to represent the Lady Allyssia at the festival competitions. You'll also represent Ayelet as her former fledgling, of course."

"Thank you very much, Ambassador Lydiah."

"You'll be going against Lieutenant Nefra and all of our best Smokeless-Flame Sisters. I do hope you're ready. It would be so demoralizing for all of your loyal local fans, don't you think, if you were thoroughly beaten and humiliated in that fighting ring?"

"I need to feed."

Lydiah nodded. "Of course. We can't have you dragging and compromised in any way. You'll fight and lose legitimately, and then you'll make a public statement about how fair the city administration has been with you, and how no harm has come to you, and how you greatly appreciate this opportunity to participate in the Spring Festival, which is a sacred celebration of Lady Allyssia, the true queen of the Jinni."

"Fine. I agree, but I need to feed now. I want Violet. Please."

"You can't have a lesbian scene with my Violet, but I'll find you a healthy male palace slave. I'll bring him personally so I can observe. I'm a fallen Mimọ expert, you see. I've written and printed a few how-to books for the privileged mistresses and masters down in the capital. I thought I knew everything about Mimọ girls, but this is a new opportunity."

## Chapter 35:

Nanka dung was disgusting. Tajee lifted a pile of it on the end of the shovel. He dumped it into the wobbly cart. He returned the shovel to the excrement, sliding the implement slowly along the floor. He didn't want to disturb the sleeping Nanka in the Lady's great hall.

Tajee scrunched his nose and picked up another shovelful of Nanka dung. One of the Nanka sighed, and a torrent of acrid gas wafted from its scaly buttocks. Tajee retreated from the cloud of foulness. The stench was giving him a headache. He'd lingered far too long with his Nanka cleanup duties, hoping to get a glimpse of Boudi-Ca being escorted out of the palace.

Boudi-Ca had been living in a cage in the palace dungeon for the previous week, or so the new rumors went. She'd returned to the city, only to be arrested. He'd tried to sneak down a number of times to the dungeon, but the Smokeless-Flame Sisters were ever-watchful with their whips.

He'd probably missed seeing Boudi. An unusual amount of traffic had flowed in and out of the palace doors that morning. Several mistresses had arrived with trunks and bags, as if they were moving into palace for some reason. Boudi-Ca had either left earlier, or somehow he hadn't seen her. At least Lydiah was allowing Boudi-Ca to compete at blades and try to succeed with her task-the Mistress Test that meant everything.

It was already the last day of the Spring Festival and the last day of the blade's competition. Boudi-Ca was doing well, according to Master Priapus. She'd reached the final rounds, which would take place that morning.

Tajee dumped one more lump of Nanka dung onto the cart. He wished he was at the amphitheaters, but Priapus had refused him permission to go to the festival. Instead, he was assigned stupid Nanka cleanup duty. He wheeled the half-full cart out through the massive mother-of-pearl palace doors, which stood three-quarters open.

Tajee shielded his eyes with his gloved hand. The sun was brilliant over the Lady's city, shining at an angle from the east under a wall of clouds coming from the west. Red flags fluttered in the wind around the courtyard. The flags bore the golden insignias of the Flames. The palace square was lined with the stalls of hawkers and vendors for the Festival, although the square itself was almost devoid of life except for a few Gypsy vendors and palace stable boys. The boys grinned at his dung-laden misfortune.

Tajee glowered at them and wheeled the cart to the very end of the palace steps, where a ramp led down behind the stable building. He wheeled the cart along the short path to the refuse heap at the base of the low cliffs along the nearby mountainside.

He navigated through clumps of thorny red umbers. He dumped the contents of the cart onto the heap, stirring up a cloud of black flies. He pivoted his cart and pushed back towards the ramp, but two men blocked his path. They were lean, hard Djinnus soldiers with helmets, swords, and steel armor stamped with the grim bearded visage of Lord Hades.

"Hello, pretty boy," one of the Djinnus said. "That's a pretty skirt." Tajee felt his stomach lurch. He released the cart and backed away, but the men advanced after him. One Djinnus grabbed his arm and yanked him towards the shadows along the stable wall. Tajee struggled, but the man's grip was like a manacle on his wrist.

"What do you want?"

"Nothing you won't enjoy," the man answered with a grin. "I'm Howard, and this is my friend Siegmar. I'll bet you need a real man, just like these lesbians."

"No! Let me go!" Tajee kicked, but he couldn't stop Siegmar from reaching low and yanking his skirt down his thighs. His legs went weak with a flood of fear.

"No one is going to hear you," Siegmar said. "Everyone is at the competition. That's an impressive cock, boy. Just relax and enjoy yourself. Have you ever been with an Djinnus? A lot of these lesbians think differently after we're done with them."

Tajee gasped when Howard shoved him against the rough, sweet-smelling pine timbers of the stable building. The Djinnus smelled like sweat, steel, and leather. His big slicked cock nosed and pressed inwards. Tajee groaned. The pain split his backside and waved up his spine.

"Lord's balls, this Mimọ boy feels like a virgin," Howard muttered. "Are you a virgin, boy? Are you a virgin Mary?"

Tajee didn't answer. The cock was driving deep from behind, pounding his words out of his stomach along with his breath. The pain slowly diminished, and the thrusts increased, lifting the pain into a slow, deep pleasure. Tajee felt his face heating, adding to his body's fever. His cock was rock stiff.

The rhythm continued for endless minutes until the Djinnus finally heaved. Tajee shuddered when the incredible pleasure inundated his core, a pleasure the likes of which he hadn't felt in forever, not since his most nectar-fueled passions with fledgling Herpessenia. When Howard released him, he slumped to his knees, but the men twirled him and pushed him face first onto the flowery ground. Howard kept him pinned with strong hands on his arm and neck. The Djinnus soldier was at least as strong as Golda.

"That's a sweet boy ass," Siegmar said gruffly. "That's the prettiest boy I've seen since my last leave in the capital city."

"I told you it was worth missing the fights," Howard said.

Tajee moaned, and he felt tears overflow his eyelids when Siegmar's cock pushed easily into his aperture. He felt no further pain. He felt only the deep pleasure, which again started to build in his body. Tajee closed his eyes. He only needed to endure the treatment, and he did, and within a few minutes Siegmar finished.

Tajee lay still amidst the rocks and flowers. The flowers were prickly against his chest and stomach. His cock finally subsided in stages, and his insides clenched oddly. He felt a queer yearning in his belly beneath the pricks. To his horror, he wanted more in that moment, as if has ass was somehow disconnected from its source of pleasure, incomplete, with something missing. His gut wanted the Djinnus back, and he tried to comprehend the queer, horrible feeling while the two Djinnus argued with each other in barely audible whispers.

Hands suddenly pressed hard on his back again, and he jolted when fresh pain hit him, this time high along his right shoulder blade. Tajee clenched his gloved fists among the thorny red flowers. The pain tore his soul and sent stars through his eyes. He cried out, and a vicious twin pain echoed on his other shoulder blade, and when he tried to rise, the men were striding away.

Tajee climbed to his feet. Hot tears were streaming down his cheeks, but he barely noticed. He'd never felt such pain. He tried not to look at his wings lying on the ground. He tried not to feel the trickles of his blood running down his back. He tried not to feel the male wetness oozing from his unmentionable nethers.

He stumbled past the shocked stable boys, who had arrived at the stable corner where the soldiers had vacated the scene. He made his way up the ramp and across the top palace step, where the wind was blowing in Sharp gusts. Lower in the city, faintly over the rooftops, came the roar of the Amphitheatre crowds. The day's fighting contests were under way.

"Nina!" Pexa was waiting inside the great hall. "Where have you been? I've been looking everywhere for you. Priapus sent me to fetch you for a bath."

"Where is the Master?"

Pexa blinked. "He's in the common area waiting, I assume. Are you alright, Nina? What happened? Why are you crying? You look scraped up and dirty."

Tajee didn't answer. He paced doggedly through the empty palace hallways with Pexa in tow. When he reached the common room of the Ahyehass quarters, Master Priapus was standing next to a large rucksack. Priapus was unusually well-dressed that morning with a leather adventurer's coat. Steel-toed boots peeked from under his long, heavy trousers.

"Master-"

Tajee turned his back to let the master see his misery.

"Nina? By the teats of Allyssia, those thrice-damned soldiers did this, didn't they? I'd kill them myself if I were capable. By the gods! These men are animals."

"They raped me behind the stables. Then they-"

Tajee bit back a sob while Priapus quickly applied a towel to his back, soaking up the drying blood. Pexa ran and wetted two more towels in the sink, and then she joined Priapus in cleaning him.

"I'm so sorry, Nina," Pexa murmured as she worked. "I was afraid to be raped, but now I wish it was me and not you."

"We don't have time for this," Priapus finally said. "Nina, you can come without your bath. The Lady said everyone could bring one Ahyehass if they wished, and I chose Pexa. Mistress Persephoneh chose you for herself."

"Where we going, Master?" Pexa's nose crinkled. "You still haven't told me."

Tajee glared at Priapus. "Yes. Where are we going? Can I have some healing herbs at least before I see Persephoneh? Can I get a clean skirt?"

"Sadly, things are happening this morning that are far more important than your wings or your wardrobe, and we're running late," Priapus answered. "As always, I'm sorry, Nina. Mimos seem to heal very quickly. You're no longer bleeding. So off we go. Come along, both of you." Master Priapus turned on his boot heel. Tajee frowned and followed Priapus and Pexa out of the Ahyehass quarters. Priapus turned and took a roundabout route through the palace back halls, down passages that were little-used.

They arrived at an ornate crystal door made of a translucent pink stone. Priapus pushed the door open to reveal a staircase of pink crystal. The tall master led the way up the spiral steps.

Tajee followed with a growing wonderment that almost distracted him from the aches and pains in his shoulder blades. The crystal stairs were yet another place in the Lady's palace that he'd never seen. They went up and up, spiraling past numerous doorways. The stairs ended at a large crystal room with an arched ceiling.

Rays of sunlight flooded into the tower room from a pair of high Gothic windows. The windows gave views of the Isandlwana sky over the Lady's city. Surprisingly, a crowd of Jinni packed the room. Nearly two dozen mistresses and an equal number of Ahyehasi mingled amidst piles of boxes, bags, and trunks of all shapes and sizes.

A small creature with the body of a winged horse and the head of a bird squawked at Priapus, who dropped his rucksack amidst the other luggage. The creature retreated to safety behind the skirts of Mistress Gonorrheah. The wizardress stood in the center of one window with a long brass tube held to her eye. Gonorrheah gripped the tube tightly with bent fingers.

"Another point for Boudi-Ca!" Gonorrheah said. "She's beaten the wyrm-rider captain and advanced to the finals."

"Well done, Boudi-Ca!" Mistress Gallinah exclaimed. "I hope she can do it. Oh! Master Priapus is here with pretty Pexa, and handsome Tajee too. Hello, dear boy. Is that everyone, Cupid?"

"Almost," Cupid replied. The love god was maskless, startling, and riveting in his ethereal youth and beauty. Cupid stood with his arm around his beautiful and reclusive wife, Psyche. Psyche's hand rested on the shoulder of their child, Voluptas. Behind the royal family stood fair Ankhises, the Lady's favorite Ahyehass.

Gallinah frowned. "Is the Lady really leaving Freyah, Pyrinnah, and everyone else behind?"

"Everyone just can't go," Gonorrheah answered. "It's enough of a risk as it is, although it's perfect timing, of course. Practically all of the Smokeless Flames and soldiers crowded into the amphitheaters to see our fledglings get beaten and humiliated."

"I'm going to miss Boudi-Ca, that poor girl." Gallinah leaned her rotund body over the edge of the window and gazed out over the city. "She's such a special fledgling. I've never known one like her. They're going to make her suffer."

"I expect she'll survive," Cupid said in his bell-like tenor. "My mother instructed me to hit Ambassador Lydiah with my magical golden-tipped arrows this morning. I struck her with two when she went through the dungeon door to get Boudi-Ca for the competition."

Priapus snorted. "That's wonderful, Cupid. Maybe if Lydiah learns a few lessons about love, she won't feel the need to tell everyone else how they should go about it. The Hell's army soldiers need lessons too. Nina was just raped behind the stables."

Cupid leaned and kissed his wife's cheek. "My mother agrees."

Tajee felt the ache in his shoulder blades take a turn for the worse. He couldn't believe that he'd heard the conversation correctly, and worse yet no one seemed to care about own encounter with the soldiers. No one looked at him, and the air in the room felt thick with tension. He'd heard the stories of Cupid's arrows. Cupid's golden arrows threw a potent love spell on whomsoever they struck.

Tajee slipped through the small crowd to look out of the window alongside Gallinah. He was high in one of the crystal towers of the Lady's palace, a hundred meters or more above the palace plaza. Red-tiled rooftops sprawled in irregular fashion through the bowl of the valley. The spired gatehouse at the foot of the city was visible against the darker, greener shades of the crossing chasm and the forested Isandlwana hills. Over the hills could be seen the hazy purple swaths of the flowery fields, and beyond the flowers could be seen the bumpy aquamarine line of a distant, island-studded sea.

"I can see Boudi-Ca and Lydiah together," Gonorrheah murmured, still looking through her spy glass. "They're ready for the final round. It looks like Boudi-Ca isn't getting much rest, and she's going against that relatively nice lieutenant. What's her name?"

"Lieutenant Nefra," Gallinah answered. "Oh, dear. Nefra's competition record in the Smokeless Flames is brilliant-second only to Ayelet's perfect record, which still stands from so many centuries ago. Boudi-Ca is a talented young fledgling, but she doesn't stand much of a chance against Nefra. Tajee? Your wings seem to be missing."

Tajee clenched his jaw. "Yes, Master Priapus just mentioned that, but no one gives a damn. Where is Boudi?" He craned to look where Gonorrheah was aiming her looking-device. The clover shaped amphitheaters near the center of the city sported a density of red flags. He could see a crowd of people like red and black ants overflowing the edges of the stony rings.

"Would you like to try the spyglass, Tajee?" Gonorrheah tapped his shoulder and offered the brass tube.

"Go on, Nina," Priapus said. "But for the love of the Lady, don't drop the thing. If everything goes well, I'd like to look through it myself when we pass over the Alpacian Mountains."

Tajee carefully took the spyglass. The tube was heavier than it looked. He levelled it and peered through. A little circular world opened up to his eye. He imitated Gonorrheah, turning the tube casing to play with the field of vision. He could see the rooftops of houses. He could see Golda's house, where he'd spent his first several moons among the New Order Jinni. He could see the little bath window where Golda had gazed across the city while bathing naked with him.

He could see Hatshepseh's house, where Boudi-Ca had told him to sneak over and pick flowers for the foyer. He could see the workshops, where he'd spent many days and weeks with Gallinah learning sewing to help Boudi. He moved the tube across the city workshops to the three-ringed amphitheaters. He could see hundreds of Hell's army soldiers, Gypsies, and Smokeless Flames mistresses in red. The crowds packed the amphitheaters below the fluttering red flags. The occupying military forces far outnumbered Allyssia's patchwork mistresses and fledglings.

"Do you see Boudi-Ca?" Gallinah asked in his ear.

Tajee focused and slowly moved the tube. He finally spotted Boudi. She wore a revealing red dress, and her honey-Brunette hair was clipped into a pony tail. He couldn't read the expression on her face, but he could see the sword in her hand.

Boudi-Ca was standing next to Ambassador Lydiah at one end of the center Amphitheatre ring. Lydiah receded into the crowd, and Boudi-Ca advanced across the ring. Her opponent met her in the center. Swords darted and flashed. Tajee steadied the spyglass. His hands were suddenly trembling.

"Boudi-Ca is fighting."

"Look for the barker at the side of the fighting pit," Gonorrheah said. "She'll raise a colored flag when someone scores a point. Boudi-Ca is in the red flag bracket, and Lieutenant Nefra is in the black." Tajee spotted the barker, who raised a black flag.

"Lieutenant Nefra just scored a point."

"Poor Boudi-Ca," Gallinah said. "It's amazing that she even reached the finals against all of those military Sisters. I would have never wagered it."

Tajee watched the combatants through the tube, which wavered in the winds outside the tower window. Boudi-Ca danced past her opponent, who was battered back. The barker raised a red flag twice. Tajee felt his heart leap. "Boudi-Ca just scored two points!"

No one said anything in response. Tajee felt a torrent of warmth wash over his aching wounds then, and his sex stirred queerly under his skirt, unbidden. Gonorrheah tugged the tube firmly from his fingers. He turned away from the window along with the mistresses.

Lady Allyssia shadowed the doorway to the crystal room. She carried a gnarled wooden elf-staff, which glowed with moonstones. Strangely, the Lady wasn't nude. She wore a dark leaden mask, a sheer Greek toga, and a golden girdle on her glorious hips. Persephoneh followed in the wake of Allyssia, equally somber and clad in blacks.

A clap of thunder sounded as the Lady strode forward. The thunder came from the sky outside, and the floor of the tower room shuddered. Thousands of tiny shards separated from the surfaces of the pink walls and ceilings, only to flutter to the floor like dead white butterflies, drained of any color. Tajee brushed the crystal flakes from his head. Another boom of thunder came, and the tower shuddered again. More crystal flakes fell.

"The wards are breaking, and the Sun Boat is beginning to form." Allyssia's voice was resonant in the room. "Everyone line up at the windows to climb on board. We are leaving for the eastern Sea of Desire."

Tajee stared at the Lady. "We're leaving? What about Boudi?"

Tajee felt Gallinah's warm hand on his shoulder. Gallinah spoke low in his ear. "Boudi-Ca is a distraction. She's helping the Lady and all of us get away from the city. She's doing her duty for the New Order, and she doesn't even know it."

"So we're just leaving her alone, to be beaten down there and whatever else?"

Allyssia's leaden mask inclined slightly. "Yes, Tajee. So will be her fate and her end, to help me make the weave right again. I accepted the gambit of Lord Tuhan and Lord Hades. Now I sacrifice Boudi-Ca back to escape a checkmate in this game of gods. They wanted a Trojan horse. I will show them a Trojan horse! I am the queen of Trojan horses! Oh, yes. Boudi-Ca will still serve Love on her journey. Will you, Tajee?"

"No. I knew you were cruel. I knew it!"

"I dreamt of something better, something beautiful," the Lady continued. "Pain twists our souls, but you can't give up on hope, Tajee. You have to believe in Love. You have to believe in me."

"I don't believe anymore." Tajee shook his head. "I believed in you at first because you're the goddess of Love. You're supposed to take away pain, not let people suffer. Well, you can let me suffer, and you can torture people and twist them around in your fingers, but not Boudi. Not Boudi!"

"I am inside of you, Tajee. I am inside of Boudi," the Lady countered in a low, dangerous tone. Her mask tipped further, and her visage grew still darker. "I am also inside of those Djinnus soldiers who took you by force for their pleasure. I am also inside of Ambassador Lydiah. I am the power, Tajee! I shall not be denied. I shall not be restrained. I shall not be caged like a beast. I shall not be subjected to laws and legalities. Love shall conquer all, and what I cannot conquer, I shall spread my legs and devour it!"

Tajee felt a chill run through his skull, and his sex stirred again under his skirt in Allyssia's overpowering presence. He wrenched away from Gallinah. He dashed towards the stairway past the Lady. He dodged the hand of Priapus. He descended the stairs as fast as he could run, crashing down into the half-gloom of the stairwell, even as another boom shook the palace tower. The crystal ceiling above him cracked and came apart.

# Chapter 36:

Boudi-Ca pivoted on the dirt, allowing Nefra to slowly circle her. The Amphitheatre was packed. Almost every soldier, mistress, and Ahyehass in the city had arrived that morning to watch the fights. Even the highest plaza railing that ringed the Amphitheatre was jammed with spectators. Mistress Isabellah started the chant again with Mistress Pyrinnah. Yenta added her voice from where she sat next to Isabellah, and Herzl shrieked louder than everyone else.

Boudi-Ca! Boudi-Ca!

Boudi-Ca! Boudi-Ca!

A counter-cheer, almost twice as loud, thundered for Lieutenant Nefra.

Nefra! Nefra!

Nefra! Nefra!

The hundreds of Djinnus and ogre soldiers from Hell's army stomped in unison with their heavy armored boots. Boudi-Ca tightened her grip on her sword and tried to focus. Nefra attacked again, taking advantage of the distraction. Boudi-Ca parried. The moves came to her fluidly-so fluidly that she shocked herself. Somehow everything was congealing in her head in that moment. She knew every nuance of every possible counterattack, and she knew it all in a split second.

Nefra launched another attack, employing the Exquisite Form of the Smokeless Flames. Boudi-Ca turned her blade and met the attack perfectly. She replied in the same form, matching the lieutenant through a little-known fifteen-move sequence, stroke for stroke until she edged ahead with her speed. Nefra retreated from the blow with a look of shock on her weathered face.

"Another point for Boudi-Ca!" the barker cried, waving the flag. "The score is seven to five in favor of the fledgling!" The crowd erupted into cheers, and Isabellah started the chant again.

Boudi-Ca! Boudi-Ca!

Boudi-Ca! Boudi-Ca!

The Hell's army soldiers roared and stomped.

Nefra! Nefra!

Nefra! Nefra!

Boudi-Ca allowed herself a small smile. Nefra's attacks were relentless, but she was turning each one away. When Nefra overextended with power, she shifted to an in-fighting style. Her blunt practice blade was a little long for her taste, but she made it work. The only way she could lose was to run low on energy reserves. She wasn't sure how she was doing it, but she was perfectly fluid. On that morning, she knew everything that Ayelet and Masad had ever told her, and much more.

Nefra changed to a defensive stance. They sparred on for long minutes. The crowd hushed, and everyone hung on the edges of their seats. Meanwhile, the late morning sun was growing very bright. A brilliant golden glow shone over the Amphitheatre rings.

Boudi-Ca pressed her attack with sudden inspiration, turning Nefra tactically into the light. Nefra squinted, momentarily blinded. Boudi-Ca lunged with a straight offense-a two-handed serpent strike. She broke Nefra's defense and struck square to the chest, launching the lieutenant onto her backside.

"Three points for Boudi-Ca!" the barker cried. "That's a victory! First place in the blade's competition goes to fledgling Boudi-Ca, fighting for Lady Allyssia!"

Boudi-Ca! Boudi-Ca!

Boudi-Ca! Boudi-Ca!

Boudi-Ca allowed herself a grim bloom of pride. She raised her sparring blade to the cheering crowd. She'd actually done it. She'd completed Ayelet's task. Meanwhile, the strange golden glow was growing even stronger over the Lady's city, throwing a harsher light across the fighting rings. The crowd went silent. All eyes turned towards the bright sky.

Lydiah descended into the ring with a taut smile on her black-painted lips. "You're very clever, Boudi-Ca. You knew all along you were this good, and you played me like a fool. I'm already thinking of the possibilities for a great future for you."

Boudi-Ca shrugged. "I have two more tasks to complete in the next two moons to finish my Mistress Test. That's my future."

"I'm declaring your Mistress Test null and void." Lydiah didn't stop smiling. Her silver-grey eyes were alight with a queer insanity. "I need some sort of damage control, or Yitzhak might flay my skin from my bones."

"Damage control? I passed my first Task of Mastery, and I didn't damage anyone!"

"Au contraire." Lydiah leaned close. "This wasn't supposed to be your day. This was supposed to be my day."

Boudi-Ca gritted her teeth. "I can't have a day? I can't have one damned day?"

"No. Now drop the sparring sword and stay close. We'll go back to the palace. We're going to prepare a public announcement. I already have an alternate plan, a way to make things right. What is that light, Boudi-Ca? Is the sun reflecting off of the Lady's palace?"

"Even if I knew, I wouldn't-"

"Well done," Nefra interrupted. The lieutenant approached and extended her hand. "I'm honored to lose to you, Boudi-Ca. I'm also deeply sorry for anything I might have done to offend you. You should join us in the Smokeless Flames. We could use more brilliant fledglings like you in the fight against Heaven."

"Perhaps the lieutenant is right," Lydiah added. "I agree completely."

"No, thank you." Boudi-Ca took Nefra's warm, strong hand nonetheless. She couldn't forgive Nefra for fucking Henne on her bed, but a grudge was no excuse for rudeness. She was furious enough already at Lydiah. Nefra smiled, bowed formally, and walked off towards the fighting pit exit ramp that led down to the ready rooms.

"Congratulations, Boudi-Ca!" Isabellah pressed forward with Henne close behind. "You passed Ayelet's task, and you showed the Smokeless Flames a thing or two. No offense, Ambassador."

"You did great, Boudi!" Henne beamed. "I was cheering for you. You're amazing."

Boudi-Ca felt her pride rise higher in her chest than ever before. Her throat warmed with so much happiness that her face tingled. "Thank you so much, Henne. Everything came together with the blessing of the Lady."

Lydiah smiled and nodded. "So if you'll excuse us, we're going back to the palace now. Boudi-Ca will be making a public statement regarding the recent events. Everyone should know how well and fairly she was treated with her Mistress Test, although there may be a problem with its authenticity. Come along, fledgling."

Boudi-Ca allowed Lydiah to escort her from the Amphitheatre, but her anger mounted as she climbed each step. She couldn't finish her Mistress Test anyway because she didn't have Violet. She'd almost been willing to play on Lydiah's terms, but she couldn't forgive Lydiah for Violet. In that moment, she hated Lydiah more than ever. When she reached the top of the Amphitheatre, she squinted and turned like everyone else to look in the direction of the Lady's palace.

The brilliant glow in the sky was an enormous golden boat-a vessel with great sails that unfurled into the shape of a yellow lotus flower. The sails filled with wind, and the boat moved, accelerating over the Divinity District towards the eastern edge of the city. At the same time, a low roar was growing, and the city itself seemed to shudder. The Lady's palace bowers were crumbling. The towers were coming down.

"Wyrm-riders!" Lydiah yelled. "To your Nanka! Rip that elf-boat out of the sky! What do you know about this, Boudi-Ca?"

"Me? Nothing." Boudi-Ca stared into Lydiah's grey-silver eyes. She thought suddenly of Ayelet's missing arms-of Ayelet's torture. More memories surged in her head-memories of unbearable, endless suffering-images like a dream. Was she psychic? How could she know of Ayelet's fate in that moment? She briefly glimpsed Ranavalona locked in a dark cage with Szenes, betrayed by Lydiah and Hell's army.

"Boudi!" Tajee ran up breathlessly. "You're safe. You're not hurt or anything."

"Why would I be hurt, Tajee?"

Tajee turned to show her his back, revealing the ragged bloody cuts. Boudi-Ca returned her gaze to Lydiah's eyes. Her anger slowly metamorphosed into hate, and her arms seethed with a curious power. It was the same strange power that she'd felt seeing Henne together with Nefra, except ten times stronger.

She wrenched her arm from Lydiah's grip, stepped to the side, and collided with the nearest Hell's army Djinnus. She yanked the soldier's steel blade from its sheath at his hip. She whirled towards Lydiah with the blade raised.

"I'm giving you a statement today, Ambassador Lydiah, but it's not the one you want. It's the one you deserve." She lunged with a serpent strike, but Lydiah's well-timed hateful kin-hex caught her full in the chest, knocking her three paces back over the paving stones. Her sword tip had missed Lydiah's corseted breasts by mere inches.

"Rebellion!" the Djinnus soldier shouted. "Assassin!" Boudi-Ca parried an attack from another Hell's army soldier. She backhanded a contretemps to his throat. It was a crazy move that she'd never tried before, but she scored a perfect hit. Blood jetted. The soldier slumped. Swords were leaving sheaths everywhere in the street. Lydiah grimly drew her narcabyss whip.

Boudi-Ca parried another blade, and another. Her intense rage poured forth. Her arms almost trembled with an unknown reservoir of unbelievable energy. She countered, slashed, and finished. Another soldier writhed in agony from a deep strike that split the seam in his chest armor. The rest of the soldiers backed away warily, waiting to be joined by more soldiers and Smokeless-Flame Sisters, who were swarming into the street in force.

"Don't be a fool, Boudi-Ca," Lydiah called. "Put down the sword, darling. Please!"

Boudi-Ca flashed. The ribbon uncoiled beneath her feet, and she slipped through space and time, through the frozen soldiers to emerge behind Lydiah. She reversed her blade and struck at Lydiah's back, but Lydiah's form strangely blurred, shifted, and slipped several inches to the side. The strike scored only a glancing blow to Lydiah's hip.

Lydiah grunted and whirled. Boudi-Ca gasped when the second kin-hex hit her, knocking her back again. Lydiah's lips muttered another spell, and the narcabyss whip in her hand transformed into flickering black tentacles.

Boudi-Ca flashed away, interposing a soldier between herself and Lydiah. She impaled the soldier from behind, and then twirled to dispatch a red-robed Smokeless-Flame Sister. Another kin-hex buffeted her, and she retreated up the street, slashing and stabbing anything in her path that wore a Hell's army uniform. Whenever a Smokeless-Flame Sister came close with a whip, she either killed the Sister quickly or skittered and flashed to a safe distance.

She didn't need to kill Lydiah. Not yet. She was a whirlwind of death. Every living thing in the street fell to her berserker fury. She slowly climbed the street towards the Lady's palace. When the tide of soldiers rose to follow her, she slaughtered them one by one, and their blood ran back down the cobblestones towards the amphitheaters.

As she approached the palace plaza, a huge ogre grunt from Hell's army confronted her with a giant club. Boudi-Ca ducked the club and rolled to the ogre's hairy, knobby knees. She speared her blade through the vulnerable soft parts beneath the ogre's studded leather skirts. She wrenched her sword free, and the ogre toppled like a tree, adding another barrier between her and Lydiah, her most formidable enemy.

Boudi-Ca battled onwards, killing uncountable soldiers as she went. When her sword broke, she disarmed an Djinnus with only her hilt and continued killing. In the palace plaza, she reached an open space and paused to wipe the blood from her hands. She gawked at the small mountain of white crystal shards.

Allyssia's palace had collapsed upon itself. The crystal bowers had all fallen. The head of a green Nanka struggled to free itself from the rubble. The giant, stinking Nanka in the Lady's great hall had apparently all been buried alive, and the brilliant sun-like boat was vanishing into the east across the open sky above the Isandlwana mountainsides.

Boudi-Ca hesitated. She felt a sudden fatigue, even as the soldiers and red-robed Smokeless-Flame Sisters surrounded her again. She could see the gates of the Divinity District on the far side of the plaza. She gauged the distance for yet another flash. Was the secret tunnel closed, or could she still escape that way? She looked back at the river of bleeding and dying bodies that she'd left in her wake. A relaxed peace came over her, a grim satisfaction.

She turned to flash just as Lydiah's whip snaked forward again. Boudi-Ca felt her heart seize. Lydiah's whip snagged around her ankle, sending numbness through her leg. She reached down to slash the whip, but the whip curled magically around her ankles instead, holding her in place.

She tried to flash, but she only lurched and tipped over. More whips snapped forward from the hands of the red-robed Sisters. Boudi-Ca toppled onto the cobblestones. Her throat made no sound, only a numb nothingness. She let her stolen sword slip from her fingers. She was done. She tried to focus on the beautiful blue Isandlwana sky, queerly sure that she was seeing it for the last time.

"Boudi!" Tajee's voice cut through the chaos. He arrived at her side and threw his body to protect her, but Lydiah grabbed Tajee's arm and dragged him back like a rag doll. Lydiah bent protectively instead. The ambassador's black-painted lips were quivering with emotion.

"You all saw what happened!" Lydiah shouted to the surrounding crowd. "Shame on Hell's army for attacking this fledgling just because she got lucky and won. I allowed this fledgling to fight in good faith on this sacred festival day. I allowed Boudi-Ca to honor Lady Allyssia with her lust for battle. In the name of Allyssia, the guilty soldiers will be held accountable for their bad behavior if they still live. I'll see to it."

~*~

"Boo! Boo!" The protests thundered through the hallowed Hell's Court chambers. "Death to the Mimǫ! Torture and the void!"

"The decision has been made, as per the will of Lady Allyssia and Lord Hades." Judge Rhadamanthus banged his ebony gavel. "Take the Mimǫ prisoner to my primum salon in the dungeon, please."

Lydiah rose to her feet as the algolagnites descended on Boudi-Ca. The Mimǫ fledgling stood a head shorter than most of the bald, black-robed devils in Hell's Court. Boudi-Ca was dragging limply from her desperate Hunger, and the girl was weighed down even more by iron chains and manacles. Lydiah watched with mixed horror and satisfaction.

"Boo! Boo!"

The bitter catcalls continued. Dozens of military wives had attended Boudi-Ca's sentencing in the capital city that day-the Jinn wives of the ninety-seven Djinnus soldiers who had lost their lives in the Isandlwana massacre. Lydiah nodded with fake sympathy to the wives who made accusatory eye contact with her. She climbed over the gold-linked cordon rope.

Judge Rhadamanthus was following Boudi-Ca's devil escort down into the dungeons of Mer. Lydiah paced to follow Rhada. A devil guard stopped her at the dungeon archway. His bored porcine eyes scanned her assets.

"The interrogation rooms and dungeon are off limits to the general public, even for a pretty Jinn."

"I'm not the public, you idiot. Are you new to this post? I'm Ambassador Lydiah, and I need to speak personally with Rhada. Many of these Jinn wives want to kill that fledgling right now, but I just saved her life." Lydiah subtly arched her back and willed the peon into submission. The devil gave a low, pitiless hiss, but he edged aside.

Lydiah pressed past on long strides into the hallway. She followed Boudi-

Ca's escort down a wide, darkened stairwell that dropped into the pits below Hell's Court, those pits that few souls emerged from, and none unscathed. Rhadamanthus turned to meet her at the bottom of the steps. Lydiah smiled at him sweetly.

"Rhada-"

"Lydiah, it's just as well that you followed me." Rhadamanthus gestured her closer with his rat-skull pipe. "There was something I couldn't mention when I passed judgment on that little rebel."

"What's that?"

"General Astaarteh, Archduke Yitzhak, and a few others have questioned your competence at Allyssia's Redoubt. They're investigating you next."

"Let them investigate. I did everything that Yitzhak requested of me."

"You're on leave from ambassador duty, Lydiah. You're not going to the Blessed Isles. You're not going anywhere. You're going home."

"Very well. I'll take a vacation. When can I see Boudi-Ca?"

"You can have your new plaything after I'm through with her. Until then, you've got the boy, or at least most of him."

Lydiah felt the bile rise in her belly. She allowed her anger to percolate and fuel her will to negotiate. She watched the devils push Boudi-Ca through a leather-clad door into Rhada's personal torture chamber. "I just wanted to ask about Boudi-Ca's interrogation. Mainly, I can't make a beauty fledgling out of the girl if she's disfigured. It's bad enough that she's a former rebel. I can't have a single blemish on her skin. I hope you understand me?"

Rhada's eyes darkened dangerously. "You called in every favor to get leniency for this freakish fledgling, Lydiah. You bypassed the normal Court channels and entertained every irregularity you could find. You petitioned Allyssia herself. You even kissed ass with my wife at the party last night, and you've loathed Breanarachelle's very soul since well before the Ukraine revolution."

"I always entertain guests and catch up with affairs when I return to-"

"Spare me," Rhadamanthus raised his urine-colored, burgundy-blotched hand. "You've become a little too used to getting your way. You're only a

Jinn. Even Fennel agrees that his wife's ego oversteps its bounds."

"This fledgling can be a great asset to our Lord and the Flames if properly turned to serve. Why do we need to interrogate her at all? Why not just give her to me now? She'll tell us nothing that we don't already know. Why waste your time?"

"Do not test me, Lydiah," Rhada answered. "I wasn't planning especially to disfigure the girl, but now I know I'll enjoy it much more. I do like her feet, but her face is pretty, and it's been a while since I used an acid drip."

"I'm not joking, Rhada. My fledglings are royalty in Mer. I can't have my Boudi-Ca with blindness, a missing nose, or any nasty scars on her skin. What do you want from me? The girl truly doesn't deserve to suffer. I'll owe you, Rhada. Please."

Rhadamanthus burst into laughter. "By the balls of the Beast, you're entertaining, Lydiah. I'll give you that. I never know what might come out of your mouth. Why don't you find a nice cock and make your mouth more useful."

"Rhada, please-"

Rhadamanthus turned on his heel and stalked to the door. With a swirl of his black robe, he closed it behind him. Lydiah strode to the door and peered through the little window. The devils were chaining Boudi-Ca to a worktable, which was carved of living stone from the Great Blue Hole mines. The table was rounded and worn from many years of use, stained the color of blackberries from Rhada's endless indulgence in his decadent devil pleasures.

Lydiah tore her eyes away from the scene. Her stomach felt queerly hollow, and Boudi-Ca's whimpering sent a chill through her bones. Boudi-Ca was brilliant. The fledgling was skilled with deadly weaponry, yet at the same time the girl's voice was like a goldfinch, and her perfect figure rivaled the most beautiful fashion plates in Mer.

Boudi-Ca didn't deserve such suffering, yet it was necessary to spare her life. Lydiah sniffed. She felt a startling, distracting tickle at her lower eyelid. She raised her fingers and wiped her cheek. She gazed down at her wet fingertips in disbelief.

"Rhada." Lydiah pushed through the door. "Wait." Rhada was unfurling a sheaf of knives and scissors at the end of his torture table. Rhada was well-known in Hell's Court for his expertise with feet, as well as a penchant for leaving his victims with permanent disabilities. Lydiah flinched. Rhada's glare of menace chilled her soul.  He gestured at his ugly algolagnite assistants.

"Arrest her for obstruction of justice. Give her a gag."

Lydiah wiped the tears that threatened to overwhelm her again.  She needed to speak, and quickly. Chains rattled. The devil men circled to cut off the exit. Their porcine eyes roamed over her flesh as they approached, eager at the prospect of inflicting delicious pain.

"I told you. I already interrogated this girl when we first captured her. The little chit knows nothing. Yes. Arrest me and put me on the table instead of Boudi-Ca. Take me instead, Rhada.  I can give you so much more."

Rhada's fingers stilled over his knives.  His froggish nostrils flared, as if testing the dungeon air.  He left the table and approached her slowly. "You're suffering, Lydiah. You're really suffering for this girl."

"Yes. I have so much more passion and flesh for your pleasure." Lydiah held still while Rhada's filed fingernail scraped and poked her cheek. He leaned and sniffed her, as if savoring the petals of a lotus flower. His ashen lips curled into a smile.

"Amazing.  I haven't seen this sort of suffering in ages, not since I had a Kishi princess on my table. She knew she'd never see the Blessed Isles again, or the love of her life, a handsome poet boy. I must have filled two buckets with her sweet elf tears, those tears of true love. Your suffering is very similar. How very, very interesting."

"Consensus ad idem, Rhada." Lydiah dared to press closer, willing her emotions to the surface of her perfumed skin. "Cut me to the bones, but leave my beautiful fledgling alone. Please. I'll do anything for you."

"Yes," Rhada finally breathed. "It's a deal. I need to see where this leads."

###

~*~

Arnett Hartwell, Born in London, UK in 1955. His parents are Ed and Liz Hartwell. Arnett studied Communications at the School of Oriental and African Studies. He overcame wrongful conviction early in his life, alcoholism, and smoking Kush (not really, he is working on giving up kush) (No that's not true either; he loves kush and is not giving that up). He worked in sales at Montanaro Asset Management. Where he challenged upper management to create a lounge area for all the employees. Arnett is Kind, honest, Loyal, funny. He is always telling great stories. And never afraid to stand up to injustice, big or small. He is most known for twerking with a coworker at an office party.

<h1 style="text-align:center">Also by Arnett Hartwell</h1>

This book was a labor of love, it really was, and the research alone was so entertaining. I really let myself go to that wonderful place called "What If"

**Deviant: Boudi-Ca Chronicles Book 1**
In an Underworld city ruled by a Love Ifreeta, (powerful Djinn) Boudi-Ca is adopted by a Jinni who sees potential in encouraging her rebellious urges. Boudi-Ca must re-evaluate her sense of self in a society where the patriarchy is turned on its head. The women are powerful, magical, and dominant.